SOUTHERN PLAYBOY

A North Carolina Highlands Novel

JESSICA PETERSON

ALSO BY JESSICA PETERSON

Lessons in Losing It (Study Abroad #4)

WHERE TO FIND JESSICA

- Join my Facebook reader group, The City Girls, for exclusive excerpts of upcoming books plus giveaways galore!
- Follow my not-so-glamorous life as a romance author on Instagram @JessicaPAuthor
- Follow me on Goodreads
- Follow me on Bookbub
- Like my Facebook Author Page

Published by Peterson Paperbacks, LLC
Copyright 2021 by Peterson Paperbacks, LLC
Cover Design: Najla Qamber of Najla Qamber Designs
Photographer: Rafa Catala
Model: Hugo Soriano
Editor: Marion Archer
Copyeditor: Jenny Sims
Proofreader: Karen Lawson

www.jessicapeterson.com

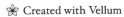 Created with Vellum

Chapter One

RHETT

I'm on my third—or maybe it's my fifth?—whiskey neat when I spot her across the room.

Short hair. Full mouth. Laughter that's real and loud.

It's been nine years since Amelia Fox broke my heart, so I don't know why my pulse skitters, sending a zip of electricity through my veins. It's the same feeling I'd get the second or two after the day's first snap. That's when the thrill of being on the field and having my legs under me used to overtake any pregame jitters.

Used to being the operative words.

My hand tightens around my glass.

One, why the fuck did my brother Samuel invite my ex-girlfriend to his engagement party?

Two, why didn't he tell me?

And three, why am I moving toward her like some dick-led deadbeat, my skull hollowed out of any thought except *damn, she looks good?*

She's wearing a floral dress. Heels that'll make her a little taller than me. She was self-conscious about being five-ten back in high school. Now she's owning it, baring legs that go on for days. Her dress clings to her long torso and those pert little tits that make—*made*—the perfect handful.

She turns her head, and our gazes collide. Her warm brown eyes widen for half a heartbeat. I hesitate, hit by the feeling of stepping in shit. I'm doing that a lot these days—acting before thinking—and I wonder if I should back off.

Too late. Amelia smiles, wide and so fucking pretty, and I'm hit square in the chest by an altogether different feeling.

God, how I loved making this girl smile.

"Hello, Rhett," she says.

I've dated models with more Instagram followers than the population of a small European nation. I've hung out with pop stars flaunting their nipples for paparazzi. I've also done some very dirty dancing with an undisclosed member of the British royal family (sorry, kids, her NDA is watertight).

I was never, ever at a loss for words in those situations.

Now, though?

Now I scramble for what to say. What to *do*. What's the protocol for greeting the girl I lost my virginity to in the bed of my brother Beau's truck? The girl I thought would be my forever?

"Amelia. Hey." I clear my throat. The whiskey's making me sound growlier than I mean to. Or maybe it's the guy in the bow tie behind Amelia checking out her ass who's got me out of sorts. "What are you doing here?"

"I'm friends with Emma." Amelia nods at the bride-to-be, who's got her arm looped around Samuel's waist over by the bar. "We were neighbors downtown before she moved up to Blue Mountain. We've been working on some educational programming together. Stuff about vegetables and growing a garden and healthy eating. My students love it."

I run a hand over my overgrown scruff—I shaved my beard when we lost in the playoffs, but I'm thinking about growing it back—and Amelia's eyes flick down to watch me do it.

"So you're teaching," I say.

She nods, her smile growing. "You'll be shocked to hear I work at Mom's preschool. I'm with the toddler class right now. It's my favorite age."

"Was only your dream to work there since, what," I scoff, "you were five?"

"Woodward was a special place," she says, referencing the Montessori school her mom founded back in the nineties. "Still is. I'm happy to report we're thriving. We were able to give twenty-two kids scholarships this year."

"Impressive! Your mom would be proud of you."

"Thanks."

Her eyes drift over my face before falling to the glass in my hand. I wait for her to say it back—that my parents would be proud of me—but she doesn't.

Not gonna lie, that kinda hurts.

I tip back my glass, vision spinning out. I probably should slow down.

"Toddlers are your favorite?"

She nods again. "Even at their worst, they're easier to deal with than moody adults."

"Why do I get the feeling you're talking about me?" I ask, lips twitching.

"I'm not."

"Liar."

She sips her drink, and my gaze moves to the lime that floats to the top of her glass. Gin and tonic? Vodka soda? "You just seem a little . . . grumpy."

"It's a new thing I'm trying out."

"Looks like you're trying out a lot of new . . . things," she replies, eyes on my scruff. "Wishful thinking? That you made it to the championship?"

Now I'm the one smiling. Amelia never held any punches.

"So you know my team lost in the playoffs," I say. "Does that mean you've been following me? My career? Maybe my Instagram too?"

"It means I'm wondering why you're sporting a semi-playoff beard while, yes, *losing in the playoffs*. Aren't you supposed to shave after you lose?"

I stroke my scruff. "Playoff beards actually started as a hockey

3

thing. I'm doing the football version, which is *post*-playoff beards. Scruff. Whatever."

"That makes no sense."

"It makes perfect sense. Season's over, and you want to relax. You don't feel like shaving, so you don't. Hence, the post-playoff beard."

What I don't tell her? I'm staring down the very real possibility that my dream of winning a title died with a missed field goal on a blustery Sunday afternoon back in December. I have one season left on my contract to make that dream come true, and then I'm retiring. Why the fuck not grow a beard at this point? Helps hide the post-season bloat too.

"So your punishment for losing is looking like Santa's erstwhile son?" she asks.

I let out a bark of laughter, making the guy behind Amelia glance over his shoulder at me this time.

Whatever. This is the most fun I've had all night.

"Yes. Although I'd like to think it's less of a jolly fat guy look and more of a Tom Hardy in beast mode idea."

Amelia gives me a slow shake of her head, eyes narrowed, clearly unimpressed. I imagine her giving a toddler the same look when time-out is imminent. *We don't bite our friends, Tommy, and we definitely don't feed them our boogers. In the corner, now.*

I feel another zing of electricity at the idea of Amelia putting me in my place. I ignore it.

"So," I say.

"So."

I should go. Clearly, Amelia has nothing more to say to me. I'm on the verge of being flat-out drunk, and I have no business chatting up the girl who fucked with my head so badly I nearly lost my scholarship, my career, and my future, all in one fell swoop.

I have way too much on the line right now to play this game.

Still, I can't seem to make myself move. I smell her perfume, something spring-y that's equal parts sexy and sweet, and I'm gripped by the sudden urge to make her laugh out loud for *me*.

Finally, Amelia straightens, shaking the ice in her glass.

"Welp, I'm going to hit up the ladies' room, and then it's time for a refill." She meets my gaze. "Take care, Rhett."

I can read between the lines. What she really means: *take care, and I'd really like us to ignore each other the rest of the night, please and thank you.*

"You too, Amelia." She's turning away when I reach out and touch her elbow, making her turn back. "And the beard—scruff—I've played five seasons in the pros, and I've followed the facial hair rules for all of them. Hasn't won me a ring yet. Figure I have nothing left to lose."

Her expression softens. "But you do have something to lose."

"What's that?"

"A shot at getting laid."

I laugh again. Amelia always spoke her mind, but she was never this ballsy.

I resist the temptation to move in closer. "C'mon, the scruff isn't *that* bad."

"It kind of is, though," she replies, smiling wide again.

"You're mean."

"I'm joking. And hey, I'm not the one growling at people."

"Maybe I'm trying to keep them away." I look at her, and she looks back. "Seems to be working with you."

She shakes her head and rolls her eyes, still smiling. "Goodbye, Rhett."

"There's probably a line for the bathrooms," I say. "Use the staff entrance past the front desk—there's an employee bathroom through the doors to your right."

I don't work at Blue Mountain Farm, but I grew up on the property. My family developed and now owns the five-star resort. I've spent count-less hours in those offices bugging Beau, our CEO, or my sister Milly, Blue Mountain's event planner. I know the place like the back of my hand.

I also know that creeper who looked at Amelia like he wanted to eat her just headed for the public restrooms. Best if she doesn't run into him.

"Okay," she says. "Thanks."

"Anytime. Night, Amelia," I reply, and I watch her disappear into the crowd.

In true Samuel form, my brother invited a hundred fifty of his "closest" friends to tonight's party, held in The Library, a large room off the lobby. It's packed, but I somehow manage to pick out Amelia until she's at the doors to the exit.

She disappears.

Growling, I knock back what's left of my whiskey and slam the glass down on a nearby sideboard, making a few nearby guests look up.

"Your conversation with Amelia went that well, huh?"

I glance down to see Milly standing beside me, casually sipping her cocktail.

"Conversation went fine," I grind out, then clear my throat again.

"Thirsty?"

"No."

"Poor thing," Milly says, shaking her head, "losing her mom like that. I still remember how awful it was."

My chest clenches at the memory. I cross my arms, wondering if I should make sure Amelia got to the employee restroom okay. "I need a drink. Wanna go with me to the bar?"

"You need many things. A drink is not one of them. Also, wouldn't getting another drink mean you are, in fact, thirsty?"

I grit my teeth. "Milly, so help me God—"

"Kidding." She nudges me with her elbow. "I'm just kidding, Rhett. Wow, you're touchy tonight. Anything you need to tell me?"

I feel my anger and my energy whoosh out of me on an exhale. I'm too tired to have this conversation. And this is a party, dammit. I'm the best at parties.

"Bar." I drape my arm over Milly's shoulders. "Let's go."

We order whiskeys and drink them in broody silence while people watching. There's Beau and his wife, Annabel, heading out to the terrace, fat cigars in hand. Then there's Hank and his new girlfriend, Stevie, the two of them groping each other like it's their mission to gross out everyone in a fifty-foot radius.

Good thing I'm just drunk enough for everything to be delightfully blurred. My brain can't seem to keep up with my eyeballs. The room jerks as I scan it, making me blink.

No sign of Amelia. Did she leave? Fuck, what if she left with that bastard in the bow tie?

I forgot to check if she was wearing a ring.

"I love our family to death," Milly murmurs. "But I also, like, hate them? With this ugly, burning, jealous passion? They're all so . . . ugh, *cute* and *in love*."

Grateful for the distraction, I raise an eyebrow. "Anything you need to tell *me*?"

"No." Shaking her head, she sighs. "Maybe. But I don't feel like talking about it."

"Would you possibly feel like talking about it tomorrow over some lunch?"

"Not sure about the talking part. But I'm definitely down to hang out." She tips her head to rest on my shoulder. "We miss having you on the farm, Rhett."

"I could hang," I say. "As long as it happens after one tomorrow afternoon."

Milly makes an annoyed sound in the back of her throat. "When are you gonna quit being such a kid?"

"When I have one," I say. "Which won't be until I'm fifty. Forty at the earliest. Until then, I'll sleep as late as I damn well please."

"Best-laid plans," she sing-songs, lifting her head, and we continue our judgmental people watching in silence.

The room spins, the minutes tick by, and there's still no sign of Amelia. I start to get worried. And then I worry that I'm worried. Amelia is none of my business. I shouldn't be looking out for her.

I'm not looking out for her.

There. The more I tell myself that, the truer it must be. Laws of the universe and all that shit.

Hank passes by. I distract myself by inviting him and Stevie over for an after-party. The idea of going home alone depresses me.

"Bongs, bourbon, and ball," I say. "Don't say no."

"No," he replies.

I turn to Milly. "Thanks, but hard pass," she says. "I don't do late night."

"Y'all are missing out," I say. I'm about to start begging when my

7

phone vibrates. Digging it out of my pocket, I see a text from an unknown number. I open the text, and my stomach swoops.

Hi Rhett, this is Amelia Fox. I have no idea if this is still your number, but if it is, I need some help. I may or may not have locked myself in a bathroom stall [smiley face emoji with gritted teeth]. Emma's not answering her phone.

"Shi-it," I hiccup, my pulse skipping a beat.

Milly goes up on her tiptoes to glance at my phone screen. "Everything okay?"

"Yeah. Just gotta take care of something." I type out a quick reply, then blank the screen and shove the phone back in my pocket. Looping an arm around my sister's neck, I pull her close and press a kiss to the top of her head. "See you tomorrow. Do me a favor, would you, and don't go home with any of Samuel's douchey friends?"

She rolls her eyes. "To quote the great Cher Horowitz, as *if*."

Chapter Two

AMELIA

I'm coming.

Relief floods through me as I read the text. I chuckle. Rhett one hundred percent means that in the literal and figurative sense. He always was a pervert.

He also always makes me smile just when I need it most.

Like right now. I glance up at the stall door in front of me. It's made of solid oak and has to be six, even eight feet tall; it goes all the way to the floor so I can't crawl underneath it. There is a space at the top between the frame and the ten-foot ceiling, but it's too tall for me to climb over without help.

I give the artfully weathered brass handle one last try. The bolt jiggles, but the door doesn't budge.

Yup. Definitely stuck. Because I didn't embarrass myself enough by trading totally inappropriate barbs with my ex-boyfriend at a very classy party.

I lean back against the side of the stall and scroll through the rest of my texts, knee brushing the toilet paper dispenser. Nothing from Jim. He's got his kids this weekend, so it makes sense that I haven't heard from him since last night. Although I'd be lying if I said I'm not

9

the tiniest bit bummed he didn't reply to my *thinking about you* message earlier.

But hey, I know better than anyone how busy you are when you're dealing with little kids. We'll talk in the morning when the kids go back to his ex.

Taking a deep breath through my nose, I hit the button on the side of my phone and drop it in my purse, which is hanging from the hook on the back of the door. Apparently, even the employee bathrooms at Blue Mountain Farm Resort are showstoppers: the three-stall room is impeccably designed, from the carved wooden doors on each of the stalls to the gleaming white subway tile and brass light fixtures hanging overhead.

It's like the set of a Nancy Meyers movie, one that would star Reese Witherspoon and Matthew McConaughey as erstwhile enemies-cum-lovers who engage in verbal fisticuffs by day and an altogether different kind of sparring by night.

Makes my heart hurt a little, being back here after all this time. The farm was so different when Rhett and I dated. Much simpler. Much more rural. But it still feels the same—wild with a sense of anticipation heavy in the pine-scented air. Like anything is possible.

For a while, it was.

Until the fairy tale came crashing down on my head.

I nearly jump out of my skin when I hear the bathroom door being shoved open, followed by the sound of heavy footsteps that echo across the rustic floorboards.

"Amelia? You in here?"

My nipples pebble at the whiskey-roughened sound of Rhett's voice. A rush of relief—relief and something else—shoots down my spine. I wobble.

Grabbing the dispenser, I steady myself. Straighten. Then I press my palms to my boobs. "Yup. Middle stall. I'm so sorry to take you away from the party—"

"No apology necessary." The shadow of his feet darkens the sliver of space at the bottom of the door. "Are you okay? You sound a little . . . out of breath."

Panic.

That's why I'm breathless. Because I'm stuck in a bathroom stall, and I'm panicking. Not because my body suddenly feels like a live wire with Rhett so close.

He came.

He looked so, so handsome. Sad too.

I hightailed it out of the party before I did something stupid and asked about that sadness. The gruffness in his voice. Why he was clearly intent on getting shit-faced.

"I'm all right. I just want to get out of here. I have no clue what happened. I closed the door and locked it, no problem. But when I went to unlock it, the deadbolt stuck."

The knob jiggles again as Rhett tries it from the other side.

The sound of his frustrated exhale is *so damn close.* I imagine I can feel it on my skin.

Despite the warm pressure of my hands, my nipples get harder.

"Y'all have a key or something?" I ask.

"No keys for these doors, no."

"A screwdriver, then, to take the whole knob off?"

"That would work, yeah." His voice strains, like he's looking up. "But I think lifting you over the door would be quickest. You seem like you're in distress, so . . ."

I look up at the empty space by the ceiling. It didn't seem so far away a minute ago, but now that I'm actually contemplating what it would feel like to fall from that high . . .

"Seriously?" I say as much to myself and the universe as to Rhett.

"Seriously. I'll catch you." His hands appear over the top of the door. "It'll take ten seconds. C'mon. I promise I won't drop you. Just climb up on the toilet, and I'll do the rest."

I'm wracked by a full-body shiver at the sight of his broad, blunt fingertips.

At the idea of him putting those hands on me again.

I close my eyes against the memories that hit me out of nowhere. That bed of pink azaleas behind his house.

That day on the river, when I kissed him for the first time, and he slid his hand inside my T-shirt. He didn't feel me up; he just pressed his palm to my bare stomach and left it there, the pad of his thumb working a slow, lazy circle over my skin.

Stop.

I have Jim now. No use revisiting all that teenage angst. Because that's exactly what Rhett and I were—*teenagers*, young and stupid. These memories are probably part fantasy anyway. Rhett couldn't have been that good. Not then.

I wouldn't want to find out about now, either. What Jim and I have has the potential to be something real.

Something good.

"How much whiskey have you had tonight?" I manage.

It's his turn to chuckle. A low, warm sound. "I've lifted a lot more weight when I was a hell of a lot less sober." He flexes his fingers, waving me on. "Time's up, buttercup. Let's do this."

It's his casual confidence, the kind that bordered on cocky in high school, that finally gets me to bend down and take off my heels.

"Incoming," I say and lift my arm to dangle my shoes by the heels over the top of the door.

Rhett grabs the toes of my shoes. "Got 'em."

A second later, I hear the click of the heels as he sets them on the porcelain ledge of the sink.

I dangle my purse over too. "And this."

"Yup." This time, our fingers brush as Rhett takes my bag. There's another rush, this one inside my skin, warm and tingly.

It must be the vodka. Thankfully, this little stuck-in-a-bathroom-stall snafu kept me from getting a refill. I need another cocktail like I need a hole in my head, clearly.

Flattening my palm against the wall for balance, I climb up on the toilet, carefully turning around to face the door.

Lifting my head, I lock my gaze on Rhett's below. His eyes are that piercing Beauregard blue, a startling contrast to his dark blond hair and darker scruff.

He's standing right in front of the door. Feet planted shoulder-width apart. He's unbuttoned his suit jacket and loosened his tie, and he looks so much like a deliciously unkempt country boy playing dress-up that my heart begins to pound.

I blink, and he grins. My legs wobble again. *This is not a good idea.* I press both palms to the walls on either side of me.

Once upon a time, having Rhett this close would've been danger-ous. Those hands. My heart.

But now? He's not a guy I'd ever consider dating at this point in my life. I'm looking for someone who wants the same thing I do: to set down roots here in Asheville, the place I love more than anywhere else on Earth.

"How do we do this?" I ask.

Lifting his arms, he takes a step forward, practically plastering his chest against the door. "Easy. You put your hands on my shoulders. I'll put my hands on your waist, and we'll ease you over the door, nice and slow."

I look down at the floor. It seems very, very far away. And very *hard*.

"You sure you don't want to just get that screwdriver?"

He cuts me a familiar look, tilting his head. "Amelia, I got you."

The thing is, he did always have me. Always had my back. Our ending was ugly and upsetting and inanely dramatic in many ways. But Rhett showed up when it counted.

I could trust him back then. Until he broke my heart.

I look down at his upturned face and eager eyes. I look down at the toilet, the water in the bowl glinting.

It appears I have no choice but to trust him now.

"I'll have you know"—I lean over, the top of the door digging into my rib cage, and put my hands on Rhett's broad shoulders—"my students really love me, and they'll be devastated if I die in a tragic accident involving a toilet, brown liquor, and my high school boyfriend."

"Noted. Now I'm gonna put my hands on your waist, okay? Let your weight fall forward."

"Okay."

I scramble to mentally prepare myself, but I don't have time. Rhett cups my lower rib cage in his enormous hands. He firms his grip, fingers curling into my sides, inviting me to tip forward.

But oh my *God*, I'm high up. So freaking high up. If I fall from this height at this angle, I'll definitely break something. My face. A leg. My pride.

For a second, my vision goes hazy. "Shit, Rhett, I'm scared. I don't know—"

"You're already halfway there, Amelia. Look at me." I do as he says. "Good. Now just keep looking at me. I'm going to pull you forward. At the same time, I want you to go up on your tiptoes, okay?"

I nod. "Okay."

I lean forward a little, slowly rolling up onto the balls of my feet. My dress makes a chafing sound against the top of the door. My heart is beating so hard I feel sick. Or maybe it's the door. It's pressing into my belly now, making the saliva in my mouth thicken.

"Focus," Rhett gently prods. "Keep looking at me."

I don't want to lose my dinner, so I try to lose myself in Rhett's eyes instead. Tonight they're the color of a Carolina sky in the morning. Light blue. Touch of green.

Kind. They're kind. And they can't possibly belong to the growly, grumpy guy I was just talking to at the party.

"Answer a question," he says.

I'm on the tippiest of my toes now. "Shoot."

He's guiding me forward with his hands. Guiding me over the door slowly and calmly, just like he said he would.

"You come here with anyone?"

"That's your question?" I glance down at his hands. They're clutched firmly around my upper torso. I follow the line of his outstretched arm to his bicep. It strains against the fabric of his suit jacket, like he's smuggling a grapefruit inside his sleeve.

Wow.

Just . . . *wow*.

Being the star player on our high school's football team meant Rhett was always in fantastic shape. But he's ridiculously ripped now, broader and bigger in a way that's making my brain short-circuit.

"Only trying to make conversation." He takes a step back, then another, his hands still on my waist as my front glides over the top of the door. First my belly, then my hips. Now we're at my thighs, and I screw an eye shut against the bite of the wood on my quadriceps.

14

"I have a boyfriend," I manage. "But he couldn't come tonight."

"Oh. Welp, he missed out."

"Missed out on what? This?" I tilt my chin toward the mirrors on the opposite wall, which capture my current predicament in excruciating, embarrassing detail. My hair hangs over my face in a disheveled mop; my dress is wrinkled, the top pulled to the side to reveal a sliver of my janky nude bra.

"You," he says, and I look down to see his eyes glued to my face. "You look fucking gorgeous tonight, Amelia."

I look away and focus my gaze on my thumbs, parallel to where I imagine Rhett's collarbones are.

"You're obviously drunk."

"You're obviously deflecting. What's wrong with me calling you beautiful? Lord knows I did it all the time back in the day."

He really did. Everyone else made me feel like a freak for being nearly six feet tall at sixteen. But Rhett? He made me feel like I was one chance-meeting-at-the-mall away from becoming a supermodel.

He moves his hands a little lower on my waist. Without thinking, I curl my fingers into his shoulders, squeezing them. "You're trying to make me blush, and I am not here for it."

His lips twitch. "But what if I am?"

The top of the door meets with my ankles. My gut tightens. This is it, the literal make-or-break moment. I'm going to have to put all my weight in Rhett's hands for a second or two until my feet fall from the door to the ground.

"Tell me about you," I say quickly, desperate for distraction. "Are you seeing anyone these days?"

He steps back again. The tops of my feet are an inch away from falling off the door. I close my eyes and send up a silent prayer that I make it out of this bathroom alive.

"Me? I'm seeing everyone."

"Of course you are," I say and open my eyes to roll them. He's smiling, this cute, careless thing that makes me want to slap or bite or maul him. Maybe all three. "That why you're alone at your brother's party?"

"I came alone so I could flirt with you."

"I wondered if you knew I would be here."

15

"I didn't, actually. But I'm glad we ran into each other. Been too long." He steps back one last time, and my feet fall. *I* fall. My pulse explodes, and Rhett grunts, his grip on my waist tightening to the point of pain.

My body flops forward, and for half a heartbeat, I feel like an ungainly, gangly teenager again, all elbows and knees and braces that color-coordinate with my track-and-field uniform. Mustard and emerald green: as unfortunate as it got.

My stomach drops as I go down, hard. Before I can even think about bracing myself for the inevitable impact of my face against the floor, Rhett is swooping me up and forward. I slam into the bulk of his body, breathless, my face prickling with heat as I jerk back a millisecond before I head butt him.

"Whoa," I gasp.

My heart is drumming so hard I feel dizzy. I just stand there, my senses coming back to me one by one.

Smell: Rhett's aftershave, woodsy and clean. Definitely not the Old Spice he wore senior year.

Touch: his arm is looped around my waist, and my front is plastered to his. The tile floor is cold against the bare soles of my feet.

Then taste: relief, mingled with stomach acid.

Sound and sight: my heartbeat. His quick, uneven breathing, at odds with the tightly controlled expression on his face.

Been too long? What does that mean?

And why is my entire *being* prickling with heat now?

Heat and something else. Something . . . delicious.

"See?" His voice is rougher. "Told you I got you. Does everything feel okay? Tell me if you hurt anywhere."

My eyes flick to his lips. They're an inch or two away. Full. Soft looking.

Nope. Not going there. Rhett and I didn't work out for a reason.

A lot of reasons, actually. He destroyed me, and it took me a really long time to move on. But I have moved on, and I'm chasing my dreams. I'm happy now. Mostly.

Wondering if Rhett's mouth tastes the same does not serve those dreams.

"Only my ego." I cringe inwardly at the breathy sound of my voice. "Thanks for the rescue. I appreciate it."

"Anytime. Nice to be needed every once in a while."

It takes more effort than I'd like to admit to peel my hands off Rhett's shoulders. As if he wants to tempt me, the bastard flexes the muscles there as I'm pulling away, flesh firming against my palms.

"Did you just pull a *French Kiss*?" I wring out my hands.

"Do you want me to pull a french kiss?"

"Ha. We watched that movie together, remember? And the lead actor, Kevin-what's-his-name—"

"Kevin Kline."

"Yes! Good memory. So Meg Ryan was afraid of flying, and Kevin Kline distracted her during takeoff by arguing with her."

His eyes twinkle. "You just answered your own question. I *do* have a good memory. We watched it at your grandma's house. She had that big old couch we loved, remember?"

For half a heartbeat, our eyes lock. This is the man I *do* remember. Kind. Thoughtful. Sweet when he wanted to be.

He always did take good care of his people. But that's just the thing —I'm not his person. Not anymore.

"I should get going," I say, stepping back. My body cries out at the sudden, cool rush of air between us, and I suppress a shiver. I turn to wash my hands in the sink. "Great catching up. And, er, being caught, I guess."

Rhett laughs. "You sure you're all right?"

I hold my hands under the dryer. "All good."

It's only when he rocks backward, catching himself on the lip of the sink, do I realize just how wasted he is.

"I think the better question is, are *you* all right?" I ask, grabbing his arm now to steady him.

He looks down at my hand. "Guess I am drunk. On you."

Can't help it. I laugh too. "With lines like that, it's no wonder you're alone."

He wobbles again. "*And high on summertime . . .*" he starts to sing.

I glance at the door. I really should go. Tomorrow will be an early wake-up call. I've got brunch with some girlfriends from college, lesson plans to work on, plus meal prep to do for the week.

I glance at Rhett. He's still singing that damn Luke Bryan song, and he's still clinging to the sink, tripping over his own feet.

"How the hell did you manage to lift me over that door without falling over?"

He turns his head to look at me and smiles. "Magic, baby."

And then he trips and falls on his ass.

"Rhett! Jesus Christ."

I lunge for him, but he waves me away. He opens his mouth in silent drunk laughter, rolling a little to the side to relieve what I imagine is a very sore butt cheek.

"I'm okay," he gasps. "Really, I'm fine."

I find myself vaguely hoping he hasn't done permanent damage to that perfect butt—yes, I noticed, it's impossible not to in those sharply tailored slacks—as I grab my shoes and slip them on. Then I squat down and loop his arm around my neck.

"What are you doing?"

"Returning the favor," I say. "You rescued me, so now I'm rescuing you. We're even, all right? Now push up on the count of three."

Chapter Three

RHETT

I wake up with the hangover from hell.

My head feels like the inside of a stadium when the score is tied with two seconds left, and we're on the five-yard line. Cotton fills my mouth.

My ass hurts something fierce.

Folding my pillow over my head to block out the light from the windows, I attempt to roll over on my stomach but stop halfway.

My dick is hard as a fucking rock.

It throbs as memories from last night hit me like a freight train. Amelia's laughter. Her bra peeking through the neckline of her dress.

How much fun it was to talk to her.

Be with her.

"Aw, baby," I groan and reach beneath the covers for my cock. Usually I sleep naked, so I'm surprised to find I still have my boxers on.

Whatever. Happens sometimes when I go to bed drunk.

I pull my woody through the slit, hissing when I give myself a slow, hard stroke. My hips jerk, and I pump into my hand with a moan, closing my eyes to relive last night's best moments.

JESSICA PETERSON

The feel of her body against mine, tits rising and falling as she caught her breath.

The spark of mischief in her eyes as we exchanged innuendo.

"Baby—"

"No baby here," a voice somewhere in the room says. "Just me. You all right there, killer?"

My stomach flips, and I wrench open my eyes, blinking hard when I see Amelia standing at the foot of my bed.

She's wearing one of my team's hoodies over her dress. Her bed-mussed hair, dark and short, is tucked behind her ears, and mascara is smudged beneath her right eye.

She smiles, and my brain scrambles. Immediately, I yank my hand off my dick and hold it up, as if to say, *look, I was definitely not rubbing one out while thinking about your tits!*

"You stayed over?" I ask, tugging that hand through my hair.

She grins. "You don't remember begging me to stay to make sure you don't, and I quote, 'drown in your own puke'?"

I suck a breath through my teeth. "Yikes."

"Yeah. You were convinced you were going to die. By the time you were asleep, it was late, and I was too tired to drive home. Here." She walks to the side of the bed and holds out a big glass of water and a pair of turquoise pills. "Thought you might need these this morning."

I blink, brain still on pause, and push up to sitting. My entire body protests, and I groan, taking the water and ibuprofen.

"Thank you." I knock back the pills with a gulp of water. "And sorry. I really showed my ass, huh?"

I glance up to see Amelia looking at my bare chest. Then she looks at my crotch. Specifically, the tent pitched there. My traitorous dick perks up even more at the attention, and I give the covers a tug, piling them in my lap.

She blinks too, and pulls the sleeves of my hoodie over her hands.

I like the way she looks in my shit.

"To be fair, I imagine it's a very sore ass, so . . . I get it."

I return her grin. A warm feeling swarms inside my center. Like bees. And then I realize something.

The weight on my chest I wake up with every day isn't there. I

20

mentally feel around for it, poking the usual suspects—breastbone, rib cage, heart—but it's gone.

"I'm sorry," I repeat. "Really. Not cool of me. I don't usually drink that much."

Amelia raises an eyebrow. "I'm not the press or, I don't know, your coach or whatever. You don't have to lie to me."

We're ten feet apart, but the space between us comes alive, vibrating with this low-frequency energy, and the swarm inside my chest brightens.

One of the (many) things I adored about Amelia when we were younger: how she knew me before I hit my stride in the game, and how she liked me for me. I won her over just by being myself. Sharing parts of my life I hadn't shared with anyone else. The dark parts. The painful ones. Not only did she never judge me, but she also understood better than anyone ever could.

We'd both had to grow up too fast, endure too much loss when we were young. I lost Daddy when I was nine. She lost her mama when she was sixteen. A big blow, considering her dad was never in the picture. He and Amelia's mom weren't married, and he left her before Amelia was born.

I'm tempted.

Lord, am I tempted to spill my guts to her.

But luckily, the remaining shred of self-preservation I have left kicks in, and I knock back the rest of the water instead. The throb in my head and between my legs lessens. But that energy between us? That stays put.

"Can I make you some coffee?" I ask.

She shakes her head. "I'm heading to brunch with friends. You going to be okay?"

I'm not sure.

"One cup," I say. "Stay for one cup. Least I can do."

Amelia presses her teeth into her bottom lip and gives me a look. The kind that is probing and a little pitying, and Jesus *Christ,* I hate it. Just like I suddenly hate the idea of her leaving. The room is lighter with her in it. Or maybe that's just the way the sun looks this early in the morning? Glancing at the watch on my wrist, I see it's only eight o'clock. The last time I was up this early was during the season. Feels like a lifetime ago.

I didn't use to be such a slob. But over the past year or so, I've had a hard time giving a shit. I know I should keep fighting. I *need* to keep fighting. I beat myself up all the damn time about not doing more, achieving more in my career. I just . . . I don't know, when I reach for my reasons, my *why*, I find them. They just don't motivate me to crush my goals the way they used to.

In fact, the pressure I put on myself to crush those goals make me pretty damn angry. Maybe that explains the constant hangovers. Alcohol is my attempt to numb the rage and the exhaustion. Escape it.

"I'm more of a tea girl."

"Shit, that's right. Still?" I fist my hair in my hand and give it a hard tug. "I could scrounge that up too. I'm sure the main house has a good selection."

One side of her mouth curls upward. "I have to go."

"Okay." *Not okay.* "Um. Well. Thanks. For not, you know, pushing me off the side of the mountain."

"So you could end up at the bottom of a ravine?"

I shrug. "Probably where I belong anyway."

"You don't belong in a ravine. A pond, maybe. A river."

Now I'm the one grinning. "Because I drink like a fish?"

"Exactly." She reaches out and pats my shin. "Take care of yourself, all right? I'm worried about you."

Even through the blankets, I feel her touch like a bolt of lightning.

What is *up* with this? The way I feel around her? It's been nine years, for Christ's sake. I'm a grown man now. One with a sense of self-control I've painstakingly cultivated over my career in the pros. I know better than to let my dick, or my past for that matter, fuck with my head.

But here I am, acting like I'm eighteen again and I don't have anything, *everything*, to lose.

I know once she leaves, I'll be back to white-knuckling it through another day, trying to pass the hours while trying not to think about how much I don't wanna do anything related to football. Like, at all. Because once the wheel inside my head starts turning, it doesn't stop.

"Where did you sleep?" I ask.

It's a clear bid for time. A stalling tactic. But Amelia doesn't call me out on it.

She tilts her head toward the bedroom door. "On your couch."

"I have a couple of other bedrooms upstairs, you know."

"Couch was fine. Pretty cozy, as a matter of fact." She yawns, eyes flicking over the mess that surrounds us. My face burns with shame. My housekeeper didn't come for her usual Saturday cleaning, and it shows. The room is a fucking disaster. Piles of clothes create a veritable landmine of shit. My bedside table and dresser are cluttered with plates and cups and bowls. My half-unpacked suitcases are half-opened, vomiting their contents onto the floor.

"Does it remind you of my room back in high school?" I ask, trying for humor.

It works. Amelia chuckles softly, the sound almost as satisfying as that big belly laugh of hers I adore. "Yup. Exactly the same, only bigger."

Our eyes meet. Hers are laughing, like she's already anticipating the dirty joke I'm about to make.

"Want to find out how big, exactly?"

She rolls her eyes.

I scramble to think of something else to say that'll stall her, but she's already pulling off my hoodie, raising her arms so that the hem of her dress creeps even farther up her legs, allowing me a glimpse of milky white thighs covered in goose bumps.

"Keep the sweatshirt." I frown. "You're freezing."

She pauses, arms up. "You sure?"

"Yes."

Better that than inviting her into bed so I can wrap my body around hers and warm her up. She was always so soft. Soft everywhere, her skin and between her legs and those brown eyes too—they were always wild.

She guides the hoodie back down, smoothing it over her stomach. My chest squeezes.

"Amelia," I say, too hungover to be mortified by the desperate note in my voice. I clear my throat. Try to clear my head. "I really am sorry I was such a fucking mess last night."

She arches a brow. "Was?"

I'm fisting my hair in my hand again, only this time I look away, face still burning. "Yeah. I'm—things are kind of crazy right now."

"Take care of yourself," she repeats. Then she glances up at the room around us. The master is admittedly swanky with a two-story ceiling, a fireplace, and a massive bed that's upholstered in sheepskin. "By the way, your house is ridiculous."

"Ridiculous good or ridiculous bad?"

She looks back down. Looks at me. Her lips twitch. "A little of both. What were you going for? Vegas meets . . . Kevin Costner?"

"Exactly. How'd I do?"

She laughs, and something catches in my center. "It's sexy."

"It's not practical, but I don't need it to be. I'm only here during the off-season."

"So you don't miss it? The farm."

"I wouldn't say that, no. I miss my family." I grin. "Sometimes."

"Stop it. Your family is the best."

"You only say that because they're not your family."

Her smile fades, and I realize a beat too late I've hit on a sore spot. Growing up the only child of a single parent, Amelia was lonely. I always thought our house of seven was pure chaos, especially when my dad was sick. But Amelia loved it.

"I'd kill to have a big family like yours," she'd say. "You have four built-in best friends for the rest of your life. I have zero."

Back then, my siblings felt less like best friends and more like pains in the butt. My brothers and I were hypercompetitive in football. Never mind that I was the youngest, and I felt like I had to compete for everything else too.

But as I've gotten older, I've realized Amelia was onto something.

"How's your family? How's Rose?" I ask, feeling a rush of warmth at the memory of Amelia's grandmother. She was always kind and cool as hell. She'd talk with me for hours about everything and nothing—books, ideas, travel. Some of my best memories happened on her front porch, the three of us just hanging, drinking sweet tea, and shooting the shit.

"She's eighty-one and living her best life. I want to be her when I grow up."

"Still in that house on Macon Avenue?"

"Yup. She's also a stoner."

"Good for her."

Amelia nods. "I gotta go. Hope your hangover isn't too awful."

They usually are these days. "Being an adult sucks."

"I wouldn't exactly call this"—she spins her hand in my general direction—"adult behavior."

"Who the hell wants to adult?"

"I do. It's not all bad, Rhett." She looks away. "Take care, all right?"

"Wait, wait. How are you getting home?"

"I have an Uber waiting out front."

"Oh. Okay. Great. Be, uh, safe."

She smiles. "See ya, Rhett."

"See ya."

I fucking hate the words and the way they sound and how hard I'm trying to be cool when I feel anything but.

Good thing I'm getting out of dodge in a couple of months, so I won't have to really interact with Amelia again. I'll steer clear at Samuel and Emma's wedding. It should be easy enough, considering they invited four hundred people to the freaking thing. Then I'm back in Vegas for the preseason. Soon.

Too soon. Or maybe not fucking soon enough.

Chapter Four

RHETT

Sweat rolls down my temples and drips into my eyes. They sting, a searing burn that matches the one in my quads.

"LFG, baby!" Tom, my trainer, barks from behind me as he yanks on the harness strapped across my middle.

I grimace, my heart screaming inside my chest. I pump my legs harder but end up tripping on a tree root. I catch myself from falling on my face just in time. "Only douches," I pant, "use acronyms. Especially that one."

"The only douche I see is the one in front of me." He keeps tugging on the harness, pulling me backward as I try my damnedest to run forward. "Now *let's fucking go.*"

These resistance sprint drills are pure torture. They've never been fun, but I was always able to dominate them, motivated by the knowledge they made me that much faster and more resilient on the field.

Now, though? I'm having trouble just getting through them. I don't know if it's because I'm another year older. I'm only twenty-seven, but in football years, that might as well be forty. Maybe I've just softened up during the off-season.

Could also be the fact that Samuel and Emma are getting married this weekend. I'm happy for them, but if I'm being honest, I'm feeling a little . . . I don't know, jealous? Maybe? Which makes no sense. I love being single. Allows me to focus on football and cut loose when I need to.

Whatever's going on, I'm sucking wind.

On account of the great weather—seventy degrees and sunny, one of early summer's last comfortable days before the oppressive heat sets in—we moved today's morning workout from my home gym to the field behind my house. There's a steep incline at the far edge, one I'm currently trying to scale. My blood is pumping, and my body's on fire, the soles of my shoes catching in the tall grass. Despite the early hour, the sun scalds my head and bare shoulders, making my scalp prickle.

It's June, which means it's almost football season. For the past decade, it used to be my favorite time of year.

But when I think about going back to it all—the nonstop travel, the politics, the injuries—something's missing. Am I just tired of the game? *Hell no.* Football's given me an extraordinary life. How could I possibly be tired of it? I love playing. Always have.

I stumble again, this time on a clump of dirt, and Tom lets up on the reins a bit.

"You okay?"

I make a noise that's partway between a dry heave and a groan. I'm definitely feeling the gallon or so of whiskey I've imbibed this week, plus those beers I knocked back last night.

But Tom doesn't need to know that. I should be cleaning up my act now that training camp starts in less than two months. But I keep pushing it off. Between Stevie's beer, Samuel's food, and Emma's cellar, feels like there are more temptations on the farm than there are in my team's new hometown, Las Vegas.

"I'm fine," I grunt. "Just need to get back into the groove."

Firming my ab muscles, I keep pushing up the hill toward the gigantic oak ahead. There's a buzzing sound that gets louder as I approach. Only when I'm at the tree do I see that my phone is lit up with an incoming call—I set it on the roots, along with my water bottle and towel.

I ignore it. This hour and a half session is for sweating and sweating only. Everything else can wait.

"All right," Tom says, dropping the harness. "One-minute recovery. Then we're gonna balance out all that pulling with a push —burpees."

I bend over and put my hands on my knees, my heart trying to crash through the back wall of my torso like a Kool-Aid man on coke. "Fuck you, Tommy."

"Fuck you right back," he replies with a grin. "How's the knee?"

"Better," I say. It's true; my recovery from a sprain last season is the one piece of good news I have to share today.

I look up at the sound of my phone buzzing again. Screen's lit up with someone's name, but I can't see who it is from here. I let it go to voicemail.

"You've put in the work, and I have no doubt you'll reap the benefits over the season. This'll be the one. I can feel it."

"That's the hope."

Four years playing ball in college. Five seasons in the pros. Three trips to the playoffs and one Super Bowl appearance.

Zero titles.

I hope this is the year that changes. It'd damn well better be because my time in the game is running out. Beau and Samuel have been pressuring me for years to retire, mostly because the risk of brain injury grows the longer I play. Now that I've hit two decades in the game—like my brothers, I started playing young, six years old—they're laying it on especially thick.

For good reason. A reason I do not want to think about right now. So I won't. I have to focus on the game and put my all into preparing for the season. It's now or never.

I straighten and my lower back spasms. I try my best not to wince. I'm gonna be sore as all get-out tomorrow.

"You sure you're okay?"

I spear Tom with a look. "How many burpees you want?"

He twists his wrist to glance at his watch. "Fifty seconds' worth. Ready?"

I'm on the ground before he even sets the timer. Burpees are the devil's work. I feel like puking as I move through one, then another and another, wondering when the hell fifty seconds got so long.

Workouts never felt so long, did they? Back in the day, I enjoyed them. Now? Not so much.

My phone starts buzzing again. My heart does that swooping thing —same as it did when I saw Amelia at the engagement party.

Tom glances at the phone. "You wanna get that? It's the third time this Melissa chick's called you."

I go still halfway through a push-up at the mention of my lawyer's name. She never calls me on the weekends. Ever. "Melissa Hanson?"

"Not sure. Couldn't see the last name well, but it looked like an H."

"Shit." As far as I know, I only have one Melissa H on my phone.

I stand, grateful for the excuse to stop moving, and brush off my hands as I jog over to my phone. Could be the spicy workout, could be the weird shadow of foreboding that moves over my center—whatever it is, my heart thrums when I pick up the phone and slide my thumb across the screen. "Melissa, hey. What's up?"

There's a pause.

Melissa, being the consummate legal professional she is, is not one to pause.

"Hi, Rhett. You have a minute?" she asks slowly. She sounds . . . bewildered almost.

I glance at Tom. "I'm actually in the middle of something. Can I call you back?"

Another pause. My heart is going apeshit now.

"You know what, this is really important. I'm gonna need you to take a seat."

"Uh." I glance at the field around me. A butterfly lands on a nearby dandelion, fluttering its wings in panic as a wasp tries to join it. I feel that flutter in the pit of my stomach. "I don't—there's nowhere to sit."

"You're gonna want to sit for this."

Now I really am gonna be sick. I meet Tom's eyes. "Listen, Melissa, I don't mean to be rude, but can you just spit it out already?"

"Rhett." She takes a deep breath. "It appears you might be the father of a two-year-old boy."

My blood rushes cold. "*What?*"

I don't know how I end up on the ground, but suddenly I'm there, the roots of the tree digging into my left ass cheek. Tom rushes over,

29

brow furrowed, but I wave him away, the saliva in my mouth thickening.

"Long story short, Miguel was going through your DMs, and he came across a . . . well, a *troubling* message from a woman named Elle Kincaid, which he forwarded on to me."

Oh boy. That's bad news. After the number of direct messages, or DMs, I got on Instagram became too overwhelming to keep up with by myself, I put my agent, Miguel, on the job. He mostly looks out for business opportunities—sponsored posts make bigger money than you'd think—but also for potential legal issues. He only forwards the trickiest stuff to Melissa.

I'm no saint. But never in a million years would I have guessed *this* would be the legal issue Melissa would find in my inbox. "I don't know anyone named Elle."

"She says she's good friends with Jennifer Williams. Do you remember meeting a woman by that name?"

A deluge of fresh sweat leaks into my eyes. I try to wipe it away with my bicep, which is equally sweaty and only makes my vision blur.

"Do you remember meeting Jennifer Williams?" Melissa repeats.

My heart pounds as my mind whirs, trying to place the name. Finally, it catches—redhead, Hollywood Hills, that Leo DiCaprio party. Or was it the Winnie Harlow photo exhibit thing? Fuck. *Fuck*, why can't I remember the details?

But I do remember both those events happened—yeah, a few years back, because that was the season I set my first record: most first-half receptions in a game during our 37-3 rout of Philly.

"Name rings a bell," I croak, throat suddenly tight. "But I wrap it up. Every time, Melissa, I swear it."

"I believe you," she replies, even though it sounds like she most certainly does not. "But condoms aren't one hundred percent effective, Rhett. There's always a chance . . ."

A chance you might knock up a stranger and end up with a kid.

Panic swarms in my veins, threatening to overwhelm me. I close my eyes and take a deep breath through my nose, moving through the familiar breath work I've relied on for years now to calm my heart rate. *In* through my nose, *out* through my mouth. *In, out.*

In. A kid. I might have a fucking kid.

Out. It's not the end of the world. It's not like—

"Jennifer passed away suddenly two days ago," Melissa continues. "She fell off a ladder and broke her neck. Elle reached out because Jennifer confided in her that you were the father of Jennifer's little boy."

"Oh," I say, the word coming out like I've just been punched in the gut. The whir in my head reaches fever pitch as the meaning of what she's saying starts to crystalize. "Oh, God, I'm so—I'm sorry. Jesus Christ, Melissa."

Tom crouches beside me and puts a hand on my shoulder. I don't know why I'm apologizing to my attorney for this woman's death. I just don't know what else to say. And yeah, maybe saying the words *I'm sorry* makes me feel like a slightly less garbage human being. She fell off a ladder?

Fuck.

Just . . . *fuck.*

Also, who gets a woman pregnant and doesn't show up for their kid?

Yeah, she didn't tell me about him. But maybe I should've, I don't know, checked in on her or something.

"I know. Rhett, I know. I'm sorry to have to bring you this news. But you're Liam's only surviving relative, at least if the paternity test comes back positive, which means you'd be in the running to get full custody. That's the boy's name, by the way—Liam James Williams."

I drag my legs apart, knees bent, and stick my head between them. Tom squeezes my shoulder.

"Keep breathing," he reminds me.

"Full custody. That means full time? Like, *all* the time? He'll be with me all the time?"

I can practically hear Melissa's gulp through the phone. "That's what full custody entails, yes."

"Oh." Jesus fuck, I sound like a lobotomized monkey.

I try to keep breathing. My lungs feel like a pair of stale prunes, small and shriveled and hard.

"Would you be willing to take custody of Liam? As his only surviving relative?"

I wince. So I'd be getting this kid because Jennifer literally had no one else. I'm the last resort. The last pick. Same as I was growing up.

I shove the thought aside. Think about poor Liam instead. Kid's probably wondering what he did to deserve losing his mom and his home all in one fell swoop. Is he confused? Inconsolable? Probably. I sure as hell would be.

I hope he's not hungry.

God, what's wrong with me, thinking about my own stupid feelings when a two-year-old kid just lost the only family he's ever known?

I lost my father when I was young, and it sucked. I'd *never* put my son through the same hell of being fatherless.

"Yes," I say. "Of course I'll take him. I just . . . why didn't she tell me about him? Jennifer."

"I asked Elle that question." A pause.

"And?"

"And she said that the two of you, you and Jennifer, never exchanged contact information."

"Okay, that's fair. I don't give out my number."

"Yes." Another pause. "But she could've reached out via Instagram. We would've seen her message."

I wince. "Also fair."

"Ultimately, I get the sense that Jennifer felt you weren't ready to be a parent."

Anger grips my windpipe. "That's bullshit. Even if that were true, there's no excuse for not telling the father of your child about, well, being the fucking father of that child."

"I don't disagree. But she did say—and I'm quoting Elle here—that Jennifer claimed you were intoxicated when the two of you were together. Very, very intoxicated and very . . . immature. Jennifer was 'not your biggest fan' after she left that morning, and so she made the decision not to raise a child with you. Y'all were strangers. Again, her words, not mine."

That anger morphs into embarrassment. My face burns. Only an asshole deserves Jennifer's description. A stupid, selfish asshole.

The thing is, I don't doubt I was that asshole back then. And yeah, maybe she made a less than stellar, too, to cut me out of my kid's life without ever asking if I wanted to be involved in the first place. But was I that big of a jerk that she'd choose to raise our baby without me?

"I was only, what, twenty-four at the time?" I say defensively. "Of course I was immature."

"What about now?"

I tear a hand through my hair. "I hope I'm not that much of an idiot anymore. But what am I supposed to do here, Melissa? Am I just supposed to take this news in stride? That I'm going to have full custody of a kid I never met and didn't know I had until now? That's *insane*. Especially when I'm staring down the barrel of my last shot at the Super Bowl."

"Before you jump off a cliff, I'd like to provide a gentle reminder that you have the resources to hire help, Rhett. Lots of it."

"Right," I clip. Because she is right. Hell, if I wanted to, I could hire a handful of nannies to be with the kid day and night, seven days a week, 365 days a year for the next 18 years, no problem.

But that—it doesn't sit right. Mama didn't raise a coward, and she sure as hell didn't dedicate her life to her family just so I could pay other people to raise my babies.

Just so I could pay other people to fix my mistakes.

"Listen, Rhett." Melissa blows out a breath. "I know I just dropped a bomb on you, so how about you take today and tonight to absorb everything? Think it all through, maybe talk it out with your family. Then call me in the morning, and we'll get you set up for a paternity test. Elle has agreed to comply. I don't mean to rush you, but the sooner we can establish the facts, the sooner we can sort this whole mess out, all right?"

Without warning, a burn joins the tightness in my throat. I turn my head just in time to empty the contents of my stomach on the ground in a neat little pile of regurgitated oatmeal, eggs, and raspberries.

Tom gags. I reach behind me and, finding the trunk of the tree, lean my back against it.

"Rhett?" Melissa asks.

I wipe my mouth on the back of my hand. "Yes?"

"Did you just—?"

"Vomit? Yup. And no, I am not all right."

"Of course you're not. That was a stupid thing to say. Look, I don't want you to panic until we know for certain that you're the father. Until then, do your best to stay calm because chances are, this kid isn't yours. Really, who does something like this to the father of her child? Why wouldn't she want your support, whether it be money or time?"

I swallow hard. "Clearly Jennifer didn't want my support at all."

She didn't want my support because she knew I'd suck at it. At parenting or consciously-uncoupled parenting or whatever the fuck people call it these days.

Did she really think Liam would be better off without me?

The idea makes my stomach hurt.

"We'll talk about everything tomorrow," Melissa says. "You have any other questions?"

I blink. I look up to see Tom standing a few yards away, still gagging.

"What happens if the test comes back positive?"

"Then we petition the court for a change of custody. Pretty simple."

"Simple. Ha."

"I'm here if you need me."

"Thanks, Melissa. I appreciate that. I'll call you tomorrow."

"Bye, Rhett."

"Bye." I've already dropped the phone away from my ear when the question hits me out of nowhere. I press the phone back to my ear. "Wait, Melissa—where's Liam now?"

I worry she's already hung up when it takes a beat for her to reply. "Liam's in Denver, where Jennifer lived."

"No, I mean, who is he with? Is he with Elle or in foster care or something?"

I hear Melissa flipping through papers. "Liam is . . . yes, he's currently with Elle. Again, Jennifer had no living relatives we're aware of."

"Is he okay?"

"I can't answer that," Melissa says.

"Screw waiting. Schedule the test," I say. "Today too soon?"

"Most likely," she replies with a laugh. "I'll get the earliest appointment I can, but that probably won't be for another day or two."

I end my call with Melissa and leap to my feet, suddenly unable to stay still. My hands shake as I try to pull up my contacts on my phone. Who do I call? Who do I tell? What do I do? What the *fuck do I do* while I wait to take this test?

I blurt the first thing that comes to mind. "Workout's over. Time for whiskey."

Tom gags again. "Thanks, but no thanks." Licking his lips, he manages to stand upright. "Did I understand that correctly? You're—"

"A dad." Just saying the word makes me want to cry. "Yup."

"But we don't know for sure, right? That you're the kid's father?"

"Not yet."

But deep down, I know Liam's my son.

Chapter Five

AMELIA

I hear the sirens approaching two heartbeats before Nuria, Woodward Montessori School's director, pokes her head in my classroom door.

"Miss Amelia? Can I speak to you for a moment?"

I look up from *Brown Bear Brown Bear, What Do You See?*, the pages so well-used they're soft to the touch. It's the copy my grandmother had in her classroom, which she passed down to my mom to have in hers too.

Nuria's face is white as a sheet.

"Sure," I say, doing my best to keep my voice cheery as I pass the book to my teaching assistant, Mr. Jake. "Y'all behave, all right?"

My stomach tightens when the sirens get louder. All ten of my students glance at the windows on the far side of the classroom.

I do the same even though we overlook an enclosed, leafy courtyard.

I still get a bad feeling about what's about to go down. It can't be an active shooter because we have protocols for that. As much as I'm relieved, I'm also bummed *shooter* is my first thought. It's a terrifying thing that violence has become a part of our everyday lives here.

Then I wonder if a student choked. Fell. Hit their head and is gushing blood. Or maybe someone had a heart attack? We have a few older teachers on staff.

As I walk to the door, my knees feel like balloons, squishy and weirdly weightless.

Nuria all but yanks me out into the hallway, closing the door firmly behind us.

"There's been an incident," she murmurs, eyes flicking to a passing parent. "A fire."

"Oh, God, where?" I turn my head, glancing at my students through the window in the door. "What about the kids? Do we need to get them out of here?"

"Not according to the fire department." Nuria shakes her head. "The fire is on school property, but far enough from the building that we should be okay. Amelia, I'm so, so sorry."

Gravity sucks my legs into the floor. "Sorry for what?"

Nuria meets my gaze. "It's your car. Your car is what's on fire."

A pulse of disbelief detonates inside my gut, followed in short order by panic.

"Are you serious?" I blurt. "My Honda?"

My beautiful, brand-new white Honda Civic hatchback with an all season package and moon roof?

She nods, blinking as the tears fill her eyes. "The fire department —" She winces at the wail of a nearby siren. "Welp, they came quickly. I'll give them that."

"Is it bad?"

Nuria flattens her lips. *It's bad.*

I take off at a sprint, mind racing as I try to figure out what the hell is happening. Did I leave it running? Was there an oil leak or something? The car is literally brand new; I bought it less than a month ago.

"Wait!" Nuria calls after me, breathless. "Amelia, there's something you should know—"

But I'm already hip-checking through the front door, the handlebar making a *clack-wheeze* as I push out into the bright sunshine.

I'm immediately assaulted by the acrid smell of burnt rubber. Turning my head, I see flames licking into the sky in the far corner of the parking lot, and my breath leaves my lungs.

Yup, that's my car, all right. There's one stroke of luck: ever since I drove it off the dealership lot, I've parked in the farthest space away from the school. What can I say? It's by far the most expensive thing I've ever bought and the only car I've driven that's not a total jalopy.

I can feel the heat of the fire from here.

The fire trucks are zooming up Woodward's front drive, sirens screaming. Without thinking, I make a mad dash for the car. I can't help—I know that much—but I also need to know why my car is currently on freaking *fire*.

"Amelia!" Nuria is shouting behind me. "Wait!"

I draw to a stop just shy of the inferno. There, scrawled on the blacktop in front of my parking spot in white spray paint, is a message:

This slut is sleeping with Jim Beasley!!!!

A married man!!!!

Homewrecker!!!!!

Nuria grabs me by the elbow, and I nearly jump ten feet into the air. My skin blisters from the heat of the fire. Flames curl into the clear morning sky, smoke billowing in violent bursts of black.

"I was," she pants, "trying to tell you about that. The note."

The fire truck pulls up beside us. Nuria covers her ears—the siren is *loud* up close—but I just stand there, staring at the words.

Why all the exclamation points?

Because *that's* the question I should be asking. God. But the real questions are too terrifying to contemplate. Questions like, since Jim is the only guy I've been seeing—the only guy I've seen for the past year—does that mean he's married?

Oh, God, is Jim fucking married?

Jim told me he was separated.

Then again, he hasn't invited me over to his new condo yet.

But he's a single dad, trying to juggle a blossoming career as a litigation attorney with the demands of being the primary parent (his ex is an alcoholic). The kids are with him more often than not, and he doesn't want to confuse them by bringing a new woman around. Considering I absolutely adore kids and would love to have a family of my own, not being able to meet them has been a huge bummer.

Still, I thought I understood Jim's predicament. I was happy to be patient if it meant being part of his family in the long run.

But what if his ex isn't an alcoholic? I've never met her.

What if his ex isn't an ex at all?

What if I've been sleeping with a Woodword Academy parent who is married?

The cherry on this shit sundae: *Jim is on Woodward's board.* Which means accusations of favoritism are going to fly.

A career at Woodward is what I've dreamed about since I could remember. Mom founded the school in the hopes of making a difference. Preschool is prohibitively expensive for many families, so she immediately began fundraising to provide scholarships for lower-income students who lived in underserved communities.

Our scholarship program has grown every year since. Mom set the goal of providing all students with financial aid, and while we haven't gotten there yet, I've made it my mission to help get us over the finish line. I teach full-time, but I'm also learning how to fundraise alongside our excellent development team. I love the work.

The pay could be better, yeah, but I feel like I make Mom proud every morning I show up for our kids.

What the hell was I thinking? How did I lose sight of that goal? My dreams?

You thought you were in love. You thought you were finally getting a family. You believed him when he said he'd put you first.

"Ma'am. Excuse me, ma'am, we're gonna need you to step back," a fireman with friendly eyes and a buzzcut says. I blink, my gaze catching on the blond spikes of his hair. I can see his scalp, red, already glistening with sweat. "Is this your car?"

Nuria gently guides me several steps back. The fireman puts on his helmet, eyes still on my face.

"It is," I manage.

And then I burst into tears at the same moment my car bursts into a ball of flames.

The neon green sign with jagged edges—the kind that pops up with a *pow* anytime Batman lands a punch in the '6os cartoon—declares this particularly cheap, and particularly bad, vodka the deal of the week.

I grab one of the plastic handles off the shelf. Contemplate grabbing another, but then I remember I just got fired with no severance and probably lit any future in my dream career on fire (ugh, the fire puns just keep coming). So cheap liquor it is.

My grandmother is going to be so, so disappointed in me. I can't even contemplate what my mom would think. The school she founded —the school that was her life's work—giving her only daughter the boot for being careless enough to sleep with a parent.

A *married* parent.

I got a grip on my tears on the Uber ride over here. Didn't want to chance the cashier seeing what a mess I am and refusing to sell me anything. But now I'm hit by a new wave of emotion that makes my eyes swim.

Guess that'll happen when your life is over.

I called Jim as the firemen doused my poor Honda in enough water to fill a lake. He didn't pick up at first, which I knew was a bad sign. Then I got a text: *I'm sorry.*

Another bad sign.

I called him three more times. He finally picked up, and when I asked him if he was married, he said he was. He kept apologizing, and I kept crying. Apparently, he and his wife had separated—for a *month*. That's when he and I started dating. He got back together with his ex shortly after, but he somehow forgot to break up with me in the meantime.

"I was just having the best time being with you," he said.

"Were you ever going to tell me you were back together with your wife?"

"Yes?" A pause. "Eventually?"

Pure, one hundred percent dickhead.

And I'm a pure, one hundred percent idiot for not seeing it sooner.

In my defense, after years of dating duds, I wanted Jim to be the one so, so badly.

Badly enough that I'd overlook a red flag or three in the hope I was being cautiously optimistic instead of willfully stupid. The sex was good. We laughed a lot. We went on some incredible hikes together and had a blast taking fly fishing lessons on our weekend getaways in Tennessee.

Now I know why Jim insisted we always skip town for our dates.

I put my head down and turn toward the cashier. I don't see the hulking figure in front of me until I literally bump boobs-first into his massive—and massively firm—chest.

"Oh my God, I'm so sor—"

"Amelia?"

My gaze catches on a pair of familiar blue eyes.

Rhett Beauregard.

Stomach dipping, I'm hit for half a second by something like relief. The kind you feel when you see a good friend, and you know everything's going to be okay, even if it really isn't.

He looks bad. I mean, he looks good—*damn, he really is smuggling grapefruits*—in his athletic shorts and sweat-stained T-shirt with the sleeves cut off. But his eyes are red, and his scruff is even scruffier than before.

He must notice the same about me—well, not the scruff, but my eyes are so swollen they probably look like chewed-up Red Hots—because his brows snap together. "Hey. Everything all right?"

Dammit, more tears.

I blink hard. "Um."

I could lie. But I'm sick of lies. I'm sick of everything and everyone.

"Bad day?" Rhett asks, voice softer now.

Swallowing the lump in my throat, I look away and nod. "You could say that, yeah."

"What happened?"

"Well." I think for a second, then decide to say it like it is because I have nothing left to lose. "My life literally blew up in my face this morning."

His turn to blink. "Sounds intense. I'm really sorry, Amelia, whatever happened."

"Thanks."

Rhett wrinkles his nose. "You smell . . . smoky. That have anything to do with it?"

"Yes." I sniff too, grateful for the distraction. "You smell sweaty."

"Yeah." He runs a hand up the back of his head, making the vein that snakes lengthwise up his bicep pop against his tan skin. "I meant to shower, but . . . my life kinda blew up today too. It's why I'm here, actually." He nods at the rows of booze around us. "Needed a little liquid fortification."

I let out a sigh of—shit, there's that relief again. What kind of monster am I, being relieved I'm not alone in my misery?

Still, I say, "Same."

He looks like he's about to cry.

"Whatever happened to you, I'm sorry too," I say, and like the idiot I am, I tap my plastic jug of cheap liquor against his shoulder in solidarity.

He studies my face for a moment, as though he's deciding whether to share the nature of the bomb dropped on his life. Napalm? Nuclear?

Instead, he reaches down and takes the vodka out of my hand.

"Don't drink this shit." He shoves it back onto the shelf. "It'll rot your insides."

"But—"

"Try . . ." He studies the shelves of vodka before grabbing a handle of Ketel One. "This. Much better. Let's not add insult to injury and drink gasoline after a bad day, all right?"

The bottle looks pitifully small in the paw of his hand. I glance at the price tag on the shelf. "No doubt that's good stuff, but it's a little rich for my blood."

But Rhett is already walking away, Ketel One in hand. He snags a handle of whiskey from another shelf, then heads for the cashier.

I glance at the neon green sign again, wondering if I should grab a bottle. For some reason, I decide against it and also hustle to the cashier, glancing over Rhett's shoulder as he sets the bottles on the counter and pulls out a wad of cash from his shorts pocket.

"I got this," he says to me, using the broad tip of his thumb to sort through the bills.

"Rhett—"

"You're not drinking bad liquor on my watch. No one has time to be that hungover."

Actually, time is all I have.

Rhett pays and hands me a plastic bag with my Ketel One inside it.

"Thanks," I say.

"Welcome," he says and holds the door open for me.

Chapter Six

RHETT

Bad idea.

Asking Amelia to have a drink is a bad fucking idea. I know it; she knows it. The universe knows it too. Last time I invited her over, I ended up attempting to rub one out because I couldn't stop thinking about her boobs.

But the thought of being alone right now makes me want to die. If anyone would know what to do in a surprise-you-have-a-kid situation, it's Amelia.

The realization hits me. Amelia literally knows what to do because she deals with kids all day, every day. Maybe she'll have some suggestions. Ideas on what I need to learn. What to buy.

How the hell I come to terms with the idea that I'm going to be a daddy.

And yeah, the fact that she looks like she's been through hell might have something to do with asking her over too. Her eyes are puffy. But it's her nose that gives her away. The tip always got bright pink when she was upset.

"Hey. Tell me to fuck off if you want—I totally get it. But you have any interest in coming up to the farm for a drink?" I lift my bag of whiskey. "Promise I won't get wasted this time."

She glances at her bag of vodka. Glances at the car idling at the curb. Did she Uber here? Sunshine ricochets off the blacktop, making her screw an eye shut. "I probably should get home."

"Right," I say, heart falling. "Like I said, totally get it."

A beat of silence stretches between us. Could be the heaviness in me searching for light, but I imagine there's warmth in the quiet. A mutual recognition of *hey, this sucks, but it sucks a little less with you here.*

"Amelia, I just found out I have a son," I blurt.

Her one eye goes wide, followed in short order by the other. She blinks, cupping a hand over her brow. "Holy shit. Holy shit, Rhett."

My throat thickens. I clear it. "Not only that. His mom passed away, so I'm"—fuck, why does my voice keep cracking?—"I'm supposed to take him. Full time, I mean. I'm going to ask for full custody if the paternity test comes back positive."

Her forehead creases, and her lips part. Before I know what she's doing, she's closing the gap between us and wrapping an arm around my neck and pulling me in for a quick, fierce hug.

How did I forget how fierce this girl could be?

Her scent surrounds me. Something inside my torso, my dead center, loosens at the familiar, comforting way her body presses into mine. Without thinking, I bury my head in the crook of her neck and take a deep, shaking breath, my arm somehow finding its way around her middle.

She's warm and soft, and shit, I'd sell my soul to Satan if he'd make her glide her fingertips tenderly through the hair at the nape of my neck, just how she used to.

I sincerely hope I don't smell too bad. I was sweating like a hooker in church during my workout. And let's not forget about the puke.

"How about this," Amelia murmurs in my ear. "I'll come up for one drink. One. Okay?"

I nod, too overwhelmed with relief to respond for a full heartbeat. "Mmfkay," I say into her neck, my stubble catching on her skin.

A tremor vibrates through the muscle halfway between her spine and side.

Amelia Fox does not like the feel of my hands on her. Not anymore.

That road leads nowhere, so it's one I sure as hell ain't gonna go down.

"You want a ride?" I straighten and look at the idling Mazda. "Is that—?"

"An Uber? Yeah. My car . . ." She shakes her head. "I'll take that ride. Just let me tell this guy real quick that he can go."

I hand Amelia her vodka soda with a slice of lime, and her brows shoot up.

"Take a sip," I say, wiping the condensation from the glass on my shorts. "Lemme know if I got it right."

Amelia sips, making a noise of appreciation that makes my skin tighten. I blame it on the fans whirring silently over our heads; it's gotten warmer this afternoon, sunlight slanting through the screens, and the air would be almost soupy without some movement.

We're on my back porch. Amelia's taken a seat in one of the rocking chairs facing the view. My house overlooks a dramatic swath of the Blue Ridge Mountains, the slopes so tall and the sky so big it takes your breath away.

But I don't think the mountains or the sky have anything to do with the squeeze in my lungs right now.

"Perfect." Amelia smacks her lips. The fans make a tendril of dark hair feather across her forehead. She doesn't touch it, but I want to. "This is just right, Rhett. Thank you. How'd you know I drink vodka sodas?"

Lifting a shoulder, I fall into the rocking chair beside hers with a small groan. My hip flexors always tighten up after a workout. "Lucky guess. Saw you drinking something see-through at the engagement party and knew it had to be either club soda or tonic. Gin or vodka. You grabbed vodka at the liquor store, and I remembered you don't have much of a sweet tooth, so tonic was out."

Amelia blinks, eyes flicking to her drink, then back up to my face. "That's thoughtful of you."

I bring my own glass to my lips and try my very best not to polish off my whiskey in a single gulp. I wince at the delicious bite of the liquor on my tongue. "I'm a thoughtful guy. Except when it comes to my own flesh and blood, apparently."

"Rhett, go easy on yourself," she says, frowning. "You said you just found out about your son. Tell me what happened."

I do. I set my whiskey down, and I tell her everything. Getting the words out is easier and harder than I thought it would be. Amelia listens intently, glass sweating in her hand as she nods, eyes kind, encouraging me to keep going when I get to the really bad parts and I want to stop. Panic threatens to overwhelm the dam inside my chest. When it finally spills over, I fold my body in half to keep the flood contained. She reaches out and glides a hand over my shoulder blades.

"How the fuck am I gonna do this, Amelia?" I ask, elbows digging into my thighs. Thumbs digging into my eye sockets.

"First, take a deep breath," she replies, pressing her palm to the center of my back, right between the blades. "That's it. Now take another."

I sit up, making her hand fall away, and immediately my pulse starts to thump again.

I swipe my whiskey off the side table and knock the rest of it back. Fire spreads down my throat and through my chest, cinnamon-y and sweet.

"The timing couldn't be worse," I explain. "This is my farewell season. It has to be my best, Amelia. I've worked too hard to go out with a whimper."

"You mean you're too scared to lose."

I manage a tight smile. "It was the last promise I made Daddy before he passed, that I'd win a championship. Didn't happen in college, so it needs to happen now. No big deal."

Amelia smiles too. "Not a big deal at all."

"Point being, I can't afford distractions. And I'm pretty sure a two-year-old kid is the ultimate distraction."

"He's two?"

Her voice perks up, which makes me perk up, turning my head to look at her. "Good age or bad one?"

"I teach preschool, Rhett. Of course I think it's a good age. Right now, I'm—" She looks away. "Well, I was with the toddler class. It's not an easy age by any means. But at that point, kids can kinda-sorta communicate with you, and their personalities really start to come out. It's fun watching them become who they are."

The swirl inside my head slows. "It really is cool that you're teaching at your mom's school. You know I'm a sucker for family traditions."

Her mouth flattens into a line that goes crooked as she blinks hard, and for a horrible second, I think she's going to cry.

"I like traditions too," she says thickly. She takes a long, slow pull from her glass, then settles it in her lap. "Not to change the subject—"

"Please, God, change the subject."

"Okay." She sighs. "I got fired today."

My gut twists. "What? Why? I don't understand how anyone would ever fire you. Least of all from your mom's school."

I scoff. "I was dating a man who was a parent at Woodward. And on the board there. And married."

Her voice rises with disbelief on the last word. *Married.*

My hand tightens around my glass. "You didn't know, though. That he had a wife."

"I didn't." She brings her cocktail to her lips, then gives the ice a shake when she drains most of the liquid. "He told me they were separated and getting a divorce. This morning, I found out that was most certainly not the case."

"What a scumbag."

"Yup." Amelia shakes her head, then lets it fall back on the chair. "How could I be so stupid? I saw the warning signs, Rhett, I just . . ." She takes another sip. "She set my car on fire today. His wife. That's why I had to Uber to the liquor store at eleven on a Thursday morning."

My glass lands on the arm of my chair with a thump. "Are you joking?"

"I wish. No, my boyfriend—ex-boyfriend—his *wife* set my car on *fire.*"

"Fuck her." I scoff. "Fuck them."

Amelia nods. The sinews of her throat work on a swallow. "Yeah."

I'm furious for her. But she's about to cry, and I don't want to rub salt in the wound. I wanna make her smile. Make this shit day slightly less awful for her.

"So basically, we've got Teacher of the Year right here," I say and hold up my glass.

Lips twitching, she taps hers against mine. "And you get the award for parent of the year."

"Does that come with a ring? Because if it does, I might not have to win a Super Bowl after all."

"No ring." She pulls a face. Fake disappointment. "Just a lifetime of unconditional love and enormous tuition bills."

She's smiling now, and so am I.

Mission accomplished.

"You're getting me so pumped for this parenthood thing." I glance through the back windows at the kitchen. I should've brought the bottles out here with me. "I'm sorry about your dude. And your car. Are you going to press charges?"

She raises her brows. "Maybe. I don't know."

"Definitely think about it."

Amelia digs her toe into the ground and raises her heel, beginning to rock. I try very hard not to look at the way it makes her calf muscles flex.

"Jim's son wasn't in my class or anything, but we still should've told the administration about our relationship. At the very least, Jim should've resigned from his seat on the board to avoid accusations of favoritism or whatever. But he wanted to keep things under wraps because the situation with his ex was pretty bad. He didn't want to do anything to hurt his chances of getting custody of his kids when the divorce was finalized." She sighs again, and I'm gripped by the desire to give this fucker the swift kick in the ass he deserves. "And then I find out via spray paint that his wife is very much still in the picture, and that he's still very much married."

I raise a brow. "Spray paint? Do I wanna know?"

"You don't."

"Gotcha." I point at her empty glass. "Another?"

She holds it out. "Like you even need to ask."

I scurry inside, slosh some whiskey in my glass, and carefully craft another perfect vodka soda in hers. Dropping a fresh lime slice into the fizz, I grab our cocktails and head back outside.

"So what are you gonna do?" I ask. "About your job?"

She shrugs. "No idea. I just became a pariah in the greater Asheville educational community, so I doubt I'll be able to get a position anywhere. Not until I can repair my reputation, anyway. In the meantime, I was fired with cause, which means I don't get any kind of severance, and my savings account is, well . . . I didn't get into education for the money." She laughs mirthlessly, tipping back her cocktail. "In short, I'm screwed."

I wince. "Fuck. I don't know what to say. That really, really sucks."

"It does," she says, sniffing. "I'm trying not to panic, but I don't have a plan B. Teaching at Woodward is what I've always wanted to do. I was just hitting my stride as a teacher. And I started working with the development office to learn how fundraising works."

"Fundraising?"

"For scholarships, yeah. Eventually, we'd like to be able to offer financial aid to one hundred percent of our students. Woodward had big plans to make that happen, and I was really excited to finally be a part of it all. I'm furious with myself for—"

"Dating a guy you assumed told the truth." Resisting the urge to grab her hand, I run my fingers through my hair. "Which would have been the case if that guy hadn't been a douchebag."

Her fingers curl into a fist. The sadness in her eyes darkens to something like fury. "He is a douchebag. He's a liar. And a fucking cheat."

"Yup."

She pulls her lips into a tight, hard line. Shakes her head. Swallows, flicking her hand. "Whatever. I don't want to talk about Jim anymore —I'm just gonna get myself all wound up. I feel like you didn't get a chance to finish your train of thought. You know, about making fatherhood work for you."

"Amelia?"

"Yeah?"

"You know you just need to say the word. Well, and give me an address."

She grins. "Tell me what's scaring you, besides the possibility of not winning a championship."

Leaning back in my chair, I say, "Having a kid—doing it on my own at twenty-seven—that was *not* part of the plan. Saying that makes me a dick, doesn't it? I'm a selfish, spineless dick—"

"Stop."

"That's just the thing, though," I say, thrusting out my arms in a quick, hard gesture of *I'm fucked*. I spill some whiskey, which lands on my forearm and beads on the skin there. "I can't stop feeling sorry for myself, even though I should feel even sorrier for this poor kid and his mother, who's *dead*. I'm not fit to be a dad, clearly. It's not like I had the best model for one."

Amelia tilts her head and cuts me a look from underneath the dark fringe of her eyelashes. "You're being way, way too hard on yourself. As usual. You're not overreacting, and you're definitely not your dad."

Her kindness makes a lump form in my throat. I swallow. "I'm not ready for this, Amelia."

"I wasn't ready to lose my boyfriend, my job, and probably my future in education either. Oh, and my reputation *and* my new car too. But here we are." She sets her drink down on the table beside her chair and digs her phone out of the back pocket of her jeans. Sitting up in her chair, she smooths her hair back from her face. The afternoon light is softening, coating her skin in liquid gold. "I can't tell you exactly what you'll need to toddler-proof the slick mountain-man bachelor pad you have here. But I can help you with developmental stuff. Books— the touch and feel ones are great for this age. Toys. Routines."

"Thank you," I breathe, even as panic sets in at the idea of reading a fucking touch and feel book to my son.

What the hell is a touch and feel book?

Is there a naughty version I can read with Amelia instead?

"I'll make a note of the most popular pediatricians our parents at Woodward use." Her thumbs move furiously over her screen. "Do you have any other cars besides the Porsche?"

"I do. I keep most of 'em in Vegas. But I've got a couple more here." I gulp my whiskey. "I don't think a car seat is going to fit in any of them, though."

Without looking up from her phone, Amelia says, "Don't tell me they're all douchemobiles."

"What's a douchemobile?" I smile despite myself.

"You know exactly what a douchemobile is. Sports car, rims, engine in the trunk. An obnoxious color like lime green or orange or matte black. Possibly assembled by hand in Europe."

My smile grows. "All my cars qualify."

"Thought so. Hate to break it to you, but I think you're going to have to buy a new one."

More whiskey. "What do you recommend?"

Her thumbs pause as she thinks. At last, she smiles. "A minivan would be perfect."

"You're hilarious."

She smiles, and my panic lessens just the tiniest bit.

Goddamn, I feel like I could do this dad thing if I had half this woman's breezy confidence.

"Most of Woodward's parents have SUVs," she continues. "Anything with four doors and a big backseat will work. Those toddler car seats can take up a lot of space."

"Okay," I say, mind immediately going to trucks that would probably qualify as douchey by Amelia's standards but have four doors. A Denali. Escalade. Would a king cab pickup work?

She continues to type, and then her phone makes a swooping noise. A beat later, my phone pings.

"Just sent you my thoughts. I'm sure I'm forgetting some things, but that list should at least get you started."

I try to ignore the way my chest lights up at seeing her name on my phone screen again and read through her list. It's thorough. Not a single typo.

Not a single mistake. It'd remind me of my own extreme attention to detail if I hadn't just found out I made the biggest, most careless mistake ever.

"I know I keep saying this, but *thank you*. I was thinking I could ask

Beau for some pointers too. He has a daughter around my son's age. God." I blink. "They'll be cousins. Maisie and my son."

Amelia offers me a soft grin. "Kinda cool, right?"

"Yeah. Assuming he doesn't hate me and run away."

"Your two-year-old isn't going to hate you." She reaches over and pats my hand. "Your teenager will. So enjoy the good times while you can."

I lift into a half-crouch. "That's it. *I'm* running away."

She's laughing again, and so am I as I drop back into my chair.

"Too late now. Do you know what Beau and Bel do for childcare? Last I checked, they both worked full time. Maybe y'all could nanny share or something. At least in the beginning until you figure out a more permanent arrangement."

My laughter fades.

Childcare. How do I even begin to figure that out?

"You think of everything, don't you?"

"Rhett, if four years of undergrad, two years getting my master's, and three years of real experience have taught me anything about kids, it's that being prepared is a superpower. A little organization goes a long way."

I look at her for a long beat, thinking.

Amelia is great at her job. No surprise there.

A job she just lost. She's unemployed, temporarily at least, and if her mention of going without severance is any indication, she's worried about money.

My stomach somersaults as the idea takes shape inside my head. Makes me think a vague outline of it has been there since this conversation began.

It's probably yet another bad one—the idea. I've had a lot of those today. Then again, I thought inviting Amelia up to Blue Mountain was a bad idea, but so far, it hasn't blown up in my face.

As a matter of fact, it's turned out to be a bright spot in a very, very dark day.

But.

Hiring Amelia as Liam's nanny would mean I'd be around her a lot. Like, a lot a lot.

But.

The way she drove me crazy and made me reckless—that was nine years ago. If I haven't matured since then, if I don't have a better sense of self-control, then I've got bigger problems. And like Amelia said, our arrangement would only be temporary until I can figure something else out for the long haul.

But.

What if Liam gets attached to her? Would she come to Vegas with us for the season? Where would she live? What about when I'm away? She'd stay with Liam, wouldn't she? The thought of her sleeping in my house . . .

But.

I'm desperate. At some point, I have to man up and push aside my own bullshit for the well-being of my son.

"I have an indecent proposal to make."

Amelia ducks her chin, eyebrows snapping together. "All right, Mr. Grey. But if it involves a red room of pain—"

"What's a red room of pain, and where do I get one?"

"You don't know about *Fifty Shades of Grey?* Where the hell have you been?"

"I've been busy going from underdog twelfth-round draft pick to one of the league's most decorated wide receivers," I reply crisply. And then, because I'm shameless, I say, "Work for me. Be my kid's nanny. You have time. I have a kid. You need money, and I need help."

Clouds gather in her eyes as she blinks rapidly, cheeks flushing with color. "Rhett, I—Jesus, are you serious?"

I stop myself from saying *serious as cancer* just in time. "Let's make a deal."

She shifts uncomfortably in her chair. "I didn't come here to ask for anything."

"I know. And I'm sorry if I'm being pushy, but there's no point in beating around the bush. We can help each other out *and* give Liam the best damn support in the world to weather a massive transition."

"Liam?" Amelia softens, smiling. "You haven't mentioned his name. I like it."

I finish my whiskey, my buzz intensifying. "Makes me think of that

Oasis CD Beau kept in his truck. Liam Gallagher—wasn't that the name of the lead guy?"

"I think so, yeah," she says.

"Just consider it, okay? That's all I'm asking. Please. I want the best for my kid. And you can't tell me you're not the best, Amelia."

Her eyes stay on mine. The smile stays in place. "I am pretty freaking awesome."

"I'll pay you whatever you ask."

Her smile tightens. She looks out at the view, and I realize at some point she stopped rocking.

Shit, am I being *too* pushy? There's something about the set of her jaw, the way she swallows, that communicates hurt.

She's hurting, and I hope I'm not adding to her pain. That's the whole point of my proposal, isn't it? To make things better for both of us?

"I'll think about it," she says at last, pushing up to standing. I'm not ready for her to go, but I guess I don't have a choice. "Do you know when you're expecting Liam's arrival?"

I stand too and reach for her empty glass. "Not yet. Is it cool if I call you? I'll let you know any details as soon as I do. We can chat about it at Samuel and Emma's wedding this weekend. Or I can send you a text. Which do you prefer?"

"Call is fine. Not like I have a lot going on at the moment, so." She scoffs. "I can talk anytime. Literally."

"Thank you." I nod at the house. "Here, come inside. I'll call you a car."

I leave our glasses on the counter and then lead Amelia out front to wait for her ride. Opening the front door for her, I slip my eyes down the length of her figure, landing on her ass.

It's such a nice ass, especially in those jeans. She was a beanpole in high school, but she's filled out since then, and I—*ugh.*

It does.

Not.

Matter what I think about Amelia's ass or her laugh. Her thoroughness. Her drive to make a difference. I can't let myself get distracted by all that awesome shit.

I can keep my body and my mind in check. My career is a testament to that.

Tearing a hand through my hair, I focus my gaze on a big old oak tree in my yard. A swing. Maybe I should put a swing up over there? My house—hell, my whole property—isn't exactly kid friendly. I have multiple staircases. Expensive furniture. Nary a gate or fence.

It's all I can do not to groan. I've got my work cut out for me.

I glance at Amelia from the corner of my eye. Her gaze is watery again, and somehow I know that she's thinking about the married loser who took down her career and her car.

In the interest of distracting myself from my ever-growing to-do list, I contemplate asking her about him. Friends can do that, right? Ask about exes? Friends *do* do that.

Also, if I'm doing the talking, then I'm controlling the conversation.

I'll still be in control.

"So this guy." I shove my hands in my pockets. "Did he break your heart?"

You weren't in love with this prick, were you?

"Not sure if it's losing the job or car or the guy," she says. "But yeah, I'm heartbroken."

Chapter Seven

AMELIA

I should go home. Cry it out. Pay some bills and throw in a load of laundry because I have exactly zero pairs of clean underwear left at the moment.

But Rhett gave me a lot to chew on—hell, life's given me a lot to think about in the past twenty-four hours—and I'm just buzzed enough to give in to my first impulse. I have the driver, a nice guy named Jeremy, who tells me he's working his way up in Blue Mountain's guest relations department, drop me off at my grandmother's house.

She lives in a fabulous craftsman-style cottage that was built in 1912. It's got wavy glass windows and a wide front porch. Towering oaks and pine trees line the house's original gilded-age footprint, which Grandma Rose hasn't changed despite a sizable kitchen renovation a couple of years back.

The house is one of my favorite spots in the world.

I climb the red brick steps onto the porch, the tightness in my chest loosening at the sight of my grandmother's mismatched decor. The upholstery on the cushy wicker chairs is mellowed with age and sun. A round, wrought-iron table is crowded with plants of every shape and size, including a cutting from the snake plant Rose gave my mom the day I was born. I have a cutting too, back at my place downtown.

"It's me," I call. I give the front door a push—it sticks in the summer, thanks to the humidity—and step inside.

I'm barraged by familiar smells. Onions sautéed in butter. Pastry browning in the oven.

My face crumples.

Because grandmothers have a sixth sense for when the offspring of their offspring is in distress, Grandma Rose appears two seconds later at my elbow. She frowns when she sees me crying. An apron is tied around her neck and waist; she's almost a foot shorter than me, five-one on a good day, so the white marble private parts of Michalengelo's *David* printed on the apron—a souvenir from her recent month-long trip to Italy—hang comically by her knees.

"Oh, lovie." She wraps me in a hug. "I'm so, so sorry."

"You heard."

"I did." Grandma Rose also taught at Woodward for the fifteen-some-odd years my mom ran the school. "Nuria called me a few hours ago. I ran over to the grocery store as soon as we hung up and started a potpie. I thought you'd be here sooner." She pulls back and studies my face again, like the answer to her unspoken question—*where* have *you been?*—is hidden somewhere in my expression.

And you know what, it just might be. Because, for a split second, I think about Rhett and the roughed-up sound of his voice when he said, *I want the best for my kid,* and my cheeks burn, and my tears dry up.

"Thank you for making my favorite meal," I deflect. "How can I help?"

Grandma Rose puts her hand on the small of my back and guides me toward the kitchen. "How about you open some wine? I've got a bottle of that Riesling Emma recommended chilling in the fridge."

I open the wine, and my grandmother opens the oven to check on her famous vegetable potpie, releasing a waft of rich, buttery goodness.

Closing the oven, she turns to me. That's when I notice the funny gleam in her eyes. "I made two pies, just in case we were especially hungry."

She pats her stomach, her fingers dancing over David's curly marble pubic hair, and she giggles when she looks down at it. I patiently unwind the cork from the copper corkscrew.

"Rose," I say. "Are you high?"

She crosses the kitchen and stands at the counter, scooping onion skins into the trash can. "Of course I am. Why? Are you?"

My grandmother, being the eternal hippie she is, recently rediscovered "the wonders of herbal refreshment." I'm happy for her. I also think she's kind of adorable when she's stoned. She laughs and talks, talks and laughs, the spark I remember so well in my mother very much alive in her too.

"No," I say glumly, dropping the cork on top of the onion skins in the trash. "I am a little drunk, though."

She raises an eyebrow. "Are you now? May I ask who you were drinking with?"

"You won't believe this, but I ran into Rhett Beauregard at the liquor store. He invited me up to the farm for a cocktail."

"On a Tuesday afternoon? Isn't he some big basketball player now? I thought he'd have things to do. Like throw baseballs or do the footballing thing and . . . stuff."

She's smiling, and now so am I. "Thanks for the joke. I needed it."

"I know you do. How many of his games did you and I go to? I remember him running up and down that football field, arms up." She demonstrates his pose, lifting a leg Heisman-style. I smile harder. "Those were fun times."

"They were." I grab a pair of antique wineglasses from the shelf and fill each with a heavy pour of ice-cold Riesling, keeping my eyes trained on the wine. "Rhett's having a bad day too. I think we both needed some company. And some hard liquor."

"Y'all were thick as thieves when you were younger." She accepts the wine I hold out to her. Taps her glass to mine. "Cheers. To being single."

I drink my wine, eyes watering all over again. "Why the hell would we cheers to that right now?"

"Because being single is far preferable to being with a cheating son of a bitch like Jim."

I consider this for a minute, crossing one arm over my torso. "Okay. Yeah. I'll toast to that." We clink glasses again. I look down, toeing at the multicolored braided rug in front of the sink. "I really wanted Jim and me to work out."

"I know you did, lovie. But I'll be honest, sometimes I wondered if you liked Jim for Jim, or if you liked him for his family. The kids."

"I never even got to meet his kids," I say, scoffing. "I saw his son Michael at school every so often. But I never got to hang out with him."

Rose shakes her head. "You know what I'm getting at. You're still young, Amelia. You have plenty of time to have children."

"Mom didn't," I say, and immediately wish I could take the words back. I see the way my grandmother's expression contracts, like she's flinching but doesn't want me to see it. "Sorry, I'm sorry. I shouldn't have said that. I just . . . I miss her."

I miss her, and I wish we'd had more time together, which could've happened if she had me when she was younger.

"I know. I do too, lovie. Every damn day. She was too young to go. We'll always agree on that. But it doesn't mean you should rush through your own life."

"I know." I wipe away a tear with the flat of my fingers. "I just want to get to wherever I'm supposed to end up."

"How many times have I told you—"

"It's about the journey, not the destination," I finish for her. "I know, I know. And I've tried internalizing that message, but—"

"You're twenty-seven, and you think you know everything."

I roll my eyes. "Ha. If I know everything, how the hell'd I end up dating a married man whose wife torched my car?"

Rose grimaces. "Is it totaled?"

"Oh yeah." I drink more wine. "Total mafia style, like someone wanted to erase evidence or hide a body."

"Oh, Amelia. I know you loved that car. The police will do something, right?"

"If I press charges."

"That woman can't get away with what she did. If you see any slick mafia men lurking around in the meantime, I keep a taser under my pillow."

A timer dings. I take the potpies out of the oven while Grandma

Rose refills our wineglasses. We sit at the little table by the window. In true Rose fashion, the table is set with mismatched china, heirloom silverware, and these cool brass candlesticks she probably got on one of her antiquing trips to Paris.

I really do want to be Rose Fox when I grow up.

She settles her napkin on her lap. "So tell me about Rhett. I don't think you've seen him since you left for college, right?"

"Right." I tuck into my potpie and groan, eyes rolling to the back of my head in pleasure. "Grandma, this is seriously insane. I can't thank you enough."

"My pleasure. I figured you could use a little comfort food. Although sounds like Rhett might've provided some liquid comfort too?"

Chewing, I eye her over the twin flames of the candles. "You're awfully curious about Rhett tonight."

"So what if I am?" She shrugs, dipping her fork into the food on her plate. "I saw him on TV a while back. He had this big old beard that made him look like a pirate. And you *know* how I feel about pirates."

My lips twitch. "You and the scoundrels. You can't resist, can you?"

Understatement of the year: my grandfather may or may not have been a moonshiner *and* a member of a motorcycle gang when she met him. He eventually settled down with Rose, had my mom, and became a professor of statistics of all things. He passed away a decade ago, not long before my mom died. But I've seen the photos from when he was young, and he had one hell of a James-Dean-meets-Duke-of-Hastings thing going on.

"It was a playoff beard," I say. "Rhett doesn't have it anymore."

"Is he single too?"

I swallow a bite of flaky pastry crust, perfectly browned, and reach for my wine. "I think so. We chatted a little about it at the engagement party, but it's been a bit, so I'm not sure now."

"Interesting."

"What's interesting?"

"Y'all didn't talk about that over drinks? Whether or not he was seeing someone? I assume the topic would've come up after you told him about what happened with Jim. It's interesting that it didn't."

I take another bite of potpie. If only Rose knew about the topic that did come up.

I should just tell her. It's not like my grandmother will judge me for considering Rhett's proposal.

Maybe I'm judging myself, though. It's a wild thing, being asked by the first man you ever loved to nanny the kid he didn't know he had until this morning.

Wild, and maybe a little too weird.

Then again, who cares how weird it is if it bridges the gap between my former and future teaching jobs? It definitely won't hurt to have a nannying gig on my résumé, especially if that gig results in a recommendation.

Especially if that gig is a chance to reestablish my professionalism. My reputation.

I bet Rhett also pays very, very well.

"He did ask me an interesting question," I say. "Rhett."

"Don't tell me he wants to get back together with you."

"What? No! No, Grandma, I just told you we didn't talk about . . . that stuff." Taking one last sip of wine, I set down my glass. Take a breath. "He asked me to be his nanny."

Rose's brows shoot up. "Rhett has a baby? I didn't know that."

"Neither did he, until today."

Her brows are practically touching her hairline now. "I feel like there's a story there. Where's the baby's mother?"

"She passed away. I don't know details, but apparently, it was sudden."

"Oh, dear."

"I know." I finger the stem of my wineglass. "I *know*."

A beat of silence stretches between us.

"What's the story with the baby?" Grandma says at last.

I sigh. "A boy. Two years old. Rhett needs to hire full-time childcare on obviously very short notice. Since I'm . . . er, underemployed at the moment, he put two and two together, and . . ." I make jazz hands. Will the floor to crack open and swallow me whole. "There's the story."

"Amelia." Rose stares at me. "I honestly don't know what to say. I find it hard to believe Rhett wouldn't want anything to do with his own son. Just seems so wrong."

"Oh, no, Grandma. The mother—Liam's mom—didn't tell Rhett about the baby. From what I understand, he only knows about Liam because the mom died, and her best friend reached out to Rhett."

Rose's hand goes to her throat. "How tragic for that little boy. But I'm glad to hear Rhett's stepping up and taking responsibility."

I am too. Not that I didn't think he was a stand-up guy. He'd just always been a little self-absorbed.

Falling back in my chair, I twirl the glass in my fingers. "I need your advice, Grandma. A part of me thinks this is a really dumb idea. But another part thinks it could be a great way to pay my bills and repair my reputation until I can get my job back. Or a job at a school *somewhere* in the Asheville area."

"What's your plan?"

I shift uncomfortably in my seat. "Nuria let me go today, obviously. It was awful. But she did give me some advice. She said to lie low for a while. Be on my best behavior. That way, when things quiet down, she and I can have a conversation about coming back to work at Woodward. At the very least, I'm hoping she'll give me a recommendation if I show her I can be trusted to, you know, not sleep with the men I work for. Work with. Whatever."

There go those eyebrows again. "And you think nannying for your very handsome, very muscular, and yes, very wealthy ex-boyfriend is going to help you prove that?"

"He's not that handsome." I sound defensive, probably because I'm full of shit. But I push ahead anyway. "It's been nine years, Grandma. I'm not in love with Rhett anymore, and he's not in love with me. I can say with perfect certainty we've both moved on. I'm also not a hormonal teenager who makes questionable decisions."

I'm a twenty-seven-year-old teacher who makes them, thank you very much.

I shove the thought from my head. I'll take my share of the blame for what happened with Jim. But at the end of the day, he's the one who lied to me. As long as I'm honest with myself, I'll be okay.

Rose chews thoughtfully for a long beat. "I loved Rhett like a son.

When the two of you ended your relationship, I think I was a little heartbroken too. But you seemed to have a good reason for parting ways."

"We did." I wipe my mouth with my napkin. "We want totally different things. You should see his house—it has to be the biggest, flashiest thing I've ever been in. And all the cars he apparently has?" I roll my eyes. "He's exactly who he wanted to be. The rich and famous athlete, living his big life in Las Vegas of all places."

Grandma smiles. "Not for you, I take it."

"Nope. I'm all about the simple life. A teaching job I love. A little house where I can raise my little family. And you, close by. I love the mountains. Always have. Don't get me wrong, you know I love to travel too. But at heart, I'm a homebody, and Asheville is and always has been *home*."

"So no chance of a reconciliation."

"None."

Another thoughtful pause. "And no chance of you having a moment of weakness? Pardon my bluntness, but you *can* keep your hands off him, right?"

The thickness in my throat returns. Is Rhett even hotter than he was when we dated? Of course. But I'm not interested in dating someone like him now. I really do want a simple life. One without the complication of Rhett Beauregard.

"I have to, Grandma. Yes."

Rose meets my eyes and nods gently, once, twice, three times. "Okay. If that's the case, then I think you should take the nannying job. Just be careful, all right? Set very clear ground rules from the beginning. Because if I were in your shoes—"

"You'd plunder that booty," I say, laughing, and she squeezes my hand. "I know."

Chapter Eight

RHETT

"Goddamn son of a *bitch*," I grunt. Sweat breaks out under my arms and along my scalp as I attempt to jam a screw into a bright green plastic table leg shaped like the trunk of a palm tree.

"Easy," my older brother Beau murmurs. "You'll break it."

"How? I can barely get this fucking screw in there. Thing's a tank."

Cutting me a look, Beau shifts, holding the plastic leg and brown plastic tub together so I can get a better angle. "Rhett, it's a water table. If this makes you lose your shit, just wait until we put together the crib."

I grunt again, giving the screw one last turn until it stops. "Kill me now."

"Not funny."

"Nothing about this is funny." I fall back on my ass and wipe my forehead. My hamstrings sing, and my pulse works double. Feels like I just crushed my record for the 40-yard dash (4.52 seconds, boom).

But instead, I'm on my family room floor, surrounded by boxes, manuals, and Allen wrenches of various sizes. So far, Beau and I have assembled a high chair (not terrible), installed a car seat (pretty terrible), and started on something called a water table (so terrible I want to chuck the thing through a window). It's shaped like a pirate ship, about waist high, with a big tub in the middle you're supposed to fill with water for kids to play in.

Beau really came through on the list I asked him to put together of stuff I'll need for Liam. This morning we took the world's worst field trip to a hellish place called BuyBuyBaby, where we knocked out the majority of the list. The two of us filled the bed of Beau's pickup with enough baby gear to set my AmEx on fire. Monitors. A crib mattress. A horrifying torture device called a snot sucker. Sippy cups and bath mats and gates for the stairs and toddler toothpaste. Actual, honest-to-God butt paste.

And diapers. Boxes and boxes of diapers.

I bought *diapers*.

I stare at the box of Pampers, Beau's preferred brand. Size 6, Swaddlers "for on-the-go toddlers weighing over thirty-five pounds."

Have I ever changed a diaper? What do you do with the poop ones? When do I potty train this kid? *How* do I potty train him?

For years now, I've wanted a dog. But I never got one for exactly that reason—I didn't want to potty train him. I didn't want to train him, period. The responsibility of keeping another living thing alive seemed too daunting. Too distracting.

Now here I am, about to be responsible for another *human life*. A life that literally shits itself several times a day.

My pulse takes off at a sprint. For a second, I worry I'm going to be sick again.

It's exactly how I felt when I told my family about Liam. Not only am I freaking out about what my life is going to be like with a kid. But I also worried that my family would judge me. Criticize me, even, for knocking up a girl without even knowing.

But as shocked as they'd been, they all hugged me and promised to help out as much as they could. Mom was actually pretty stoked about getting another grandbaby, and Beau and Annabel were obviously thrilled Maisie was not only getting a cousin but one her age too.

Me, though? I'm still stressed as fuck.

I'm going to be raising a little boy. *Me.*

"How'd the conversation with Elle go?"

After I hung up with Melissa the other day, I reached out to Elle via my agent, Miguel, and got her number. I called her this morning. I asked about Jennifer. What her relationship with Liam was like. Any tips or tricks Elle had for me. I also asked for some pictures of Liam and Jennifer together. The woman raised him on her own for more than two years. I think it's important she's still a part of his life.

"Hey," Beau says, cutting me a look. "Let's take a break. Want something to drink? I could go for a beer."

I spear a hand through my hair. "No beer. I'm supposed to work out this afternoon."

"If you're overwhelmed, you can skip a workout, Rhett. You won't lose the Super Bowl because you didn't work out one day."

"I don't *want* to skip a workout," I growl. "Sweat is my medicine." Or was, before I started hating the gym.

Beau frowns. Nods at the mess around us. "If this stuff freaks you out, we can return it. Nothing's set in stone yet."

"You and I both know the paternity test is going to come back positive."

"We don't know that, actually."

"I have this feeling, Beau." I shake my head. "Kid's mine, and I need to come to terms with that fact ASAP. I'm not gonna be some deadbeat dad. I thought shopping for this shit might get me excited or whatever. At the very least, I thought it'd help me focus on the task at hand—focus on getting my son settled into his new home. But instead, it just freaked me out even more."

Beau flips off his hat and runs a hand through his hair. His is much longer than mine, long enough to curl out from under the baseball hat he perpetually wears. He puts it back on his head, backward this time, and pulls his legs into his chest, resting his elbows on his knees. "Have you seen a picture?"

"Melissa's supposed to send one over this afternoon," I say, and I'm hit by a new wave of nausea. I push up to my feet and head for the fridge. I grab a beer and hold it up. "IPA okay?"

Handing Beau a can, I crack open my own and fall heavily on the couch. "I'm sorry if I'm grumpy. I'm terrified. And hungover."

Beau grins. "Get your hangovers in now while you still can. Being hungover with a kid is legitimately the seventh circle of hell. Worse than that, even."

"Can't wait."

"Samuel says he saw you with a woman in your car yesterday." Beau sips noisily on his can. "Said she had short brown hair. Didn't Amelia cut her hair? She looked great at the engagement party."

Jesus fucking Christ.

"I see what you're doing."

Beau holds up his hands, can clutched between his thumb and first finger. "Just trying to distract you. Change the subject for a bit."

"Amelia is a subject that's off-limits, understand?"

"Understood, yes," he replies, although the gleam in his eye tells me he doesn't understand and will probably bring her up again sooner rather than later because he's nosy as all get-out. "I don't wanna lecture you. I know there's a lot going on inside your head, and the last thing you need is everyone giving you their unsolicited opinion. But because I'm your older and much wiser brother, I'm gonna do it anyway."

"Gee, thanks."

Ignoring my sarcasm, Beau forges ahead. "I was scared of being a daddy too. You remember the shit I put Annabel through. I was so scared and so sure I'd suck at being a partner and a parent that I pushed her and Maisie away. But turns out I'm a pretty decent dad. And you know what? I was totally unprepared for how hard it was, sure, but also how fun it can be."

"Fun?" I scoff, gesturing to the carcass of the water table at my feet. "You think this shit is *fun*?"

Beau grins. "Doesn't seem like it now, but I'm telling you, Rhett, there's this joy in having a tiny human live in your house that just . . . it's awesome. Especially at this age, when they're generally pretty happy, and you can actually play with them. Having a kid means *you* get to be a kid again. Only it's better the second time around because you can eat as many cookies as you want." He pats his stomach.

"You have filled out since y'all got married."

"Thank you," Beau replies, this dumb, dreamy look on his face. "Annabel loves my dad bod. Like, *loves* it. This morning, she—"

"Please," I groan. "For the love of God, don't brag about your sex life. Whatever sex life I had is about to go down the drain, so . . ."

"That's not true."

I look at my brother. "It is, though. Everything's over. The life I knew is gone for good."

"Maybe that's a good thing." Beau looks up. "You have a cool place here, but ever thought of building something new on that lot? The one on the east side of the mountain?"

A couple of years back, I bought some acreage from The Farm as an investment. I got it pretty cheap—I am part of the family that owns the place, after all—and while it hasn't appreciated the way some of the other properties in my portfolio have, it's a gorgeous spot. Views for days, a stream, and lots of trees.

"I haven't," I reply. "I don't need a new house."

Beau lifts his eyebrows.

"What?"

"Nothing. I just wonder what you're gonna do when Liam runs head first into that glass over there." Beau nods at the glass-encased wine room tucked underneath the stairs. It's like a little box, the wine racks that run from the floor to the ceiling packed with pricey bottles. "And that two-story master closet you have? Just wait until he climbs to the top and falls trying to reach for your hats."

I close my eyes. "We bought gates. I thought you were done giving me your opinions."

"Don't hold your breath."

"Baby Jesus, give me strength," I growl, shaking my head.

Somewhere in the room, my phone rings, momentarily startling me from my self-pity. I make a dive for it, finding the phone underneath a package containing a stuffed giraffe that's attached to a pacifier.

Amelia.

My stomach flips. Was I hoping to hear from her this soon, less than twenty-four hours after she left my place? Yes. But I certainly wasn't expecting it. Hell, I half expected her to never get back to me at all. The question I asked was that indecent.

"Hello?"

"Rhett," she says, and something inside me unlocks at hearing the familiar-yet-not sound of her voice. "Hey, it's me. Amelia. You have a second to chat?"

"I do. Of course I do. What's up?" I glance at Beau. He's got his eyebrows raised. *Who is it?*

"I've given your proposal some thought."

"And?"

"And"—I hear her take a short, sharp breath—"I'm in."

My eyes bulge. "You'll really do it? Oh, fuck, Amelia. Fuck. Thank you."

"Amelia?" Beau asks.

"Is that Beau?"

"Yeah," I say, waving my brother away as I turn back toward the kitchen. "He's here helping me set up some kid stuff."

"That's nice of him."

"It is. Thank you, Amelia, really I"—I pull my thumb and forefinger across my eyes—"I seriously can't thank you enough. You're a lifesaver."

She makes this sound, not quite a scoff but not quite a laugh either. "Wait until you hear my terms before you thank me."

"Anything." I slump over the counter in relief. "Ask me for anything, and it's yours. Can you start today?"

I'm kinda joking, kinda not, and she laughs. "Let's draw up a contract first. I'm looking at a template I got from a friend. It's pretty basic, covers hours and pay and all that stuff. I can email it to you if you'd like to take a look while we chat?"

"Sure. Yeah. That'd be awesome, thank you." I give her my private email address.

"Amelia's going to be your nanny?" Beau asks.

"Is your brother still there?"

"Go away," I tell him. "This is a private conversation."

"Not when things just got juicy," he says, and pulls up a stool. "Put it on speaker?"

I ignore his request and lean down, settling my elbows on the countertop.

"Tell him I said hi," Amelia says. "Let's dive in, shall we?"

My pulse skitters at her decisiveness. Her willingness to jump in with both feet from the get-go. No judgment. No shame. Just facts.

"Let's," I say, oxygen filling my lungs. The relief is so sudden I'm light-headed for a beat. For the first time since I got that call from Melissa, I feel like this might not be the end of the world after all.

I feel like I can actually do this—be both the stud wide receiver who wins championships *and* the single dad of a two-year-old.

"I'd like forty hours guaranteed every week. I'm flexible in terms of hours, but Grandma Rose and I have standing dates on Wednesday for dinner and Sunday for yoga, so it'd be great if I could block those times off. Anything past forty hours will be considered overtime."

"Done," I say.

"What are you thinking in terms of housework? Would you like me to cook, do laundry, tidy up . . .?"

"Um." I shift my weight to rest on my right elbow. "I haven't given it much thought, to be honest. I was just ordering in from the Barn Door for the past couple of months. But now that training camp's on the horizon, I've been having these paleo meals delivered from a service downtown." I scoff. "How do toddlers feel about lean meats and veggies?"

"Hard to say. If Liam will eat healthy stuff, great. If not, we may need a plan B."

"How about I talk to Samuel and get his thoughts on what we can do in terms of family-friendly food? As for housework, I have a housekeeper who comes three times a week to help with cleaning and laundry and stuff. But I don't know what a two-year-old's laundry situation is going to look like, so I may need your help with that every so often." I glance at the nearest box on the floor, a small one that contains a faucet cover shaped like a whale. "Baths too, if I'm not able to be around for that."

"Sounds good. And speaking of training camp, what's our time frame looking like for this arrangement?"

I imagine Amelia's sharpened pencil poised over a neat pad of paper, each sheet printed at the top with her name in pink. Her favorite color.

I tell myself my heart skips a beat because this is the part of the conversation where the rubber meets the road. The part where I have to think ahead, make decisions, recognize that this arrangement really is temporary, and that I really do need to start thinking about what life with Liam will be like in the long term.

Because, yes, having Amelia on board while we're still on Blue Mountain is all great and good. But I'm fairly certain she won't want to come out west with us. She made clear she wants to teach again, for one thing. For another, she's always been attached to Asheville. What was it she said when she broke up with me? Something about the fact that she had roots here, and she couldn't imagine ending up anywhere else.

"I have to be in Vegas at the end of July. Camp begins the twenty-eighth."

"Okay." Now I'm imagining that pencil scratching over the paper. "Okay, let's set that as our end date. Gives us a solid month or so together."

But now that I'm thinking about it, the last thing I need is to put Liam through yet another transition just when I'll need to focus most on football. "What about the possibility of extending it? The contract? Past the twenty-eighth, I mean. Would you be willing to come to Vegas with us?"

She hesitates. "Since you've met all my terms so far, I'm willing to put some language in the contract to that effect, sure. But I need you to know, Rhett, I'm not moving to Las Vegas for the long term."

"Ha," I say mirthlessly. "This argument sounds familiar."

"We're arguing?"

I glance up to see Beau looking at me. He does nothing to hide the judgment in his eyes.

I glance back down, determined to backpedal hard and backpedal fast. "No. No, definitely not. I totally understand where you're coming from. But in the off chance I can't secure childcare in Vegas between now and then, I may need you to bridge the gap for a small period of time. Is a month really enough time to repair your reputation anyway?"

She hesitates again. I've hit on a sore spot. My chest clenches at the realization—she's more scared than she's let on.

I know the feeling.

"I'm sorry," I blurt. "Didn't mean for it to come out like that."

"You're not wrong," she says. Quieter now. "I don't know if it's long enough. But for now, let's be optimistic and assume it will be. If not . . ."

"Right. We'll cross that bridge when we get there."

"What about screen time? Typically children Liam's age should have a limited amount, but there are some really great kids' shows that are educational."

I finally put the phone on speaker so I can pull up the contract. "You're the expert. Whatever you think is best is fine by me."

I hear the smile in her voice when she replies. "You really trust me, huh?"

"I always trusted you," I say, and I mean it. Amelia was the one thing I could rely on when I was younger. Her kindness. Her belief in me. She was my steady Betty, and I loved her for it.

I sure as hell never got that steadiness at home. Not from Daddy, anyway. We didn't know it then, but he was sick pretty much from the time I started kindergarten. While my older brothers had a good chunk of time with him before the CTE really took hold, I didn't. I had maybe five, six good years with him. Years I don't remember all that much. After that, he became the man who alternated between ignoring me and cussing me out. If I'm being honest, sometimes I think I associate fatherhood with yelling. Aggression.

Such a great example I have here, clearly.

But that shit's bleak, and I can't do bleak right now. So I do like a good millennial and shove those memories way down deep, telling myself I'll deal with it later.

Amelia negotiates the rest of her contract like the pro she is. Pay. Taxes. Rules around driving and medication for Liam (something about two-year molars and ear infections). She talks about doctor's appointments. Sunscreen. I scroll through each section of the document on my phone, nodding as I go.

I agree to her terms for all of it. When we're done, I stand, surprised to find I feel lighter on my feet. Literally lighter, like my shoes got an extra layer of magic moon foam or something.

I *will* do this.

I'm not alone in it. Not anymore.

Beau, who's still sitting beside me, smiles, and I'm kinda shocked to find that I almost feel like smiling too.

"One more thing," Amelia says.

Beau raises his brows. I take the phone off speaker and bring it to my ear.

"Shoot."

"This goes without saying," she continues slowly, carefully, "but you and I—our relationship remains strictly professional. We have history. That's no secret. But this? Me nannying for you? It has to be separate from that. Our relationship has to be different this time around, Rhett. You're my boss, I'm your employee, and our focus needs to be on Liam. We operate according to this contract. No coloring outside the lines."

My almost-smile fades. Like I'm remembering all over again exactly why having Amelia around is not the amazing idea I want it to be.

Need it to be, more like.

Like the reminder she *won't* be my steady Betty again pisses me off. Which is complete bullshit, my midmorning woody that weekend she slept over notwithstanding.

She's doing me a solid. Allowing me to dedicate myself to the game I love while parenting a toddler too. I can take this shit seriously. And taking parenthood seriously means keeping my hands off the nanny.

I don't know my son yet. But I do know I'm going to give him a good life. The kind of life and *stability* I never had. You don't get stability with a revolving door of nannies, women chased out of a job by a daddy who crosses lines he shouldn't.

And yeah, I'm gonna need her to stick around if I'm going to stick to my strict pre-camp regimen. My days just get more and more intense the closer that date gets. Longer workouts, then two-a-days. Recovery becomes more serious with things like ice baths and regular massages.

I'm dreading every fucking minute of it.

I need a lot of sleep to perform at my highest level. Like, *a lot*. Toddlers sleep through the night, right?

Whatever the case, there's more at stake now than just my feelings. Or my dick.

"You have my word, Amelia," I say. "You also have my word that I'm going to fully participate in raising my son. I want to do it all. When I'm able to, at least. I just ask that you be patient with me as I learn."

A pause. Then: "That's really sweet. Of course I'll be patient if you'll be patient with me too."

"Looking forward to it," I say.

I ignore the flutter inside me that repeats, over and over again, *bad idea*.

The next morning, the paternity test comes back positive.

I get the news just in time for Samuel and Emma's wedding, where I have yet another semi-breakdown in front of Hank and Stevie, who hadn't been around when I told my family about Liam. Coincidentally, Amelia is a no-show. When I check in, she tells me she picked up a stomach bug from school. Apparently, it was going around, and Amelia said it was only a matter of time before she got it. "Whatever the kids get, I get. My immune system is garbage."

I don't realize how much I was looking forward to seeing her again until that phone call. I'm more bummed than I should be that we don't get to hang.

Whatever the case, if I pass the home visit from social services, Liam will be arriving here on the farm sooner rather than later.

Chapter Nine

AMELIA

"You sure you want me to meet Liam with you?" I ask, frowning at Rhett from across the kitchen table.

His knee bobs frantically up and down, his khakis making a *whisk whisk whisk* noise as he checks his phone for the hundredth time.

His cup of coffee sits untouched on the table in front of him.

"Of course I do. You and I are going to be the ones who are with him the majority of the time." His eyes remain glued to the screen. "And yeah, I need someone there to catch me if I faint."

"Which is why I'm here, dummy," Samuel says. He's standing at the stove, giving a pan of scrambled eggs a stir. "I got you."

"*We've* got you," June corrects, reaching for her youngest son's hand. "It's going to be all right. Between the—wait, I have to count now." She quietly counts out the number of Beauregards gathered in Rhett's kitchen. Beau and Annabel are here with little Maisie, who's sitting on her Uncle Hank's lap while Stevie leans in and reads *On the Night You Were Born* to her for the third time this morning. Emma and Milly are sipping their coffee at the far end of the table. "Between the nine of us, including Amelia—thank you, sweetheart, for helping out Rhett—we'll make it work."

I give Rhett a meaningful glance, ignoring the way my heart flickers

76

at June's term of endearment. It's been a while since she smiled at me in that warm way of hers and first called me *sweetheart*, but I still get that feeling I did back then. The sense that I belonged here. That I was an honest-to-goodness member of this family and not just a girl-friend, a temporary addition.

It was something I very much needed after losing my mom to breast cancer at sixteen. Mom was barely forty-eight, and had been sick for close to five years before she passed. It was a dark time in my life. But the Beauregards showed up for me in a way no one else did.

"Your mom is right," I say. "You have the best damned safety net there is."

Rhett blanks his phone screen. "Thank y'all. I appreciate you being here. I do. But I still think it's best if it's just Amelia and me meeting Liam for the first time."

June nods. "Of course. We don't want to overwhelm him. But we're here if you need us, all right? All you have to do is call."

His Adam's Apple bobs on a swallow. "Thank you."

"I get that you're still in shock," Milly says to her brother. "But I, for one, am pretty excited to have a nephew."

Beau grins. "I think Maisie may be the most excited of all. She's been telling us for a while how much she'd love a new cousin. Not gonna lie, I thought Samuel and Emma would be the ones to do the kid thing first, but—"

"Hey," Samuel says in mock offense. "Give Emma and me a little time, all right? We've been married for, like, twelve minutes."

"No rush, baby," June says.

"I still feel terrible about missing the wedding," I say. "From what I hear, it was one hell of a party."

Emma waves me away. "We're just glad you're feeling better, friend. Stomach bugs are no joke."

"Amelia, you sure you can catch this guy?" Beau asks, nodding at Rhett. "He may be the smallest Beauregard brother—"

"By five pounds," Rhett shoots back.

Beau's grin deepens. "But he's still not light by any means."

I lift my arm and flex my bicep. "I've got him. Turns out lifting little kids all day keeps you in pretty decent shape."

"Dang, girl," Beau says appreciatively. "I'm impressed. No doubt you got my little brother, but you ever need help, you come to me. Got it?"

"Or me," Hank says.

"But I was always Amelia's favorite, so she'll come to me, obviously," Samuel says, pointing his spatula at me.

There's that flicker again. The love in this room is real, a palpable thing that invades my middle and makes the organs there feel like they're about to burst.

I smile. "A good teacher doesn't play favorites. But in y'all's case . . ."

"It *is* me, right?" Samuel says.

Hank lets out a bark of laughter. "I'm the prettiest Beauregard. And the funniest. Stevie says so, so it must be true."

"Of course it's true," Stevie says, and leans in to peck Hank's cheek.

"I throw a flag on that one," Rhett says, lips twitching.

"Y'all smelled too bad back then to be anybody's favorite," Milly interjects. "Clearly, I was and still am Amelia's favorite. I'm cooler than Hank, and I definitely smell better than Samuel or Beau."

His family is doing this on purpose—teasing me, baiting each other —to lighten the mood, and it's working. I can't stop smiling.

"Mama, tell Milly I don't smell," Beau says.

June grins at her only daughter. "Milly, Beau doesn't smell . . . *too* bad."

"It's true," Annabel says, turning to smile at Beau. "He only smells some of the time."

"Y'all are children," Hank mutters.

Samuel meets my eyes. "So? What's the verdict? Who is your favorite Beauregard?"

"Am I allowed to say everyone is my favorite?"

"Absolutely not," Beau says.

Samuel shakes his head. "Nope."

"Total garbage non-answer," Milly replies. "But because we all have to be nice to you and Rhett on account of this secret baby situation—"

"Y'all are never nice to me," Rhett says.

"We'll accept it, just this once."

"Thank you," I say, laughing. "And you know, there's nothing wrong with a secret baby."

Rhett finally looks up from his phone. Looks right at me, running a hand inside the collar of his shirt. "Really? Ask Darth Vader and Luke Skywalker. I think they'd have a very different opinion."

Hank's barking with laughter again. "Are you comparing yourself to Darth Vader?"

"But you were never a Darth Vader," I say in mock seriousness. "I thought we agreed you were more of an Ewok."

Samuel pulls a face. "What the fuck is an Ewok?"

"Language," Junie says and points at Maisie, who's now running circles around the ottoman in Rhett's family room.

"Sorry, sorry."

"No," Rhett says to me, "*you* were the Ewok. I was Han Solo."

Milly rolls her eyes. "In your dreams. PS, how did I forget what huge dorks you two are? Those movies were always on when y'all were around back in the day. I bet I can still quote *The Empire Strikes Back* by heart. Ew."

"You're wrong," I glance at Rhett. "I was Jabba the Hut, remember?"

"Oh God," Hank says, "if this has anything to do with Amelia's tongue—"

Rhett laughs, the kind of belly laugh that rumbles in his throat, and a ribbon of feeling unspools inside my rib cage.

"No comment," he says.

Luckily, he leaves it at that because Samuel's setting plates piled with eggs, toast, and bacon in front of us, giving me just the distraction I need to focus on anything but these mushy feels I keep getting.

I've missed the Beauregards. Emma is so damn lucky to have married into this family.

"Y'all got a long day ahead," Samuel says, taking a seat at the head of the table. "Time to carb load."

I tuck into my eggs. They're perfectly cooked, scrambled with chives and this rich, tangy goat cheese that's out of this world. It's the first meal I've eaten in days that hasn't come out of a can or a styrofoam takeout container, and it's so delicious I want to cry.

"I adore all of you," I say around a mouthful of buttery sourdough toast, "but I think Samuel is my favorite today. This food is insane."

Rhett groans as he nibbles on a piece of bacon. "You're insane. Samuel is the worst, clearly."

The fact that Rhett can joke around shouldn't make me smile this hard, but it does.

"And by worst, you mean the best," his brother replies. "Clearly, I'm the handsomest, and clearly the least smelly too. Also the best cook, but that goes without saying."

We eat and trade barbs for the next half hour. I can't stop wishing I'd grown up in a big family. My chest hurts when I begin to think I may never have this for myself.

I may never have a family like this, one of my own.

Rhett's phone chimes just as Hank shuts the dishwasher after loading it with our dirty dishes. The Beauregards grab their things, wishing us luck. Milly is the last to leave.

"Hey." Rhett curls an arm around her neck at the door and kisses the top of her head. Milly leans into his chest, the obvious familiarity between them making me think this is an embrace they've shared a thousand times. "Thank you for coming over. I know I'm being a grumpy asshole, but I appreciate your support, Milly."

Looking up at him, she says, "You'd better. Amelia's right—your family's pretty fucking fantastic, Rhett."

"Like I could ever forget, considering how often y'all remind me of that fact."

My heart squeezes as I watch Rhett pull her in for one last quick, tight hug. "Tell me I'm gonna be okay."

"You're gonna be okay." She runs a hand up his back. "I promise."

"Love you."

"Love you too, Vader."

Something I love? How fiercely Rhett adores his family. Makes me think he really will be okay. He loves his people, and he'd bust his ass to make them happy.

It was one of the many things that drew me to him as a lonely sixteen-year-old who could count the number of family members—immediate and extended—on one hand.

Milly leaves. Not long after we hear the crunch of tires on Rhett's gravel driveway. Glancing out the family room window, I see a small white Ford with a Buncombe county sticker on the side pull up.

My stomach drops, but by some quirk of physics, it ends up in my throat. I glance at Rhett. He wears a stoic expression, the kind I imagine inhabited the faces of French royals on their way to the guillotine. The only sign that he's about to lose it is a tic in his jawline.

He's shaved today. All traces of the overgrown scruff I've seen on him lately is gone. He's dressed in pressed khakis and a blue-and-pink checkered button-up. It's not a bad look—in fact, I very much like the way his chest and shoulders fill out that shirt—it's just not very . . . him. I actually miss the scruff. And even now, he plucks at his pants and gives his belt a tug, like he's wearing a stockbroker bro costume that's one size too small.

Rhett wouldn't want my pity. But right now, I can't help but feel bad for him.

Then a car door opens and shuts, and I remind myself he's about to get a kid, not a cancer diagnosis.

"Okay." I blow out a breath. "Let's go meet your son."

"Let's," he says grimly and heads for the door. I follow a step behind. Close enough to catch him if he really does pass out, but far enough to give him some space.

He puts his hand on the knob and drops his head. Breathes deeply. Then he looks up and opens the door.

The morning is overcast, but the light that pours into the foyer is still bright enough to make me blink. A black woman in shiny clogs and a cardigan stands on the stoop, a navy blue quilted tote bag slung over one shoulder. Rhett told me her name is Natasha. She was here earlier this week for a home visit—child protective services wants to make sure kids go to stable, secure homes—which Rhett said went well.

Beside Natasha, his hand in hers, is a little boy with bright blue eyes and the thickest, blondest hair I've ever seen on anyone other than Rhett. He's holding what must be his lovey in his other hand, a worn stuffed puppy attached to a small gray blanket.

Oh my God, he's a mini Rhett Beauregard. Right down to the shape of his eyes, the olive tone of his skin, and the uncertain frown he wears.

He is beautiful.

I'm flooded by emotion ferocious enough to clog my throat and make my eyes water. Without thinking, I reach down and grab Rhett's hand. It's warm, dry. Safe.

It feels safe. Even as a zip of awareness darts up my arm, making me want to lean into him, into the solid breadth of his body.

He turns his head, and I see that his eyes are full of tears too. He squeezes my hand. *Thank you.*

I squeeze back. *I'm here.*

"Mr. Beauregard," Natasha says, extending her hand. "Good to see you again. I'll get right to it, as I know you must be anxious to finally meet the newest member of your family. This is your son, Liam. Liam, this is your dad."

Rhett drops my hand and offers it to Natasha. "Good to see you too." He falls into a crouch, his knees cracking, and gives Liam a watery smile. "Hey, buddy. It's nice to meet you."

"Can you say hello?" Natasha asks gently.

Liam looks at Rhett. And keeps looking. I can already tell he's a serious little guy.

"No," he says at last in his high-pitched toddler voice, and the three of us adults burst into mostly relieved, slightly nervous laughter.

Rhett's wiping away tears with the crook of his thumb, sniffing as he stares at his son. Is Rhett thinking about everything he's about to gain? Or is he still dwelling on everything he's going to lose?

Probably a little bit of both.

I don't want to ruin the moment. But I also know Rhett could use a little backup at this point. So introduce myself to Natasha as Liam's nanny, and then I turn to Liam himself.

Using my best teacher voice, I smile and lean down, flattening my palms on my thighs. "Hi, Liam, I'm Amelia. Can you tell me who that is?" I point at his lovey.

Liam is looking at me. His eyes are wide, the expression in them uncertain.

"Tell Amelia who you're holding," Natasha says. "That's Pup Pup, right?"

Liam buries his head in Natasha's leg. "Pup Pup," he says, the words muffled.

"Would you and Pup Pup like to come play? We have lots of new toys."

"So many toys," Rhett adds.

Liam looks back at his father. Turns his head to study me.

"Toys," he says.

"Yes, sir," I reply. "We have a slide, and a shopping cart with all kinds of food to put in it, and a school bus—"

"Bus!" Liam turns his head to look at me. "Bus! Bus!"

I glance at Natasha. "I take it he's a fan of *Wheels on the Bus?*"

"Oh yeah," she replies. "That, and *Twinkle Twinkle Little Star.*"

I straighten and hold out my hand. "Liam, would you like to come play with the school bus? You can bring Pup Pup too."

Liam doesn't take my hand, but he does look up at Natasha and say, "Bus."

"All right then. Let's go play with your new bus."

Natasha leads Liam inside. Rhett closes the door behind them and lifts his arm to wipe his nose on his sleeve.

"Hey." I nudge him with my elbow. "You're doing great."

He offers me a tight smile. "I'm not, but I appreciate you saying that."

"Did you or your son try to kill each other yet?"

He blinks. "No?"

"There you go." I pat him on the shoulder. "You're already doing better than Darth Vader."

"He's not that hard to beat." Rhett thinks about this for a minute. "But he probably doesn't know the words to *Wheels on the Bus.*"

"You do?"

"Hank plays it all the time for Maisie."

I grin. "See? No one on the Dark Side sings—you always did have a nice voice. Me, on the other hand . . ."

"Atrocious." He manages a grin too. "C'mon, Jabba. Remind me just how terrible it is."

Chapter Ten

RHETT

The poop happens the second Natasha leaves.

Thanks to a show called *Mickey Mouse Clubhouse*, she was able to slip out without upsetting Liam, leaving the three of us—him, Amelia, me—on the floor of my family room. Liam is standing entirely too close to the TV, head tilted all the way back as he stares at Mickey and Minnie singing a pretty painful song about pancakes.

Liam has these nubby knees and big, square hands. His hair is straight, a little unruly, just like mine was at that age. He's not a towhead with the almost white hair Milly had as a kid, but he's definitely blond, and he's definitely a Beauregard.

I can't stop staring. The lump in my throat refuses to budge as I wonder if he'll be tall, like Beau and Samuel, or on the shorter side, like Hank and me.

One minute, he's stomping a foot in time to the pancake song.

The next, Liam is bending his knees into this half-squat thing, going completely still as his eyes flick to meet mine.

His little face turns red. He grunts and starts to shake, and I don't know whether to laugh or call an ambulance.

"He's all right." Amelia puts a hand on my forearm, presumably to keep me from leaping into action and performing the Heimlich maneuver (yes, Beau hooked me up with an infant and toddler CPR class, where I was able to practice the Heimlich on a plastic dummy even scarier than Dwight's on *The Office*). "I think he's just going to the bathroom."

My heart dips. One thing I haven't been able to practice? Changing a diaper.

"Please tell me it's just a number one," I say, even as I get a whiff of something that doesn't smell promising.

Amelia's lips twitch. "Hate to break it to you, but I think we're looking at a number two situation."

"Already?"

"Just you wait." She laughs. "The amount of poop in your life just increased exponentially."

"Poop," Liam repeats, and then his eyes are on the TV again.

Amelia pushes up to standing. "Is that what you have in your diaper, little man?"

My eyes, traitorous bastards, flick to her legs. They're bare—she's wearing denim shorts—and they are long, all smooth skin and lean muscle, light catching on the fine hair on her thighs.

"C'mon, Liam, let's go change you," Amelia says, holding out her hand. She glances at me over her shoulder. "You come too, Daddy."

Good.

It's good she's here to stop that train of thought in its tracks.

Thoughts like that are why I'm in this pickle in the first place.

Speaking of pickles. I get up, squirming a little at the not-so-good feeling in my pants. I don't care that Amelia called me daddy—not my kink—but I do care that I'm suddenly aware of her sweet, summery scent, and how it's suddenly making the inside of my house feel like summer too, the air still and a little too warm and full of possibility.

Liam is still glued to the TV. Amelia carefully wraps her hand around his and starts walking toward the bedroom, where Beau suggested I set up a changing station. When Liam doesn't budge, she gently tugs on his hand. "How about we go outside after we change you?"

That gets Liam's attention. "Oss-ide?"

"That's right." Amelia smiles warmly at him. "I bet you like to play outside, don't you?"

"Oss-ide," he repeats, and by some miracle, he follows Amelia.

I turn off the TV and follow, lowering my voice when I say, "How?"

"How what?"

"How'd you get to him to listen?"

"Kids his age love going outside." She looks down at him. "It's kind of like a magic bullet—take them out there, let them run around and play, and everyone's happy."

"Noted."

"Bonus points for the water table y'all bought. He's going to love that."

Liam is still wearing his shoes, a gray pair of scuffed-up sneakers, and I'm struck by the quick pitter-patter sound of his stride. Watching those little knees work, his hair flopping in time to his steps, my chest hurts.

He is really fucking cute.

The changing table is set up opposite my bed in the master. Despite it being the most expensive one I could find, it still required an obscene amount of time, patience, and beer to assemble. Beau's presence—his silent judgment—was the only thing that kept me from totally losing my shit and abandoning the project altogether.

He and Annabel gifted me something that's apparently called a diaper caddy, filled with diapers, wipes, and every kind of diaper cream ever manufactured. The caddy sits on the table beside the little changing pad thing Beau warned me needs a plastic cover, lest literal shit get on it and ruin the thing.

I'd laughed at the idea of baby shit then. But now that I'm faced with the very real possibility of the very real mess I'm about to make —*where do I even begin?*—I sway on my feet, feeling seasick.

The three of us look expectantly at the table, Amelia still holding Liam's hand.

"You said you wanted to participate," she says at last. "It's not as bad as you think."

I tug a hand through my hair, face burning. "It's not that. I've never

—this is embarrassing, but I don't know how. To change a diaper, I mean. I've never done it before."

"Really?" Amelia's brows snap together. Liam makes a run for the door, but she reaches out and grabs his hand. "But you have a two-year-old niece. You've never—"

"No. I'm not proud of that fact. It's just . . . I guess I've never really thought about it."

"How Maisie's a human being who pees and poops?" She looks at me like I have something stuck in my teeth: equal parts wonder and disgust.

A look I absolutely deserve.

"How do you not know how to do this?" she continues. "You're one of five children. You have, like, thirty-eight first cousins."

"Um." I scratch the back of my head, the heat in my face becoming acute. "Toxic masculinity? An unhealthy sense of entitlement? General laziness?"

The furrow in her brow deepens. "Down with the patriarchy."

"Amen."

"I'm serious," she says, and my blood jumps at the flicker of passion in her eyes.

"I'm serious too." I unbutton my cuffs and start rolling up my sleeves. "Patience, remember?"

"I do, yes."

"I have no excuse, and I'm sorry. But I want to change that—I want to participate—so from now on, things will be different. I'll be different. Teach me, please. You know I'm a fast learner."

If she picks up on the innuendo I'm laying down, she doesn't show it. Instead, she looks at me for a long beat. Maybe I'm imagining it—definitely imagining it, we're in the middle of a diaper change, for crying out loud—but something in her eyes changes. Gets softer.

Hotter.

But then she looks away and scoops Liam into her arms, giving his side a tickle and making him laugh. She sets him down on the changing pad.

"Grab a diaper," she says, opening the plastic top of a packet of wipes. "A lot of kids his age don't like getting changed. If he starts wiggling around, just do your best to keep him contained."

"You make it sound like we're dealing with a nuclear disaster."

Amelia's eyes meet mine, and this time they're full of laughter. "Don't call the devil."

On cue, Liam moves, twisting at the waist as Amelia tugs off his shorts which, luckily, move over his sneakers with ease.

"Here, you hold his arms." She tugs at the velcro-like tabs on either side of his diaper, and I do as she tells me, taking Liam's little arms in my hands. I'm surprised by how strong he is; the kid really doesn't want to stay still, and he fights me, starting to cry.

Sweat breaks out along my scalp. Amelia opens the diaper to reveal an adult-sized turd, and I kinda want to cry too.

I try not to gag. "Wow, buddy, that's impressive."

But as I look down at Liam's tear-streaked face, I wonder what he's thinking. Feeling. Clearly, he hates having his diaper changed. Judging by the wails, he's got a good set of lungs on him too. Is he wondering where his mom is? Where Natasha went?

Looking into his little eyes, so clearly the Beauregard blue, my chest tightens. Is he gonna be okay?

"Wipes," Amelia says, and I kick myself for not knowing to hand them to her without her asking. I can't remember the last time I experienced such excruciating embarrassment. High school, maybe?

I hand her a wad, and she shakes her head. "Just one at a time. Okay—okay, yes, exactly, thank you. See, you just clean him up like this, making sure you get all the nooks and crannies."

She moves quickly and confidently, probably because she's done this five thousand times. It throws my own lack of experience into even starker contrast. While I wanna shrivel up and die a little bit, I'm a dad now. Dying is not an option.

Not even when faced with a nuclear number two.

"You got it?" Amelia asks.

I nod. "I think so, yeah."

She steps back. "I'm a big believer in learning by doing. So." She gestures to Liam. "Do."

"Okay." I let out a breath. Grab a wipe. "Okay. You sure I don't need a hazmat suit?"

"No hazmat suit necessary."

"What about an oxygen tank?"

She shrugs, ducking her lips. "Nah. Save that for the bad ones."

I grin, appreciating her playing along with me more than she'll ever know. "This doesn't count as bad?"

"Oh, Rhett," she says with a chuckle. "You have *so* much to learn."

I press my tongue to the back of my mouth to plug my nose and dive in. I wipe, and Liam squirms. Amelia grabs his legs this time, cooing *Twinkle Twinkle Little Star*. She could shatter glass when she hits the high notes, but Liam stops crying, so it seems like he doesn't mind. He still wiggles, though, and my arms tangle with Amelia's as she tries to keep him still, our shoulders brushing.

I should be too distracted for my body to warm at the contact. But I'm not. Guess I like the feel of her next to me. It's comforting.

It's comforting and not at all arousing.

Not one freaking bit.

It takes approximately seventeen thousand wipes, but I somehow manage to clean up my son. By the time I'm done, his cute little heinie literally shines.

Meanwhile, I'm practically sweating bullets.

"Good?" I ask Amelia, lifting my arm to wipe my forehead on my bicep.

She ducks her head to get a better look. "Great. Excellent job, Daddy."

Can't help it. I smile so hard it almost hurts. I've gotten lots of praise for lots of big accomplishments over the course of my career. But I can't remember the last time praise hit home this way. It's like Amelia's words land right where I need them, right in the center of my chest between my heart and my gut, rearranging the panic there into something way less painful.

Way more pleasant.

"You're the one who deserves kudos for being so patient with an entitled ass"—I cut a glance at Liam, who of course is looking at me, listening intently—"an entitled *jerk* like me."

"Such a jerk, changing your son's diaper."

"I'm the worst, yes." I nod at the dirty diaper. "I just roll it up and put it in that Jasmine thing, right?"

She laughs. I get even warmer. "The Diaper Genie? Yes. Then we'll put a fresh diaper on him and head outside."

"Oss-ide!" Liam says.

Amelia shows me how to do the fresh diaper thing—lift the butt, slide the diaper in, fold it up, secure it with those tabs—and then she lifts Liam onto her hip while I go wash my hands.

Lathering up, I try to parse through what I'm feeling. I haven't shaken the dread and disappointment that's haunted me ever since I got the call from Melissa. And there's this weird edge of something in my center—anger, maybe—that appeared out of nowhere this afternoon.

But there's also relief. Gratitude too. I'm so fucking grateful Amelia is here, and that I have my family around. I can't imagine how difficult this would be if I were on my own, the way poor Jennifer was.

Difficult and lonely.

And still, she didn't reach out to let me know Liam was mine. Didn't give me the chance to be a dad. To be someone other than Rhett Beauregard, star wide receiver.

Most days, that's all I am.

Who did Jennifer lose when she became a mother? Was she always alone looking after Liam?

The thought hits me out of nowhere: *have I been lonely this whole time?*

But that makes absolutely no sense. If I want company, I get it. I have four siblings. Fifty teammates. Eight coaches and twice as many trainers, masseuses, acupuncturists, reflexologists. An unlimited travel budget and guaranteed company in all my favorite places around the world.

Why do I drink like I do, then?

Why this creeping sense that I'm missing something, something big that has nothing to do with MVP awards or pretty girls in tiny bikinis on white sand beaches?

"Today is not the day for an existential crisis," I murmur to myself in the mirror. Time to put my head down and keep going. Today is going to be the hardest part of this whole thing. I canceled everything to be with Liam today. After this, it will get easier, and life will get back to normal, and I'll return to my routine in no time.

People juggle parenthood and work all the time. If they can do it, so can I. Even if the thought of returning to said routine ties my stomach in knots.

So I dry my hands and head out into the family room, determined to have the best time ever doing whatever one does with a water table.

"Who's ready to play pirates?" I ask, and Liam smiles.

Chapter Eleven

RHETT

Amelia stays late to help me bathe Liam and put him to bed. By the time I walk her to the front door, I am bone-tired and in desperate need of a beer (or twelve).

I had no idea feeding, bathing, and getting a two-year-old to go to bed took so much damn energy. Liam is a cute little fucker. But he's definitely not sold on me. I'm not a natural, not like Beau or Amelia. Hell, Liam smiled at her all through bathtime but whimpered when he looked at me, even when I put on a little show with a rubber duck and a miniature bucket stamped mystifyingly with frogs and a spaceship.

Now Amelia's leaving for the night.

I really, really wish she wasn't.

I open the door, and she adjusts the bag on her shoulder, a Woodward Academy tote embroidered with her initials. In pink, of course.

Reaching up to fold my hand over the top of the door, I say, "Thank you, sincerely, for all your help today. I would legit be curled up in a ball on the floor right now if it wasn't for you."

"It's my job, remember?" She gives me a tight smile, eyes flicking to my outstretched arm. Flicking back to my face. "I'll be here at eight fifteen tomorrow. Just keep doing what you're doing, all right?"

"Keep fucking up?"

Her smile softens. "Keep trying."

"Right." I want to ask her to stay for a beer. Badly. I'm not ready for Amelia to leave yet; the idea of being alone in the house with Liam scares the shit out of me. Maybe because the reality of my situation is finally settling in. I may have help—lots of it—but at the end of the day, I'm the one who's ultimately responsible for my son.

The idea of being alone, period, scares me in a way it hasn't before. Maybe because my house has been full of action today, people too, and the sudden silence that presses in from behind me is at once a welcome relief and a terribly depressing turn of events.

How many beers am I allowed to have with Liam here? He's sleeping now, sure, but what if he wakes up and, like, runs a fever or something and I have to take him to the ER? Probably can't have the handful I'd like to slam.

Then what the fuck is gonna dull the restlessness I feel at this time every day? That sinking feeling I get, equal parts exhausted and bored? Will I be able to fall asleep?

"Do yourself a favor and go to bed early," Amelia says. "It will be better in the morning, I promise."

"Only because you'll be here."

"Damn right." She puts a hand on my shoulder and looks me in the eye. "You can do this."

"I don't know if I can, Amelia."

She takes a breath. Lets it out. "Let me rephrase: you *have* to do this. So eat a good dinner, get some good sleep, and we'll regroup in the morning. Night, Rhett."

"Night," I say miserably. "Thanks again."

I watch her climb into her car—a navy blue Chevy Malibu, the rental her insurance company gave her while they process her claim—and manage a grin when she waves before pulling out out my driveway. I make a mental note to offer her the Porche if she wants to use it. Not like I'll be driving the thing much anymore.

The quiet she leaves in her wake rings with shit I don't want to think about.

I close the door and lean my forehead against it. I can just hear the whir of Liam's noise machine upstairs. The soft buzz of my refrigerator in the kitchen.

Once upon a time, this used to be my favorite time of day. I love to eat, so dinner's always something to look forward to. It's always nice to revel in the feeling of having had done shit, relaxing on the couch while patting myself on the back for everything I accomplished that day: exercised, practiced, pushed.

But over the past year or so, nighttime's brought with it this weird . . . unhappiness. I don't know how else to describe it. I've tried mitigating it with more exercise. More doing and going and accomplishing. But the harder I work, the crankier and more tired I seem to get.

The more anxious I seem to feel.

I push off the door and head for the kitchen, grabbing a beer out of the fridge. I pop the top and take a long, hard sip, the sudden deluge of carbonation burning the back of my throat.

I take another sip, and another, waiting for the hard edge of . . . whatever it is to go away. These days, it takes more and more booze to make that happen, so it's no surprise I stay anxious, despite the second beer I open, and the third.

I stand by my statement: I love the game.

I just don't know if I love my life anymore. Maybe because I don't have a life outside of football. I've sacrificed everything to win this goddamn championship. Family. Fun. Relationships. Hobbies.

I thought living this way was the right call.

Now I'm not so sure. And I don't know if Liam's going to make the doubt I feel any better or worse.

I wake with a start at the sudden, high-pitched screech.

"Mama," someone moans. "*Mama!* Lili want mama!"

Groping blindly on the nightstand for my phone, my hand bumps into something unfamiliar. Bigger than a phone. More solid.

That's when it hits me: the sound isn't coming from my phone.

It's coming from the monitor *beside* my phone.

My son is making that sound.

My eyes fly open, and my stomach dips when I see the grainy video of Liam standing up in his crib, sobbing.

The monitor tells me it is 11:52 P.M. I think—I hope—I must've passed out sometime around nine?

I push up to sitting, my brain sloshing around inside my skull. I wince and run a hand over my face, taking in the disaster that is my bedroom. A half-empty beer bottle stands beside a water glass on the nightstand. My khakis and shirt are in a pile on the floor, along with my shoes and belt. The sheets are hanging off the bed. I must've kicked them off after I fell asleep.

The TV is still on. At least I had the peace of mind to mute it.

"*Mama*," Liam screams.

Heart clenching, I climb out of bed. Poor little dude. Is he scared? Maybe being in a new place with new people is freaking him out?

I scurry to the bathroom, angry with myself, and maybe the universe too, for the throb in my head.

I scurry up the stairs and into Liam's room.

He's hysterical now, the kind of crying that almost sounds like a series of breathless hiccups.

"Hey, buddy," I say, using the low, soothing tone Amelia did as I lift him out of the crib.

He only cries harder, asking over and over for his mama.

It's fucking heartbreaking.

I try rocking him the way Beau showed me. I bounce him, doing laps around the room. I sing, wanting to cry myself when that doesn't help either. At one point, Liam arches out of my arms and accidentally clocks me in the nose with his little hand, clearly fed up with my attempts to soothe him

Hours pass. Or maybe it's minutes. There is no concept of time when a screaming kid is involved. Liam cries and cries. I feel bad for him.

I feel bad for myself too. Then I start to get frustrated. And *then* I start to panic.

What if this kid never gets over losing his mother? What if I can't give him the help he needs?

And what the fuck am I gonna do about the call I have with my agent tomorrow at nine, followed by a two-hour workout at eleven, if I'm up all night?

I'm angry with myself for thinking about this stuff. Slogging through a call is small beans compared to losing a parent. But I can't seem to help it. I'm more than a little obsessed with my work, which, up until now, was a good thing.

Mostly.

Heading downstairs, I try to give Liam his sippy cup.

Doesn't want it.

I try snacks. Goldfish. A yogurt pouch. A banana. I fumble with a syringe of bright pink children's Tylenol. I turn on Mickey. I give him Pup Pup.

Doesn't want any of it.

By now, Liam's practically purple from crying so hard. I'm tired and panicked, and my throat has started to hurt from the tightness there. Grabbing my phone, I wonder if I should call Beau. Or maybe my mom? But Liam hasn't met them yet, and I don't want to introduce him to a stranger when he's mid-meltdown.

My thumb goes still when I scroll to Amelia's number. *What if she quits? What if her phone is on silent? What if she has whatever magic sauce this kid needs right now?*

Fuck it. I don't know what else to do, so I press down my thumb and bring the phone to my ear.

All the while praying her phone isn't on silent.

Praying she doesn't quit on me for calling her at two in the morning on her second day on the job.

Chapter Twelve

AMELIA

Rhett's house is weirdly silent when I walk through the front door.

"Hello?" I call softly.

"In here," comes an equally soft reply.

I head for the sound of Rhett's voice, pulse kicking up a notch as I pass the kitchen. It's a complete disaster. There's food everywhere; a pair of sippy cups are on the floor; the necks of brown beer bottles peek over the lip of the sink.

I make a beeline for the master bedroom, not bothering to take off my vest or shoes.

Rhett is on the bed, wearing nothing but a pair of boxers and polka-dot socks. Can't help it—his chest and arms are so egregiously *naked* and *huge* that my gaze locks on his body and stays there.

You son of a bitch, I think to myself.

You beautiful, ridiculous son of a bitch, giving me a hot little tingle when I'm half-asleep and determined to keep my feelings about you, my employer, above board.

Summoning the entirety of my willpower, I tear my eyes from the striations of muscle in Rhett's right shoulder and look at Liam. He's curled up beside his daddy, his sweet little face bright red and swollen. But his eyes are closed, and Rhett is gently stroking his features, making a quiet *wooshing* noise as he swoops his index finger over the curve of Liam's cheek.

I bring my hand to my chest when my heart dips. A futile attempt to catch it.

"Y'all are alive," I whisper.

Rhett turns his head to look at me. His eyes glisten, and the skin around them is puffy. "He just calmed down. I'm so sorry to call you, but I didn't know what else to do. He was hysterical."

"I heard him on the phone." I drop my bag and head for the bed, settling my hip on the edge of the mattress. *Must not look at Rhett's nipples. The boss's nipples are a hard no.* "But you did it. You got him to go back to sleep."

"Amelia, he's been up since before midnight."

I make a face. "Ooopf. That hurts."

"I'm just glad he finally stopped crying. He kept asking for his mama." Rhett's Adam's apple bobs. "I hate feeling so helpless, you know?"

As someone who lost her mother—who watched cancer rob every smile, every ounce of energy—I absolutely do know that feeling.

Poor little Liam. He'll never even know his mom.

I change the subject and nod at his hand. "What's that you're doing there?"

"This?" He lifts his index finger, hovering it over Liam's nose. "My mom called it the skier. See how he whooshes down the slopes? I remember her doing it with me when I couldn't fall asleep."

My heart dips again. Tingle gets hotter. This time, I'm the one who swallows hard. "That's sweet. And apparently a winner."

"At this point, I would've sawed off a limb to get him to stop." Rhett blows out a breath. We watch Liam's chest rise and fall, rise and fall. "Beau tried to prepare me for this—for the exhaustion. The wakings and stuff. But lemme tell you, I was *so* not prepared."

Shaking my head, I say, "I can only imagine how much it sucks."

He scoffs. "You don't have to imagine. You're here. You got up in the middle of the night and drove across town to be here. Amelia, you know the suck as well as I do."

I ponder this for a moment, feeling a pinch of pride. "Okay, yeah. Sure. I'll accept that dubious honor."

"Dubious honor," Rhett repeats, rolling his eyes playfully. "You're *such* a teacher."

"And you're *such* a dad, with your skier and your socks."

"Hey." He wiggles his toes. "I happen to like my socks."

"I see the scruff has made a comeback too." I nod at his five o'clock shadow.

He runs a hand over it. "I'll shave again in the morning."

"Don't."

His face creases into a grin. "So you do like the beard."

"I thought it wasn't a beard."

"I'll keep it."

"Good."

I attempt to keep my focus on the lime green polka-dot on his left big toe. Are we flirting? Or am I just delirious?

Either way, I need to get Rhett and his cute ski trick and taut stomach out of the vicinity before I combust.

"Why don't you get some rest and head upstairs? I know you have a busy day ahead."

Before Liam's arrival, Rhett and I sat down and hashed out our calendars. While his schedule isn't crazy at the moment, he still has a heap of commitments. Workouts, appearances. Meetings and calls and social media marketing stuff. Makes sense that an athlete of Rhett's caliber is so busy; I just had no idea that the business of being Rhett Beauregard was exactly that—a business that's run with the same intensity and dedication to perfection that Rhett clearly applies to his instrument.

That is to say, his body.

His rock-hard, mostly naked body that's so close and emanating so much heat right now I feel short of breath.

"Kinda freaking out about it," Rhett says, groaning as he gently disentangles himself from Liam. "Getting through it all tomorrow. This is the kind of tired that makes you nauseous. Working out feeling this way—it's gonna blow. If I can even do it."

I keep my eyes trained on Liam, who slumps awkwardly against a rumpled pillow. "You'll do it. It won't always be this way, Liam not sleeping."

"What if it is, though?" Rhett looks at me and runs a hand over his scruff, clearly stricken. "A, I can't lose this season. I can't."

Ignoring the nickname Rhett uses—*A for amazing?* I'd ask, and he'd smirk and say, *A for amazing ass*—I unzip my vest. "We'll figure it out. Now go upstairs—"

My insides clench at the sudden wail. Liam is awake, and he is not happy about it.

Neither is Rhett. His head falls back on the headboard with a *thunk*, his eyes pulled into a squint and his lips into a flat line, like he's about to cry.

Time to lighten the mood. Do something to save this man and this kid from each other.

"*Twinkle, twinkle little star,*" I begin.

Rhett closes his eyes. Liam cries harder, fat tears leaking out of his eyes.

Reaching up to wipe them off his cheeks, I keep singing. "*You're gonna send me straight to the bar.*"

Rhett scoffs, cracking an eye open. "I'm not up on my lullabies, but are you sure those are the right words?"

"Of course they're the right words." I smooth Liam's hair away from his face, and he sticks his thumb in his mouth. "You do the skier. I'll do the singing."

Rhett lets out a breath. He's clearly had it, but to his credit, he leans over and starts running his finger over his son's forehead, soft, patient swooshes.

"*Up above the world so high, when you don't sleep, I want to die.*"

Rhett's massive shoulders heave on a chuckle. Liam hiccups around his thumb, then misses the next wail, his curious eyes moving between Rhett and me.

"*Twinkle twinkle little star,*" I sing.

"*I'm running away now in my car,*" Rhett finishes, then glances at me, eyes laughing. "Too far? Ha! Look at me, dropping rhymes."

"Calm down, Hova. And it's three A.M. Singing 'Big Pimpin' to this kid wouldn't be too far."

Rhett looks down at Liam. "It's working," he whispers. "Keep going."

"Five little monkeys, jumping on the bed."

"Oh! I know this one," Rhett says. *"One fell off and bumped his head. Mama called the doctor, and the doctor said, please let Daddy sleep in his bed."*

Fingers of lightness tickle my sides. *"Four little monkeys, jumping on the bed. One went off and said I'm fed."*

"What? That makes no sense."

"Go with it."

"Okay, lemme think . . . got it! *Mama called the doctor, and the doctor said, that's what happens when your girl's legs are spread."*

He's really laughing now, and so am I. Liam's lips twitch, even as I move to jokingly cover his ears.

"Inappropriate," I say.

"I know," Rhett replies. "Best line yet, right?"

"You're a poet, and you didn't even know it. Okay, Mr. Pervy, let's move on. What about . . . oh! *The itsy bitsy spider crawled up the water spout, down came the rain—"*

"And made Miss Amelia pout."

"Why am I pouting?"

"Because you drank that shi—that *shifty* vodka you almost bought at the liquor store the other day."

"Li-whoa store?" Liam says.

I meet Rhett's eyes over his son's head. "Your fellow parents are going to hate you."

"Why? Because Liam's the coolest kid in his class?"

"You really want your son to peak in preschool?"

"Yes," Rhett replies gravely. "If only so he steals that vodka so you don't end up drinking it." Rhett blows out another breath, but this one is less annoyed, more . . . playful, I guess? "Okay, let's stay focused. Next verse: *Out comes the sun and dries up all the rain, and the itsy bitsy spider knew better than to drink that garbage again."*

I wrinkle my nose, holding back another laugh. "You're the worst."

Rhett points his finger down and whispers, "You mean the best."

By some miracle, Liam is asleep again. This time Rhett doesn't have to untangle himself, and the two of us slide off the bed.

"I wish we could leave him here, but he could fall off the bed," I whisper. "I'll take him up to his crib. You go back to sleep."

Rhett shakes his head. "He's heavy. I'll carry him up."

Liam stirs when Rhett picks him up, moaning. We freeze; Liam blinks, then lays his head on Rhett's shoulder; he goes limp, and I let out a silent sigh of relief as Rhett adjusts his son's body against his own. His massive forearm is looped under Liam's butt, making the sinews and veins there stand out against ropes of hard muscle.

Rhett's eyes still laugh, but his expression is serious. These two look so sweet together: tired daddy, sleeping baby. It's a thing for a reason, Chris Hemsworth cradling kids in his Thor-worthy arms.

There's a twist in my center, urgent, a little painful. I look away. Cross my arms. As much as I'd like it to be, this is not my moment. For a second, I wonder if this feeling isn't longing but jealousy. All I ever wanted was a family of my own, and I thought I'd be well on my way to having one by this point in my life.

But thanks to some bad luck and worse decisions, I'm further from that dream than ever.

Yet here's Rhett, being handed a family when he didn't even want one. Here he is in his beautiful house, cradling his beautiful son, worrying about being too tired for his workout tomorrow.

Yeah, that's definitely a flare of ire inside my gut. I get that the timing of Liam's arrival isn't ideal and that Rhett was totally taken off guard. But at least I have the balls to own my mistakes. In many ways, Rhett's still fighting his.

I shove the idea from my head and follow Rhett upstairs. Now is the time for grace, not judgment.

Now is the time to stop being angry that things fell apart and roll up my sleeves. This little boy needs us to keep calm and carry on, so that's exactly what I'm going to do.

Only problem? I can't stop staring at Rhett's ass as he climbs the stairs. He has a true athlete's butt. Big. Slightly bulbous. Deliciously firm yet fleshy, like a peach that isn't quite ripe yet. I've watched enough porn to know what a butt like that looks like when its owner is thrusting. The way each cheek tightens on the forward motion, the muscles hollowing out on the sides. Hardening.

Imagining the feel of being fucked by an adult Rhett, a guy who's broader and stronger and more experienced, I don't realize I've reached the top step until I miss it completely.

"Oh!" I gasp. At the last minute, I manage to grab onto the banister before I face-plant onto the carpet at the top of the steps. My stomach somersaults at the almost disaster, heart elbowing against my rib cage.

Rhett whips around, eyes wide. "You all right?"

"Yeah." My face burns as I straighten. "Yeah, I'll be okay."

But fantasizing about fucking your boss is definitely not okay.

In my case, it's downright dangerous.

Chapter Thirteen

RHETT

It's five o'clock, and I'm dragging ass after the longest day ever.

Workout: sucked.

Calls, meetings, emails: sucked so hard I wanted to die.

Massage: sucked worst of all, thanks to a knot in my neck/shoulder area that just won't quit.

I half limp, half tiptoe into my kitchen, praying Amelia and Liam are . . . well, anywhere else. I need a minute to catch my breath.

I need a beer, stat. And then I need to go to bed for about a week. Except I have a kid who doesn't sleep, so I'm not sure what I'm going to do about that. Thought's crossed my mind to ask Amelia to stay overnight, at least until Liam is on some kind of manageable sleep schedule. But she's with Liam all day, and the girl needs a break so she can come back tomorrow morning rested and recharged.

And yeah, let's be real. Amelia and I are doing a decent job keeping things professional so far. But having her in my house all night, every night, knowing she's right upstairs, probably wearing very few items of clothing, gives me ideas that are not at all appropriate for a boss/employee situation. What if we run into each other? What if there's an emergency and I have to, like, go save her or whatever, and she sleeps naked now—I didn't see any panty lines in those yoga pants she wore over last night—and all of a sudden, she's pressed up against me without so much as a sock on, burying her head in my chest as I whisk her and Liam to safety?

What then?

Thankfully, Liam and Amelia are nowhere in sight. I grab a beer from the fridge and take a long, cold pull. Jesus Christ, what is wrong with me? I feel like death warmed over, but apparently, I have enough energy to pop a half-chub thinking about my nanny's panty lines (or lack thereof).

I gotta stop thinking about this shit. So naturally, I think about Amelia's bogus take on nursery rhymes instead. Being up all night with a two-year-old isn't what I'd call fun. But trading adult-flavored lyrics to the tune of *Twinkle Twinkle Little Star?*

Not gonna lie, that *was* fun. Even now, I can't help smiling at the memory of Amelia's lyrics. They were cheesy as hell but also witty in that unself-conscious, adorable way of hers. She made me laugh when I felt like crying, and the idea that she did that on purpose—that she gave enough of a shit not to only rush over at 2 A.M. but also to crack jokes to get me to smile—has me feeling downright squishy inside.

Am I in trouble?

Fuck me, I cannot get into trouble. Not now, and not with this woman.

I'm gulping the rest of my beer when I hear it: a scream, followed in short order by a grunt.

My blood rushes cold. My already fertile imagination shifts into overdrive. What if Liam fell? What if he broke something? I was an accident-prone kid, starting with a broken ankle at thirteen months after I launched myself off my parents' bed in the middle of a diaper change.

And if Amelia's hurt, or she can't help Liam because something happened—

My half-empty beer lands with a clack on the counter. I sprint toward the direction of the sound, pushing through my back door onto the porch.

I scan the length of my backyard and draw up short, heart tripping. There, on a flat expanse of grass, are Amelia and Liam, giggling like lunatics in the shade of an oak tree as Amelia helps Liam hit a bright orange shuttlecock-birdie thing with a racquet. There's a canvas bag off to the side, a net spilling out of the open zipper.

The badminton set I bought a while back. For a party, I think? Whatever the case, I never used it.

I flatten my hand over my chest. Let out a breath.

Liam and Amelia are safe. *Thank fuck.*

Not only that, it looks like they're having a blast together.

"Good job!" Amelia says as Liam runs after the birdie, yelping with joy when he finds it buried in the grass. "You're practically Forrest Gump at this point, Liam."

They haven't seen me yet, so I could easily go back inside. Finish my beer, maybe scroll dead-eyed on my phone for a bit.

Instead, my feet start moving toward Liam and Amelia, taking me down the steps. I can't explain it. I'm drawn to something that's going down here. Sunshine? My kid's smile?

Whatever the case, I want to be a part of it.

Shoes catching in the grass, I say, "Didn't Forrest play Ping-Pong?"

Amelia, who's bent over Liam and is about to help him hit the birdie again, looks up. Our eyes lock across the sun-dusted expanse of the yard, and a sudden, merciless rush hits me square in the chest. I reach for air, scrambling to draw a breath, but come up empty.

I've always thought Amelia was beautiful. But right now—brown eyes lit up, wavy hair everywhere, smile growing—she's a fucking stunner.

The space between us simultaneously expands and contracts on a swell of feeling.

I can't.

But God, do I want to. Right now, I wanna erase the space between us and take her face in my hands and do . . . everything.

"Same idea." Amelia's hand is clasped around Liam's on the racquet handle, and together they lift it. He smiles at me, toothy and big, and the swell of feeling grows. "Ready to get your heinie handed to you, Vader?"

"Let's see what y'all got, Jabba." I jog over to the bag and grab a racquet. "No net?"

Amelia's smile moves into a teasing grin. "Liam's on the shorter side like his daddy, so no net. Not yet, anyway."

I crouch in front of Liam and give his tummy a tickle, just like Amelia did. He pulls back a little, pressing against Amelia's legs, but his smile deepens, and Lord, if I don't smile so hard myself, I feel like my face'll crack in two.

Okay, maybe this parenthood thing isn't a total hellscape.

"Son, it's not the size of the boat that matters, but the ride it provides. Got that? So keep your engine clean and your gas tank full, little Yoda, and you'll keep the fish in your sea content."

"You're talking about badminton, right?"

"Of course." I swipe a stray birdie off the ground and straighten. "What did you think I was talking about?"

Amelia scoffs, rolling her eyes. "So Liam's Yoda."

"Liam's Yoda." I point my racquet at my son. "That's you, right? Y'all are both serious little dudes, wise beyond your years, and y'all talk funny too."

This time Amelia laughs, and a feeling takes flight in my chest.

I'm making her laugh. The kind of laughing—real laughter, not flirty or forced—I haven't shared with someone since . . .

God, it's been a long, long time.

She furrows her brow. "You're right. That's kinda perfect. So it's Jabba and Yoda versus Vader."

"Bring it." I grip my racquet and stand in front of them. Sunshine hits the crown of my head and pours over my neck and shoulders, not hot but just warm enough to get me sweating a little.

Feels good.

This feels good, being out here.

"Ready, Liam?" Amelia asks, holding out the birdie.

Liam shuffles those little legs in excitement. "Lili, hit it!"

"You got it, buddy," I say.

I watch Amelia help Liam make contact with the birdie. It goes flying into the air, and the two of them—Amelia and Liam—shout their praise while I go after the birdie, raising my racquet only to miss completely, nearly falling over in the process.

"Look!" Amelia says, pointing at me. "Look, Liam, you beat Daddy! Yay!"

"Yay!" Liam says.

"Not yay," I say, gasping for air as I'm racked by laughter. Again, I don't know why. Here we are, playing badminton without a net. I probably look like I'm swatting flies with this ridiculously tiny racquet.

This is stupid. Silly.

But maybe silly isn't a bad thing. It's making me laugh more than my very serious, very studious dedication to the game I claim playing "is the most fun I've ever had" did.

The last time I laughed like this playing football was . . . so long ago I can't remember.

Yeah, I laugh for the cameras. The smiles I give them after making a play or winning a game are genuine.

Now, though, I'm wondering if they're joyful.

Amelia and Liam hit it to me a few more times. I miss twice and make contact on the third serve, only to send the birdie flying into the tree above us. This makes Liam literally scream with delight, and without thinking, I scream too, this high-pitched monkey sound that has all three of us in stitches.

Maybe Amelia really was onto something when she said adulting wasn't all bad.

Hell, it can be downright fun.

"Can I help you now?" I ask Liam, nodding at his racquet.

He glances up at Amelia, uncertain, but she smiles encouragingly. "Daddy *is* an athlete. Apparently."

"Watch it." I hold up the birdie. "Give us a few tries, and we'll have deadly aim."

"No doubt," Amelia replies, throwing up her brows in disbelief. "All right, Liam, Daddy's gonna show you how *not* to play. I'll be right over there, okay?"

Amelia takes her position across from us while I bend down to help Liam. To my surprise, he lets me cover his hand with mine on the grip, his little body tucked against mine.

The fact that he's trusting me makes my chest tighten. He's so *little* and so sweet. Sweaty too, but in that cute, pink-faced way kids are when they're playing.

"Let's show Miss Amelia who's boss," I whisper in his ear, glancing at the woman in question.

"Lili show We-wa," Liam repeats.

Together we manage to send the birdie soaring through the air toward Amelia.

I'm holding up my hand to Liam for a high five when she leaps up and hits the birdie back to us.

Immediately Liam darts after the birdie, dragging the racquet behind him. Because he's my son—strong, determined, yet somehow hopeless—he tries to swing the racquet on his own but can't quite manage it. Instead, he drops the thing and runs to where the birdie landed in the grass. He picks it up and proceeds to keep running, holding the birdie above his head as he circles the tree.

"Kid's got endurance," I say, and bend down to pick up Liam's discarded racquet.

Amelia tucks her hair behind her ear. "Yes. He took a surprisingly great nap and had a big snack, so he's got some energy to burn."

I hold up my racquet. "I'll school you while he runs?"

"You forget I'm the teacher." Her lips twitch.

"You forget I'm the athlete." I take a pair of birdies out of the badminton bag and tuck one into my pocket. I serve the other up and watch, mouth going dry as Amelia goes after it, the muscles in her calves flexing.

"So is that"—she lobs the birdie back to me with a grunt—"how you pick up chicks these days? Telling them you're rich and famous?"

"Yes." I return the birdie, hitting it a little too far to the left. "Do you whip out your ruler and entice guys with your mastery of the disciplinary arts?"

"Uh-huh." Amelia lunges for the birdie and hits it back. "Broke my ruler on the last guy."

I hit it back. "A naughty one, then."

She jumps into the air to return it, grinning. "Naughtiest since you."

"Aw, thank you," I say on my own return.

"No." Amelia reaches up, and with perfect form she slams the birdie at my face. "Thank *you*."

Lifting my forearm, I block the birdie just in time. "Body shots are illegal!" I cry, gasping with laughter.

She puts her hands on her hips and smiles. How did I not notice she was barefoot until now? "Not for the master of discipline."

"Lesson learned," I say, and now she's laughing too.

I bend over and put my hands on my knees, glancing at Liam. He's dropped the birdie and is currently shoving a handful of dirt into his mouth.

"Whoa, buddy, let's not eat that." I stand and hustle over to him, gently taking his hand and brushing away the dirt. He looks up at me, mouth open. His lips and tongue are black. "Welp. Let's hope that wasn't deer poop."

"Poop," he repeats. Must be his favorite word or something.

Amelia shuffles over and wipes his mouth with her shirt.

I rub his back. "Everybody poops, little man. Everybody poops."

A loud whistle sounds from the house. I look up to see Samuel standing on the back steps, fingers in his mouth as he makes another ear-splitting whistle. "Meat's here!" he shouts.

"Meat?" I ask.

"Me-e," Liam says.

"Y'all are still making meat puns?" Amelia asks, shaking her head.

"I brought y'all dinner," Samuel replies, descending the steps. "Meat loaf, mashed potatoes, and some minty peas. Hope you don't mind that I stopped by."

"I always mind," I say, although my mind's already leaped twelve steps ahead, and I'm grateful for the excuse to spend more time with Liam and Amelia at my kitchen table. Will this be the first time I've ever used it? "Come and meet your nephew."

I look at Liam. Take in his bright pink face and dirty hands and big blue eyes. His cuteness is a punch to the gut.

"Are you hungry, Yoda?" I ask.

He looks back at me. Looks at Samuel. Then to my delight and surprise, Liam wraps his arms around my legs and buries his head in my thighs.

"Aw." I pat his back, doing that smile-so-hard-it-hurts thing again. "I also think Uncle Samuel's face is scary."

Samuel claps me on the shoulder. "Your face will be too if you don't adjust that attitude." He crouches. "Hi, Liam. I'm Uncle Samuel. Can you say 'handsome'?"

Liam turns his head and stares at Samuel.

"Just like you when you were a baby," my brother says, glancing up at me.

"Cute and perfect and therefore the favorite?" I ask.

"Silent and serious," he replies. Then he turns back to Liam and smiles. "And you're my favorite nephew because of it."

Amelia laughs softly. "He's your only nephew."

"Semantics."

Samuel tries to give Liam a high five, but Liam says, "No!" and hides his face again.

Laughing, I lift my son and settle him on my hip. I like the feel of having his solid little weight in my arms. There's something . . . I dunno, almost soothing about it.

"Let's go eat." I turn my gaze to Amelia, heart thumping as hope, stupid and wild, fills my center. "Would you like to stay for supper?"

By the way she blinks, hard, she wasn't expecting the invitation. I feel the heat of Samuel's gaze flicking between Amelia and me, but I ignore it.

It's the polite thing to do, asking her to stay for dinner. No doubt Samuel brought enough food to feed an army.

Yeah. Yeah, I'm also still terrified to be alone with my son. He likes me now, but I'm not sure what will happen if Amelia leaves.

"I don't want to interrupt family time," she says at last.

"Amelia, you are family," Samuel replies, and the thump in my chest gets louder.

"No pressure," I reply. "But Samuel's mashed potatoes are out of this world."

My brother wags his eyebrows. "So's my meat."

"How does Emma put up with you?" Amelia asks, laughing. She turns to me. "Terrible meat puns notwithstanding, I'd love to stay for supper."

Chapter Fourteen

AMELIA

"Mo-wa."

"More? Really?" I stare at Liam in disbelief. "This'll be your third slice of meatloaf."

He stares right back, his serious expression a hilarious counterpoint to the smears of potatoes and peas that cover his sweet little face. There are even morsels of ground meat in his hair. No clue how those got there, but it's cute as all get-out.

"Mo-wa," he repeats, this time gesturing to the plate in front of me.

I move to hand over what's left of my meatloaf, but Rhett waves me off. "You finish yours, Amelia. Little man, you can have the rest of mine. Growing baby needs to eat!"

Rhett cuts his meatloaf into tiny pieces. He uses his fork to ferry them onto the tray of Liam's high chair, which we've pulled up to the table in the kitchen. Liam immediately digs in, grabbing a fistful of meat and jamming it into his mouth.

"Mmm!" he says with a smile.

Rhett smiles back at him, leaning over so their noses are almost touching. "Aw, yeah, that's the good stuff, isn't it?"

"Goog," Liam repeats.

I set down my fork and rub my fingers over my breastbone. There's a nudge right there, a tug I keep getting as I watch Rhett and Liam together. Sitting at this table with them sure as hell isn't helping, the three of us cozy and comfortable as we polish off a delicious, home-made meal (Samuel had to head to work at the Barn Door Restaurant for dinner service, so he couldn't stay).

I'm full and exhausted and bewildered by the ache spreading inside my chest. It's not a bad ache. More of a bittersweet one.

I wish it would go away.

I wish I could stop smiling.

"This might be a weird thing to say." Rhett shakes his head as he glides a forkful of peas into his mouth. That *mouth*. Full lips and cocky smirks, and *oh God, I gotta stop thinking about this stuff.* "But it's really satisfying to watch him eat. Like, it's almost fun, seeing how much he enjoys food."

I nod, training my gaze on the single bite of mashed potatoes left on my plate. Samuel put bacon bits, cheese, and scallions in them, and they are out of this world. Can't help but think what a pleasure it would be, living up on Blue Mountain and eating like this every day. Real food at a real table with the cutest company imaginable.

But I learned a long time ago that that life wasn't meant for me. I let that fantasy go because that's exactly what it always was: a fantasy, born of teenage horniness and pubescent hormones.

I have my own life and dreams now. Real dreams, ones that matter. Ones that I hope will make a difference in the world if I manage to make them come true.

That won't happen if I sit here and pine after my boss-slash-ex-boyfriend.

I've let the fantasy of what *could* be sabotage my life for the last time.

"It is fun," I say. "Reminds you of the simple pleasures in life. Kids get so happy over the smallest things. You saw how much Liam smiled when he woke up this morning. That's all it took —waking up."

"And then whooping his nanny's behind at badminton. But that made me smile too, so . . ."

I really gotta stop smiling myself. My face hurts. Looking up, I say,

"I thought *I* whooped *your* behind? Are you forgetting that winner at the end there?"

Rhett meets my eyes across the table, wiping his mouth on his napkin. I can't see his lips, but his eyes are bright blue and playful, and they're locked on mine. It's the kind of look that gives you goose bumps: vulnerability in the feeling I see there, confidence in how long he's looking at me.

The combination—or maybe the juxtaposition—is so hot I have to look away, a pulse of liquid desire hitting me between my legs.

"We must have different recollections of the event. What about you, Liam?" Rhett turns to his son. "Who do you think won? Daddy or Amelia?"

Liam grins, eyes sliding to my face. "We-wa!"

"Oh yeah!" I throw my arms up, grateful for the distraction, and reach over to give Liam a high five. He doesn't quite get the concept, so Rhett gently takes Liam's wrist and guides his sticky hand to meet with mine. "That's right, Liam, you're giving me a high five."

"Great job, buddy," Rhett says, and helps Liam give him a high five too. "Although I am, in fact, high-fiving you because you're my kid, not because I agree with you. Daddy won, fair and square."

Laughing, I say, "You are *such* a sore loser."

I glance up and see Rhett looking at me again. This time I can see his mouth, and he's giving me that *fuck*ing smirk of his, the one that dares me to call him out or kiss him or *something*.

"Makes me a better winner," he replies.

Crossing my arms, I tilt my head. "Do you always have to win?"

"Yes."

"Why?"

"Because losing sucks."

"That answer sucks."

"Who cares? It's true."

I look at him expectantly in reply. A part of me wants him to keep brushing me off. I have no right to dig. I *shouldn't* dig. I should get up, get my bag, and get the hell out of here.

But another part—the stupid part—is secretly thrilled when Rhett says, "Ugh, fine." He picks up his napkin again and starts wiping off

Liam's hands. "Maybe there's a daddy issue or two in there. Some bogus idea about, I don't know, winning my dad's love or whatever because I felt I never had it when he was alive."

My heart clenches. "Wow."

"Therapy. I tried it for a while."

"Good for you. But still—that idea, it qualifies as bogus?"

Still wiping down Liam, Rhett meets my eyes. His aren't playful anymore. "Yes. And no."

But before I can ask him what that means, Liam starts to throw a fit because Rhett is wiping off his face. In true toddler style, Liam goes from happy meatloaf man to inconsolable ball of ire in the space of two seconds.

"Liam, buddy, you are a *mess*." Rhett tosses his napkin onto his plate and yanks the tray off Liam's highchair. "How about a bath? You liked that last night."

My cue to go, for real this time.

"Y'all go do bath time." Standing, I grab our plates. "I'll clean up here, and then I'll take off."

Rhett glances at the table as he unclips Liam, who narrowly avoids hitting his daddy in the face with the foot that he's flailing. "Just leave that stuff. I'll take care of it."

"I got it."

"You sure?"

"Absolutely. I think Liam's going to be ready for bed in about twenty seconds, so you'd better hurry."

"I'm on it."

I load the dishwasher while Rhett takes Liam upstairs. He stops crying not long after, and as I'm wiping down the table, I hear him laughing and splashing—his room is right above the kitchen—and then I hear Rhett laughing too.

Glancing around the kitchen, I notice a half-empty beer bottle on the counter by the stove. I frown, trying not to think about what Rhett said about his dad. What it means, and why he'd share something like that with me after all this time.

But then I notice that Liam's left Pup Pup down here, so I focus on that instead. It's safer. Easier.

I walk into Liam's room, lovey in hand, just as Rhett is getting him out of the tub in the en-suite bathroom.

"We-wa!" Liam cries when he sees me.

Holding a naked, squirming toddler in his outstretched arms, Rhett glances over his shoulder. "Shoot, I forgot to grab a towel."

I grab one off the pair of hooks on the wall beside the tub.

"You mind drying him off while I hold him?" Rhett asks.

"No problem." I make quick work of it, wiping down Liam before wrapping him up in the towel, mummy-style, and pressing a kiss to the tip of his nose. "Is there anything better than a clean baby?"

"Yes. A sleeping one." Rhett shifts Liam in his arms so that he's cradling him against his chest. "T-minus five minutes. Not like I'm counting."

Crossing into the bedroom, I dig a pair of pjs covered in red monkeys out of a dresser drawer while Rhett sets Liam on the bed and puts a diaper on him. I gotta give the guy credit; he still fumbles a little with the tabs, losing one, finding it, then losing the other. But he gets it, tongue jammed between his teeth as he holds Liam down and attaches both tabs in the general vicinity of where they're supposed to go.

I set the jammies on the bed beside Liam and grab the baby lotion on the nightstand. We discovered pretty quickly that Liam has super sensitive skin, with bumpy, dry patches on his back and arms. Luckily Beau put lotion on the list he gave Rhett.

Rhett sits Liam up and holds his arms out for me to lotion up. We did this last night too, but it's still surprising how coordinated our movements are. I stand beside Rhett and rub lotion onto Liam's little arms, Rhett bends him forward a little so I can get his back. Tilts him upright again so I can lotion up his tummy, making him squirm with laughter before I move to his little legs.

I'm close enough to Rhett to catch his scent. No cologne or after-shave—just skin, a hint of detergent.

Liam practically cackles when I get to his chubby feet, kicking out and sending my arm into a collision course with Rhett's side. The contact is quick, my elbow and forearm meeting with his rib cage, but a spot of warmth blossoms inside my skin nonetheless, quickly spreading up my arm and down my torso.

"Sorry," we say at the same time, and then we're laughing when it happens again as Liam keeps kicking.

"It's almost like he wants us to smush," Rhett murmurs.

I hook my hands underneath Liam's armpits and hold him still, taking half a step to the left to put a little space between Rhett and me. "Sorry, little man, that ship has sailed."

"But oh, what a ride that ship did provide." Rhett tugs Liam's pajama top over his head. Then Rhett shoots me a look, one eyebrow lifted. "It was a good ride, right?"

"Decent," I say, lips twitching. Liam's arm is stuck in his pajama top now, and I reach down to help Rhett push it through the sleeve.

More contact. Fingers. A brush of wrists and forearms, his warm and firm in a way that makes the heat inside my skin pulse in time to my rising heartbeat. The small space between his body and mine comes alive, sparking with something I'm too chickenshit—too smart —to name.

He smells so, so good.

This *feels* good. Working together, getting Liam cozy.

"Aw, come on, A, it was better'n decent." Rhett's focused on Liam now, eyes averted like he's very much aware of the tension sparking between us.

How did this happen? And how can I stop it?

"You know what's not decent?"

Rhett lets out a soft grunt as he yanks on Liam's pajama shorts. "What's that?"

I scoop Liam into my arms and hold him against my chest. A barrier? A life vest?

"How cute this kid looks in his pjs." I give Liam a quick squeeze. He doesn't hug me back, but he does rest his head on my shoulder, and my heart about melts. *This*. I need to focus on this, the connection I'm making with Liam.

I need to remember the only connection I have with his daddy is a contract. A legal document that states he's my boss and I'm his employee.

117

That's.

It.

Even if I'm already thinking I'm not going to press charges against Jim's wife because I've got better things to do.

Because I'm busy being a part of something awesome. Something I'm not going to let my past ruin.

"He likes you," Rhett says softly and runs a hand over Liam's back. "I want him to like me that way too."

My heart swells, and I look away. Look at the blue-green light that peeks through the slats of the shutters on a nearby window. Everything feels heavy—this kid, my feelings. The moment.

"Here." I pass Liam to Rhett. "Y'all enjoy a bedtime story. I should —I'm going to go."

My face feels hot as I pull the door shut behind me.

"Amelia?" Rhett calls quietly.

I pause with my hand on the knob, pulse thumping as I reopen the door a crack. "Yeah?"

"Thank you. For everything. I had no appreciation for how much time and effort it takes just to keep kids clean and fed. It's a lot of really hard work that's somehow invisible—"

"Screwed up, right?"

"Totally. The point being, I see all the work you're doing for us, and I appreciate it. So damn much. I'd be dead in the water without you."

My eyes fill with heat, and I close them, even as I grin. "You're never going to let that boat pun go, are you?"

"Nope."

"Good night, Rhett."

"Night, A."

Chapter Fifteen

RHETT

"*Morning, baby,*" *Amelia says with a grin.*

Padding into the kitchen, I bend down and press a scruffy kiss to her lips.

Soft. She's so fucking soft.

She sets down the paper she's reading at the table—The New York Times, *naturally*—*and her grin deepens into a smile.*

Her brown eyes are hot, and suddenly so am I.

She's wearing this nightie and robe set thing. Pale pink. I look at her tits, and her nipples pebble to hard points underneath the fabric.

"*Aw, honey, you're beautiful.*"

Amelia reaches down and unties her robe. The nightie underneath is trimmed in lace. It's gossamer thin. My mouth waters, and this feeling—*this full, happy, excited feeling*—*settles in my center.*

Heat prickles low in my groin.

"*Show me how beautiful you think I am,*" *she murmurs.*

I glance at the monitor on the counter. "*Liam still sleeping?*"

"*Hasn't made a peep.*"

The kitchen smells like coffee. Sunlight streams through the windows. I have nowhere to be and nothing to do, and the sense of freedom I feel is glorious.

"*Good.*" *I turn back to Amelia and drop to my knees in front of her chair. I gently part her legs, and Amelia bites her lip, running a hand through the hair at the nape of my neck.*

My dick gets hard. Only when I reach down to stroke it do I realize I'm naked.

Aw, fuck yeah.

Pushing her nightie up her thighs, I see that she's bare, wet, and swollen.

"I fucked you last night," I growl, distressed. "Why didn't you tell me you needed me?"

Her smile softens. Touches her eyes. "I've always needed you, baby. That hasn't changed."

And then she curls her fingers into my hair, makes a fist, and pulls, tugging me none too gently down to her center.

My dick pulses at her urgency, her decisiveness, and I fall face-first into her pussy. I nudge my nose up her slick folds, inhaling the scent of her, reveling in her heat and her willingness and the way her stomach hollows out when she sucks in a breath.

I open my mouth and kiss her. Kiss her clit, lick her clit. Bite it and play with it and she laughs, and I laugh, and the whole time I'm telling her: See? See how good this is?

"You're good," she breathes, hips rolling against my mouth.

"You read my mind now?"

I stroke myself and look up to see her smiling down at me. "You're not exactly a mystery, Rhett."

I pause at a faint ringing sound.

"Ignore it," Amelia says.

I do.

My balls tighten. I put my other hand on her thigh and inch my thumb up the tender skin there until I reach her pussy. I use that thumb to open her wider, and then I press the pad of it inside her. Her hips buck, and I'm stroking myself faster, and she comes, clamping down on my thumb as she cries out.

"Say my name," I bite out.

And she does. She says it over and over again, loud enough to blot out the ringing.

I come too, a wet explosion in my hand that has me shouting nonsense.

"Stay," I yell. "Be with me. Be with us. You belong here, A."

I must be shouting really loud because Liam starts to cry, the monitor making his wail sound tinny.

The ringing is still there.

"Shit," I say. "I'm an animal, aren't I?"

Amelia throws her head back, hands still on my neck, and laughs. Loud. Real. Happy.

"You are, and I love it." *She rises to her feet, then bends down to kiss me on the mouth.* "I just finished my tea anyway, so the timing's perfect. Almost like it's meant to be, isn't it?"

The moment would be perfect if it wasn't for that damn ringing—

I wake with a start. Heart pounding, head spinning.

I'm covered in sweat and something sticky. My hand is on my dick. Lifting the covers, I groan.

Fuck me.

Blinking, I see that the light outside the windows is warm but pale. Early. It's early.

I immediately glance at the monitor beside the bed. Liam is snoozing peacefully on his belly, face turned away from the camera. I wait until I see his back rise and fall, rise and fall, to let out a breath.

He's alive. And he only woke up once last night.

Maybe the fact that I got a good stretch of uninterrupted sleep is why I had a sex dream about Amelia. Because really, when was the last time that happened?

My phone is ringing. Wrinkling my brow, I grab it with my clean hand. The damn thing's on silent, which means only my favorite contacts calling would make it ring. My stomach clenches as I run through the possibilities. Mom? Melissa? Miguel, my agent?

Looking at the screen, I see it's Miguel.

"What the fuck, dude?" I grumble when I answer it. "It's not even seven yet."

"Good morning to you too, sunshine. Sorry for the early call, but I thought with your kid you might be a morning person now."

I laugh. The throb in my head lessens, and it hits me that I actually feel . . . decent. Might have something to do with the fact that I didn't drink my usual six-pack last night.

"Definitely not a morning person yet. Liam was up at two, so."

"How is the little guy? How are you?"

Tugging my thumb and forefinger over my eyes, I flip onto my back. "Liam's doing all right, all things considered. He's cute as hell. I lucked out and hired an amazing nanny, Amelia, which has been huge. I'm . . ." *Tired. Hopeful. Scared. Confused.* "Hanging in there, I guess."

"Glad you hit the nanny jackpot. I've been thinking about you guys. You get the baby gift I sent?"

I scoff. "The last thing my kid needs is a mini G Wagon, but yes, we got it. Thank you."

"Just trying my best to turn him into an L.A. douchebag."

"You would know how."

"Indeed. So." I can practically hear Miguel clapping his hands together. "I have news. Big news. That's why I called so early."

"What's up?"

"It's Nick."

My heart trips to a stop. Last year, the team drafted stud wide receiver Nick Kapakos in the first round. He performed well in his first season, thanks in no small part to guidance from yours truly. It's no secret he's being groomed to take my place when I retire.

"What about him?"

"He joined Kanye's cult."

"Stop it."

"I'm serious. God came to him in a dream and told him Yeezy's the Messiah. Nick was on the next flight to Wyoming. He's done with football."

I pause for a second, waiting for Miguel to tell me he's joking.

When he doesn't, I say, "You're serious."

"I am. His poor agent is going to have one hell of a time getting the kid out of his contract, but that's not our problem. Our problem—or, really, our opportunity—is this: the Sharks want to sign you for another two years. Yeah, yeah, you only wanna play one, but what if I told you they're willing to pay you what Kim is probably paying Kanye in their divorce settlement?"

"I'm retiring at the end of this year," I say, but my heart is pounding so hard, and so loud, I have to sit up. "Kim's paying Kanye?"

"She's the billionaire. They're offering you a two-year extension for eighteen million. Six million signing bonus, which I'll negotiate up to eight, and ten million guaranteed, which I'm confident I can make twelve."

My eyes bulge. "Twelve million guaranteed?"

"Yes."

"I'm retiring," I repeat.

"Of course you are."

Another pause. I honestly don't know what to think. At this point in my career, it's not about the money. I have plenty enough to keep me comfortable for the foreseeable future.

I've been smart. I've made some investments in real estate that have panned out pretty well, bits of land here and there, some commercial properties in booming Southern cities.

But the guaranteed cash the team's offering would take my portfolio to the next level. It's the kind of money that would establish generational wealth. I don't have to worry about money, but if I take this deal, neither would Liam.

And yeah, the two-year timeframe would give me some more breathing room to win that elusive championship.

I run a hand over my head. But my body, and more importantly my brain—and the fact that I find myself wanting to hang with Liam and Amelia more and hit the gym less, be on the phone less—

"So that's a no?" Miguel asks.

"Don't be a dick. Let me sleep on it, okay? When do they want an answer?"

"Before training camp starts."

"Okay. Yeah. Yeah, I'll let you know by then."

I hang up and drop the phone onto my lap. Stare at it for a long beat, my stomach working itself into a neat little knot.

What the hell is that about? Excitement? Dread?

"Hi," a little voice says, and I glance at the monitor and see Liam sitting up in his crib. "Hi. Lili say hi."

I'm bone-tired and not at all excited for the day ahead. My feelings about—well, everything and everyone are all over the place. I just blew a load into my sheets having pornographic dreams about my high school girlfriend for Christssakes.

My *nanny*.

Everything's a fucking mess. Still, I watch Liam babble to himself and smile.

"Hi!" he says when I walk into his room a couple minutes later. I smile. He doesn't smile back, but he does let me pick him up and cuddle him against my bare chest.

"Morning, buddy. What should we have for breakfast? Some waffles?"

"Waffle," he replies.

"Done and done. But first"—I sniff his diaper—"whew, we gotta change you. Son, that's downright rude."

This turd isn't nearly as traumatizing as the first. Maybe because I'm actually getting the hang of this diaper changing gig, and it feels good to kinda-sorta know what I'm doing.

Liam watches me, his expression serious. When I'm done, I take his little hand and put it on my chest. "Dada." I move his hand to his chest. "Liam."

"Lili and Dada eat waffle," he repeats. It's a simple thing, small, but him saying my name—adding his—it makes my chest swell.

Grinning, I pick him up and head down the stairs. "That's right. Dada and Liam are going to eat some waffles for breakfast. Do you want blueberry or chocolate chip?"

"Lili want bee-is," he says, which I take to mean blueberry.

I put Liam in his high chair while I wash my hands, turn on the coffee pot, and pop some frozen waffles into the toaster. Liam starts to fuss, and I scramble to make him a sippy cup of milk—shit, or is it water first thing? Whatever, milk it is—which he eagerly grabs out of my hand and gulps down.

Watching him, his blue eyes wide and his blond hair sticking up every which way, I smile again.

"You're cute. I'll give you that," I say, smoothing back his hair.

I do not smile when Liam gets maple syrup in that hair as he scarfs down one waffle, then another, plus a handful of blueberries (the "bee-is" he was talking about) and half of an overripe banana that just adds to the enormous, and enormously sticky, mess.

He screams when I wipe him down. Throws his toothbrush and

toothpaste on the floor when I offer them to him. Flails as I unbuckle him, finally calming down when I have him in my arms.

"Poop," he says.

"Again?" Lifting him up so I can smell his butt, I groan. "You've gotta be kidding me."

Another diaper change later, and I'm legitimately sweating. Who knew caring for a toddler was a total-body workout? I make a mental note to call my mom and thank her for not running away. I can't imagine doing all this for *five kids*.

I put Liam down with his toys in the family room, and then I hustle back into the kitchen where I scrub down a sinkful: high chair tray, toddler plate and spork, the other spork I gave him when he threw the first one on the floor, bib, sippy cup.

I glance at the clock on the microwave. Good Lord, it's not even eight o'clock yet. I feel like it should be ten. At least.

Is this how it's going to be every morning?

Twenty-seven minutes until Amelia arrives.

Only when I start to get a headache do I realize I forgot my coffee. I pour myself a cup and head for the couch. Liam's playing happily with his little kitchen. Another good call by Beau—he said it's Maisie's favorite toy right now. He also mentioned something about limiting screen time, but I'm beat, and I need to take a minute to finish my coffee if I'm going to get through this day. So I put up my feet and turn on *SportsCenter* and sip.

Just as I'm starting to relax, Liam marches over with *Llama Llama Red Pajama* in his hands.

"Dada book," he says.

"Can you give me a minute?" I hold up my cup. "Dad's trying to finish his coffee."

"Dada book," he repeats, this time setting the book on the couch beside my leg.

With a sigh, I take a gulp of coffee and set my cup on the table beside me. "All right, Dada will read you a book."

Elle, Jennifer's friend, told me one of Jennifer's favorite things to do with Liam was read books, especially ones about animals.

I pick up *Llama,* and I'm about to start reading when Liam hooks a leg onto the couch and climbs on up, scurrying over to me and sitting on my lap. Sticking his thumb into his mouth, he turns his head to look at me and says, "Dada book!"

I'm annoyed. I just want to finish my coffee in peace. Is that too much to ask?

But then Liam rests his head on my chest, and I'm smiling. *Again*. His little body is solid against mine, and I brush my lips over the top of his head, catching a whiff of maple syrup.

"I heard your mommy loved to read to you," I say. "Thanks for letting me read to you too."

I read the book, and he listens quietly. I discover he likes turning the pages, so I insert my thumb between each one and hold it open, making it easier for him to do.

"Mama," he says, pointing at the Mama Llama of the title. His delight—his loss—makes my heart contract.

The thought hits me out of nowhere: I could give Liam so, so much if I played another couple of years. But what would I be taking away?

What would he be losing? What would *we* lose as a family?

Speaking of losing, Liam loses interest in the book a few pages from the end. He wiggles in my lap, rolling off the couch, turning his head to watch the TV. Then he rolls back up, settling in my lap again, and—holy God, did I hit the kid jackpot?—he quietly watches Sports-Center with me.

Granted, the moment lasts all of five minutes. Probably a good thing, because again, apparently screen time and kids don't mix. Or they mix a little too well or . . . something.

Whatever the case, my son and I sit like that, Liam cuddled up on my lap. We watch highlights from last night's games and matches for five glorious, uninterrupted minutes. He sucks his thumb, and I finish my coffee. Toronto gets routed by Boston. A Spaniard makes it to the semifinals at Wimbledon.

It's been an exhausting morning. But it's also a good one.

A really good morning. For the first time, I feel like I can maybe—someday—be the kind of father I always wanted but never had.

Chapter Sixteen

AMELIA

I walk into the family room, and my heart swooshes.

Rhett and Liam are curled up together on the couch, both bed-mussed, their hair sticking up in nearly identical spikes at the backs of their heads.

Rhett isn't wearing a shirt again.

And again, I'm hit by a pulse of desire taking in his chest and arms. His broad shoulders and the smattering of hair across his chest and belly.

But really, it's his face I can't stop staring at. Cuddling his son, he's got this glow about him. This soft, easy energy I remember from high school but haven't seen in him since.

It was why I fell in love with him. Why I wanted a future with him too.

Before Rhett's football career took off, he'd give me what he did have—time—without restraint. He came to all my track meets. He'd drive over to my grandmother's house when she was working and I was lonely.

He lingered with me in his backseat long after the sex was over, trailing his fingers over my skin, my ear pressed to his chest as it rumbled with laughter at whatever terrible joke I cracked. Even the sex itself was a testament to Rhett's generosity. He was eager, sure, but he never rushed, and he *never* let the orgasmic scales go unbalanced.

Not once did he ever make me feel like I was too much. Too needy or demanding or weird. When I was with him, everything about me felt right-sized.

Maybe I've been chasing that feeling ever since.

Someone taught this boy how to love and how to love well. Because Rhett doesn't have time anymore, but he's giving Liam what he can. Who knows what that will look like when the season starts? But right now, he's doing the right thing. The kind thing.

Rhett turns his head and sees me. He smiles, blue eyes soft, and the feeling in my torso tightens even more, making my knees wobble. I reach for the back of the sofa, setting a hand there to steady myself.

"He likes you," I manage, nodding at Liam.

Rhett looks down and brushes his son's hair off his forehead. "You think so?"

The sleep-roughened sound of Rhett's voice makes my nipples tingle.

Should I quit? I should probably quit.

"I do."

"Thanks." He looks back up at me. "Morning, A."

"Hey. Hi. How's everybody doing today?"

"We-wa!" Liam cries. He launches himself off Rhett's lap, elbowing Rhett in the process. Rhett makes an *oompf* sound that's exaggerated and adorable, sitting up on the couch while I pick up Liam.

I tickle his side, and we giggle together. "Hey, sweet pea. I missed you."

"He did much better last night." Rhett puts a hand on the back of the couch beside my hip. "Only woke up once."

"That's great news. And you?" I venture a glance in Rhett's direction. He's looking at me with those eyes, and I remember with searing clarity how good he smelled. "How'd you sleep?"

He lifts a massive shoulder, making the muscles along that side of his body tense. "I would've slept pretty well if my agent hadn't woken me up at the crack as—early. He woke me up way, way too early."

"Everything okay?"

"Yeah." Rhett runs a hand over his scruff, the skin around his eyes tightening. "Well—everything's fine, it's just . . . he put more on my plate, that's all."

I set down Liam. "I'm sorry. You have a really full plate as it is. He knows about you unexpectedly getting full custody of the son you didn't know you had, right?"

"He does."

"Kind of lame of him, then, to add to the chaos."

Rhett shakes his head. "It's not his fault. It's just how football is. Great at times, frustrating at others." He pauses, and my heart begins to pound as I wait for him to continue.

See, this is where the line gets blurred. As Rhett's employee—as an educator trying to get my dream job back after being unceremoniously fired—I shouldn't want him to confide in me. But as Rhett's friend, I do want that. I want that very badly. If only so I can make him feel better, the way he made me feel better the day I lost my car.

But I have to remember that we're not friends. Even if we have fun together, and even if we make a good team, and even if he makes me feel safe and valued and respected, we *are not friends*. Which means I have no right to the thoughts inside his head or the things he's feeling. And he has no right to share them with me.

"I'm being offered a contract extension," he blurts. "A big, fat extension that has the potential to be life-changing."

Oh, fuck, he's sharing, and I love it.

My idiot heart *loves* it.

"That's exciting."

"I know."

"Why don't you sound excited, then?"

He scoffs. "I was planning to retire. I had the whole thing set up. All the pieces were in place, you know? And with that little guy in the picture"—he nods at Liam—"it definitely felt like it was meant to be, me saying goodbye to the game. But now I'm not so sure."

Liam wiggles, and I sway my hips. I have the peace of mind to look away while I consider Rhett's words.

I do not, however, have the self-restraint it'd take to brush them off altogether. "Why do you say that?"

"The guy who's supposed to be my replacement quit to join Yeezy's followers."

I blink. "Yeezy as in Kanye West?"

"Yup. Kanye and all those people in matching beige sweatshirts he preaches to every week? Nick ran off to be one of them. So now I either let down the team or let down myself and my family. If I retire before the team finds another Nick, I'd be leaving 'em high and dry. I'd also be leaving a shit ton of money on the table."

Glancing up at the extravagantly furnished room around us, I say, "I don't get the impression you need to worry about money."

"This would be money I could leave Liam. He'd be set for life."

"Okay." I nod, pulse skipping a beat at the idea of Rhett already planning for Liam's future. "That's definitely something to consider. But—and I hope you don't mind me bringing this up—so is the fact that your dad suffered from CTE caused by a few too many hits to the head after a few too many years playing football."

Rhett furrows his brows. "Why would I mind you bringing that up?"

"I'm the nanny." It's my turn to lift a shoulder. "Not exactly my place to talk personal stuff with you."

"Well, yeah, you're the nanny, but you're also the girl I lost my virginity to, so . . ."

Blurred lines. We're looking at them, right in front of us. And because my heart really is an idiot, I find myself smiling at them. Smiling at *him*, the guy who's being relentlessly charming this morning.

"You keep bringing that up. I'm that memorable, huh?"

"Please." Grinning, he rolls his eyes. "Does anyone forget their first?"

"Not really, no." I move Liam to my other hip. "Although some might want to."

Rhett rises to his feet and pads over to us. He holds out his hands to Liam. "But not you, right?"

"This is healthy," I grunt as I hand Liam over, trying very hard not to blush at Rhett's kindness. His consideration. "You and I are talking about doing it as teenagers in front of your son."

"What a wholesome upbringing I'm providing." Rhett smooths

Liam's shirt over his belly. Liam glances over Rhett's shoulder at the TV. "Maybe you really would be better off if I wasn't around so much."

I cuff Rhett's shoulder, once again amazed and aroused and slightly angered even, by the firmness of his build. "Stop. You're doing great. Maybe that's why this extension thing is throwing you for such a loop —because you care so much about everyone and everything."

"Could be." He cuts me a look. "Or it could be me rebelling against all this responsibility that's been piled on my plate all of a sudden. I wanna win that Super Bowl, A. So, so bad. As things stand now, I only have one more season to do it. But this would give me more time, which means less pressure."

"Higher risk of brain injury."

His eyes stay locked on mine.

I know, they say.

I know.

"You're new to this dad thing," I say. "But you've always had family around you. You've always had them to consider, and they've always considered you too. They've always had your back, Rhett, and I think we can agree you've learned how to be a good brother, son, and parent from the best."

Rhett scoffs, even as his Adam's apple dips. "My dad was hardly the best."

"But your mom is. I'll fight you if you say otherwise about Junie. And from what your brothers and sisters say, your dad was pretty great too, before he got sick. My point is, you've learned how to make good decisions from good people. Trust yourself to make the right call here."

"Lili want bus, We-wa. Bus," Liam says, looking at me.

"Okay, buddy, go get your bus," Rhett replies. He sets down Liam, who scurries over to his toys. He picks up his bus but then quickly abandons it for a Cabbage Patch doll. Rhett's been lucky so far; Liam is a pretty independent player, which isn't usual for a two-year-old.

"That's just it, though," Rhett continues. "I don't disagree with you about making good decisions. It's just that I've always known what the right call is—my gut always knows what's right—but this feels differ-ent. Everything about the past two weeks has thrown me off my game, and I'm struggling to find my footing." He runs a hand up the back of his head as he watches Liam bang the doll's head against a rainbow-colored xylophone. "I don't know what to do."

Do me, I want to say.

"Do you," I say instead.

He turns his head and smiles. "Do who now?"

"Don't go there," I reply, but I'm smiling too. "What I mean to say is, you do you. Just keep doing what you're doing. One foot in front of the other, one day at a time—Rhett, you'll figure it out. You're always, always doing better than you think, all right?"

He looks at me for a long beat. "You are too, you know," he says at last. Softly, like he knows it's a blow that'll land right where it hurts.

And it does hurt. But not in the way I thought it would.

It's a good hurt, the kind that has my throat tightening not with regret but with hope.

"Thanks," I whisper.

And then I grab Liam and start our day. If I don't, I'm worried I'll do something stupid like kiss my boss.

Ex-boyfriend.

Whatever.

Chapter Seventeen

RHETT

Chest heaving, sweat dripping into my eyes, I squint at the hill. It's steep and high, the kind that makes your quads scream and your glutes burn just looking at it. Even my traps hurt from using my arms to gain momentum when my legs gave out on my tenth sprint up the grassy slope.

"One more," Tom says.

But I'm dead. Literally dead inside from my first two-a-day since the season ended six months ago. Despite my best efforts, I can't summon the will to go on.

Putting my hands on my knees, I hang my head, feeling dizzy. "I'm done."

"No, you're not." Tom checks his watch. "First two-a-day always sucks. Dig deep and power through. This is where you're gonna build that endurance."

That's just it, though. I'm digging, and I'm coming up empty-handed. It's like the wind's gone out of my sails. Not only am I out of gas but I also have no desire to replenish the stores. I could guzzle some water, grab a bite of the nasty protein bars I always keep in my gym bag for times like this.

But I just wanna be done already.

I wanna go home. Grab a shower and hang with Liam. Maybe even have dinner with him and Amelia. If I leave now, I could probably make it. Hell, I could probably squeeze in a quick round of badminton too. That was fun.

This is not. None of what I did today was fun, and I'm bone-tired of the slog. Especially knowing what waits for me back at the house.

Straightening, I put my hands on my hips. "Dude, I appreciate what you're trying to do, but I'm beat. My kid was up last night, and the night before that, and . . . yeah. I just can't. Let's try again tomorrow."

Tom looks downright panicked. It's a reminder that I should probably be panicking too. But again, I can't seem to summon the shits I'd need to give about cutting a workout short. Instead, I feel . . .

Relieved.

Excited because I get to see Liam. He may be a pain in the ass, but I miss him. His cute little mop of hair. How he insists on using a spoon even though he makes a huge mess. The way he screams when he laughs, all eyes and teeth.

I didn't know Jennifer all that well, but she did an amazing job raising our sweet boy. I hate that she won't be around to see him grow up.

Makes me wonder, though, if she would've ever introduced me to Liam. Could I have potentially never known I had a kid? The idea makes my stomach seize.

Tom takes off his sunglasses and peers at me. "Is there something you're not telling me?"

"Like what?"

"Like you're dying," he says matter-of-factly. "Is it cancer? Oh, God, it's cancer. Rhett, why didn't you—"

I let out a bark of laughter. "I'm not sick. Just tired as hell."

"You've never quit on me," he replies, still baffled. "Not even when you had the flu, or bronchitis, or that weird parasite thing you got."

Jogging over to my bag, I take out a clean towel and wipe my face. "Yeah, well. I didn't have a kid then, and lemme tell you, kids take more out of you than a parasite, my ravaged intestinal tract notwithstanding."

"Promise me this is just a one-time thing? Because you're paying me to get you in Super Bowl shape, and I can't do that if you aren't showing up."

A shadow moves across my excitement. I jostle the towel in my hands. "I know. You're right. I guess I just need a little more time than I thought to adjust to being a daddy."

"Your nanny not working out?"

My nanny's working out too well, and that's part of the problem.

I can't stop thinking about Liam, and I can't stop thinking about her either. Amelia. I'm having the worst case of FOMO—fear of missing out—ever. A part of me couldn't wait to leave the house this morning. But another part hated to go. Like a jerk, I wanted to stay, I wanted to keep confiding in her because—

God, because she made me feel *okay*. The problems I have are admittedly ridiculous. Or, at the very least, privileged in the extreme. But she didn't judge me. She also didn't blow smoke up my ass. She listened, and she called me out when I needed to be called out.

She was honest and real in a way few people are with me these days.

She was also able to make me smile. Laugh. I want more of that.

I'm sure as hell not gonna get it here in a field with my trainer.

"It's going great," I say. "She's excellent with Liam. But he's my kid, and at the end of the day, he's my responsibility, not hers. I guess I . . . I wanna be around more."

Tom looks at me for half a beat too long. "Okay." He puts his hands on his hips. Looks out over the view in front of us. Looks back at me. "I'll let you go just this once. But we can't make this a regular thing, okay? Get help at night if you need it. We don't have time to fuck around here, Rhett."

I think about this as I drive home. If I'm being honest, I like the idea of Amelia spending the night. Or maybe just my dick likes it, which isn't helpful because . . . reasons.

I promised I'd keep my hands off this girl.

Asking her to take the night shift in addition to full days with Liam is probably asking too much. She has to rest too. She has a life outside my kid, same as I do. It's not fair to monopolize her time, even if I hate the idea of not having her around.

Turning onto Blue Mountain Farm's main drive, I look up at the sound of a honk just ahead. Milly's making her way down the mountain in her cute little Mini Cooper. A glance in my rearview mirror tells me no one's behind me, so I hit the brakes and roll down my window.

"Hey," I say.

Milly offers me a tight smile as she ducks her head out her window. "How's it going? I spoke to Samuel, and he said it looked like y'all were doing okay. I haven't wanted to bother you . . ."

"It's no bother. Honestly, you're welcome to stop by anytime now that we're over the hump of these first few days. Liam seems to be adjusting well, all things considered."

"I'm so glad. He's really freaking cute, Rhett."

"Just like his daddy." I swallow. "Being a single parent—it's tough. Really tough. I keep thinking about Jennifer, Liam's mom. I give her so much credit. She clearly was a great mom. Her friend Elle—the one who reached out to me—told me Jennifer and Liam were super close. I wonder how she did it, to be honest. I've got help and money out the wazoo, and it's still hard."

Milly's expression softens. "It's not your fault she didn't tell you."

"It is, though. I wish"—another swallow—"I wish I could've been there for her. For Liam. I wish I'd been less wasted when we met. Maybe then—"

"Rhett. Don't beat yourself up like that. You can't change the past. But you can be a good dad *now*. And the fact that you're sweating this stuff shows you care. A lot. I'm not a parent, but I'm pretty sure the definition of a good dad is one who gives a shit about his kid. Think about it—you signed up for full custody of Liam seven seconds after you found out he existed. You're taking responsibility, and that's gotta count for something."

Glancing through my windshield, I will her words to sink in. She's right. I'm right too. But at some point, I gotta let the past go. I have to move on. If not for me, then for my son.

Easier said than done.

"Can I stop by tomorrow?" Milly continues. "Maybe bring some food?"

"Sure."

She arches a brow. "And Amelia? How is she?"

"Perfect," I say without thinking.

I hear Milly put her car in park. "That sounds interesting."

"You know what I mean. She's perfect for Liam. I'm learning, slowly, but I couldn't have done this without her. It's nice having help. Having people around. I actually should get going—"

"Eager to get home, huh?" Milly narrows her eyes.

I look away, face burning. "I have a kid now. Shouldn't I want to get home?"

"Absolutely. I'm just astonished, frankly, at how quickly you've gone from holy-shit-my-life-is-over to damn-I-gotta-get-home-to-my-kid-and-girl."

Sticking my tongue into my cheek, I roll my eyes. "You're baiting me, and I'm choosing to ignore it."

"All I'm saying is you look happy. Tired, but happy. Beau was right —fatherhood looks good on you. So does having a crush."

"I don't—" I slam the heel of my hand on the wheel. "Jesus Christ, Milly."

"What exactly happened with y'all, anyway? You and Amelia. I was away at college when you guys broke up, so I only got the Spark Notes."

Easing my foot off the brake, I let my car roll forward a little. This conversation is bullshit, and I want to get home. But I'm getting butterflies talking about Amelia—thinking about her—and I like the feeling too much to let it be.

I hit the brake again. "Senior year, Amelia was late. We were mostly careful, but sometimes . . . not so much. For a hot minute, we were sure she was pregnant. When she told me, I cried. I had my scholarship, I was going to pursue this big career I wanted, and a kid was not part of the plan. Amelia cried too. She wanted to have the baby. Stay in North Carolina to raise it. On the drive to Target to get the tests, we got into this huge fight when I told her how I felt."

"That you didn't want to have the baby."

The blacktop ahead wavers in the heat as I glance through my windshield. "Not that, no. I said she should come with me to Alabama. We could both go to school, and I could play football. We could raise the baby there together. But that's not what she wanted—her mom had just passed away, and she wanted to stay close to her grandmother. She'd also gotten an academic scholarship to App State, and she didn't want to give that up. She wanted to get her degree in education, come back to Asheville and teach at Woodward, and have a family."

"Is that admiration I hear in your voice?"

I shrug. "But I didn't want to give up football. And yeah, maybe I didn't want to give up my shot at fame either. So basically, we realized we wanted different things—that we had different priorities, because she wanted to stay close to family, to have some kids of her own, and I wanted the opposite of that. So when she took the test, and it came back negative, we were like, yeah, why the fuck are we together if neither of us is willing to bend?"

I don't realize I'm holding the wheel in a death grip until pain arrows up my forearm. I loosen my fingers.

"But you were still in love with her."

"Hell yeah, I was in love with Amelia. You remember how crazy I was about her. Our split fucked me up for a long time. I nearly lost my scholarship freshman year because I was so torn up about it. I was wrecked, and it showed—I played like absolute shit. I constantly wondered what would've happened if the test were positive. I missed her, Milly. So damn bad. But eventually, my feelings faded, and hers did too, I guess, and . . . yeah. That's basically it."

Milly's eyebrows are halfway up her forehead. "The *drama*. Y'all were having your own little redneck version of *Varsity Blues*, weren't you?"

"There were no whipped cream bikinis—"

"A shame."

"I know. But it was a lot, the way teenage breakups usually are."

"The way any breakup is," Milly says, and the mirth in her expression fades.

I frown. "What's up with you? I'm sorry I haven't checked in."

"You had a new kid to deal with." She waves me away. Glances out her windshield and sighs. "Promise not to say anything to Beau?"

"Cross my heart and hope to die."

"I just agreed to do Nate Kingsley's wedding."

My eyes bulge. "Nate Kingsley's getting married? To who? You?"

Milly looks down at her lap and shakes her head, her blond waves falling into her face. "Not to me, no."

"But I thought y'all are a thing." Nate is the owner of a local whiskey distillery. He also happens to be the son of Daddy's old enemy, Mr. Kingsley. Our families had a little Romeo and Juliet type feud going on back in the day. Thankfully it ended, but there's definitely still some bad blood between Beau and Nate.

"We *were* a thing." She glares at me. "But we broke up a while ago."

I lift the fingers on my steering wheel in surrender. "You don't tell anyone shit, Milly. Don't be mad at me for not knowing what you didn't share."

My sister swallows. "Sorry. You're right. I kept things close to the vest because, well, Nate is Nate, and Beau hated his guts for a while, and—"

"You liked having a dirty little secret, running behind everyone's backs and falling in love."

"I never said I was in love," she replies with a scowl.

"But you are."

"I was. Yes. I'll admit that much. But Nate's getting married to someone else now, and she's dead set on me planning their wedding. So, yeah, fun times."

"You still love him?"

Milly sighs again. "Doesn't matter. Anyway, I've already kept you for too long. I really am happy for you, Rhett. I'm happy you're happy."

"Thanks."

"And Rhett?"

"Yeah?"

"Don't make the same mistake I did. If Amelia's perfect, don't let her get away this time."

Chapter Eighteen

RHETT

I walk through the door to the sound of laughter.

Tiptoeing through the house, I find the back doors flung open to the gorgeous summer afternoon. As I take in the view, my heart does a backflip and lands in my throat.

Amelia and Liam are leaping through a sprinkler shaped like a duck —*where the hell'd she get that?*—the two of them giggling when the spray hits Amelia squarely in the face.

"We-wa get owie!" Liam howls. "Lili want owie."

"Owies are actually bad things, but we'll roll with your interpretation today. Let's do this, sweetpea," Amelia replies, then uses her foot to direct the spray in Liam's direction. He takes off running, laughing so hard he falls onto his knees in the grass.

She jogs over to help him up, and that's when I notice her bikini.

Her pink *fucking* bikini. It's not scandalous or especially revealing. But what it does show is glorious. Pert tits, long legs. An expanse of naked, lily-white back.

Blood gathers between my legs. Legs that are suddenly moving down the steps and into the grass. I reach behind me and yank off my shirt, and Amelia's face is lighting up when she turns around and sees me; she's giving me this huge, unguarded smile, and I'm hit in the chest by a bullet I don't wanna name.

"You're home early," she says.

"Dada!" Liam says.

My heart thumps.

My son called me *Dada*. I don't think I'll ever get over how cool that is.

"Thought I'd join y'all." I nod at the sprinkler. "Looks fun."

Amelia's eyes catch on my stomach before moving to Liam, who's squirming on her hip. "Your son is quite the little fish. He can't get enough of the water."

"Lili get down," he says.

She slides him off her hip onto his feet, pulling down the tie of her bikini bottoms in the process. I'm gripped by the vicious desire to hook a finger through that tie and pull it back into place.

Pull the damn thing loose and make the bottoms fall off. Would her pussy be groomed? Bare? Wild, the way it was in my dream?

I look away. Silently remind myself not to be a dog and to focus on my kid because that's what this is about.

He's what everything is about from now on.

I ignore the throb in my dick, and I leap through the sprinkler, sucking in a breath when a lash of ice-cold water hits me across the torso. I bounce on my sneakered feet, chanting, "It's cold. It's cold. It's so freaking cold!"

Amelia's eyes get this wicked gleam in them. She bends down—*do not look at her ass, you fucking animal*—and loops an arm around Liam's waist.

"Daddy says it's too cold," she tells him. "Should we get him wet, Liam?"

Liam grins and nods, and then Amelia's helping him put his hands in the sprayer so it's aimed right at me. I yelp, and Liam roars, Amelia literally falling over from laughter.

"Y'all are the worst," I say, "but two can play this game."

Instead of running away from the water, I walk toward it, firming my abs so I create a wall that redirects the spray. It lands on Amelia first, then Liam. He holds out his arms and makes a run for me, slamming into my legs.

"Whoa!" I say, wheeling my arms as I pretend to fall backward from the impact.

Delighted, Liam keeps pushing me back. I fall onto the grass and, reaching for him, take him with me, lifting his little body above my own as I flatten my back against the ground. It's warm, the ground, and the sun glints between the leaves of the tree overhead.

There's this green smell in the air—earth, grass, heat—that screams *summer*.

It's a time of year I always seem to miss. Between gearing up for the season, training camp, and then the preseason, summer just kinda whizzes by without me really noticing.

But I'm noticing it now, and it takes me back—way back—to when I was a little kid. Older than Liam, but young enough that Daddy was still the good guy, and I wasn't on high alert for one of his outbursts.

I was free then. Free to be a kid, to play and have fun, the way I'm playing right now.

A feeling elbows its way into my center. It's clean and simple and really fucking nice, and a voice inside me says *I'm done*. Not with this feeling, but with *not* feeling it. If that makes, like, any sense at all.

Makes me think . . . I don't know, that maybe I'm not playing football for the right reasons anymore. Maybe being around Liam and Amelia is making me realize I'm no longer motivated by the fear of disappointing a dead man.

Which begs the question: What does motivate me? And what does that mean for my career?

"Mo-wa, Dada, mo-wa," Liam says, water droplets falling from his hair into my face.

Flexing my biceps, I bring Liam down and kiss the shit out of *his* face—amazed at how natural it feels—then push him back up again. He squeals with laughter, wrinkling his adorable little nose.

I love this kid.

"You're heavier than you look, little dude," I grunt.

"He's a workout, that's for sure. And you've already had, what, three of those today?"

I grin, turning my head to look at Amelia. "Just two."

"Just two." She scoffs and rolls her eyes. "You're getting lazy on us, Beauregard. Tired?"

"I was before, yeah. But I must've just gotten a second wind or something because I feel pretty damn good right now." I give my son a wiggle. "Maybe it's his cuteness."

"It's definitely his cuteness."

Amelia watches me lift Liam up and down, up and down, her expression softening as her gaze roves from my arms to Liam to my face and back again.

She looks the way I feel.

Happy.

Dare I say it, she looks turned on. Cheeks a shade of pink that's a tad brighter than her bikini. Brown eyes warm. Liquid.

I imagine her nipples are hard underneath the cups of her top.

"Aaaand that's enough of that," I say. I set Liam down and push up to sitting, groaning. I'm already sore pretty much everywhere.

Amelia holds out her hand. "Need help?"

I look up at her. Our eyes meet, and a pulse of pure, naked need moves between us. Her lips part, allowing me a glimpse of her pink, slick mouth.

"I'm good." I somehow manage to leap to my feet despite the ache in my hips and pinch in my lower back. I grab Liam's hand. "Should we see who can jump the highest over the sprinkler?"

"Yay!" he says.

"Let's do it," Amelia replies. "You two go first."

"All right, Liam, let's show Amelia what we got. On the count of three—one, two, *three*!"

I take a running leap through the sprinkler. Liam follows me half a step behind, doing this hilarious hopping thing that has Amelia and me in stitches.

It's a good distraction from the throbbing in my head. *That* head.

Amelia takes a turn, and because she's a track-and-field gazelle, she nails it, soaring through the air in this elegant arc that has me shamelessly checking out her legs. The muscles there, how they flex against her skin—

"That's a tie," I say.

Amelia rounds the sprinkler to cuff my shoulder, and I am very much aware of how close she is. Another step forward, and her tits would brush against my chest. Imagining how good that would feel—imagining how I'd yank her against me and roll my hips into the cradle of hers—I see double.

"Hardly," she says. "But we can do two out of three."

"So you can show off your moves?"

She wags her brows. "Exactly."

Liam and I do our leap, and Amelia follows. Only this time, she launches off a slippery patch of grass and stumbles, throwing out her arms in an attempt to catch herself.

Before I know what's happening, I'm dropping Liam's hand and pouncing forward. My heart makes a hollow sound inside my chest as my brain goes from perv to parent in the blink of an eye.

I imagine Amelia getting hurt. Bloody nose? Broken wrist?

Not on my watch.

Grunting, I grab her, looping an arm around her middle. The momentum of her leap sends her body crashing into mine, our skin meeting with a muted *slap*.

Skin on skin on skin.

My blood jumps, and I die for the second time today. Only this death is way fucking better.

Her bent arms are caught between us. She tries to regain her footing, but she just ends up slipping again, so I firm my grip, my arm wrapped so tightly around her waist my fingertips graze her belly.

"Amelia," I say. It's an admonishment, or at least I mean it to be.

"I'm okay."

"You sure?"

She looks up at me. Our mouths are half an inch apart. "I'm sure."

I hold her for a beat too long.

She *lets me*.

She lets my fingers flex against her bare skin as I flatten my palm against her side. I can feel the quick, hard *pound, pound, pound* of her pulse here. A flare of awareness ignites in my center.

She feels the connection between us too. She's not trying to hide her curiosity, and the fragility this exposes—the vulnerability—makes my heart hurt.

But the way her eyes flick to my mouth? That makes my dick hurt in the most pleasurable, most maddening way possible.

"This keeps happening," she breathes. "You catching me."

Yeah, but this time, I'm not blackout drunk.

This time, you're really trusting me, and it's driving me wild.

I search her eyes and beg. I beg her to ask me to kiss her. Beg her to tell me to back the fuck off.

Please.

"And you told Beau *you'd* be the one catching *me*," I say.

Her lips curve into a smile, and she catches the tip of her tongue between her teeth. "We're only on day three. You've got plenty of time to fall."

I got a feeling that's already happening, honey.

"Dada jump with Lili," Liam says, tapping on my calf and breaking the spell. For half a second, I panic, not wanting to let her go but knowing it needs to happen *now* before I do something I can't take back.

I'm her employer. She needs this job. The money, the recommendation. The time.

And I need her, desperately. For Liam.

For. Liam.

I'm putting all that in jeopardy by acting like a lunatic with nothing to lose.

It still kills me to loosen my arm, allowing her to step back. Allowing her to step away feels all kinds of wrong but is, at the end of the day, totally the right call.

It's wrong, and it's weird, but I let my fingertips trail over her side as she moves. Our gazes lock one last time, and the naked desire I see in hers—the fear too—it makes me feel—

A lot of things. Ashamed. Angry.

I don't wanna dig too deep into that shit, so I don't.

Instead, I ask Amelia to jump with Liam for me, and I jog inside under the guise of ordering us some dinner from The Barn Door.

I order the food—a whole barbecue chicken for Amelia and me, grilled cheese and steamed broccoli for Liam—and jump in the shower. Only then do I take my dick in my hand and let the floodgates open.

I think of her, and I come.

I lean my forehead against the wall. The tiles are cool, a welcome antidote to the burn that fills me.

Aw, hell. No use beating around the bush. I'm in trouble.

Chapter Nineteen

AMELIA

My hands shake as I rinse the dishes after dinner.

I tell myself it's because I'm tired. Today was fun, but it was also exhausting. I took Liam to the park this morning, then swung by my favorite local hardware store to grab a sprinkler before heading home to do the whole lunchtime rigamarole. While the little guy napped, I folded his laundry, set up a sensory table exercise, and gathered the courage to send Nuria a "checking in" text. It was off to the races after that when Liam woke up, and Rhett came home an hour early, culminating in what shall henceforth be known as The Great Sprinkler Foreplay Incident.

How stupid was I, falling into his arms and staying there?

What the hell was I thinking?

It just felt so nice, being held like that. Being looked after the way Rhett looks after all the people he cares about.

It felt nice, indulging my simmering need for a split second. I won't allow myself to have this man, but it seems I have no control over whether or not I want him.

Today showed me I want him. Badly.

Hence the shaking hands. I don't know who I think I'm kidding by calling it exhaustion, whatever this feeling is. It has nothing to do with being tired.

It has everything to do with the man who's currently upstairs, reading his son a book before he puts him to bed.

My eyes squeeze shut as I drop the plate I'm rinsing. I rest my hands on the lip of the sink and take a deep breath, a futile attempt to calm the tingly rush inside my skin. It intensifies as I relive the feeling over and over again of Rhett's naked torso pressed against mine, his body warm and solid, his hands certain as they moved over my skin.

He'd looked at me, and I'd looked back, and my heart exploded not because I realized we were about to kiss—don't get me wrong, that was great too—but because the whole thing felt *right*.

At that moment, it felt right and uncomplicated and real in a way things with Jim never did.

But the reality is, wanting Rhett is very complicated and not at all right. And who even knows if it's real? There was no mistaking the hard-edged lust in his eyes. I'm not questioning that.

I'm questioning his intentions. Because if there's one thing that hasn't changed, it's that we're different people who want different things. He still wants big fancy titles and a big fancy life. I don't.

But then watching him with Liam—watching him choose to come play with us rather than keep working out—has been a bit of an eye-opener.

We're only on day three, so that could obviously change. He might lose interest and go back to his single-guy hedonism. This . . . it's not real yet. We're also not in Vegas, where football will once again dominate his life.

But he's stepping up and being a great dad. Is that part of his winning-is-what-matters mentality, I wonder? Or is it just confirmation that Rhett Beauregard is the excellent person I knew he'd always be?

Ugh, I don't know what to think anymore, and the seed of doubt planted is suddenly sprouting desire so potent I'm having the hardest time fighting it.

Lord, I really need to quit before I do something stupid and seal my fate as a horny outcast in the educational community of Asheville forever.

"You all right?"

Startling, I glance over my shoulder to see Rhett standing behind me, his brow furrowed. He's barefoot, dressed in jeans and a white T-shirt that's somehow as deliciously revealing as him being naked would be: biceps that bulge out of the sleeves, pecs for days, shoulders that strain against the fabric.

I imagine putting my hands on him there. I imagine the feel of the fabric, broken-in, soft. The subtle shift of the muscles underneath as Rhett moves to take me in his arms. I imagine I loop mine around his neck, I play with his hair as I pull him down for a kiss.

The blue in his eyes deepens as though he knows exactly what I'm imagining because he's imagining it too.

Yep, definitely need to quit. Tomorrow, when I'm not on the verge of an emotional breakdown.

Of sexual combustion.

"Long day." I turn back to the sink and shut off the water, putting the plate in the dishwasher. "I'm gonna head out."

Grabbing a towel, I use it to dry my hands before reaching for my keys on the counter.

"Wait," Rhett says, extending his arm just short of touching me. "Can we talk for a minute?"

My heart takes off at a sprint. "Okay."

"I'm sorry. About this afternoon. I . . . um, touched you in a way I shouldn't have, and I feel like an ass. I know how much your work means to you, A, and I respect you as a professional. It won't happen again."

But what if I want it to?

"Thanks for that," I manage, balling my fingers into a fist around my keys. "To be fair, I got a little carried away too, so you're not the only one at fault here."

My words—my confession—hang between us. My face burns.

"You're really good at this," Rhett says at last. "With kids, I mean. You know how to make it fun."

"You don't? You literally play a game for a living."

He shrugs. "Meh. The more I'm with Liam, the more I'm starting to think football stopped being fun a long time ago."

149

Now it's his confession that hangs between us. I really should go, but I'm too curious not to ask, "So you don't think playing football is fun anymore?"

"Playing with you and Liam feels like real *play*, you know? It's fun for fun's sake." He meets my eyes. "I haven't had this much fun in forever, Amelia. Maybe that's part of the reason I got carried away. I missed it, playing the way we do. There's no pressure. No expectation to make it capital Best Thing Ever. It's like . . ." He looks down and digs his toe into the floor. Looks back up. "It's a breath of fresh air I really needed."

I know the feeling, and it's lovely.

So lovely I'd risk things I shouldn't to keep having it.

"I'm not sure I should work for you anymore," I blurt. Now it's my eyes that burn.

Rhett's go wide, and he takes a step forward, the creases in his forehead deepening. "What? Amelia, no, please—do you feel like things aren't going well? Are you not enjoying it? The job?"

"No!" I say. "The job has been great so far. Hard, but great. I do miss the classroom, and I miss the company of other people. Kids and adults. The isolation of nannying is tough. But Liam is such a peach, and you being around . . ." *You being around is making it so much better and so much more difficult all at once.* "It's a good job. That's not the issue."

"Was it what happened this afternoon? I promise—"

"Can we really trust ourselves right now? We're not even a week in, and we're already crossing lines left and right. Maybe we should quit while we're ahead before Liam gets too attached—"

"He's already attached."

A flare of anger ignites in my gut. "Don't you dare guilt me into staying."

Rhett holds up his hands. "Sorry, sorry. Low blow. I'm just trying to do what's best for Liam, and Amelia, you're the freaking best. You know it, I know it. He knows it."

"Thank you," I grumble. "I am pretty great."

"We've established that fact. Now tell me what you need to make this work, and you'll have it. Talk to me, Jabba."

He keeps making me grin when I should be going. I want to hate it, but I don't.

"Listen, Rhett, I want the world for y'all—for you and Yoda. I can already tell you two have a special bond, and I want to nurture that. I want to see Liam grow and thrive, and I want to see you thrive right alongside him. But I want to thrive too. I want the best for myself. And I'm putting that in jeopardy by, you know, casually falling into the arms of my employer."

"Hey, that was an accident," Rhett says with a smile. "What was I supposed to do, let you break your face? It's such a pretty face, A."

I give him a look. He looks back. At last, he drops his arm. "Liam fucking adores you, and so do I. I'm not gonna beg, but I am gonna tell you you've turned what could've been a nightmare into a dream. Is it perfect? Hell no. But you can't tell me it's not good. Having you around —it's allowing me to fall in love with my son in a way I didn't think was possible a week ago. Please, A. Please don't go."

I swallow the lump in my throat that's appeared all of a sudden. "It's cool of you to say that. Thank you."

"Now tell me what you need."

"Honestly?" I catch a tear in the crook of my first finger. "I don't know what I need. You're right to say this is good, which makes me think we shouldn't change a thing. But this . . . this *thing* between us—"

"The tension?"

"Yes," I breathe, hugely relieved and secretly thrilled to know I'm not the only one caught in its throes. "We have to nip it in the bud. To make that happen, I'm not sure if we need a time-out, or if we need to communicate more, or, I don't know, jump each others' bones and get it out of our system . . ."

I mean it as a joke, but I know it's a bad one the second the words come out of my mouth because the look in Rhett's eyes sharpens and my pussy clenches, and I'm inundated by very graphic, very tempting fantasies of what "getting it out of our system" would look like exactly.

"Wow," I blurt, because blurting shit is apparently my MO today. "That was a stupid thing to say. Stupid and unprofessional."

Rhett laughs, making my embarrassment fade ever so slightly. "It's all right. I told you I'd give you whatever you asked for, and if that's it, well." He looks up at me, suddenly shy. "I take it you haven't heard from the Married Asshole?"

It's my turn to laugh. "I'm going to have to change his name in my phone to that."

"How about you delete his number instead?"

"How about you mind your own damn business?" But I haven't talked much about Jim since everything went down, and I guess I'm lonelier than I thought because I find myself saying, "And no, I haven't heard from him."

"I'm sorry."

"Don't be. It's better this way. To be honest, I've been so busy with y'all, I haven't had much time to dwell on what happened."

"You miss him?"

I ponder this for a second. "My grandmother asked me if I liked Jim for who he was, or if I liked him for what he was—a family man. Because I loved the idea of getting everything I wanted in one fell swoop. Love for the long haul, kids. A home."

"Grandma Rose, always asking the hard questions."

"Right? She's the best. I don't think I miss Jim. Do I miss the excitement that comes with the possibility of a future with someone? Yes. Yes, I do miss that. But I'm not, like, waiting by my phone to see if he'll call or anything. Makes me think . . ."

Rhett looks up, our gazes colliding. "What?"

I look, and he looks, and the tension we've now named in the hope of bursting its bubble swells between us.

"Makes me think Jim wasn't the one."

"Bummer," Rhett says, standing, not looking bummed at all. "I never took you for the sister-wife type anyway."

"One of the things I'm not good at is polygamy."

"Thank God for that. I sure as hell never wanted to share you, and anyone who does, well." Rhett shakes his handsome head, and I'm not sure if I want to slap him across the face or tear his clothes off. "He's a scumbag who doesn't deserve your awesomeness."

"That's sweet."

"I am getting sweeter, right? Being a dad?"

"You are," I say, and I mean it. Our eyes keep meeting, and my pulse keeps thumping, and I have to get out of here. I have to go.

Rhett just makes it so hard to go sometimes.

"So tomorrow. Eight fifteen?" I reach for my bag and loop it over my shoulder.

Rhett taps the bottom of his fist on the counter, gaze still on mine. *Stay,* it says. *Let me show you just how sweet I can be.*

"Works for me. Here, I'll walk you out."

I head for the front door on unsteady legs, painfully aware of Rhett's presence two steps behind me. He lunges for the door before I can get to it and opens it to the dusk outside. Still air, darkening sky, a symphony of crickets.

Summertime in the mountains at its finest. A reminder of what I love, what I want.

What I'm not willing to leave behind.

I pause on the threshold, and Rhett reaches up, settling his hand on the top of the doorframe in that I'm-so-hot-I'm-gonna-melt-your-face-off way of his. He's a foot away from me, maybe more, but I still get the feeling of being surrounded by him, the scent of his body wash filling my head.

"Thanks." I lick my lips, Rhett's eyes following the motion. "For the apology. And for checking in on how I'm feeling. It's great we can talk like this."

"I always wanna talk with you, Amelia." His eyes flick back up to lock on mine. "And look, I'm not gonna let some leftover teenage hormones hold us hostage here. I want you to feel good about this, okay?"

"Okay." Desperate for a change of subject—I need space, time to think—I say, "by the way, I couldn't help noticing the beers in the fridge."

He blinks. "What about them?"

"They've been there since Monday. Hard to miss because there are so many."

"Oh yeah. Yeah. Now that I'm gearing up for the season, I gotta be good."

I smile. "You gotta be good for the season. Not for your son."

He smiles back. "I didn't say that."
Maybe he really is changing.
Maybe I am too.

Chapter Twenty

AMELIA

My grandmother is waiting for me when I pull into the parking lot outside the brewery.

Taking in her outfit—trendy leggings printed with pink and blue skulls, matching pink tank and visor—I smile.

She's so damn cute it kills me.

"Look at you, Rose! Your pirate friends would approve of your legging selection." I pull her into a hug and give her an extra tight squeeze.

Like she knows I need it, she squeezes me back. "How was your day, lovie? I've been thinking about y'all. That Liam, he's a cutie."

Rhett gave me permission to send Rose pictures of his son, so of course I've shared my favorites with her. Like his daddy, he's pretty damn photogenic.

"He's such a lover. The day was long but good. At school, I handle a lot more kids, obviously, but somehow being responsible for one is way more exhausting."

"Of course it is." Rose turns and starts walking toward the entrance, and I follow. "You have assistants at school. And part of your new job description is helping out around the house. That's not something you have to do at Woodward—feed the kids, do laundry, cook. It's a lot, isn't it?"

I grin. "Makes me really appreciate all the work caregivers do."

"We're the best." Grandma cuts me a look. "Does Rhett appreciate the work you do?"

My heart skips a beat. "He does. He sees it, and we talk about it. He says he wants to learn from me."

"Of course he does! You're an expert in the field."

"And a pariah in that field, but that's neither here nor there. I thought for sure Rhett wouldn't be as involved, you know, with the season coming up and everything. I thought he wouldn't be around much." I glance at the crowd already gathered on the brewery's massive lawn, people rolling out yoga mats and clasping their hands above their heads to stretch. "But turns out he's around a lot, and when he is, he's very hands-on. He tries. I think he's also having fun being a dad. Today, he came home early and ran through the sprinkler with us—me and Liam. I haven't seen Rhett laugh that hard in a long time."

"Hm."

I turn to see Rose smiling. "What does that mean?"

"You're gushing."

"I'm not a gusher," I say, pressing a hand to my face. My skin is warm.

"I know." Rose finds us a spot in the shade, and together we roll out our mats and set down our water bottles. "That's why I mention it."

I fall onto my knees. Smoothing out the corners of my mat, I keep my gaze trained on its slightly pebbled surface. "Nothing happened if that's what you're asking. Between Rhett and me."

"I didn't ask a question."

"Yes, you did. And I'm giving you my answer."

She's still smiling. "But is that your final answer?"

"Yes," I say, even though we both know I'm full of shit.

The instructor, a ripped man in shiny bike shorts and sunglasses, takes his place at the front of the lawn. Adjusting the microphone on his headset, he leads us in a chant about the power of claiming our truest selves by shaking our asses, and then we get to work.

Technically it's a "Hip Hop Yoga" class, but really, it's an hour of dancing your heart out underneath the evening sky with a few sun salutations thrown in.

My grandmother jumps in with both feet, literally, doing this little samba move to a Maroon5 song that draws claps of approval from the young hipsters around us.

"So tell me," she says, not at all breathless. "What is it about Rhett, exactly, that makes you want to plunder his booty again after all these years?"

"I like her," the guy next to us says, tossing his thumb in Rose's direction.

Meanwhile, I'm already sweating bullets. I could lie. I could blow her off. But no one knows me better than Rose, and I need her advice.

"I think he's—he's changed," I pant. "Or he's chang*ing*. He still says he's all about winning championships, but I think—I don't know, I think he's finding a lot of joy in the simpler things."

"Things that you've always valued. Time spent with loved ones, having fun, being outside."

"Yes." I don't know why I'm still stunned by my grandmother's ability to *get it*, to get me, so quickly. But I am, and for several beats, I just stare at her, letting the SZA song pass on by while I draw to a stop. "Yes, that's it. Exactly."

"Which means the two of you might not be so different after all."

I start moving again if only to distract me from the butterflies taking flight inside my stomach. It's like my gut is catching onto something, an idea, a possibility, that my mind can't grasp yet.

"It's not that we're different—"

"It's that you want different lives. Yes. You've mentioned that a couple hundred times already. But what if—hear me out, lovie—what if y'all always wanted the same life, but you're just realizing it now? Or, really, maybe Rhett is learning what he thought he wanted and what really makes him happy are two different things?"

"Damn, that's deep," the dude beside us says, shaking his head as he falls into a plank position on his mat.

The butterflies are swirling inside my torso now, tickling my sides.

"Even if that were true, it doesn't change the fact that my career will be over if—*if*—we were to . . ."

"Bone?" Rose asks.

"Do the dirty thing?" the guy adds.

I grunt as I attempt the Superman pose. "I don't even know what to say to that."

"Say you know your mother would be proud of you, whether or not you follow in her footsteps," Rose says.

My pulse thunders as my heart twists, making a lump form in my throat. Rose and I talk all the time about my mom; she was Rose's only child and my only parent, and she looms large in our collective memory.

But we haven't talked about the pressure I feel to honor her memory by making her proud. By finishing the work she started.

Or, really, I've never talked to my grandmother about it. But of course she'd know. She pays attention; it's one of the things I adore most about her.

"Woodward means a lot to me," I say. "Teaching means a lot. And the scholarship program—"

"Will continue whether or not you're there. I don't mean to offend you, but we both know that's true."

"Of course it's true. I just . . . I love the *idea* of Woodward. I loved being a part of something, a program that really is making a difference. And yeah, the fact that I'd get to finish the work Mom wasn't able to . . ." I swallow. "I don't want to give that up. And I'd have to if Rhett and I got together. They aren't going to hire someone who slept with not one but *two* employers. Parents. Whatever."

"Jim was your employer?"

"Well, not technically, no. But he was a board member and the parent of a student, so you could say he was my boss in some ways."

Rose nods, pursing her lips to breathe out, then breathe back in as we hold a warrior pose. "Right. That's a fair assumption about your future employers. But it is an assumption. Maybe you wouldn't be able to work at Woodward again. Who's to say, though, you couldn't make a difference somewhere else? Maybe you take what you learned at Woodward and start something new. I love how passionate you are about your career. I'm not saying you should compromise on your mission to change the world. But maybe you should revisit what you want that mission to look like. Tweaking your dreams doesn't mean you're giving up on them. Just means you're getting closer to who you really are. What really makes you the happiest. Is teaching at *this* school in *this* city really the hill you want to die on? Why not follow a different path and see where it leads you? I very much doubt it'll be a dead end."

"But you," I say, jumping twenty steps ahead and making some really huge assumptions I probably shouldn't. "I don't want to leave you."

"Lovie, it's why they make airplanes. Lucky for you, I love to travel almost as much as I love pirates."

"Where does one find a pirate these days?" the guy asks.

Rose shoots him a disbelieving look. "Boats."

"Ha."

"And books. Really, the best ones are in books, so I'd recommend starting there."

"Noted."

I fall into child's pose, which is supposed to count as "resting" but actually makes my knees scream bloody murder. A thought hits me, distracting me from the pain, and I turn my head to look at Rose, our eyes meeting underneath our outstretched arms.

"How is this different from Jim? What if I just want Rhett because I'll get the whole package. Family, kid, all that stuff?"

Rose just smiles again, shaking her head. "Don't insult Rhett by comparing him to Jim. You adored Rhett before Liam showed up. You're not in this for what you'll get. You're in it for what you'll become."

"Oh?" I smile. "What's that?"

"The heroine of your own story."

"That's—"

"Beautiful," the guy says.

"But I'm not in it," I say.

"Yet. You're not in it *yet*."

My head is spinning on the drive home.

Windows down, cool night air blowing in my face, I listen to emo John Mayer and try to make sense of it all.

The thing is, none of it makes sense. Not losing my job because I dated a married man. Definitely not Rhett asking me to be his nanny.

It doesn't make sense how I could miss Liam after being with him for all of three days.

It's *ridiculous*. Embarrassingly, awesomely ridiculous.

This is not at all what I thought my life would look like at twenty-seven. It's messy and uncertain and scary in a way I hoped it wouldn't be. But I like my grandmother's suggestion that maybe that isn't a bad thing.

Maybe I need to stop forcing things so I can step back and listen.

Listen to what my true self, whoever the hell she is, is telling me.

Listen to the way my heart sings when I'm with Rhett. It may sing dirty nursery rhymes, but it's still singing.

To be honest, I'm not sure it's sung this way since Mom died.

But what if Rhett's not on the same page? What if I'm wrong, and he's only like this because it's the off-season? He's seriously considering that contract extension. What if he does end up like his dad because he played too long and too hard?

What if he *doesn't* sign the extension? It's still a whole year away, and he'll be so busy.

What about Liam? If things didn't work out between Rhett and me, Liam stands to lose just as much as we do. I'm not sure it'd be worth the risk. That little boy's already been through so much. I don't want to put him through yet another change. Another transition.

Then again, a transition is coming the way things stand right now. I'm only contracted to work for Rhett through July. I'll have to leave Liam anyway.

Unless I still don't have another job lined up and Rhett needs me to stay on. Not hard to imagine, if I'm being honest. But could I handle being in Vegas for the next six, eight, ten months? Away from Rose, from the place and people I love?

And if I'm struggling to keep my attraction to Rhett in check now, what would happen if I was with him for nearly a year straight?

I know the answer to that. The guy was my first love. First everything. I haven't found that kind of closeness—that connection—with anyone else in the years Rhett and I have been apart.

And then there's Grandma's question: *What if y'all always wanted the same life, but you're just realizing it now?*

My heart skips a beat, just as it did then. This strange, heady joy rises up inside me.

Him.

I want him. Rhett. The man who laughs with me, not at me. The one who looks at me with fire in his eyes. The man who trusts me with his son.

Oh, fuck.

I'm falling in love with Rhett Beauregard.

Again.

Chapter Twenty-One

RHETT

The front door opens, accompanied by the chime of the security system. My heart twists.

Liam, who's taking tiny groceries in and out of his tiny shopping cart for the fiftieth time since he woke up an hour ago, looks up.

Looks at me.

"Is Miss Amelia here?" I ask, dunking the tea bag—English breakfast—into the mug of hot water one last time before tossing it in the trash. I add one teaspoon of sugar and a couple more drops of milk, just like I've seen her do it.

"We-wa!" Liam cries and takes off running.

Amelia appears a beat later, arms outstretched, a huge smile on her face. "Liam! Morning, sweetpea. Oh, thank you, you give the best hugs."

Her eyes flick to meet mine over Liam's tiny shoulder, and I can't breathe for a full heartbeat.

She's wearing a white dress—casual, cotton, cute as hell—and lip gloss, and fuck me for life, but I'm wondering if she wore it for *me*. If she got dressed up for *me*, the way I did for her.

It wasn't lost on me how her gaze roved over my chest and arms in the white tee I wore last night. So I wore it again today. Like a jerk off.

But it's the joy in her eyes that really gets me. She's completely transformed from the defeated, weary girl I ran into at the liquor store. It's like a light's been turned on inside her, illuminating the things I adore most about her: her fearlessness. Her fierceness.

She's gorgeous, and if I had my way, I'd spend the whole fucking day with her. I'd feed her. Pick her brain. *What are you into these days? Where do you hang out? What are your thoughts on Robert Pattinson as Batman and the culture divide in America and TikTok?*

I want to know what she thinks about everything and everyone. And then I wanna get her naked.

"Morning," I manage, holding up the mug. "Said you were tired yesterday, so I made you, uh, tea. More tea. I know you drink a cup before you get"—I clear my throat—"here? Right?"

Wrinkling her brow, she releases Liam and straightens. "That's awful sweet of you. Thanks, Rhett."

She walks over to the kitchen and takes the mug from me, our fingers brushing. The contact lasts for all of three milliseconds, but it's enough to make my skin ring with awareness.

Aw, shit. Somehow I don't think "communicating more" is gonna keep us from crossing lines. We're beyond that.

Somehow we're already beyond that. It should scare me—and it does—but really, it's exciting.

Liam follows Amelia into the kitchen. I hand him his sippy cup. Amelia sniffs the tea. "English breakfast?"

"I pay attention."

A part of me expects her to make a face. A *that's-weird-why'd-you-do-it* face. But another part is downright thrilled when she smiles instead, and this time it's my stomach that dips.

That smile means something.

Something's changed, and I am here for it.

Would giving in to these feelings mean I'm letting go of the past? That I've let go of my fears that she won't wreck me again?

Or would giving in mean I'm still the reckless asshole I was when I knocked up Liam's mother and disappeared the next morning, too hungover to even offer her breakfast?

"I would think putting all your focus into prepping for the season wouldn't leave you a lot of space to remember this kind of thing." She sips. I stare at her lips on the rim of the mug. "Delicious."

"I do have to focus on the season," I say, patting Liam's back when he wraps himself around my legs. "But maybe I wanna focus on y'all too."

She makes this noise in her throat, half scoff, half moan. "What if one interferes with the other?"

I notice she doesn't blow off my comment and what it means.

"I probably should care more about that, yeah." I sip coffee from my own mug. It's still too hot, and it scalds my tongue. "But I'll be honest, I'm having trouble giving a shi—caring that much about football with y'all around."

"That a good thing?" Amelia raises her brows. "Or a bad one?"

Liam starts to fuss, so I set down my coffee and pick him up. "You tell me."

She frowns. "Well. How are you feeling about your contract extension?"

"I haven't thought too much about it."

"Why is that?" Amelia crosses her ankles and leans a hip against the countertop, holding her mug in both hands.

Liam's fidgety, but when I try to set him down, he starts to fuss again, so I hike him back up on my hip. I grab a nearby canister of apple-flavored toddler puffs and open it, offering it to Liam. He smiles and digs a hand inside.

"He loves these things," I say.

Amelia shakes her head. "Kid has the appetite of a small horse."

"But yeah, I guess I don't want to think about it. The extension. I'd rather . . . I don't know, think about what I should order us for dinner or what other ridiculous backyard sports we can pick up. By the way, I think croquet could be cool. My point is, that stuff is way more fun."

"And that's a problem because . . ."

Liam offers me a puff. "Dada eat," he says. I open my mouth, and he pops it inside with a giggle. I bite down on it with exaggerated crunch. He giggles louder, and for a second, I'm so happy I feel like my chest's going to burst.

"Because it's fun," I reply to Amelia. "And fun isn't what it's about."

"Life, you mean—you're not supposed to enjoy it?"

"No," I say with a mirthless laugh. "You're supposed to work all the time and be miserable, obviously."

She elbows me in the side. "You know, I was talking to Grandma Rose last night, and she floated this idea that I shouldn't base all my decisions on whether or not they'd make my mom proud. Like, why is it so important that I teach at a particular school? Why do I have to follow this very straight and very narrow path? Maybe it's limiting me in the long run. Maybe she'd be prouder of me for being brave enough to follow my own path, even if it's different from hers."

God, I love when Amelia gets real. Makes the hard stuff in my center soften, like her vulnerability is a reminder of what I should be chasing.

How I should feel. *Free*, like I really have let go.

"What did you say?" I ask, heart thumping.

She purses her lips.

"Dada, eat!" Liam yells, stuffing another puff in my mouth. "We-wa, eat!"

"Okay, little man," Amelia answers with a smile.

So we much on puffs for the next minute or so. I just wanna continue my conversation with Amelia, but Liam refuses to be still.

She claps her hands, grabbing Liam's attention. "Would you like to play with your doggie puzzle, Liam?"

"Doggies. Lili play doggies," he replies and scrambles out of my arms.

She moves to follow him to the family room, but I grab her hand.

"What were you saying, A?"

"Let me get him started with his puzzle."

We head to the family room and sit on the floor as Liam starts to pull the pegged pieces out of the puzzle board.

Is this how conversations will always be as a parent? Fragmented? Constantly interrupted?

"How about this," I say. "Let's finish this conversation later this afternoon when he's napping. That way, we can actually talk."

"You don't have to work out?"

"Not between twelve and one."

She grins. "Okay."

"Okay."

———

I'm waiting at the bottom of the stairs at noon on the dot when Amelia comes down from putting Liam in his crib.

"Hi," I say.

She furrows her brow, smiling. "You really do want to talk."

"I do. Kitchen?"

"Sure."

I hold out my arm. "After you."

Amelia plugs in the monitor and sets it on a nearby counter. Then she sits on a stool at the island. I stand opposite her.

"So you were talking about how your mom would be proud of you for following your own path," I begin.

"Right. Definitely something to think about. Maybe it's something you should think about too—why you put this pressure on yourself to earn this much money or win this championship. Why do you need to be that guy? The one who runs harder and faster than anyone else?"

My heart continues thumping as her words barrel into me again and again.

I don't want to talk about this stuff. But Amelia's honesty is magnetic, or maybe contagious is a better word for it. I'm not gonna leave her hanging.

And yeah, maybe opening up will help me find some answers. Or at least feel a little less lost.

"My older brothers had a very different experience with Daddy than I did," I say. "I was just so much younger, you know? Dad mentored Beau and Samuel in a way he wasn't able to mentor me. I remember when Beau committed to Clemson. The pride in Daddy's eyes was unmistakable. And when Beau won a championship there? Good Lord, Daddy smiled for a month straight. *That,* I used to think. I want to make him smile like that. The CTE had already gotten pretty bad by then, so for him to be so happy . . . it was a miracle. You know how angry and mean he was at the end. I was all of eight, but I promised him I'd win one day too."

Amelia's brows curve upward. "I remember."

"I put all my time and energy into football. I guess"—I swallow, hard—"I just wanted to make him happy. He and Mama. They weren't, though. I thought, hey, maybe if I just work really hard and win that championship I promised him, I'll make them happy. I'll save Daddy, and I'll give Mama the life she deserves."

There are tears in Amelia's eyes, and when I blink again, I realize I have 'em in my eyes too. Happens when I think about my father's suicide.

"I couldn't save him, obviously. But I still . . . I think about him, Amelia. All the time. I think about whether or not he'd smile if he saw me now."

"You think about whether or not he'd love you," Amelia says softly.

Aw, shit, now I'm really crying. "Damn, you're good."

Amelia stands up. Rounds the counter and wraps me into one of her fierce hugs. "Your dad always loved you, even if he wasn't capable of showing it."

I sniff. "How do you know?"

"Because I see how you love. Someone taught you how to love by loving *you*. Junie had a big part in that. But your dad did too. Look at you with Liam." She leans back a little to look me in the eye. "You've been with him less than a week, and you're already telling me how you're falling in love with him."

"Maybe that's because I'm trying *not* to be like my dad."

"Your dad was sick," Amelia replies softly. "Of course you're not going to be like him. It wasn't his fault he was mean, and it wasn't yours either. It was bad luck. But you have the good luck of knowing better. It's not your job to save anyone, Rhett."

"Oh yeah?"

"Yeah. Pretty sure your dad would want you to be happy at the end of the day. And if trying to save everyone isn't making you happy, well . . ."

She reaches up and wipes a tear off my cheek. When she moves to pull away her fingers, I catch her wrist, holding her hand against my face.

I can't.

I can't let her go.

The thing is, *she* doesn't let *me* go. She stays like that, holding my face in her hand, eyes steady as they move between mine. Acute desire mingles with hard, throbbing pain inside my body.

"All right, Oprah," I sniff again. "I wasn't expecting to have an existential crisis in my kitchen in the middle of the day, but here we are."

"Here we are," she replies, voice still soft. "Hashtag parenthood."

"Hashtag daddy issues."

"I want to believe you, A," I say.

Her thumb inches toward my mouth. Or maybe I just want it there. I want her to touch my lips so I know it's okay to lean in and kiss her.

"I want that too."

I blink, confused for a beat—is she reading my mind?—but manage to recover, saying, "I'll work on it."

One side of her mouth quirks upward. "You take everything so seriously. What if you don't need to 'work on it'? What if you just—God forbid—try to enjoy life a little more and go from there?"

"Okay," I say, even though I wonder what enjoying life would even look like.

And then the answer comes: it'd look like kissing Amelia.

Right here. In the kitchen on a Friday afternoon while my son naps upstairs.

I use my thumb to urge hers closer to my mouth, the edge of her palm scraping against my scruff. "Can I?"

Her gaze lingers on my lips before flicking back up to look me in the eye.

"Yes," she breathes. "*Yes.*"

Chapter Twenty-Two

AMELIA

What are you doing? What the hell *are you doing?*

Ignoring the chant of my runaway pulse, I let Rhett guide my thumb to his bottom lip. It's soft, hot to the touch, and because I'm wildly, frustratingly turned on, I tug at that lip, pulling it down. The look in his eyes ignites.

The inside of his lip is slick, a deep, gorgeous pink that, if memory serves, matched the crown of his dick.

I should not be thinking about Rhett Beauregard's dick.

But like the man himself said: here we are.

Here I am, about to kiss the man I absolutely, positively *should not touch*, much less make out with.

If only he hadn't confided in me.

If only he hadn't listened to my ideas and responded intelligently and earnestly to them.

If only he hadn't verbalized willingness to change. Not who he is—I'd never ask that of him, nor would I want to—but what he believes. About himself, about the truth.

He's after the truth, and if that isn't the sexiest thing ever, I don't know what is.

Stepping forward, I plaster my body against Rhett's and urge him backward, so we're hidden from our view of the stairs. There's no way Liam could catch us kissing—he'd have to climb out of his crib, open his door, and walk down the hallway—but it still feels weird to do it out in the open.

"Yeah," Rhett says, reading my mind. His voice husky. "He is a little young for the birds and the bees talk."

"We've talked enough," I say.

"But you said—nip the tension in the bud—"

I look him in the eye. "Maybe I'm changing my mind."

He swallows. "Doesn't change everything we have to lose."

"It's complicated. But I'm not sure that makes it wrong. If you don't want—"

"I do. Christ, A, I don't think it's any secret how bad I want you," he says, eyes searching mine. We're almost exactly the same height, him barefoot, me in my sneakers. Neither of us has to look up or down. We're equals this way.

He's ceding control to me, though. I can tell by the slant of his neck and the heat in his gaze he wants to make a move. But he's waiting for me to decide what happens next.

His consideration makes me ache.

"Fuck you," I whisper. "Fuck you for getting this so right."

And then, before I can chicken out, I tilt my head and kiss Rhett's mouth.

My pulse is drumming a wild, uneven beat, and I close my eyes against the riot of sensation that ripples from the place where our lips meet.

Need.

Tenderness.

Warmth.

I move my mouth, and Rhett responds in kind. It takes a second to find our rhythm, like we're trying to remember the lines of a play we performed a long time ago. They're there, the moves are there, but I have to reach for them. Remind myself it's okay if I don't remember it all perfectly because it's not meant to be the same.

It's *good* that it's different now.

And it is different, if only because neither of us gives up. Our noses bump, and we both pull back for a second to laugh, Rhett's chest barreling out to press more firmly against my breasts.

The pressure is divine.

He finds my mouth again with his, and this time we get it. The seam of his lips opens, allowing the taste of tea and coffee to mingle on my own lips. His are soft and slow, moving like we have all the time in the world.

I put my other hand on his chest, drawing my fingers into a fist around the fabric. He responds with a grunt, putting a hand on the wall beside my head and melting his hips into mine. My eyes roll to the back of my head as he sips me, small caresses that become thirsty pulls. We're breathing hard now. I lick inside his mouth, and he tilts his head, opening his lips to me, and his tongue finds mine, playing, toying. Asking.

The fire I saw in his eyes spreads inside my skin, heaviness gathering low in my core as Rhett kisses me, and *kisses* me. Our heads move in tandem, and he sucks on my bottom lip, just the way I like it. Only this time, he goes back to nip at it, pulling at it with his teeth, something he didn't do before.

My blood jumps. His taste and the way he moves are both familiar and thrillingly new. His stubble chafes my chin, making the throb between my legs grow hotter.

We've had practice since high school, and it shows.

His hand moves to my neck, cupping it, his thumb grazing my jaw. My heart squeezes.

Please. Please don't let this blow up in our faces.

Please don't let me fall for this man just to lose him all over again.

"Lili want We-wa, now!" Liam's little voice plays through the monitor.

Rhett pulls back with a groan, but when I open my eyes, I see that he's smiling, the kind that touches his eyes.

"Sorry."

"Don't be." I glance over my shoulder at the monitor. Liam is standing up in his crib, Pup Pup in hand. "Here, I'll—"

"Dinner. Tonight. Let me take you out for a real date so we can . . . er, connect without being interrupted."

My pulse skips a beat. What if someone sees us out together?

What if we have the best time ever?

The thought of being able to make out with Rhett again—

"Yeah," I say. "But wait, who's gonna watch Liam?"

"I'll have my mom come over. She can meet him, and we can put him to bed together. That way, we won't interrupt his routine."

I flatten my palm against his chest. "Can we go somewhere a little off the beaten path? Just in case—"

"Of course. Actually . . ."

"What?"

He grins, rubbing his hands together. "Nothing. I have an idea. Pick you up at seven thirty?"

"Okay." I blink. "Should I wear anything special?"

"Whatever's comfortable. And cool. We'll be outside."

Of course we will. Because I love any excuse to head outdoors, and Rhett knows it.

"We-wa now!"

My turn to laugh. "Enjoy your workout, all right?"

"Pssshh," Rhett says, rolling his eyes. "But I am gonna enjoy thinking about you without feeling like a scumbag. I really wanna kiss you again, A."

"And your son really wants not to go down for his nap."

"Tonight." His eyes burn. "I can't wait to have you all to myself."

Nuria calls me a little later when Liam is finally asleep.

"Thanks for reaching out," I say, stomach clenching. "How're things looking over there?"

"Your car's been towed, but the parking lot still hasn't been cleaned up, so that's been a bit of an ugly reminder of the whole thing. Kids seem to be okay, though. They miss you."

I look up at the ceiling. "I miss them too. They do a good job of singing happy birthday to Monique yesterday?"

"They sure did. Her dads brought in cookies and balloons for everyone. It was sweet." Nuria lets out a breath. "How are *you?* I've been thinking about you, Amelia. A lot."

A lump forms in my throat at her kindness. I swallow it.

"I'm better. The job is good. The little guy I'm nannying is a sweetheart."

"Glad to hear it. Think you'd want to do it in the long-term?"

Her unspoken question: *What are you going to do if you can't come back here? Because it doesn't look like that's a possibility yet. Or maybe ever.*

The implication stings. But it stings a lot less than it did two weeks ago. I haven't stopped turning over Grandma Rose's words of wisdom inside my head, and I think they're starting to stick.

That doesn't mean I'm over the death of that particular dream yet. I still have no idea what dream is going to replace it. I'm trusting the universe to keep me safe during this (not so?) awful in-between period, and while it's been liberating in many ways, it's also terrifying.

"I miss being around people too much," I say. "No offense to nannies because this job is important. Rewarding too, and a lot of fun sometimes. It's just not for me."

Nuria sighs. "Amelia, my heart breaks for you. I'm so sorry about what happened."

"I am too."

"The more I think about it, the more I'm convinced you were seriously, seriously wronged here. Losing your job because a man lied about being married? And his wife doing that to your car? That's just . . ."

"Insane?" I say, tongue in cheek. But I secretly mean it. Who torches a car?

"Well, yes. That too. Apparently, Jim and his wife split again. Or so I've heard."

I wait for my stomach to clench again, but nothing happens.

Not a damn thing moves or leaps or falls inside me at the mention of Jim, and despite the lump in my throat, I smile.

Being kissed by Rhett Beauregard must've confirmed my growing suspicion—Jim wasn't the one.

Which begs the question, what if Rhett is?

"I feel terrible for their kids," I say.

"We all do. But I feel terrible for you too. We removed Jim from the board, and his wife—ex-wife—whatever—she's not allowed on school property."

I scoff. Swallow. "Probably for the best."

"No kidding. I wish we could do more—"

"I'm not going to press charges."

A pause. "You'd be well within your rights, Amelia."

"I know. And I've thought about it, believe me. But at the end of the day, I just want to put it behind me. I have a good thing going here, and revisiting all that . . . it feels like a step backward. I don't want to drag Woodward's name through the mud."

"Okay." Nuria sighs. Her relief is palpable through the phone. "Thank you." Another pause. This one is longer. "Listen, Amelia. As much as I hate to say it, we're nowhere near to bringing you back on board. I tried to broach the subject with a board member I'm friendly with this morning, but I was immediately shut down. I'm trying my best, but . . . I'm sorry. I keep saying that—"

"It's okay," I say. "Well, it's not okay, but I'm working through it. Or trying to, anyway."

"Hang in there, all right? And stay in touch. I'll reach out if anything's changed."

"I really appreciate it. Take care, Nuria."

"You do the same."

I stare at my phone for a long time after we hang up. I'm so ready to move on from all this already—I want to know where I'm headed next—but I still cry a little, holding the flat of my hand against my eyes as the silence of Rhett's enormous house presses in around me.

Talk about emotional whiplash. I was on cloud nine this afternoon. Still am at the thought of going on a date with Rhett.

But I'm also seriously bummed. Scared too. What if I'm shooting myself in the foot, career-wise? What if it's the wrong move, giving in to the feelings I have for Rhett?

It's just *so much*, all at once. The good and the bad.

The problems and the possibilities.

But then I hear Liam's little voice over the monitor—*hi, hiiiii*, a happy scream—and I remember what Rose told me last night.

Why not follow a different path and see where it leads you?

I just don't get why it's so hard to *trust myself.*

Trust Rhett not to tear my heart out again.

But I trust myself and the universe anyway. What choice do I have? I could sit here and mope, or I could keep going. Keep seeking.

Keep hoping.

I get Liam up and give him a snack. I decide to take my own advice to enjoy life more, and together we head to Blue Mountain's pool. Thanks to Beau, we have unlimited access to all of the resort's insanely great amenities.

It's a glorious Friday afternoon, sunny and hot, so the pool is packed. Well-heeled families claim cushy recliners poolside while waiters in khaki shorts, navy blue polos, and sneakers dart in and out of the main house, trays laden with delicious-looking cocktails and sandwiches.

I slather Liam and me in sunscreen. Then I put on his swimmy, buckling it at the back, and velcro his little sunhat underneath his chin. He giggles, shying away from me. I take his hand and head for the water. Elle told Rhett that Liam has taken swimming lessons, so he's not totally new to the pool.

He's hesitant at first, so I jump in and hang by the stairs while I try to coax him in the pool, one step at a time. A couple of older kids do cannonballs nearby, splashing Liam with water. At first, he's horrified, his expression so twisted up with disgust I have to laugh. But then the kids do it again, and Liam actually splashes back a little, bending down to slam his hands into the water.

"Lili make wa-wa go boom!" he says, clearly proud of himself.

I slam my hands down too, soaking both of us, and Liam screams with delight.

"See? The water doesn't hurt. Should we try to swim?" I hook my hands underneath his arms and gently pull him with me deeper into the pool.

This time he screams with terror.

"Oh! Oh, I'm sorry, buddy," I say, taking him back to the steps. "We can stay right here and do boom if you want?"

"Lili go boom."

Liam splashes, and I sit on the steps and splash with him, sipping a Coke I ordered because I'm not going to make it to my date with Rhett if I don't caffeinate.

"It's a full-contact sport, isn't it? Hanging with a toddler all day?"

I look up and see Beau's wife, Annabel, smiling down at us, her little girl, Maisie, slung on her hip.

Smiling back, I reply, "Absolutely. I practically face plant into bed every night."

"It's no joke, that's for sure. Y'all mind if we join you? Maisie is all about the pool these days."

"We'd love that," I say, and I mean it.

Liam stares at Maisie with his big blue eyes.

Turns out Maisie is completely and utterly fearless, leaping into the pool with abandon and refusing help from her mommy as she paddles her way through the water. Liam watches her intently and finally allows me to take him a step deeper, and then another step, and then he's floating, still watching Maisie as I hold him.

Maisie kicks her way over to us, lifting her little arm to touch Liam's. He shies away, clinging to me, and while I want him to warm up to his cousin, I can't help but feel a surge of joy.

He trusts me. This little guy who lost the only parent he knew is learning to trust someone again, and it's such a bittersweet moment I almost want to cry.

"It's all right, Liam," I say. "Maisie just wants to say hello. Can you say hi, Maisie?"

"Mimi," he says. "Lili say hi Mimi."

Annabel grins. "He's two and a half, right? He's talking really well. Maisie's just starting to string words together."

"She's a little adventurer."

Grabbing Maisie, Annabel lifts her out of the water and smiles up at her. "We call her Bam Bam. Kid acts first and thinks later, just like her daddy."

"Uh-oh. Y'all are in trouble."

"No kidding." Maisie starts to fuss, so Annabel puts her back in the water and turns her attention to me. "I'm glad we're finally getting to hang out. I've been dying for these two to meet. Things going okay so far?"

"All things considered, things are going pretty well." Liam starts to kick his legs, mimicking his cousin, and I hold him by the stomach to let him move. "It helps that he's such a good kid."

"So I've heard. And Rhett? How's he handling everything?"

Liam bumps into Maisie, making her laugh, and he shouts, "Mimi!"

"I wasn't sure what to think when Rhett told me about Liam," I reply. "But I think he's really enjoying it so far—fatherhood. I think he could use a little more sleep—"

"Every parent of young children can use more sleep. Maisie was up with strep throat two nights in a row this week."

I wince. "Ouch."

"Yup. But during those moments, you just have to remember that this too shall pass." Annabel lifts Maisie onto the pool steps, and immediately Liam cries out to join her. Smiling, Annabel lifts him too, and to my surprise, he lets her. "Hey, buddy. I'm Auntie Annabel. I'm so happy to meet you. Welcome to the family. We're not perfect, but we are a lot of fun."

"The most fun." I look up to see Emma standing at the edge of the pool. Putting her hands on the small of her back, she smiles. "I heard y'all were out here, so I thought I'd swing by to say hello. I also haven't met Liam yet. Hey, buddy."

I reach for him and settle him on my hip, pointing at Emma. "Can you say hi to Auntie Emma?"

In true Liam style, he just stares at her, tucking his head into my neck. She laughs.

"Stranger danger?" she asks.

"Yup," I reply. "Big time. I've missed you, friend. How's married life? And the honeymoon planning?"

Because Emma and Samuel are in the middle of their busy season here at the resort (rooms are sold out through August), they decided to delay their honeymoon until the fall.

"It's going great," she says. "Samuel and I agreed that Italy is our happy place, so we basically plan to drank and eat our way through the lakes region, with stops at some fabulous hotels along the way."

"Sounds heavenly," Annabel says. "Beau and I are long overdue for an adults-only trip."

"How's the nannying gig going?" Emma asks, turning back to me.

I nod at Annabel. "We were just talking about that. It's going really well."

"Amelia told me Rhett is dominating the dad thing," Annabel says. "No doubt helped by Amelia dominating the nanny thing too."

"I knew you'd kill it," Emma says. "You two make a great team, huh? You and Rhett?"

She gives me a look. The kind that makes me blush and turn away.

I want to tell her about my date with Rhett tonight. Emma and I have become pretty close, and we've talked plenty about our love lives. She knows Rhett and I were together in high school; she also knows things didn't end well.

Emma would never judge me. But she would tell me the truth, and right now, truth is this date could very well be a bad idea. Still, it'd be such a relief—a thrill too—to say those words aloud to someone: *Rhett asked me out on a date.*

But that news belongs to him too. And Emma is part of his family now. I'd trust her not to share what I told her in confidence with Samuel. Still, this . . . *thing* between Rhett and me feels too new. Too delicate. I don't want to jinx it. I also don't want anyone to judge us. Yes, we have history. But more importantly, we have a third party involved now—Liam.

Liam always comes first.

"Anyway," I say, smoothing his wet hair out of his face. "I'm having a blast with this little guy."

Emma beams. "I can't wait to hang out with y'all. He looks like Rhett's mini-me, doesn't he?"

Chapter Twenty-Three

RHETT

I don't even get to finish the question when Mom yelps, "Yes! Yes, I'd *love* to babysit Liam. How soon can I come over?"

Because my family is my family, Milly shows up too, a laptop bag slung over her shoulder and a gigantic box tucked against her hip.

"What the hell is this?" I say, taking the box. I study the picture splayed across the front of a red inflatable monstrosity. "A bouncy house?"

She lifts a shoulder as she breezes into my foyer, glancing past me in a clear attempt to look for Liam. "I'm the cool aunt."

"This thing is going to take up my whole backyard."

"So? It's not like you use your yard anyway."

Mom leans in to press a kiss to my cheek, smiling. "I'm so glad we finally get to meet the little guy."

"You look nice." Milly's eyes move over my jeans and blue plaid button-up. "Where are you going again?"

"Out," I reply crisply. I'm not telling anyone about my date with Amelia. The Beauregards are nosy motherfuckers, clearly. The second I tell them I'm going out with the girl we all fell in love with ten years ago, they're going to start asking if we've set a date yet.

This thing is complicated enough without them meddling in our business. I need to go into it with clear eyes. The pressure they'll put on me to make it something more may cloud my judgment.

Then again, I'm taking my kid's nanny out for a date after kissing her in my kitchen this morning, so my judgment is . . . questionable at best.

Whatever. I'm excited. Excited to hang with Amelia one on one, and excited for Mom and Milly to meet my son.

"Y'all come on in," I say, and lead them into the family room. I set the box on a console table behind the sofa, and then I fall into a crouch, gesturing to Liam. "Li, are you ready to meet Grandma and Auntie Milly?"

Liam, who's been busy pushing his dump truck in manic circles around the room, pauses long enough to look up at me. His big, serious eyes dart to Mom and Milly, and he immediately abandons his truck and runs over to me, launching himself into my arms.

"Ooopf!" I smile and, settling Liam on my hip, stand and point at Mom. "That's your grandma. Can you say hi?"

"Hi, Liam," Mom says with a big, watery smile. "It's so nice to meet you. Can I get a high five?"

I duck my head to whisper in his ear. "You know how to give high fives, buddy."

Liam just stares at my mom and her outstretched hand for a full beat. I laugh, and so does Mom. I gently take Liam's hand and guide it to Mom's. Their palms make a neat little *clack* when they meet, and Liam giggles, burying his head in my chest.

"Aw, buddy, that was great," I say, brushing my lips over the crown of his head.

"Oh my God." Milly fans her hands in front of her eyes. "Y'all are, like, the cutest thing ever. I'm dead. Legitimately dead from the sweetness." She puts one of those hands on my shoulder. "Rhett, he's perfect, and so are you."

Goddamn it, now my eyes are misting over.

"Thank you," I say with a sniff. "Liam, this is Auntie Milly. She tells it like it is, which isn't always a good thing, but today—well, today is one of those rare occasions where it is."

"We don't tolerate bullshit in this family, Liam," Milly says, pointing at him. "You remember that."

"Language," Mama warns.

My sister has the grace to look sheepish. "Sorry. But now he knows."

Liam stares at her too, clinging to me.

"Why don't we blow that thing up?" I nod at the bouncy house. "That might get him to warm up a bit."

"Should we go outside and play?" Milly asks Liam.

He finally smiles. "Ous-side."

My trick works. I leave Liam with Mom and Milly while I blow up the bouncy house. They help him pick dandelions and ooh and aah when he shows them his water table.

When the bouncy house is ready, Liam lets Mom take his hand, and she helps him climb inside. He's hesitant at first, testing out the floor, the walls. But then he gets the hang of it, small jumps that get bigger and bigger until he's literally bouncing off the walls. He laughs so hard he poops.

We take him inside, and Mom and Milly fuss over him as they elbow me aside to change his diaper.

"Y'all sure you wanna do this?"

"We're sure. Now make yourself scarce."

But instead, I stay and watch, and later the three of us put Liam to bed together. Because watching the people I love, love up on my son?

It's loud, and it's messy, and it's kind of the best thing ever.

I leave my house with a full heart and a smile that won't quit.

———

I don't do dates.

Not in the past year and a half or so, anyway. Our team was a Super Bowl contender last season, so I put all my focus into football, no distractions of the female variety allowed. When we didn't make it past the playoffs, I jumped right into Hank's not-so-little retirement bender, jetting around the world in search of . . .

Forgetting, I guess. I wanted to forget how high the stakes just got and how down I felt.

So, yeah. I'm nervous as fuck when I knock on Amelia's door. I want a beer so bad I can taste it, but instead, I'm holding a bouquet of pink Gerbera daisies in one hand and my hopeful heart in the other.

Dear Lord, please don't let me screw this up.

Also, please don't let her think I was assuming anything if she finds that sleeve of Trojans in the glove box.

Again, I have no idea how to date, so I don't know what the protocol is anymore for that stuff. Are we allowed to have sex on the first date? Will Amelia want to? Should we run the bases first, a little warm-up before we swing for the fences? This is our first date in nine years, yes, but technically, it's probably our five hundredth overall. What are the rules for that? And do the condoms show I'm an arrogant jerkoff or a man who learned the hard way never to be careless again with the woman he adores?

Amelia opens the door, and my mouth goes dry.

She's wearing a strappy dress, dark blue and short, her bare shoulders and chest and legs tanned and soft looking. I don't think she's wearing a bra because I can see the outline of her nipples through the thin, silky fabric, which of course makes me wonder if she's not wearing underwear either.

My eyes flick to her waist. I can juuuust make out the lace of what appears to be a thong arching over her hip and disappearing into the curve of her ass.

Dear *Lord*. Is a thong sexier than going commando?

According to my cock, yes. Yes, it is.

Amelia smiles, her entire being lighting up. "Hi."

"He—" I clear my throat. Try again. "Hey. Hello. Hi, are you trying to kill me with that dress?"

She laughs. "I am. Luckily I'm certified in CPR."

"You're gonna need to use it, 'cause I think I just went into cardiac arrest. You look gorgeous, A." I thrust the daisies in her direction like a dickhead, eager and embarrassed and weirdly proud too. Proud I actually had the balls to make this date happen. "For you."

The fancy florist paper the flowers are wrapped in crinkles as

Amelia takes the bouquet. "Aw, they're beautiful, Rhett, thank you." She wraps an arm around my neck and pulls me in for a hug, enveloping me in the smell of her perfume.

Flowers. Summer. Sin.

"My pleasure," I say huskily. "You ready to head out? I'm not trying to be rude, but if you invite me in, we sure as hell ain't coming back out anytime soon."

The look in her eyes sharpens. "No problem. Lemme get my purse."

I'm not sure whether or not to grab her hand on the walk to my truck, so I flip my keys to keep from reaching for her.

"*That's* your idea of a family car?" she asks when I open the passenger side door of my brand-new, gunmetal gray F-250.

"Just got it this afternoon. It's a king cab, so there's plenty of room for a car seat. You'll see. It's also got a five-star safety rating. So the thing's not just a dad car. It's a safe *and* sexy dad car."

Amelia rolls her eyes and grins. Her dress moves up her thighs as she takes my hand and climbs inside, and I have to bite the inside of my cheek to keep from staring.

I drive away from Asheville proper, where Amelia lives, the setting sun slanting through the windshield as we wind our way through the mountains.

Folding down her sun visor, Amelia crosses those fucking legs and says, "So where are we going?"

I adjust my hand on the top of the steering wheel and cut her a glance. "Somewhere way off the beaten path."

"I have pepper spray."

"Good. We can use it on the bears."

By the time I pull into the clearing, the light is golden, and the air is on the right side of warm. I back up so my taillights are facing the river.

"You weren't kidding," she says, turning around to peer out the back windows. "We are *out* here."

I put the truck in park and roll down all the windows. The steady hush of the nearby water fills the car, along with the sound of crickets.

"Honey, we can run naked through these woods for miles, and no one would know."

"Scary." Her eyes flick from my face to my crotch. "And hot."

"Keep looking at my dick, and I can't promise it'll behave."

"What if I don't want it to behave?"

I punch the ignition button with excessive force, cutting the engine. "I gotta—I wanna feed you first. I'm trying to be a gentleman here, A, but you're making that really damn difficult."

She looks at me, lips twitching. "I appreciate that, actually."

"Actually?" I furrow my brow. "C'mon, Amelia, we aren't horny teenagers anymore. We're horny adults. Which means we eat first, *then* we . . ."

"Engage in some heavy petting?"

"Exactly."

"Great. Let's do this." She opens her door, and I follow suit.

I open the tailgate and set up our picnic. I went all out, basket and blanket and this heavy marble canister thing to keep the wine cold.

Amelia's eyes widen as I set up our spread in the bed of my truck beneath a canopy of trees, the fading sky purpling above, the water rushing below.

"What can I help with?" She puts her hands on the small of her back and glances up at me.

"Nothing," I grunt, tucking the edge of the blanket into the corner of the bed. I turn around and hold out my hand. "Time for supper."

I pull her up onto the bed. For a second, we stand there, bodies touching. Looking down at the spread I set out, Amelia slides a hand into the back pocket of my jeans and rests her head on my shoulder.

Fu-*uck*. Fuck, I like that.

I will my gaze to stay on the blanket. We've got a crudite of heirloom carrots, cucumbers, and radishes served with pimiento cheese. Platter of fried chicken, served cold in true Southern style. Cornbread with honey butter and deliciously mayonnaise-y potato salad made with purple and red potatoes from Blue Mountain's garden.

Let's not forget the ice-cold bottle of Albariño—Emma's recommendation—and the slab of chocolate sheet cake beside it. I've got some music playing on a small but mighty speaker, my favorite acoustic country playlist cued up.

"Rhett." She sighs. "This is so romantic."

"Cheesy romantic or good romantic?"

"Cheesy *is* good."

My chest swells. "I get an A, then, Miss Fox?"

"A plus."

We kick off our shoes and sit down. I try not to watch Amelia eat because that's weird. But she makes these throaty little moans as she chows down. She reaches for more chicken, and those moans get progressively louder.

"Are you being porny on purpose?" I ask, drinking my wine. I'm trying to take it slow—I'm driving—but I'm nervous and a little strung out on how gorgeous Amelia looks.

"Yes," she says, wiggling her eyebrows. "This food is really freaking good."

"I made it."

She laughs again, and I get the same happy, fizzy feeling I got watching Mom and Milly with Liam earlier.

When was the last time summer felt this good?

When was the last time life felt this good, period?

"You did not make this," Amelia says.

"Fine. I ordered the food from the Barn Door. But I did organize everything else"—I gesture to the silverware, the basket, the plates —"on a few hours' notice. Aren't you impressed?"

"*So* impressed." She narrows her eyes, pulling back. "You're not expecting to get a blow job out of this, are you?"

"Blow jobs? Psh. Who likes those?"

"You do, if memory serves."

"Don't," I warn.

But her smile deepens as she leans forward, eyes locked on mine. "Don't do what, Rhett?"

"Tease. Tempt. Generally make me want to jump your bones right here, right now." I cover my crotch with my napkin. How many inconvenient boners is this girl gonna give me? "One of us has to keep our head screwed on straight. And the thought of you putting your mou—"

"Is yummy enough to make your head explode. Pun absolutely intended." Amelia stretches her legs out in front of her, crossing them at the ankle. She rests her weight on the arm she's got propped behind her and looks out over the woods. "So now that the first week's done—how are you feeling about everything?"

I stretch out my legs and rest my weight on my arms, my shoulder brushing Amelia's. "Right now? I'm crushing a date with a girl I really like. I'm full. My son's asleep." I glance at my phone, its screen blank. "Yeah, I'm feeling real good."

She nudges my leg with her knee. "You know what I mean. How are you feeling about suddenly becoming a dad?"

"It's way harder than I thought it'd be." I notice lightning bugs are starting to appear, marking the pink-purple air with flickering dots of bright yellow. "But also way better? I'll be honest, I used to wonder why people had kids. It seemed kinda miserable. Thankless, I guess."

"So what's changed?"

I tap my foot against hers, and she taps back. Our feet stay like that—her ankles are crossed, but mine aren't, so the bony outer ridge of mine meets with her big toe. "I had no idea about the joy that comes with parenthood. It's the fun and the laughter, sure. That's awesome. But I feel . . . a lot less lonely than I did before. I feel like I'm connected to life or the universe or whatever. Like I'm *in it*, and it's urgent and real in a way life is meant to be."

"Kids have a way of keeping you present," Amelia replies. "It's excruciating and exhilarating, all at once."

Yes. Yes, that's how it feels. The fact that Amelia understands has my heart swaying like the drunk I used to be.

Still am, maybe.

All I know is I haven't wanted to drink like I used to.

The emptiness I was trying to numb isn't as deep. Looking into Amelia's eyes—they're translucent in this light, the color of honey—it suddenly clicks into place, what's been slowly but steadily filling the hole inside me.

People.

My people.

Time spent with them. Putting them first. Doing fun things with them. Making them a priority instead of work.

It's always, always been work that's ruled my life.

"I think I'm re-learning what being happy feels like," I say. "What happiness really is. What if . . . I don't know, what if I've been chasing the wrong things?"

Her expression softens, and the impulse to kiss her punches me in the gut. "What do you think you should be chasing?"

"I'd like to chase you, if you'd let me."

The words feel dangerous, and for a split second, a warning—a premonition—catches inside my head. Am I making promises I can't keep? There's still so much we haven't talked about. So much to decide. But here I am, holding out my heart like it's available for the taking.

And here she is, looking like she might want me to take hers too.

Be. Careful.

"Let me think on it," she says, but there's a smile in her eyes.

A smile I haven't seen on her as an adult. It's not reserved. Cautious.

This is the smile of a woman who feels safe and seen.

Fuck careful.

"You're getting me all hot and bothered." I stand and start unbuttoning my shirt. "I'm gonna go for a swim."

Amelia looks up at me, brow furrowed but eyes still smiling. "You didn't tell me to bring a suit."

"Way I see it, that leaves you with two options. Swim in those clothes"—I nod at her dress—"or take 'em off."

She bites her lip. "How about you take all yours off first, and then I'll decide?"

Rolling back my shoulders, I take off my shirt. Then I get to work on my jeans. "Honey, I think you're gonna like what you see."

"I'll be the judge of that." She picks up her wineglass and sips. "Now strip."

Chapter Twenty-Four

AMELIA

I don't miss the way Rhett's eyes darken at my command. "Yes, ma'am."

Standing on the bed of his truck in the fading light, he looks like a mirage. The skin on his bare chest and thighs shimmers, the hair there catching the last rays of amber and orange from the sun. He kicks off his jeans and his ab muscles tense. If I didn't appreciate his insanely beautiful body before, I sure as hell do now.

And then there's his dick.

My eyes catch on the impressive erection that tents his briefs. He's making no effort to hide it now, and my skin throbs at his confidence. There's an earthiness and a steadiness to his desire, his acceptance of it.

His eagerness to share it with me.

I can just make out the soft curve of his crown. There's a wet spot there.

Heat floods my pussy. He's leaking.

"I'm going full monty if that's all right with you," he asks, hooking his thumbs in the elastic waistband of his briefs. "Speak now or forever hold your peace."

I swallow, clenching my thighs. I am soaking wet, and hot, and indescribably thrilled at the prospect of having this man tonight.

Who am I kidding? I knew we'd get naked the moment I opened my door and saw Rhett standing there, looking like a goddamn snack in his checkered shirt and scruff.

"Rhett, if you don't take those undies off right fucking now, we're gonna have a problem." I finish my wine. "Do it already."

And he does.

Oh, Lord, does he, and I'm left staring, mouth watering at the sight.

Rhett's not huge, just the right side of satisfying. His shaft is smooth, marked by a thick vein that forks toward the broad, pink head. The slit there is wet with pearlescent fluid. His pubic hair is dark, the same shade as his scruff, neatly trimmed but still lush.

My body responds fiercely, my pussy smarting and my nipples firming at the suddenly erotic sensation of rubbing up against my dress. I wince.

Rhett frowns. "You okay?"

"You're delicious." I get up on my knees and scoot over to kneel in front of him, looking up to meet his eyes. "Can I? Taste you?"

His nostrils flare. The ridges of the truck bed dig into my knees through the blanket.

The pain just makes it hotter.

Was it ever this hot when we were kids?

Eyes locked on mine, he takes his dick in his hand and gives it a long, slow stroke.

"Just for a second," he says, taking half a step forward. "Otherwise, I'm gonna come, and that can't happen because you come first. Open your mouth."

I do as he tells me, anticipation ricocheting inside my skin as he thumbs his head down a little, lining it up with my mouth.

Reaching up, I put my hands on the hard planes of his hips. His skin is hot to the touch.

I burn, knowing he's burning for me.

I extend my tongue and lick up the length of his slit. His stomach caves. He sputters *fuck*, and I smile at the salty taste of him on my tongue.

Rolling my lips over my teeth, I take him inside my mouth. He grunts and jerks his hips, thrusting a little too deep. I gag, my eyes watering at the sudden intrusion. He pulls back, horrified.

"Oh, shit, A. Shit, I'm sorry."

I shake my head. "Don't be. It's hot, knowing I can make Rhett Beauregard lose his mind."

"That was the problem with us, isn't it?" He cups my chin in his hand, his blue eyes hazy. "There was no controlling it. Whatever we felt, it was wild."

This time, I take his dick in my hand, pumping it just the way he did. "What if we chased the wild? Just for tonight."

"Chase the wild," he grunts. "I like that."

Gaze locked on his, I lean in again and lick him. Suck the tip, then take him deeper, deeper still, his crown hitting my soft palate. He starts to roll his hips, putting a hand on my head to guide me in time to his movements.

I accidentally scrape him with my teeth. He hisses.

I pull back, face burning. "Damnit, I didn't mean—"

"To bite off my dick because I promised to keep my hands off you, but I'm fucking your mouth instead?"

I let out a bark of laughter. "Maybe"—I give his shaft a firm squeeze—"you do deserve to have your dick removed."

"I definitely deserve it." He takes my chin in his hand again and leans down to give me a quick, hard kiss on the mouth. "But if you wouldn't mind sparing me just this once . . ."

I laugh harder, and now he's laughing too. He's reaching down to play with my breast, thumbing my nipple, and I arch into his touch. Behind my closed eyes, I see stars.

Taking his cock in my hand again, I guide him back into my mouth. More confident this time around because there's literally nothing to be afraid of.

Nothing to prove.

I'll be honest: I rarely, if ever, enjoy giving blow jobs. I *never* lose myself in them.

But this—I do lose myself. The desire to make this man feel good, to put into action the feelings I can't seem to put into words, is overwhelming. It's easy to be passionate and playful when you've already laid down the law, and that law is: be vulnerable.

Be *you*.

"Ooookay," Rhett says, pulling out my mouth. "Let's get you naked. It's your turn."

I gesture to his engorged dick. "But—"

"I can handle it. I think."

He literally handles it as he watches me tug my dress over my head. He strokes himself slowly, expression sharp when it lands on my tits.

"No bra," he breathes. "I was right."

"Makes me feel sexy, not wearing one."

"The panties. Off, honey."

I step out of my thong. Rhett rakes his gaze over my pussy, and I feel it like a physical caress, a pair of fingers gliding through my slit, back to front.

He actually does reach for me. He runs the crook of his first finger over my pubic hair.

"I like this."

"Good," I manage, practically panting, "because I do too."

He falls to his knees, cock bobbing between us, and hikes one of my legs over his shoulder, spreading me wide. "Can I taste you?"

My skin ignites at the sudden rush of cool air against my folds. "Yes. *Soft* biting allowed."

"Noted," he says, and leans in.

I almost combust from the anticipation. When his tongue meets with my clit I throw my head back, unsteady on my foot, but Rhett grabs my ass and holds me upright as he licks inside my folds. Slow, steady strokes that make my need tighten to an almost painful degree.

"I wanna—I wanna scream," I say. I'm legitimately panting now.

Rhett glides a hand up my side to cup my breast, circling the pad of his thumb over my nipple. Sensation bolts through my center, and I grab onto his shoulders. "So scream."

I do. "Oh, God, yes!"

"Louder." He sucks on my clit. Moves his hand from my breast to my hip. Moves it lower so that he presses his broad thumb inside me, thrusting it a little as he keeps sucking on my clit. "Pornier."

"Baby! Oh! Yes, baby, *yes!*"

He laughs, and I can feel the vibration in my folds. I'm rolling my hips now. Seeking, seeking.

Needing.

"Can you go even pornier than that?" he asks, nudging his nose against my clit as he slips his thumb all the way inside me. I feel myself stretching around him, then tightening, little flutters that come before the release.

"Aw, yeah, baby, eat this pussy. You know you want it."

"I want it!" Rhett shouts back, shoulders shaking. "You'd better give it to me, or I'll spank you."

"Spank me! Do it!"

"I'm actually not into spanking!"

"I respect that!"

"Boundaries are sexy!"

"Communication is too!"

Our voices echo through the woods. I'm laughing so hard tears are streaming down my face.

"Time to come for me," Rhett says, and he nibbles gently on my clit while pressing his thumb to the front wall of my pussy.

I reach up to play with my nipple, plucking it between my fingers. Rhett watches me from between my legs, his entire face lit up, and seeing the joy there—the challenge—

My pussy clamps down on his thumb, and he growls, literally *growls*, as my orgasm rips through me. I close my eyes and hold on to him for dear life. Sensation pounds low in my core, its shockwaves spreading through me with alarming fierceness. My legs shake, and I arch my back, and Rhett kisses my clit, a slow, soothing motion that helps bring me back to earth.

I open my eyes to see this funny expression on his face. His eyes are soft—soft and hot—and his brows are curved upward, his brow adorably wrinkled.

My heart dips.

What the hell did we just do?

Can we do more of it?

"Don't tell me you're already having second thoughts," I say.

"No," he replies forcefully, shaking his head. "No. The opposite, actually. Because communication is sexy—well, I'm gonna communicate that I just might be catching feelings."

My heart dips harder. I don't know what to say. "Wow. Wow, okay."

"Are you?" His eyes flick over my breasts, my belly. "Having second thoughts?"

His dick brushes my calf. I look down. "Little late for that. Do you have condoms?"

"Sex on the first date," he says.

"Something wrong with that?"

He runs a hand over his face, grinning. "I thought you said I wouldn't get laid with this scruff."

"Maybe I've changed my mind."

"Hallelujah."

"Told you getting older doesn't always suck."

"You're right." The look in his eyes sharpens. "You are so fucking right, A."

I look at him, and he looks back. I unhook my leg from his shoulder and fall to kneeling, one knee at a time. I take his face in my hands and kiss him. He tastes salty this time, salty and a little sweet from the wine.

He kisses me back hungrily, hand on my face. Hands all over me, my neck and my shoulders and my tits. He curls an arm around my waist and guides me down onto the bed of the truck, the blanket soft against my back.

He lays me down and kisses me so well and so hard my body rises into the caress. He lays on top of me, the weight of his body making me breathless, warm, needy.

I loop my arms around his neck and dig my fingers into his hair. He groans, trailing his mouth down my jaw to my throat. I gasp, turning my head to give him access. Closing my eyes to revel in the sensation of being loved this way. Wholly.

Recklessly.

We're being reckless. But I'd be lying if I said reckless didn't also feel right.

Chapter Twenty-Five

RHETT

I tear through my glove compartment, cursing when I can't find the condoms I put in there earlier.

I'm going to fuck Amelia Fox.

Amelia Fox is lying naked in the bed of my truck, waiting for me.

Blows my mind she's as hot for me as I am for her.

For once, *she wants what I want*. What if that's the case for more than sex? What if the things I've believed about myself for so long aren't true anymore?

What if they were never true?

What if this is? The anticipation thrumming through my veins, the ache in my ribs from laughing so hard. The feeling that I'm exactly where I'm meant to be, with exactly who I'm meant to be with.

If that's our story, well, I don't know if it's a book I should buy, or if it's one I'm better off burning.

All I know is I am fucking burning for this girl.

Finally finding the Trojans, I slam the passenger door shut and jog back to the bed of the truck.

And then I really do almost have a heart attack.

Amelia's legs are spread, and she's toying lazily with her pussy, fingers gliding through her folds as one of her bent legs moves back and forth, back and forth. Her tits are right out of that song "Night Moves": full, pert, the bottoms slightly heavier so her nipples point thirstily upward.

The sound of the crickets pulses around us.

"*Honey*."

Her eyes are hazy. One side of her mouth curls into a smile. "I was thinking about you."

My dick surges. I tear a condom off the sleeve and toss the sleeve to the side on the bed.

I get why our breakup fucked with my head so badly. This girl is heaven.

Just gotta hope she doesn't put me through hell again.

"I was gone for two seconds."

"Long enough to miss you. Miss the way you touched me."

"*Argh*," I bite out, rolling the condom on in short, brutal strokes. I climb onto the bed, leaning down. I brush her hand aside and give her pussy one last, long lick with the flat of my tongue. She moans, and my balls tighten, and I work my way up her body, stopping to bite one nipple, then another. I drag my stubble up her neck, kissing her there. Sucking her.

By the time my mouth reaches hers, she's clawing at my chest, arching up against me. I grab one of her knees and hike it over my hip. Then I grab my dick and circle the tip over her clit, moving down, then back up again, down far enough to notch at her entrance. I get a whisper of resistance, a taste of her tightness.

I capture her mouth in a deep, bruising kiss, my breath coming out through my nose in a noisy exhale.

Pulling back, I look her in the eye.

No words. None needed. But she knows, and I know that we're safe, and we're okay like this. For now, at least.

I nudge my hips forward and sink the tiniest bit inside her. Her lips part, and her smile grows, her hands roving up my chest to curl around my nape.

I push a little more. Her pussy stretches around my head, the heat of her making sweat break out along my scalp. The tips of her breasts press against my chest. Sparks erupt at the base of my spine.

Brushing my nose against hers, I bite the corner of her mouth. *Can I go?*

She tips her head forward so our brows meet, both damp. *Yes.*

With a grunt, I bury myself to the hilt. She lets out this sound, half pleasure, half agony, and I freeze.

"No," she says with her mouth as it covers mine. "Don't stop."

So I begin to move. A slow thrust that has her body going languid beneath me. She's so wet and soft and swollen I go easily.

Knowing I turn her on this way—knowing I delight her enough to get her soaked—makes the heaviness in my core throb. I bite down on the inside of my cheek.

I gotta make this last.

I tell her this with a swivel of my hips, a bite on her neck. She was playful with me, so I'm playful with her, grabbing the leg wrapped around my hip and guiding it up to her chest, then using it to guide her onto her side. I fuck her like this for a minute, reveling in the sight of her tits bouncing in time to my thrusts.

Then she gets on her knees and elbows, practically shoving her ass in my face. I pull one cheek aside, my blood jumping when I glimpse her asshole, and I give her a little swat as I glide back inside her pussy. She yelps, I laugh.

"I thought you weren't into spanking?"

"Maybe I am."

I take her from behind, sweating and swearing as our bodies meet with rude little slaps. I wanna move fast and hard, so I do, and Amelia keeps up. She rolls her pelvis at the apex of each of my thrusts, a motion that makes the muscles in her back flex against her smooth skin. I run a reverent hand over those muscles, massaging them with firm strokes of my thumbs.

I could come like this, easily. But I wanna look at her when that happens, I want her to be with me, so I dig my hands into her hips and turn her around. I sit on the blanket, stretching out my legs. I hold my dick in my hand, and she squats above it, resting her hands on my shoulders. She lowers herself onto me inch by inch.

Together, we watch the lips of her pussy spread around my girth. The tightness in my balls becomes painful.

"Fuck, you're perfect," I say, thumbing her clit.

She hisses. "It feels full this way. Really full."

Furrowing my brow, I tuck her hair behind her ear. "Take your time, honey."

She's sitting on my lap now. Eyes closed. Bottom lip caught between her teeth. My chest swells, and so does my need for release.

She is so damn pretty it hurts.

A few heartbeats pass. Amelia keeps her eyes closed but begins to move, eyebrows coming together like she's focusing. Memorizing.

I would know because I'm trying to memorize this too. Who knows what's gonna happen next? Who knows if we'll ever feel this free again to be ourselves? To be together?

The thought of Amelia being with anyone else, especially someone like that married piece of human garbage, makes me want to tear apart the world with my bare hands.

It makes me angry and unfocused.

I can't afford to be either of those things right now.

So I try to memorize the feel of her body instead as it milks mine to completion. The smoothness of her skin and the determination in her eyes when she opens them. The small, sly smile she gives me when I hold her by the thighs and spear her with a hard, sudden thrust. Her laughter when she really begins to move, and I move with her, sweat flying everywhere, the echoes of that sound loud enough for the forest to send them back to us.

I can't hold on anymore. Not with this laughing, languid woman in my arms, riding my dick like it's her fucking job.

Curling my fingers into her waist, I grit my teeth and prepare myself for the onslaught.

And oh, does it come. Release rises up to meet me and slams through my body like a vicious tackle, the kind that leaves me breathless. Bruised.

There's a howl in the woods, and only when I feel the condom fill with cum do I realize that howl belongs to me.

I'm howling like a goddamn animal.

Amelia digs her fingers into my hair and fists them, holding my face still while she kisses me hard, licking her tongue into my mouth. Stealing the howl and turning it into something else.

A plea. A confession.

"Are you actually a *werewolf?*" she murmurs into my mouth, and the sound morphs into laughter.

Opening my eyes, I give her thighs a squeeze. "Only with you. Jesus, A, you made me lose my goddamn mind."

"Your human form too, apparently." She pulls back, searching my eyes. "You okay?"

A knot forms where my heart should be. "Nah."

"Rhett."

"Funny—you don't have a curfew anymore, but now all of a sudden, I do."

Her expression softens. "What made you think of that?"

"I hate that this night is going by so fast. I wanna take you home, A. I wanna lay you down in my bed and fuck you like a civilized human being. We never got to do that as kids, have a sleepover. A month ago, we could have. But now I can't—we can't—and it's kinda killing me."

Amelia arches a brow. "Rhett, you're literally still inside me. You had time to think all this through?"

"Yes."

"Think of it this way, then. A month ago, we *could* have had a sleep-over. But we wouldn't have because Liam wasn't around yet, and he's the reason our paths crossed again in the first place. So there."

I let out a sigh. "Why you gotta be so smart?"

"To drive you crazy." She gives my bicep a squeeze. "Same reason you're so sexy."

I tilt my neck to look up at her. "So you think the truck is a sexy dad car after all."

"In its own gas-guzzling way, sure. Bed is cozy."

Wrapping my arms around her, I pull her close. Bury my head in the crook of her neck and hold her tight. "Was it ever this good before?" I ask softly.

"No," she whispers. "This was . . ."

So good it's scary.

I'm not sure if that's the right thing to say, though. Communication may be sexy, but leading people on isn't. I'm changing. I'm questioning things, and I feel the ground shifting underneath me. That doesn't mean Amelia and I are suddenly on the same page, and we're ready to ride off into the sunset.

I have to think of Liam, first and foremost, and what's best for him. Is that me taking my foot off the gas pedal in my career? Or is it me hitting that pedal hard?

And if hitting it hard is the right thing for Liam, I'm going to lose Amelia. She wouldn't commit to Vegas for a few *weeks*. No way is she gonna leave the town and the people and the job she loves for *years*. I'd be an asshole to even ask her.

Fuck. *Fuck,* there's a very real chance I'm making a very big mess right now.

I take a deep breath. Let it out. I know if I let my mind spin out, I'll panic, and that won't serve any of us right now. So I carefully guide Amelia off my lap, wincing when my dick slips out of her.

"I want you to know I brought you out here to go swimming, not to have sex," I manage.

Amelia stands up. Gloriously, gorgeously naked. The fantasy hits me out of nowhere: a sliver of my cum leaking down her thigh. I've taken her raw, no protection. Just a promise that I'll do whatever it takes to keep our family together this time.

Because I'm starting to think I might want a family. Maybe even a big one—siblings for Liam.

A woman like Amelia to raise them with.

"Really? Because I came for the sex," Amelia says. "Food wasn't bad, either. But I'll go swimming if you still want to."

I blink, snatched back to the present where what I want isn't clear. It's muddled. Or maybe that's just me flailing around in what would otherwise be still water, the kind that lets you see all the way to the bottom of the riverbed.

"I want to."

I tie off the condom. Leap down from the truck, still naked, and hold up a hand to Amelia. "C'mon, honey. Let's get you cooled off after the hot sex I just gave you."

She slips her hand into mine. "Please tell me the weird porny exchanges end here."

"But the hot sex—it doesn't, right?" I help her down. Keeping her hand in mine, we walk to the water.

"Hell no," she says. "Because I'm the one giving it to you."

And then she takes off at a sprint and launches herself into the water, diving in headfirst.

Amelia in a nutshell.

She emerges from the water with a yell. "Woo*ooo,* that feels nice!"

"Cold?"

"Not at all."

I debate whether or not to test it out.

Screw it. I dive in after Amelia. The water's pretty shallow, so I'm careful not to go too deep. My knuckles still scrape the rocks on the bottom, my lungs squeezing at the onslaught of cold, *cold* water.

Coming up for air, I flick my head, moving the hair out of my eyes. Amelia's right there waiting for me, grinning like a Cheshire cat.

"It's fucking freezing!" I splash water at her. "Thanks to you, I may have shrinkage that lasts for days. Days, Amelia. *Days.*"

She splashes me right back, then loops her arms around my neck and climbs me like a tree. "Let's see how bad it is—"

"Hey—don't you—" But she's already reaching down, and then I am too, grabbing her wrist. She writhes against me, face split open with a smile as she struggles to reach for my junk. I hold her, but she still struggles, calling me every name in the book. *You bastard, let me feel. Dickless jerk—and yes, I mean that literally, because I can only assume your dick has indeed disappeared if you're trying so hard to keep it from me. I didn't even need to bite it off!*

I throw my head back and laugh. A big old belly laugh that fills the night around us.

Chapter Twenty-Six

AMELIA

I wake up sore and horny.

There's a strange new feeling inside my torso. A lightness that makes me smile, even though for several beats I have no idea what I'm smiling about.

Then it hits me: I had sex with Rhett last night.

Porny, feely, rock star sex that was satisfying on a soul-deep level.

Not only that. We had the best date *ever*. The clearing in the woods? And that food? The conversation and the wine and the way we clung together in the water, keeping each other warm until the stars came out and our hands and feet were pruny?

Chase the wild.

Flopping onto my back, I cover my eyes with my hand.

"Oh no," I say aloud.

Oh yes, my heart says, making me wince and smile harder, all at once.

I grab my phone off its charger beside the bed. My pulse races as I tell myself not to be disappointed if Rhett hasn't texted. I've gotten my hopes up before, and I keep saying I'm not going to make the same mistakes again.

201

Does sleeping with your ex nine years after you broke up count as the same mistake?

I don't want to dive too deep into the answer to that question, so I hit the button on the side of my phone instead, the screen blinking to life.

There's not one but two texts from Rhett Beauregard.

Night A. I had a great time and hope you did too.

And then today at 7:01 A.M.: *Morning. Sorry for the early text, but Liam was up before six. We may have left you a little something on your doormat.*

Heart lurching, I hop out of bed and run to my door. Yanking it open, I see a tidy paper bag marked with Blue Mountain Farm's fancy insignia waiting for me on the mat. I open it to find a to-go cup of tea —English breakfast from the smell of it—and a bacon, egg, and pepper jelly sandwich wrapped in foil.

I glance down the hallway. First to my right, then to my left. I feel a surge of regret at having missed them.

And then, looking at the egg sandwich, I feel a surge of something else. Something big and happy, and it threatens to crack open my rib cage.

I drop the sandwich into the bag and start to cry.

"Are you crying?" Rhett asks when I call him a second later. "Don't tell me they fucked up the order. Did you get coffee instead of tea? I'll wring Samuel's—"

"The tea is perfect." Sniff. "Same goes for the sandwich."

Also, I'm in love you.

"Aw, honey, why the tears then?"

"It's just sweet of y'all. Thank you for thinking of me."

I hear the smile in his voice when he replies. "Told you I was getting sweeter. You need me to come over? Liam and I are still in the car. Can you say hi to Amelia, Li?"

Li. Rhett's got a nickname for his son now. I love that too.

"We-wa hi!" The sound of his little voice has a hand gripping my heart and squeezing.

"Hey, buddy! I miss you."

"We miss you too," Rhett says. Lowers his voice. "How are you feeling?"

Letting out a breath, I take a sip of tea and reply, "In the interest of honest communication—great. Really, really great. I had a blast last night. You?"

"Best I've felt in years."

"Stop being an ass."

"I mean it, A. I spent Friday night with you. Now I'm spending Saturday morning with my son. He woke up at the crack of dawn, but having a buddy to watch *SportsCenter* with is pretty nice. We also looked at some pictures of Liam's mommy."

"Oh yeah?" Another sip of tea. "That's right, Elle's package arrived yesterday."

Rhett connected with Jennifer's close friend, Elle. He told her he wants to keep Jennifer's memory alive for Liam, and so she agreed to send a photo album Jennifer had been working on for her son. Apparently, it contains lots of photos of them together.

"He loved seeing his mom again. They looked happy."

"Aw. I'm glad. She clearly was a great mom. Liam is such a good boy."

"Most of the time."

"Ha. What else do y'all have planned for the day?"

Rhett's turn to sigh. "Not much, which is nice, actually. Thought we'd hit up the sprinkler this morning before it gets too hot. Then nap time for both of us because I didn't sleep all that great last night."

"You didn't?"

"Naw. Too busy thinking about you."

A tear works its way down the slope of my nose. I catch it in the crook of my finger. I don't know what to say, so I don't say anything. I just sit in my kitchen and sip my tea while my heart runs riot inside my chest.

What the hell are we gonna do?

And would Rhett be down to have a quickie later?

"Are you really not okay?" he asks.

"None of this is okay. It's also wonderful."

He chuckles. "Agreed. I really did mean it when I said this is the best I've felt in forever. Bonus points for no hangover."

"Ha. I imagine that does feel nice. Because that morning after the engagement party—"

"I was a mess."

"It wasn't a good look."

"You're not wrong." A pause as he thinks. "I was just coming off my bender with Hank. I don't think I was, uh, in a good place then."

"But now?"

Another pause. "I used to get this feeling at night. *Used* to, before you and Liam. I was lonely, I guess. Empty? Unhappy? I have this big life, but I also had no life, you know? Working all the time."

I swallow. He's opening up to me again. Talking about things I don't think he's talked to many people about. "Are you saying you're not lonely anymore?"

"I'm starting to think I'm not, no." Liam fusses in the background, and Rhett scoffs. "Which is a good and a bad thing. All I know is, I want to remember the time I spend with y'all. You and Liam. Hangovers suddenly feel like a waste of life."

"I love that idea," I manage. "Let's keep talking, yeah?"

His voice is gruff when he replies. "Thank you, honey. Just listening —that helps a lot."

"I'm here. Always."

One last pause while our inconvenient, squishy, lovely feelings get the better of us.

"So," Rhett says at last. "Since this is already not okay, I'm going to ask you another not-okay question."

"Go for it."

"Hank and Stevie are having everyone over their house tonight for a cookout. Liam's going to meet everyone he hasn't yet—just a few Beauregards left to scare the crap out of him. No worries if you want the day to yourself, but would you have any interest in coming with us?"

My pulse skips a beat. "I'd love to come again, sure," I deflect.

"There's my girl."

I set down my tea and unwrap the egg sandwich, inhaling the

scents of butter and freshly baked bread. I wait for my stomach to grumble, but it doesn't. Already too full of butterflies I guess.

"What are you going to tell your family?" I ask. "About us?"

I imagine him lifting a massive shoulder. "That's something we can decide together. We can say you're coming to keep Liam company—say we're keeping familiar people around him or whatever. We can also say nothing because what's happening between us is none of their damn business."

"But they're going to ask."

"Of course they are. Doesn't mean we'll have to answer."

I pause. Ponder. I *love* Rhett's family. Love them. It'd be the best Saturday night I've had in a long time, hanging out with Junie and Milly and Beau and Samuel and the rest of the Beauregard clan. Good food. Good company.

Probably great sex afterward.

What's not to love?

"Of course I want to come. To the cookout, I mean. But—gah. I can't decide if it's a good idea or a bad one."

"Why don't we try it out and see?"

"Since when did you get so persuasive?"

"Since I grew the fuck up."

"Hey. Watch the language in front of Liam, would you?"

"Sorry, Ms. Fox."

"You should be."

"Look, I'm just going with what feels right here, A. You've been a part of our family for a long time, and it doesn't feel right not to include you tonight. You're as much a part of Liam's life as I am. You've worked your ass off this week to take care of him and help me out. This is a celebration of the fact that we survived. *We.* You and me. Which means you should be there."

I'm a part of his family.

My throat closes in. I clear it. "That does feel like a big milestone."

"Mama's bringing that peach ice cream you love."

"Oh, God, that stuff is good. Don't tell me you asked her—"

"To make it just for you? Maybe."

"Then she already knows something is going on between us."

"Something *is* going on, A."

"I know," I say quietly. "That's kinda the problem, though. I don't think we have any idea what that something's going to turn out to be."

His turn to pause. "I can't make any promises right now, honey. But I love spending time with you, and I'm missin' you when you're gone, and I can't help wanting to be with you. I'm sorry if I'm making this hard for you. I really am. I just woke up today, and . . . I dunno." His voice gets rough. "I wish I woke up next to you. Everything's better when you're around."

More tears. More sniffles.

"I'd love to come tonight," I manage. "What can I bring?"

"Just yourself. And maybe some extra condoms, because when Liam goes to bed . . . well. If you're down to fu—fun, down to have *fun,* we're gonna need a lot of 'em."

Chapter Twenty-Seven

AMELIA

Hank's house is set on top of a hill about a mile or so past Blue Mountain Farm's signature blue barn. It's beautifully understated, with a swooping cedar shake roof and white shutters. I arrive at five on the dot, but the gravel driveway is already crowded with *very* fancy cars: a G Wagon with gold rims. A matte black Bentley coupe. A cute little white Mini Cooper that has to be Milly's.

The Beauregards weren't wealthy when Rhett and I were in high school. They weren't poor either, like a lot of their neighbors—the infamous Kingsleys among them—but I don't think any of us ever dreamed all five siblings would do so well for themselves.

The amount of wealth here is something out of an Edith Wharton novel. Who, coincidentally, visited the Vanderbilts back in the day at Biltmore, their castle-like home about five miles or so down the road.

It's a gorgeous night, a little on the warm side. But the sky is clear, and the day's earlier humidity has been replaced by a soft breeze. I hear voices and music the second I open my car door. I can also smell a smoker, the rich, tangy scent of applewood heavy in the air.

Smells homey. My stomach finally rumbles. I didn't eat much today. Too excited—too anxious—about tonight.

Rhett and I decided to be as vague as possible with his family.

Probably not the best choice, but all our options kinda suck at this point, so we went with it. He told everyone I was coming to the cookout and let that be that.

No doubt they've already made some very uncharitable and very correct assumptions about what's going down between us.

Too late to do anything about that now, though.

Walking up the steps to the front door, I get feeling that I'm wading into something. My steps feel purposeful, *fateful*, my legs heavy like I'm drawing them through water that gets deeper and deeper.

It's only a matter of time before I'm in too deep.

Then again, maybe I was in over my head the second I signed that contract.

"Amelia!" Milly says when she opens the door. My heart swells at the familiar sound of her voice, the way her words lilt with a solid southern accent. She wraps me in a hug too tight to be polite, and the heaviness around me evaporates. "It's so good to see you again. Come in, come in, please. Rhett told us you were coming, but we didn't want to get our hopes up."

"Yeah, because she's still way too good for him, and we're all wondering when she's gonna figure it out," comes another voice. I glance over Milly's shoulder to see Hank, a big smile on his clean-shaven face. "Hey, Amelia. So? How did it go this week? Liam is freaking adorable, but Lord above, does that boy have a pair of lungs on him."

He pulls me into a hug too, and now I'm smiling so big it hurts. "He's precious, right? All things considered, this week went well. What about you? I hear your new lady love is in town visiting again."

He steps back, and I see that he's blushing a little. The same way Rhett used to blush when he caught me looking at him in chemistry class. It's adorable, and it makes me ache.

"She is. And she brought some of her new beers. Here, I'll grab you one. Stevie!" He turns to Milly. "Did she come out yet?"

Milly shakes her head, then glances at me, pointing her thumb in Hank's direction. "These two can't keep their hands off each other. They just had a quickie in the bathroom—"

"We did not," Hank says. His blush intensifies.

"Hank, the neighbors could hear you," Milly replies. "Anyway, Stevie's cleaning herself up. She'll be out in a minute. You're going to love her. C'mon, I'll pour you one of her beers. You drink beer, right?"

Beau appears and puts a hand on Milly's shoulder. "Of course Amelia drinks beer. I used to buy it for her and Rhett back in the day. Natty Light, remember?"

"As delicious as we were smart," I deadpan, and Beau lets out a bark of laughter.

"Get in here, girl." He curls an arm around my neck and presses a kiss to the top of my head, just like Rhett did to Milly the day Liam arrived. My chest contracts. When is this going to stop feeling so great? "Thank you for helping out my brother."

"We were worried about him," Hank says, lowering his voice.

"Very worried," Milly says. "But here he is, laughing and horsing around and *smiling*."

"You know he hasn't smiled this much in ages," Beau says seriously.

"*Ages*," Hank emphasizes. "Y'all aren't having quickies too, are you?"

Milly elbows him. "Hank! I thought we agreed to get her tipsy, *then* ask about the quickies."

"Sorry, sorry." He winks at me. "We're just kidding about getting you tipsy so you'll answer our inappropriate questions. Kind of."

There's nothing to tell. But that's a lie, so I don't say anything.

Milly loops her arm through mine and leads me inside. Hank's house is more compact than Rhett's, but the view outside the open doors out back is just as breathtaking. The sun is still high enough to coat everything in a late afternoon glow, all amber-washed greens and clouds the color of cotton candy. Mountains undulate in tree-covered waves as far as the eye can see.

But the man casually chatting with his sister-in-law Annabel nearby, bottle of water in hand and baby on his hip, is what catches *my* eye.

He looks up and smiles. Eyes and everything. He raises a hand, the one holding the water, and lifts what fingers he can in greeting. "Hey!"

Liam sticks out his head to get a better look. "We-wa!" he yells, squirming in Rhett's arms.

I see that they're dressed in matching white tees and dark jeans.

Even their hair is styled the same way: a deep part to the left that's hipsterish and hot on Rhett, cute and clean on Liam.

My knees wobble, a sensation that's quickly becoming familiar. I know if I don't do something with myself, I'm going to either maul Rhett or start crying again.

"Hi, guys," I manage, my voice wobbling too. I reach for Liam. "Here, I'll take him."

Rhett and I lock gazes, and for a second, neither of us knows what to do. Hug? Kiss? Shake hands in a horrifically awkward show of faux-professionalism?

"Amelia, you're off the clock tonight. I've got him." Rhett leans in and presses a scruffy kiss to my cheek. A shiver darts up my spine, and for half a heartbeat, I close my eyes to revel in the sensation. "You look beautiful."

"So do you," I say, and then quickly add: "You do too, Liam." He's leaning up for a cuddle, so I squeeze him tight. I love this little man's hugs.

Rhett arches a teasing brow. "We're beautiful?"

"Men can be beautiful, yes," Annabel adds. I turn to see her eyes moving between Rhett and me, a small smile on her lips. "And the Beauregard boys are definitely beautiful."

"The women too," Junie chimes in from a nearby sofa, where she's camped out with Maisie on her lap. "My kids get it from their mama, clearly."

"Mama's the most beautiful of all," I say.

Junie smiles, waving me over. "We didn't get to have a proper catch-up last time. Tell me how you've been."

I glance at Rhett. Before I can ask if he's sure he doesn't need help, he says, "Go sit, A."

Junie and Annabel exchange a glance at the nickname. Now I'm the one blushing.

But it doesn't feel weird, knowing they know. Maybe because they treat me like they always have: as one of their own.

Junie asks me about my grandma and my work. I ask her how much she loves being a grandmother and how happy she must be seeing her kids pairing off with such excellent people. Milly wanders over and makes us laugh with tales of her most recent scumbag client (her words, not mine). I chat with Stevie and immediately form a girl crush on her when she tells me about her newest creation, an amber ale called Tennessee Brunette.

Emma joins in too, and I don't miss the way Samuel hovers behind the sofa, giving Emma's shoulder a squeeze, ducking down to ask if she needs a wine refill.

Maisie wedges herself between Junie and me, and together we count her toes and make several unsuccessful attempts at "Miss Mary Mack." Liam gets bored with his daddy and joins in, happily slapping his hands on my bare knees in time to our singing. Maisie starts to fuss, and Beau appears, hiking her onto his shoulders and disappearing into the house with the promise of a snack.

Then it's just us ladies—well, and Liam too—which I don't mind one bit. I love being surrounded by women. I think because I was raised by them, but also because I miss the woman I loved more than anyone else in the world. The woman who would enjoy the hell out of a party like this.

I dig my fingers into my chest, a fruitless attempt to ease the pain that suddenly jumps there. I always seem to miss my mom the most when I'm having a good time. Grandma Rose says it's because I get my sense of fun from my mother. She also says I shouldn't feel guilty when *I* have fun.

I don't. I just miss my mom, and I wish she could be here.

I wish she were here to tell me what to do. I fell fast and hard for Rhett, and now I'm falling fast and hard for his family too. How do I keep heartbreak from meeting me on the other side of all this? Is it inevitable? Or is there a way for us to find some semblance of happiness together?

I don't see it. Not yet.

Startling at the touch on my neck, I glance up to see Rhett standing behind me, brow furrowed. "You look hungry. C'mon inside, A. We'll get you fed."

"Y'all don't rush on my account," I say.

Hank sticks his head through the doors and smiles. "No rush— food's ready. There's a lot of it, so I hope you brought your appetite."

"We don't let anyone go hungry here on the farm," Junie says, taking my hand and giving it a quick, tight squeeze. "I'll make you a plate."

I offer to help Rhett with Liam, but he waves me away with strict instructions to *sit*.

So I sit at the giant farm table in Hank's kitchen. Rhett's siblings and their significant others jockey for the seats on either side of me, Beau and Hank coming out the winners. I dig into the plate Junie made me, piled high with more food than I usually eat in a week: smoked chicken thighs smothered in Alabama white sauce; succotash made with sweet white corn; a watermelon, arugula, and feta salad that's out-of-this-world delicious. There are chive-and-cheddar biscuits with sour cream butter. Swiss chard sautéed with bacon and sugar. Roasted sweet potatoes. I wash it all down with a crisp, Italian chardonnay Emma recommends, and more than once, I wish I'd Ubered so I could keep drinking it. It's that good.

I plow through everything, keeping an eye on Rhett as he puts Liam in his lap and feeds him dinner. Rhett gets flustered when Liam refuses to let him put on his bib and again when Liam chucks his sippy cup onto the floor. But once Rhett offers him food—pieces of chicken he carefully cut into tiny chunks—things start to go much more smoothly. Rhett helps Liam dig his little blue plastic spoon into the potatoes, and together they bring it to Liam's mouth.

"Mmmm!" Liam says, kicking his legs against the table in delight.

Junie claps while the rest of us laugh.

"Kid likes his food," Rhett says.

Samuel pats Rhett's belly. "Just like his daddy."

"You're the one with the beer gut."

Samuel smiles and pats his stomach proudly. "It's a wine gut, thank you very much. My lady here"—he wraps an arm around Emma—"happens to like it."

"Do you really?" Rhett asks, casting a disbelieving glance in her direction.

"I do," Emma says with a grin.

"Ew, y'all," Milly says.

"Don't hate on love," Beau teases.

Junie smiles. "Lovers, let them love."

"Just not too loudly." Milly points her knife at Hank and Stevie. "I'm talking about y'all."

"Sorry," Stevie says.

"I'm not," Hank shoots back.

"More," Liam says, glancing up at his daddy. Rhett patiently spoons another scoop of potatoes onto his plate. This time Liam doesn't bother with the spoon; he just digs both hands in, smiling when we laugh as he shoves giant handfuls into his mouth.

When Liam finishes that, Rhett spins his plate so the chicken pieces are front and center. Rhett pops one into his mouth, making exaggerated Cookie Monster noises as he chews. Liam pops chicken into his mouth and does the same thing. He doesn't eat a ton of chicken, but he eats enough to count.

Using the wet paper towels he set beside his plate, Rhett wipes Liam's hands when he's done. He offers him his sippy cup, and this time the little guy actually drinks out of it in big, audible gulps.

"There you go." Rhett unscrews the top to the sippy cup and refills it from his own water glass. "Gotta stay hydrated, buddy."

That's when I realize it's quiet at the table.

The Beauregards are never quiet.

I glance around to see we're all watching Rhett and Liam. Scratch that. We're watching Rhett *with* Liam. And we're witnessing firsthand how good he is with his son.

Is he perfect? No. But he's trying, and it's obvious he's getting the hang of it. This is one of those times Rhett could easily pass off his kid and let someone else do the work. I offered, and I'm sure his mother and most of his siblings did too.

But he wanted to do it himself. From the looks of it, he's having fun doing it.

Beau's eyes shine, and even Milly looks a little emotional as she watches her brother care for his son. I've thought a lot about how, as a society in general, we give men way too much credit for doing way too little when it comes to family life. Women rarely get kudos for doing the lion's share of that work; it's just expected of us, and we certainly never expect to be thanked for it. Just look at my mother, who raised me by herself from day one.

But I'd like to think this isn't an example of that double standard. I'd be impressed by *anyone*, man or woman, who jumped into parenthood as quickly and as joyfully as Rhett has under the circumstances he's in.

My throat tightens. I'm so freaking proud of him.

I'm so, *so* freaking turned on. Despite the obscene amount of food I just consumed, there's this gnawing hunger in my center that grows brighter and hotter the longer I watch Rhett across the table.

He'd be a great family man. The kind I always dreamed I'd end up with.

Rhett looks up to see us all watching him. "What?"

"Oh, Rhett, sweetheart," Junie says thickly. "The two of you—you just look so happy together."

"Never thought I'd say this," Hank adds, shaking his head, "but you're good at this dad thing. Like, shockingly good."

"Should I be offended by that?"

Hank keeps shaking his head. "No. It's just this time six months ago you were in total playboy mode. Now you're all, like, Mr. Rodgers or whatever. It's cool. Although if you show up wearing a cardigan, I'mma have to draw the line."

Rhett's gaze darts to me. I look down at my plate, embarrassed for us both.

Playboy.

We haven't talked much about the nine years we spent apart. We haven't needed to. Actions speak louder than words, and Rhett's actions this week definitely don't fit that description.

Still, the mention of the word makes the niggle of doubt in my head reappear. The one that's been there since this whole thing started —the one that's gone dormant over the course of this week.

I believe he's changing. I'm watching it happen right before my eyes. But change takes time, and so does building trust.

Please.

Please, God, let this time around be different.

Chapter Twenty-Eight

RHETT

Beau falls heavily into the rocking chair next to mine.

"So." He hands me an ice-cold beer. It kills me not to take a sip, but by sheer force of will, I set it on the ground. "What are y'all gonna do about it?"

My stomach clenches. "Who's going to do what about what?"

"Don't play dumb. I see the way you look at her." Beau glances over his shoulder through the big picture window. Amelia is hanging out with Samuel and Emma in the great room. Liam's running circles around them, apparently not winded from Capture the Flag like the rest of us. "How long did it take for you to fall back in love? An hour? A day?"

Sweat rolls down my temples. I came out to the porch in an attempt to cool off underneath the ceiling fans. It *was* working, until now.

"We're not—I'm not—" I sigh, tearing a hand through my hair. "Fuck."

"She's your nanny."

My face burns. "I know."

"Then you know what you're doing is wrong, and you gotta make it right."

"Oh, yeah? And how do I do that? Since you're the expert."

"An expert at being a bonehead, yeah. That's why I'm talking to you about this, *playboy*. I already told you I don't want you to make the same mistakes I did. You have a kid now, which means you can't screw around. You're either in"—he slices his hand through the air—"or you're out. All or nothing."

"Beau—"

"Just listen for a second. Are you? In love with her? Look at me when you answer."

Takes me a second to gather the courage to do as he tells me. I look up, meeting a pair of blue eyes identical to my own. "Yes."

"Are you good to her?"

"I try my best, yeah."

"She good to you?"

"Always."

"Good to Liam?"

"Course. He adores her. I'm really starting to worry about what'll happen when we leave."

"Then put a ring on it, brother."

My pulse explodes. So does my tempter, even though I'm not sure why. Somewhere deep down, I know there's some truth to what Beau is saying. But listening paradoxically requires more effort than raging, and I am *tired*.

"It's not that simple," I say, holding the chair arms in a death grip. Somehow I manage to keep my voice to a low growl. "It's been one fucking week, Beau."

"More like twelve years for y'all. And we're not kids anymore. We know what we want, and when we see it, we go after it. You've been around the block—you know what's out there. And none of it compares to Amelia."

"You're not wrong about her," I say gruffly. "But you are wrong on another point—I'm not sure what I want."

Beau raises an eyebrow. "I don't buy it."

"I got offered an extension. Two years, twelve million guaranteed."

He leans back in his chair. Lets out a breath. "I know."

"Who told you?" I bite out.

"Doesn't matter. What matters is doing right by the people you love. You really think chasing a championship is how you do that?"

"Sure as hell wouldn't hurt."

"But you already have money. Money you've invested well."

"I'm providing for my family, Beau, just like Daddy taught us to."

"Horseshit," he spits. "I guarantee you Daddy would want you to stay in Asheville with Amelia."

Now my eyes are burning. "You have no fucking idea what Daddy would want."

"Rhett," he says, voice softer now.

"What?"

"Why the anger?"

I glare at my brother. For a split second, I consider standing up and walking out of here. I have every right to end this conversation. Beau's poking his beak into matters that don't concern him. This is my life. My kid. I can do what I want.

But for some reason, my ass stays glued to the chair. I drop my head and dig my thumbs into my eye sockets, pressing hard enough to make neon stars explode behind my closed lids.

"I fucked up," I bite out. "I missed out. Chasing this goddamn championship, I missed out on so much. Girls came and went, and I kept it that way so I could put all my time and energy into the game. I never gave out my number, and I *never* went back for seconds. So, yeah, there was no chance I'd see Liam be born because his mom had no way of reaching me. I didn't get to hold him or cut the cord or any of that shit. Two whole years, gone. Never mind the time she was pregnant. Beau, she was *alone*. Can you imagine how rough that was? I didn't think I'd care, I didn't know to care, but now I do, and it hurts."

A beat of stunned silence.

Then a hand covers my shoulder. Squeezes. "That's heavy."

"No kidding."

I run a hand over my face, "I'm an asshole."

"Well, yeah."

I turn my head and spear my brother with a look. He's smiling, the shithead. "I thought you were supposed to be on my side."

"Of course I'm on your side. Sometimes that means telling you things you don't want to hear. You were an asshole, but I don't think you meant to be. I think you genuinely believe your reasons are good."

"Right. I thought I was doing the right thing, chasing. Working."

"And why is that?"

"Because." I let out a long, low breath. "Work and wealth are how you gain respect."

"Daddy's respect."

I swallow hard. "Yeah. Yes. And by extension, everyone else's respect too. Sounds ridiculous when you say it out loud. He's gone. I know that. And when he was around, when I was a little older, at least, he was sick. Even so, the lessons I learned living in our house . . ."

"They shaped you. They shaped all of us, Rhett."

"Even after everything that's happened, and everything I've lost, part of me still thinks if I just get there, you know, get the Super Bowl, I'll be happy, and he'll be happy up in heaven or hell or wherever the fuck he is, and *then* I can live my life. *Then* I can put a ring on it."

Beau frowns thoughtfully. "But that's magical thinking. Why not live your life now?"

I shrug. "Wish I knew how."

"You give yourself permission. You say, 'Hello, self, please stop torturing me, it's stupid and pointless, and I'm telling you I deserve to be happy right now, whether or not I win.'"

Scoffing, I reply, "I just give myself permission. It's that easy?"

"It's that hard. What I'm saying is, it's up to you. Not whether you'll end up with the perfect life you always imagined. But whether you'll give yourself a shot at happiness. We're lucky motherfuckers to have everything we do. You don't have to sweat money. You're surrounded by people who love you. It's an incredible privilege to be in your position, and it'd be a sin to waste it. Also—lest we forget the elephant in the room—you're definitely not gonna find happiness if you die a slow, awful death from CTE. Which, if you play another couple seasons . . ."

Sitting up, I offer him a tight smile. "Right."

"Take it from a fellow father—Liam doesn't need a trust fund. He needs you."

I glance over my shoulder through the back windows. Amelia has

Liam on her hip and is spinning around in quick, tight circles. I can hear him giggling.

As I watch them, a fist grips my heart and squeezes.

Do I really get to just . . . have them? Be with them? Enjoy them?

I don't have to earn their love or anyone else's?

I don't have to earn, period? I just *let myself be happy?*

"Why?" My voice is hoarse. "Why do I get to be happy?"

Beau claps my shoulder now. "Because you're not the piece of shit you think you are. You were born the same way Liam was. Don't you think he deserves happiness?"

"Of course."

"Then so do you." He looks me in the eye. "Turn down the new contract, Rhett."

It's that simple.

It's that hard.

I close Liam's bedroom door softly behind me. Amelia's a step ahead of me in the hallway, her bare feet making a quiet sound on the carpet.

We were quiet too, as we put Liam down together. It's become a well-practiced dance: I change his diaper, Amelia reads him a few books, I rock him until his little head lolls on my shoulder. I put him in the crib. Amelia turns out the lights. I close the door.

But tonight feels different.

I feel different. Raw. Needy. Heavy.

I should tell her to go home, but I can't. Maybe that makes me the hero, maybe that makes me the bad guy. Whatever the case, I'm done denying the hunger inside me.

My dick gets hard as I devour the sight of her legs and ass. I grab her by the hand and spin her around, yanking her against me. Our hips meet, and she lets out this hot little pant. I duck my head and kiss her neck, opening my mouth to lick her. Nick her with my teeth. She tastes like sweat. Wine.

"Lemme have you, honey," I murmur. "Stay."

"I'm here. I'll stay."

Her hand finds the back of my head. She gently glides her fingers through my hair, like she knows it's tenderness I need tonight.

My heart twists.

The words pound through me in time to my thundering pulse. *How. Did this. Happen.*

I kiss her mouth in a way I haven't before. I suck. Plunder. I pour my fury and my confusion and my adoration into her body. Our lips catch, release, and my dick throbs. I thrust it into the cradle of her pelvis, blindly seeking release, and she reaches down and unbuttons my jeans.

I grab her wrist. "To bed. My bed."

Resisting the urge to throw her over my shoulder, I lead her downstairs and into my bedroom. It's still light outside, the kind of soft, white-blue light you get just after the sun slips below the horizon.

Amelia's eyes are wet when I pull her around to face me. A line of buttons trails down the front of her dress, and I unbutton them one by one, pressing my forehead against hers as I work. My fingers falter on the last button, and I curse. Smiling, she reaches down to help me, our fingers tangling, then moving in perfect tandem as we guide the button through its hole.

And then—

Heaven.

I reach inside her dress. She's wearing a bra, a simple but sweet nude-colored thing, so I reach inside that too, cupping her breast. My skin tightens at her softness. I press my palm to her nipple, growling when I feel it bud into a hard point, and I flick my thumb over it, making her arch against me.

"I like that."

"I've noticed."

I guide either side of her dress over her shoulders. It falls to the floor with a small *whoosh*. My dick surges against my zipper, and I wince.

"You okay?"

"You're too damn gorgeous for your own good," I murmur, and then I unhook her bra and use my thumbs to shove down her panties.

For a second, I just stare. Pale skin dotted with a handful of freckles—one beneath her right breast, another on her collarbone. The small, pink puckers of her nipples. The curving slopes of her hips, somehow both luscious and bony.

I put a hand on her hip. "When I touch you, how wet are you gonna be?"

"Very," she pants. "Since this morning—I woke up and . . ."

"Tell me what you did. How you played with yourself when you thought about me."

Her gaze darkens. "I used my fingers. Went slow because I wanted to make it last."

I reach down and gently—slowly—glide my middle finger between her lips. She's soaked, soaked and hot, and she lets out a breath when I circle my fingertip over her clit.

"Holy shit," I grunt. "I love you like this. What did you do next?"

"I—I did exactly what you're doing. I thought about your head between my thighs, and I—yes, just like that."

I nudge her leg with my knee. "Wider, honey."

She steps to the side, opening her to me. I slip my finger deeper, slip it inside her, pressing the heel of my hand to her clit.

"Oh." She tips her head back, eyes rolling shut. "Rhett, that feels —*good*."

My dick is throbbing, and so is my pulse. I lean down and take her nipple in my mouth, sucking hard, seeing stars when she steadies herself by putting her hands on my shoulders.

"I want you to come on my dick," I say. "You'll go first, always you'll be first, but this time I'm inside you when it happens. Understood?"

She nods, breathless, hips rolling against my hand. Her pussy flutters around my finger, and I know we don't have much time.

I carefully remove my finger and then my hand, and I tell Amelia to lie down on the bed.

Reaching behind me, I tug my shirt over my head and shuck off my jeans and briefs. All the while watching Amelia make herself comfortable on the left side of the bed. She pulls back the covers—my housekeeper came today—and climbs inside, and my chest about damn near explodes seeing her here, in my room, hair a dark halo around her head on the pillow.

And then she sighs. Eyes soft, pussy hot, the woman *sighs*, like she's never been more content in her life.

Fuck chasing the wild.

I am wild. I yank open the top drawer of the bedside table and grab a condom, tearing it open with my teeth. I roll it on.

Amelia holds up the covers. "Don't keep me waiting."

But I have waited.

I've waited my whole life for this. The girl. The feeling.

The permission to finally, *finally* let go.

I let go. And pray like hell it doesn't come back to bite me in the ass.

Chapter Twenty-Nine

AMELIA

Rhett wastes no time.

He climbs into his massive bed. Climbs over me, my legs falling apart as he settles himself between them. He does this insanely hot half push-up thing, using his arms to lower himself just enough to capture my mouth in a searing, hungry kiss.

I clutch his sides, huge slabs of muscle and warm skin, and do my best to meet him stroke for stroke. I rise into the kiss to keep up, bewildered at the sudden onslaught of intensity.

Don't get me wrong, our connection has always been intense. But this—this is different, more ferocious, and I wonder what's changed between this morning's breakfast sandwich and Liam's bedtime to make Rhett burn this way.

My stomach hollows out as he kisses me. It's too much. It's not enough.

It's everything, being wanted this way, *loved* this way, and it makes me almost sick with want.

I want this man more than I've ever wanted anything, but I'm afraid he was never mine to have.

I'll let him have me. I'll show him how it's done, the surrender, and

I'll hope he'll reciprocate. I'll hope he'll set himself free from the things that hold him back. And if he doesn't—

He'll destroy me.

Then again, he's doing that right now with this kiss. I'm done for, whether or not he sticks around.

Shit.

Oh, shit, it feels nice when my nipples brush against his chest as he rises on one hand, using the other to reach between us. My blood leaps in anticipation, my pussy throbbing and needy. The sheets are cool against my back, a welcome antidote to the rising heat inside me.

He takes his dick in his hand and glides it down my slit, back up again, making me moan. Eyes locked on mine—my *God*, the look in them, fire and possession, feral lust and focus—he notches himself at my center and shoves inside me with one hard thrust.

I cry out, body igniting, and he curses.

"You're still sore, aren't you?" he says, keeping very still. "I'm sorry, A."

I shake my head. "No. I mean yes, I'm still a little sore, but this— you being this way—I like it. Keep going."

He brushes his lips over my forehead. "You sure?"

"If I tell you something, I'm sure. Don't make me repeat it."

His lips twitch. "Lesson learned, Miss Fox."

And then he pulls back his hips and thrusts again. Harder this time, deeper, nearly splitting me in half. He thrusts again and again, taking his time, the muscles in his sides and back flexing beneath my fingers.

All the while, his eyes never leave mine. He watches me, watches me writhe and moan, his gaze serious. Soft too.

How can lust like this be soft? Makes no sense.

It is, though. I feel equal parts soft and hard. Soft with feeling. Hard with need.

"Show me," he says, hitting me with another gutting, athletic thrust. "How you touched yourself. Show me and make yourself come."

"O-okay."

I'm overwhelmed, but I somehow manage to do as he tells me,

touching my clit, closing my eyes against the urgent sensation that bolts through me.

"Rhett," I breathe, sweaty and surrounded, throat tightening.

"Do as I say," he growls. "Don't you dare stop. Lemme feel you, honey. I need to—"

His voice catches, and he doesn't finish the thought. Instead, he kisses the corner of my mouth, my closed eyelids. My jaw and my earlobe. Both nipples.

The need for release spirals between my legs, and my fingers move more urgently now. Slippery circles and scrapes have me bucking my hips. My pussy contracts, one hard, long squeeze, and Rhett shouts, an unintelligible sound made through gritted teeth.

His flat belly sticks to mine as he moves now. Sweat.

I want more. Need more. I put a hand on the firm globe of his ass cheek and guide him deeper inside me. He kisses my neck. I arch upward, fingers curling into his flesh, fingers working my clit.

I want this to *end* I want this to last forever.

Whether or not it lasts is in Rhett's hands now.

"I feel you," he breathes. "You feel so sweet. C'mon, honey, give it to me."

I press the pads of my first two fingers against my clit at the same time he hits me at the crest of a thrust, swiveling his hips.

I close my eyes, and I come.

I clamp down on his dick, release ricocheting through me with such force I bite down on my lip and taste blood.

"Rhett!" I shout, not thinking. I close my eyes.

Covering my mouth with his hand, he breathes, "Shout all you want, A. Fucking lose your mind."

Now I'm biting down on the fleshy part of the heel of his hand. It's calloused, hard, just like the way he pounds into me now, his rhythm suddenly uneven, hips jerking.

I come, and I come, and I *come*, sensation that spirals through my pussy and spreads through my pelvis, making the muscles in the small of my back tighten.

I come down just as Rhett rises up.

He takes.

I let him.

He drives into me blindly, and I keep my eyes closed. A last-ditch effort to keep my feelings in check. If I see how much he wants me, how much he needs me, it's over. That's the kind of love that makes me stupid.

Stupid and desperate.

The muscles along Rhett's sides seize. He rises on one last quick, punishing thrust.

He goes still inside me, our bodies throbbing in time to his release. He groans.

He's groaned plenty. But this one is different. It ends on a slightly high-pitched note that sounds suspiciously like a whimper.

He's helpless, a feeling I know all too well.

My heart clenches. I feel like I'm finally a part of something—a couple, a family—and this, the sex, it's part of the affirmation. Everything I've ever wanted is *right here*.

After a beat, Rhett collapses on top of me and lets out a long, low breath, tucking his head into the crook of my neck. He stays like that for a while, and I tangle my fingers in his hair. Soothing him.

It's all right, it's all right, it's all right.

If you just let me in, I say with my touch, *we'll all be all right.*

Or maybe that's just me being an idiot.

"You're not leaving," he grumbles against my skin.

My fingers go still. "I didn't say I was."

"You're thinking about it, and like you suggested, I'm nipping that thought in the bud."

Sighing, I draw my knees away from his body, straightening my legs. "Last night, you said you couldn't do sleepovers. But here you are, already breaking that rule. Liam—"

"You're not fucking leaving, A. It's late, you're tired, and I wanna make love to you again."

Now my heart is tripping to a stop.

"And yes, I know what I said, and I one hundred percent meant to say it."

A happy, floaty feeling fills me. It ripples outward from the center of my being, making my toes tingle, making every hair on my body stand on end.

But then I think about what his words mean and what they don't, and there's a heavy twist in my chest.

I want those words. There just has to be more to them, though. I want *more*. Always have.

I've worked hard not to hate myself for that. So many people, guys especially, said I was difficult or crazy for not only knowing what I wanted but for asking for it too.

Respect. Romance.

But Rhett? Rhett always liked what I had to say. Until he didn't.

Has that really changed?

I do and don't want to find out. Because this right here—it's so, *so* good. But it's just a repeat of what we had in high school. And that didn't last for a reason.

I flatten my palms against his chest and gently press upward. "You can't do that."

"Do what?" he asks, pushing up onto his hands. Our eyes meet, and his flash with panic.

Panic that spreads its wings inside my breastbone.

"In one breath, you say you can't make promises right now. In another, you say you're in love, and you *know* the kind of love I want comes with a promise. You know that, Rhett. So either you're full of shit, or you're breaking my heart."

His eyebrows push together, and his lips part. For half a heartbeat, I expect him to fight me.

For half a heartbeat, I consider backing down. A familiar refrain darts through my head: *I'm asking too much. I'm being a pain in the ass. Why can't I just be grateful for what he's offering? Who do I think I am to deserve more?*

But then I think about my mom, and I think about Rose, and I stand my ground. Losing Rhett is preferable to losing myself. I think.

I know.

My pulse thunders as I wait for Rhett to say something. Instead, he rolls onto his back and runs a hand over his face.

"I am in love with you," he says hoarsely, not looking at me. "I'm trying here, Amelia. You think I planned this? I didn't want to make a mess."

My throat thickens. "It doesn't have to be a mess."

He turns his head and looks at me. "I need time, honey."

"Time's either going to make this much better or much worse."

"So take a gamble with me and bet on it getting better." He reaches down and grabs my hand. Brings it to his mouth and brushes his lips over my knuckles. "Give me a week to get my head straight, all right? The kind of—the decision you're asking me to make requires a significant change that doesn't happen overnight. And you're gonna have to bend too, A."

I swallow. "I know. And I will. It's just hard for me. I want to let go and let this road take me where it's going to take me. But I can't see what that destination looks like. I can't envision it, what me going to Vegas with you and Liam would look like, and that scares me. Do I teach there? Can I teach there? Do I do something completely different? I'd be dependent on you, at least at first, and I've worked too hard to end up—"

"An athlete's girlfriend?" he says, smiling tightly.

A spark of anger ignites in my gut. I do my best to ignore it. "Lost. I've worked too hard to end up lost."

His Adam's apple bobs. He runs a hand over his face again. "A week, A. Give me that. If I don't have my shit together by then, you're free to go. I just—I need you. We need you. Please."

So much can happen in a week. I know that now. If he decides he's going to take the extension—if he chooses his work over his family, because that's what it comes down to—I'll be left with nothing. No job, no future, no family. Liam, too, stands to lose. He'll get over me not being around. But combine that with the fact that Rhett *isn't* going to be around all that much either during the season, and it'll be a double whammy.

But if Rhett chooses us?

I get everything I've ever wanted. And that's a gamble I'm willing to take.

It's quiet. Dark.

But I'm awake, thinking. My mind won't stop spinning, and I'm in need of relief.

I need a little comfort.

I put a hand on Rhett's stomach. He still sleeps on his back, one arm bent behind his head, one leg bent at the knee, which brushes against my leg beneath the covers.

He stirs but doesn't open his eyes. "A?" His voice is rough with sleep. "You all right?"

I walk my fingers lower. He chuckles, a low, throaty sound of consent, and I wrap my hand around his dick. He's hard, and he fills my hand. Heat and girth.

My pussy clenches.

Rhett's hand lands heavily on the bedside table. He rummages around for a minute, knocking something—his phone, probably—to the floor. Wordlessly he hands me a condom.

I roll it on, then give his balls a gentle squeeze as my eyes adjust to the darkness. His breath comes out on a grunt, and he grabs my thigh, hiking it over his hip. I climb on top of him, straddling his torso, and his hands move to my hips.

"Stay up," he says, and then he scoots down a little. Just enough so that my knees meet with his armpits. He lifts his arms and guides my hips forward, and now his face is squarely between my legs. "Now lean forward and put your hands on—yes, perfect, just like that."

I've got the headboard in a death grip, hot anticipation streaming through my veins as I look down and watch him lower my pelvis onto his face, my knees gliding apart on the sheets.

I'm spread open, pulsing, and when his mouth meets with my center, I melt.

I melt against his tongue. His scruff catches on the inside of my thighs as he laps at me, tongue flat and warm and firm, and I gently rock my hips to aid the motion, my legs already shaking.

Rhett sucks on my clit. Reaches up to play with my breast, plucking the nipple between his thumb and first finger. I throw my head back and smile into the darkness.

When we're like this, I feel invincible.

I feel cared for in a way I haven't in years.

I feel like I know Rhett, I know his heart, and it's a heart that would choose me.

Maybe if I show him my willingness to compromise, he'll do the same. It's a huge risk. But one of us has to make the first move. If not now, when?

His hands move to my pussy, making the heaviness there throb. Using his thumbs, he opens me wider and rewards me with an open-mouthed kiss, head moving, lips grazing. His tongue dips inside me, and then it's on my clit, swirling, teasing. Licking.

No rush.

No sound.

Just us, taking time.

God*damn,* this man gives good head. Doesn't take long for me to come, my head falling forward as the earthquake hits.

I'm Jell-O. Rhett puts on a condom. Guides me onto my side and wraps his body around mine, the big spoon to my little spoon, and lifts my top leg. I'm still coming when he slips inside me from behind. This angle makes me feel full to the point of pain, but I want the friction, I seek it out.

I love the feel of being surrounded by him. Our fingers tangle. He kisses my neck. Bites my shoulder. Cups my tits and thumbs my nipples.

He comes, heart pounding through his chest against my spine.

We clean up in his bathroom and climb back into bed, still naked. Holding up the covers, he curls an arm around my waist and tugs me against him. Back to front.

We wake up that way, too tired and too sore to fuck again.

But we do. We're desperate.

We're chasing the wild because neither of us knows if—when—the chase is going to end.

Chapter Thirty

RHETT

I stare at my phone.

The screen is lit up with Miguel Fuentes's contact info. I just have to hit his number and make the call.

That's it. Ripping the Band-Aid off will suck, but living the life of my dreams after it's done won't.

Why, then, can't I make the damn call?

My knee bounces frantically, my jeans swishing as I move. I'm sitting behind the desk in my office, morning light streaming through the windows. The door is closed, but I can still hear muffled sounds: Liam sobbing for his water, Amelia opening and closing the fridge. It's like the kid knows when we're exhausted and/or strung out because he picks those days to wake up on the wrong side of the bed. He hasn't stopped throwing a fit since he woke up an hour ago.

Amelia, being the sexually satisfied saint she is, offered to take him while I handled some business. She didn't ask, and I didn't elaborate, but I think we both know it's good news for us.

I'm just conflicted. Guess that'll happen once you decide you're done climbing the mountain that's been your whole life, whether or not you reached the peak.

What if?

Guess questions like that'll happen too. I still have this season to win a championship, but what if we don't? What if the season after this one is the lucky pick?

What if I hate being retired? What if I'm bored?

What if Daddy would've made a different decision?

Maybe these questions are a natural part of the grieving process. I'm making the call out of love, but that doesn't mean there isn't death involved. I love the game, even if my passion for it has faded. I love making big money. I love making the people I work for proud.

But turning down the extension is going to make *my* people—my own little family—proud. It's time to climb a different mountain, one that's all my own. It's time. I went from being miserable and slamming six-packs like it was my job to this. Full heart, full house.

I'm not the selfish dickweed I was when I met Jennifer. But is it as simple as what Beau said yesterday? The bit about giving myself a shot at happiness and how Liam needs me, not a trust fund?

Seems like the right call.

Still, I can't seem to hit Miguel's number.

Chucking the phone across my desk, I run a hand through my hair. Stand up.

Guess I really did mean what I said when I told Amelia I needed time. That's not a crime, right? I'm being intentional. Thoughtful. Turning down twelve million bucks is not a choice you make in four days.

Ignoring the weird stomachache I just got, I leave my phone in the office and head for the kitchen.

Amelia looks up from handing Liam his sippy cup. "How'd it go?"

She's trying to play it cool. But her eyes are warm and hopeful, and I know she'd love to hear some news. *Hey, honey, I actually don't need any time at all. I choose you. You and Liam.*

I'm chickenshit.

"Meh," I say. I curl a hand around her nape and pull her in for a quick, hard kiss.

She kisses me back, and my body lights up, a welcome distraction from the weird seasick feeling in my gut.

I drop my hand and wrap my arms around her waist, seeking. Needing. Amelia was always so sure about who she was and what she wanted. Maybe if I hug her tight enough, keep her close enough, I'll get some of that certainty I'm looking for.

I also want to take her back to bed. But that's what nap time is for.

"I know you said you wanted to think about things," she murmurs into my neck, running her fingers through my hair. "I've been thinking too. I'm willing to go to Vegas with y'all. Not just for a little while, but for the whole season."

My heart dips. I smile. "Whoa, whoa, whoa, Miss I-Love-Asheville-And-I'll-Never-Ever-Leave. Are you bending?"

"Don't act so surprised." She gives my shoulder a playful shove. "Bending's a beautiful thing, isn't it?"

Just say it. Tell her you're turning down the contract.

"It is," I say gruffly. "I'll be honest, A. I'm not sure I deserve you."

She pulls back to look me in the eye. A cute little crease appears between her eyebrows. "You okay?"

"No." I blow out a breath. Jut my hips so my half-chub presses against Amelia's belly. "Here you are, showing some serious character. Being brave. And here I am, asking for time, getting hard every five seconds. It's . . . a lot to process."

She smiles and I don't know if her kindness makes me feel better or worse.

"You asked for time. If that's what you think you need, that's what you'll get. Just don't leave me hanging too long, okay? Because two weeks ago, I had my dream job in the city I love more than anywhere else on Earth. Now I'm moving to Vegas with my ex-boyfriend and his kid."

Raising a brow, I say, "Don't do me like that. I'm your boyfriend now. Time to drop the ex."

"How boring of you, Vader."

"Call me old-fashioned, Jabba."

"We should celebrate."

233

To be honest, I'm not in the mood to celebrate. Feels a little premature. A little . . . unearned.

But Amelia's lit up, a ball of fucking sunshine that practically radiates happiness. If she thinks we should celebrate, so be it. I'm not gonna piss on her parade, even if I'm not quite ready to have mine yet.

"Invite Rose over," I say. "She can meet Li, and we can all go to the Barn Door for dinner. They're doing this new veggie paella on Sundays that is out of this world."

Amelia's grin broadens. "Emma's idea, no doubt. She loves Spanish food."

"I love her for bringing you crashing back into my life."

Speaking of crashing—I'm aware of the pitter-patter of Liam's feet, followed in short order by a distinct, stomach-wrenching *thud.*

He lets out an ear-splitting wail.

I glance over Amelia's shoulder to see him splayed out on the kitchen floor, holding his little foot. He wails again, making my head throb, and I glance at the clock above the stove. How long until nap time again?

"I got him," I say.

I take care of his stubbed toe—BandAid that's completely unnecessary, a kiss, promise to go ous-side—and then, because I can't stop wondering *now what,* I open the fridge.

I waver between grabbing water or a beer. Water is the right choice. Clearly.

But then Liam starts crying again, stomping his feet when Amelia won't give him the knife she's using to butter some toast.

I grab the beer.

Amelia eyes me as I sip.

"I'm celebrating," I say.

"Rhett, it's ten A.M."

"And? I'm brunching so hard. Want one?"

"I'm good."

Liam stomps his feet when I refuse to let him sip too.

"You sure about that?" I ask Amelia.

"You sure you're drinking that beer for the right reason?"

Liam's melting down again. I gesture to him. "Yes."

Amelia bends down to pick him up. "C'mon, little man, let's change your diaper and head outside. Rhett, you wanna blow up the bouncy house? The dishwasher just beeped too."

"Sure. Yeah. I'll get it."

But I don't want to blow up the bouncy house or empty the dishwasher or think about what we're gonna give this kid for lunch. I want to flop on my couch and nurse this beer and maybe another one and watch *SportsCenter* for the next five hours.

This time a month ago, that's what I would have done. Relaxed.

Now, I want to numb all these feelings that won't quit contradicting each other. Relief and regret. Excitement and dread. Love and annoyance.

But I'm a dad and a boyfriend and family man now, and I don't have that option.

It pisses me off.

Gulping my beer, I know I'm being an ass. Feeling sorry for myself accomplishes nothing. Like Beau said, I'm in a position of extreme privilege. I have health, wealth, the woman of my dreams, a son who's happy and cute as hell. I *get* to choose this. I *get* to live this beautiful life. A lot of people never get that chance.

The idea flashes through my head nevertheless: a similar scene to the one I just witnessed, played out over the next few dozen years. Waking up too early. Dealing with a kid who's too grumpy. Standing at a sink that's too full of the same dirty dishes, and counting down the minutes until nap time. Rinse and repeat. A slow, tedious slide into . . . what? Angry old age?

Maybe I've stopped wanting to please Daddy. But now I've started wanting to not become him.

If I don't take the extension, I'm staring down the barrel of a similar gun. Not the CTE, but the being tied down part. The boredom of everyday life here on the farm. The monotony of raising kids, keeping a house, cleaning up after a family.

How can parenthood be both the most and least fun thing ever?

Why would I give up my old life for this?

You're panicking.

The voice inside my head is right. Liam's just having a bad day, that's all. I'm being a stupid, selfish idiot to add fuel to the fire of this ridiculous existential crisis, and that needs to stop. Right now.

I am *not that fucking guy anymore.*

I breathe. Drink. Breathe some more.

I *am* a guy who wants freedom. Who wants to run life his way.

But then Amelia emerges from the bedroom with Liam on her hip, and Liam is saying, "Dada! Dada ous-side! Dada go ous-side with Lili!"

He's so fucking cute.

See, this is what I'd be missing if I went back to being *that guy*.

I drain what's left of my beer and open another. I drink it as I inflate the bouncy house outside.

"Vegas," Rose says with a twinkle in her eye. "I love that town. Y'all are going to have such a wonderful time out there. What an adventure! I can't wait to come visit."

I lean down to pick up the crayon Liam threw on the floor. "I'm just happy I finally convinced Amelia to come with us."

"I'm happy you're finally together." Rose tucks into her bacon, ranch, and heirloom tomato salad. "I wondered how long you'd fight it."

"Grandma," Amelia says, dropping her fork.

Rose dabs her lips with her napkin. "What? Everyone knew you'd get back together. Well, everyone but the two of you, apparently."

"What made you think that? That'd we'd get back together?" I ask. Then I sigh when I hand Liam the crayon, and he throws it back on the floor, shooting me a nasty look while he does it. I grab it off the floor and tuck it into my pocket. Liam kicks his feet and starts to whine. "Too bad, son. You throw it; you don't get it."

He whines louder. It's half past five, so the Barn Door is mostly empty. My face still burns. Is this always what it's like when you take a toddler to a restaurant?

Becoming a dad didn't kill my sex life. It could, however, kill whatever social life Amelia and I might've had because going out is *so* not worth it. Doesn't help that I'm the tiniest bit hungover from all the beer I had earlier. I went from happy buzz to house of pain somewhere around two or three o'clock, and it *sucked*.

Rose offers Liam his snack cup of goldfish, but he shoots her a look too, tucking his chin.

"I'm really sorry," I say. "He's usually not like this."

"What about some milk?" Amelia asks, offering him his sippy cup. She looks as tired as I feel: dark hollows underneath her eyes, hair a little messy. Liam didn't nap, so we're all running on fumes. "No? Okay, then."

"Don't apologize." Rose waves us away. "This is life with kids. I remember when Amelia was this age. She literally never sat still. I flew to Toronto once with her and her mother, and she screamed so loud because she couldn't leave her seat that the captain came out of the cockpit. He wanted to make sure she was all right."

"Sorry about that," Amelia says with a smile.

Rose pats her hand on the table. "It gets better. Just look at you now! You sit *and* you use your utensils."

"I'm advanced," Amelia replies with a shrug.

"So what is your arrangement going to be now that the two of you are together?" Rose glances between Amelia and me. "Is Amelia still going to nanny, or . . ."

Amelia cuts a glance in my direction. Lifts her wineglass and sips.

"We haven't talked about that yet, actually," she says carefully. "This is still so new."

Liam is kicking the table again, so I lift him out of his high chair and set him in my lap. "I know you said you missed teaching. Maybe we look for a position for you out there."

"Maybe." Amelia winces. "But it'd have to be temporary, right? We'll be in Vegas until, what, February at the latest? No one's going to hire me for six months. Not for the kind of position I'd want, anyway. And I'm not sure if Nuria would even give me a recommendation, so . . ."

"All things to consider, certainly," Rose says. "Y'all are also going to have to figure out childcare for Liam if Amelia does get a teaching job."

My chest tightens. Liam squirms, trying to get down, and it's all I can do not to let him in the hopes a passing server kidnaps him and takes him home with them. I grab the crayon from my pocket instead and hand it to him. "Definitely lots to think about."

"Yeah," Amelia says, that furrow between her brows reappearing. It's the first time I've seen her excitement flagging. "It is a lot."

"You'll figure it out," Rose says. "In the meantime, I'm here to help. And remember: at the end of the day, the three of you get to be together in a fabulous city in what is no doubt a fabulous home. Think of it as an adventure. One that won't last forever, just like the toddler stage." She nods at Liam, who's now breaking the crayon into tiny pieces. He pops one on his mouth and gags; Amelia and I both lunge for him at the same time; he screams when I hook my finger inside his mouth and dig the crayon piece out. Then I almost scream when he bites down on my finger, hard.

"God*damn* it!"

"Rhett—"

"That's it," I spit, tossing Liam onto my shoulder. I stand and throw my napkin onto the table. People are staring, but I don't care. "We're going home. You ladies enjoy your dinner."

Amelia's staring too. So is Rose.

"Rhett," Amelia repeats. "Take a deep breath."

I shake my head. "I really am sorry, y'all. I don't mean to lose my mind, it's just been a long day. Rose, can I get a mulligan? I promise we'll both"—I gesture to my son and me—"be in better moods next time. Thanks for coming." Ducking down, I kiss her cheek, and then I hightail it out of there.

Amelia comes home an hour or so later. I'm finally on the couch, beer in hand; by some miracle, Liam went down with barely a whimper. And that means I've had an hour or so to think. And think. My thoughts are still jumbled, thanks to real life interrupting the little honeymoon phase we have going on at home.

But is this home? *My* home? *My* life?

How do I switch off years of competitiveness and drive and purpose?

I don't have the answer. All I do know is that I owe my girl an apology.

"I'm sorry," I say for what feels like the millionth time. "I really am, A."

She nods, resting a knee on a nearby ottoman. "I don't need to ask if you're punishing us, right?"

I blink. I've shown my ass today, but I have the peace of mind not to ask what she means.

It's a fair question.

"If I'm going to punish anyone, it's myself." I pat the empty spot on the couch beside me. "Now come sit. I've been waiting all damn day for this."

Chapter Thirty-One

AMELIA

It's noon on a Monday. Outside, the early July heat shimmers on the blacktop, blanketing the mountains in a heavy, humid haze.

Liam, poor baby, went down for his nap fifteen minutes ago. This morning, he woke up with a slight fever, which I've been nursing with Tylenol and lots of liquids, per the pediatrician's orders. If his fever peaks at 102° and stays there, I have instructions to bring him into the office. Could be a sign of an ear infection.

Rhett is in the shower after his first workout of the day, so the house is quiet, as is the farm itself. It's one of those hot, lazy summer days when there's no one around and nothing to do.

So I nearly jump out of my skin at the firm, loud knock on the front door. I quickly run through the possibilities of who it could be. Housekeeper? She comes on Wednesdays and Saturdays. A Beauregard sibling? But they're all working, as is Grandma Rose.

Rhett has one of those doorbell camera things, but of course it's on his phone, not mine. I creep toward the front door, ducking my head to look out the sidelight windows on either side of the door. My pulse kicks up a notch when I glimpse two people on the front step. From what I can tell, they're dressed in suits.

My pulse kicks up again. I have a funny feeling about this. Not a bad feeling, per se; Blue Mountain's front entrance is closely monitored, so I don't think these guys are here to murder me or anything. Maybe it's some police officers who are here about my car? I haven't pressed charges, so I'm not sure what to expect next.

Nah, they can't be here for me because this isn't the address I have on my driver's license. Which means these men are here for Rhett. And Rhett doesn't get visitors who aren't family all that often, which means this must be important.

Hovering my thumb over the emergency call button on my phone screen, I reach for the knob and open the door.

"You must be Amelia," a man with a blindingly white smile says. He extends his hand. "I'm Miguel Fuentes, Rhett's agent. And this"—he tilts his head toward the unsmiling hulk of a middle-aged man next to him—"is Kevin Scott, head coach of the Las Vegas Sharks. May we come in?"

───────────

"Y'all did not fly all the way out here to see me," Rhett says with a smile as he emerges from the bedroom, freshly showered and handsomely dressed.

He's dressed a little too handsomely, actually. I ran into the bathroom earlier to tell him about Miguel and Coach Scott, and he clearly abandoned the broken-in jeans and tee he'd laid out for something much slicker: gray slacks, pressed button-up, shiny Rolex and shinier shoes.

My insides slosh in the beginnings of a stomachache.

"Don't act like you're surprised," Kevin replies. "I'm not gonna let my star running back go that easy."

"So *now* I'm your star," Rhett shoots back. But his smile grows, all teeth and eyes that sparkle.

"Hey. You were the one teaching Nick, not the other way around."

Rhett takes Kevin's hand with such enthusiasm their palms clap when they meet. "But I'm done. After this season, anyway. That was always the plan."

"Kapakos leaving changes everything. So I'm gonna wine and dine you and hope you'll come home with me at the end of the night."

Yeah. I'm not Coach Scott's biggest fan.

But Rhett? Rhett's smiling so big you'd think he just won the lottery. "Not likely," he says.

Kevin grins. "Aw, hell, quit flirting. You know I like a challenge."

"So." Miguel brings his hands together. Looks at me. "Any chance you guys can get a sitter for the day? We'd like to take you out."

"Oh?" Rhett says. "Where we going?"

Ire pokes me in the rib cage.

"PJ is fueled up and ready to go," Miguel says.

"PJ?" I ask.

"Private jet," he explains. "How do you feel about dinner in Charleston? I got us a reservation at The Pearl."

Rhett's eyes bulge. "But you can't get a reservation there. They book up months in advance, don't they?"

Miguel shrugs, lips twitching. "I know a guy."

"Of course you do." Rhett shakes his head. Looks at me. "What do you think, A? You up for a fancy dinner date? We sure as hell could use a break."

I want to tell Rhett that dinner with his agent and his coach doesn't count as a date. But that would be rude, and I'm not a rude person. Unlike some people in this room.

"We've never left Liam with anyone," I say.

"That's not true," Rhett replies. "Mom and Milly watched him the other night, and it went fine. Here." He digs his phone out of his pocket. "I'll give Mom a call. I'm sure she'll help us out."

I'm hit by a wave of nausea.

This is a bad idea.

This is pissing me off. In a show of good faith, I put myself out there with Rhett. I put my own personal bullshit aside so I could put him and Liam first.

I thought—hoped—Rhett would eventually do the same. But this? Him welcoming Coach Scott and Miguel into our home? Well, it's not *our* home. It's Rhett's. But having these men in *Rhett's* home feels like a betrayal.

It's a step in the wrong direction, and the fact that Rhett's considering it at all hurts.

"Wait." I put a hand on Rhett's shoulder. "Can we chat for a sec?"

Frowning, Rhett looks up from his phone. "Sure. Yeah. Give us a minute, fellas."

He follows me into the bedroom, and I close the door quietly behind us.

"I'm going to be honest," I begin. "I'm not thrilled about this. It feels wrong."

Rhett blinks. "Wrong? How? I told you—"

"Time. Yes. But . . ." My mind spins out. Do I even have a right to feel angry? Rhett's been totally transparent about where he's at and what he needs. I was the one who took a leap of faith; Rhett never asked me to move to Vegas with him full time.

Oh, God, am I being a gigantic idiot?

"I guess I just hoped you'd turn these guys down, like, right away. I hoped . . ." I shrug. "I hoped you wouldn't want to go because you knew you'd just be wasting their time."

Rhett tilts his head, eyes moving to the windows over my left shoulder. "Amelia," he says, letting out a breath, "I get what you're saying. But I'm still working with these guys, at least for another season, so I have to play nice. Doesn't hurt that we'll be getting an awesome trip out of it too."

I don't know what to say to that. Or maybe I have too much to say.

It's not just you anymore, Rhett.

Shut them down and stay.

But my tongue is like stone in my mouth. What I say at this moment matters. He's in a vulnerable position, and I don't want to push him away or piss him off. I haven't been a part of Rhett's life while he's played in the pros, and I have no idea how all this works.

Still. There's a nudge inside me, one that says I'm pulling the same shit I always do when I get scared: I'm making myself small. That works out for everyone but me. But what else can I do? I'm terrified I'll lose Rhett if I say or do the wrong thing.

"I'll trust you to make the right call," I say slowly, choosing my words with care. "And if you think the right call is getting on that jet,

I'll go with you. But we've got a sick baby on our hands, plus a lot of talking to do on our own to get our plans ironed out. I want you to consider that."

His eyes are serious when he nods. "I know. But I do think we should go to Charleston. I gotta show my respect. Play the bullshit game. The politics involved in this sport are fucking ridiculous. Plus, I know I could use a break."

My anger sharpens. "*You* could use a break? I'm the one who's with Liam most of the time.."

"Of course you are," he says quickly. "I'm sorry. I just meant we might enjoy a little breather from a whirlwind week. We've both talked about feeling overwhelmed."

I nod, swallowing the sudden ache in my throat. "Yeah."

"Besides, my mom kept all five of us alive. I think she knows how to handle a fever. And I promise when we get back, we'll figure our shit out. We'll sit down and make plans for everything, all right?" He leans in and kisses my mouth. "I won't let you down."

I kiss him back. "It's just a game."

"Yup. Now let's go have a sexy night out."

I can't kick this bad feeling. I hate that neither of us will be here for Liam if he wakes up tonight. I hate that Rhett's thinking about politics instead of parenting right now.

Still, I told him I trusted him. Now I'm going to show him that I really do.

So I get dressed and head to the airport in a limo with Rhett and his entourage, hoping I'm wrong to doubt him.

Hoping I was right to trust him.

Chapter Thirty-Two

RHETT

Amelia's head lolls on my shoulder as we make our descent into Asheville.

Mom, being the awesome human being she is, offered to stay with Liam overnight, so we were in no rush to get back from Charleston.

The sun is just coming up over the mountains. It pierces my eyes, making them water. I already have a headache; we were drinking until 3 A.M. at some dive bar on Upper King Street.

I'd say I'm regretting that now, but I'm not. I had a fucking ball hanging out with Miguel and Kevin, getting away, cutting loose. Eating amazing food at one of the South's best restaurants.

Maybe it makes me bougie, but I like being entertained in fancy-as-fuck style. I like being chased. I've missed it.

I did my best to show Amelia a good time too. She needed a break just as much as I did. It took her a minute to warm up to the idea. I get it, I do. But the second she sipped her first vodka and soda, whipped up by none other than Chef Elijah Jackson himself using sweet potato vodka and this deliciously refreshing basil-infused craft soda, she was in.

Now it's almost six o'clock in the morning. She's asleep. I'm hungover.

Hungover, and so damn confused.

Miguel and Kevin put on the full-court press. *You're at the top of your game. Don't quit now when you're on the cusp of becoming a legend. You're twenty-seven; you have plenty of time to grow your family later. What's another two years? Your brain scans looked good.*

"Y'all are shameless," I said.

Kevin looked me in the eye. "Son, I'm not gonna push you to do something you're not comfortable doing. But I've been coaching for thirty years, and I've come across very few players with the kind of drive you have. I genuinely believe you'll come out on top if you give us an extra couple years. We need you."

Miguel's gaze said it all. *You'd be an idiot not to take this deal.*

Letting my head fall back on the seat, I look out the window. We're still high enough that I can pick out Blue Mountain just west of the city. The mountain is actually blue in the early morning light. I take in its familiar, sloping shape, the cap of pines on its peak. The neatly tended clearing where the barn and the gardens are at the bottom of the hill.

Daddy would be proud of what we've done with the place.

Liam will be proud to inherit it.

And to think of the even more extravagant things we could do with an extra twelve million bucks. After funding a hefty trust for Liam, I could invest what's left in the resort's holding company. Use it to get the next phase of development underway, the sports complex and ten-thousand-square-foot spa Beau's been dreaming about for years. It'd be an amazing place to raise my son.

Add a championship to that? Makes me feel all puffed up in the chest.

Makes me feel like shoving this inconvenient desire for fun and family to the side, at least for the next couple years. Two years for literally generations of security and purpose seems like a solid trade to me.

Like Coach said, my scans still look good. Maybe a couple extra years won't come with such enormous risk.

Think of all the good I could do with that money. For everyone.

I'm trying to let this go, the idea that happiness lies on the other side of a pile of money and a Super Bowl ring. But even though I know, rationally, it's a bullshit idea, I keep coming back to it. I keep pressuring myself to nab that ring already.

Old habits die hard.

The plane dips, and so does my stomach.

Amelia stirs, tucking her head into the crook of my neck, and now it's my heart that's dipping. She's *right here*. She's not an idea or a ghost or a hang-up. She's the one who promised to put my son and me first. But now I'm hesitating to promise her the same, and it makes me feel like the world's biggest piece of shit.

Then again, that's the scaffolding holding up my whole life, isn't it? The idea that I'm only worth something if I win.

Because here's the thing: now that I can take in the ten-thousand-foot view, I realize I wanted Kevin and Miguel to convince me to sign the contract. I wanted to escape my new life for a taste of the old. I was ripe for the picking the second I saw them standing in my living room.

Getting on this plane was an asshole thing to do, and I did it anyway. I was reckless.

The same way I was reckless one night three years ago with a woman I'd never see again.

God fucking dammit, what is wrong with me?

"Christ," I breathe, running a hand over my face.

"You all right?" Miguel asks softly. We're the only ones awake; Coach is snoring softly in the seat across from mine.

"Tired." I yawn. "Just really tired. Can't party like I used to."

"Rhett, I'm forty. You're too young to be saying shit like that."

The words slip out before I can stop them. "I'm too young for a lot of things, but I'm stuck with them now. I've become the lame old guy."

"Adulting sucks sometimes, doesn't it?"

I look out the window. "Yeah. Yeah, it really does."

I know something's wrong when Amelia's quiet on the ride home from the airport.

I know something's *really* wrong when she grabs her bag off the bedroom floor and starts throwing her shit inside it. Luckily Liam and Mom are still asleep upstairs, so I can handle Amelia before I deal with them.

"Hey." Standing beside her, I put my hand on her wrist. "What are you doing?"

She pauses. Looks at me.

The tip of her nose is pink.

"I'm leaving."

For a heartbeat, I just stare at her, my brain drowning in the thirty-two drinks I had last night. "But—"

"I thought you were past the whole getting-old-is-such-a-drag bit. Having a family sucks that much, huh?"

My stomach bottoms out. I try to grab Amelia's elbow, but she yanks it out of my grasp.

"That's not what I meant."

She finally looks up from her bag. "What did you mean, then? What about your life sucks? Your million-dollar house? Your beautiful son?" She swallows. "Me? Am I what's holding you back, Rhett?"

More staring like a mute idiot. Somewhere in the back of my head, I know I need to quit drinking for good—booze is not the friend I thought it was—but I'm too panicked to give it much time.

This.

Here.

Now.

I have to stop what is happening right here, right now. Because the thought of going to bed without Amelia—

It's the fucking worst.

"I was talking about being hungover."

"No, you weren't." She lets out a breath, closing her eyes, and her shoulders fall, deflated. "You can't do this, can you? You can't pass up another shot to make 'your dreams'"—I wince at the air quotes she uses—"come true. We moved way too fast."

You know what's also the fucking worst? Lying to the people you love.

The anger I felt talking to Beau the other night on the porch flares to life inside my gut. Anger at myself, at her, at the world—I don't know where it comes from, but I do know where I'm aiming it.

"Maybe I can't," I spit. "But that's something you wouldn't understand."

"Oh?" She opens her eyes. "And why is that?"

"Look how easily you gave up on your dreams. You just let them go, didn't you? That teaching job you wanted so badly, you messed up, and you quit fighting the second it got hard."

Her eyes go wide, mouth falling open. She looks like I punched her.

I feel like I punched her. It gives me this horrible, hollow feeling, and at that moment, I wish for nothing more than to be the one who took the blow.

What is wrong with me?

"You know," Amelia says after an excruciating pause, "you don't have to push me away with your bullshit. I'm already done."

"What? I say one stupid thing, and you quit?"

She pierces me with a glare. "Yeah. Apparently, I'm good at that, but so are you. Here you are, quitting after one hard day with Liam."

"I'm not quitting," I snarl. "I'm doing what a good parent would do and thinking about his future."

"That's bullshit, and you know it."

"You can't run away from this, A." Which makes no sense because I know I'm pushing her away. I fucking *know* I'm contradicting myself.

Then again, none of this adds up. Not the way I'm acting or the decisions I'm making or the how I'm making her feel.

"But you can run away from me real easy, huh?" She bends down to pick up a pile of clothes. She stuffs them into her bag, and something about seeing her shirts and dresses all wrinkled makes a lump form in my throat. "I should've known this would never work out." She laughs, a brittle sound. "God, I really am an idiot."

"Amelia, please."

She tears the bag's zipper up its center. "I should go before Liam wakes up. I'll ask around for a replacement for y'all." Hiking the bag over her shoulder, she turns toward the door.

Something about the proud set of her shoulders, the way she holds her head high despite the nasty things I've just said—it makes me panic. She's excellent. She deserves better.

What's the right call here? Asking her to stay and fight? Or letting her go?

"So what?" My heart hiccups inside my chest. "So what if I play another couple years? We'll be back in Asheville often enough. Holidays. The off-season. What the hell is so wrong with me taking the extension?"

Amelia whirls around, mouth set in a hard, straight line. "It's wrong because it shows your priorities are still out of whack. I'm not waiting around for you to figure your shit out. I know what I want, and this?" She gestures back and forth between us. "This isn't it. You're free to take all the time in the world to dick around and feel sorry for yourself. But I'm not gonna let you take *my* time. And I'm not going to watch Liam spend the next few years missing his dad because you're too busy playing football. I know what it's like to grow up without a dad, Rhett —you do too—and it's not fun. But at least you had your brothers and sister. A mom who didn't die when you were sixteen. But I was literally *orphaned*. You're all that little boy has right now."

Oh fuck. Fuck, *fuck*, how do I—

"But you've made your choice, Rhett. It's obvious nothing's changed."

"I have changed," I say fiercely.

"If that's true, prove it to your son. If he doesn't make you change your mind about putting your brain and your body at risk, well." She smiles tightly, tears leaking out of her eyes. "That tells us everything we need to know, doesn't it?"

I'm not that man.

Aren't I, though?

"I hate that you're making me choose," I say.

She looks at me for a beat, lifting her hand to wipe underneath her eyes. "I hate that you think it's even a choice. You're breaking my heart, Rhett. You're breaking everyone's hearts by doing this."

I swallow the lump in my throat. "I'm sorry."

"I am too." Amelia looks down at her hands. "I knew taking this job was a bad idea from the get-go. I should've never accepted the offer, and I definitely shouldn't have let things go so far."

I shake my head, crossing my arms because I'm afraid I'll reach for her if I don't. The longer this fight lasts, the more I'm convinced letting her go is the right thing to do.

I'm so fucking bad at doing the right thing.

"Don't blame yourself." My voice cracks. I clear my throat. "It's my fault. But if you'd just consider—"

"*No.*" She flattens her palm on the center of my chest. "Don't take this out on Liam, okay? He's a good boy. You're lucky to have him. Make sure he's lucky to have you too."

"Rhett?" Mom's voice floats down the stairs. "Rhett, is that you? Is everything all right?"

"I should go," Amelia whispers.

Now I'm crying too. Sniffing, I say, "I wish you wouldn't."

"I'm going to ask you not to reach out," she says. "We have to make this a clean break. Liam . . . I love him, but . . ."

I nod. My throat is so tight I can't breathe. "Right. Okay. I don't know what the fuck we're gonna do without you, but okay."

She pats me once on the chest. "You're gonna keep going."

She turns and walks out of my room.

Walks out of my life. For good this time.

Chapter Thirty-Three

AMELIA

My grandmother hands me a steaming mug of tea.

"Thanks," I say, fingers stinging as I wrap them around the mug. I sip. Cough. "Did you put whiskey in this?"

"Breakfast of champions." She takes a seat across from me at her kitchen table and frowns. "Really, breakfast of the heartbroken. Drink up."

I do as she says and get my 7 A.M. buzz on. Tears trail silently down my face as the smell of Rose's strawberry muffins baking in the oven fills the room. Rose doesn't ask, and I don't tell. We just sip our spiked tea in blessed silence.

I'm exhausted to the point I'm almost delirious. My head is pounding, and I feel weirdly hot. We partied *hard* last night. Looking back, I think I just wanted to dull the creeping sense that the proverbial train was going off the tracks.

"It all just happened so quickly," I say, staring out the window over Grandma Rose's shoulder.

"To be fair, you and Rhett have history. Lots of it."

"Yeah, but even this—like, Rhett getting the contract offer one day, telling me he has serious doubts about it that morning, then getting on a plane with his agent and his coach to talk about signing it a few days after that . . ." I scoff. "And yeah, then there's the whole thing about us falling in love over the course of one freaking week. What a ridiculous whirlwind."

The oven timer dings. Grandma rises and pulls a tray of muffins out of the oven, their tops glistening with a turbinado sugar crust. The heavenly smell is enough to momentarily stop my deluge of tears. "You were blindsided." She pulls off her floral oven mitts and drops them onto the counter. "By love."

"I was blindsided by my idiot heart." My face crumples. "Again."

Rose settles an arm across my shoulders. "Oh, lovie. I'm so sorry."

I nod, too emotional to reply for several heartbeats.

"I'm embarrassed," I say at last. "Acting like I did with him, it *was* ridiculous. Who does that? Falls in love in five days? Makes plans to move across the country? Grandma, there was a *kid* involved. I feel horrible."

My grandmother rubs my shoulder, a steady, slow motion. "You were excellent with Liam, Amelia. Don't beat yourself up about that."

"I can beat myself up for disappointing the little guy. The two of us were just hitting our stride, and now I'm abandoning him." I shake my head. "I hate him. Rhett, I mean. And I hate myself for believing him."

Rose's hand pauses on my upper arm. Squeezes it. "Whether or not you believe it now, you were doing the right thing—acting in good faith."

"Yeah, but that's the problem. I keep believing the best about people—I keep believing them—and I end up getting burned." I set down my mug harder than I mean to, making the liquid inside jump. "Now here I am, out of a job. Zero career prospects. Having brown liquor breakfasts because my high school boyfriend broke my heart again for the same fucking reason he broke it the first time."

And this time, the stakes are so much higher. I can forgive him for going after his dreams ten years ago. He was right to chase them then. But doesn't he have enough now? The money, the health, the family?

Rose keeps rubbing. I keep crying.

We stay like that until the muffins cool. Grandma scoops two of them out of the pan and cuts them in half, slathering each half with butter. It gets all melty and delicious, and even my emotional and mental breakdown can't keep me from scarfing a muffin.

I feel the teeny-tiniest bit better.

"Sometimes, all it takes are some carbs to do God's work," Grandma says, smiling. "Why don't you lie down? Get some rest. When you're ready, we'll figure out what your next steps are, all right? Nothing is as bad as it seems after a good nap."

I take a breath. Let it out. My chest is sore, and so are my eyes. "Thank you for letting me crash here. I don't want to be alone right now."

"You're welcome to stay as long as you like." Rose smooths my hair. "Does Rhett know you're here? I'm sure he's worried."

I shake my head. "I told him to let me be."

"Amelia, are you sure—"

"We're done, Grandma. Fool me once, fool me twice . . . yeah." I lift my mug and bring it to my lips, draining the tea's lukewarm remains. "I don't need to learn that lesson a third time."

Her hand moves to my forehead. She frowns again. "You feel warm."

"I'm fine."

"I'll make some chicken noodle soup while you're sleeping."

Her kindness makes my eyes burn all over again. "I really appreciate it."

"I know you do, lovie. Would you like a toke before you head upstairs? It helps me fall asleep. I've got this delicious lemon love strain that's very mellow."

I laugh softly, my face arranging itself into some semblance of a grin. "I should probably be careful, considering I'm on the hunt for a new job. But thanks for the offer."

I give myself twenty-four hours to wallow. Despite the whiskey and the exhaustion, I can't sleep. Instead, I lie very still in the guest bed, which somehow manages to be both creaky and comfortable all at once. I lie there with my eyes closed and my head thumping, waiting for the time to pass.

I throw off the covers. Turn on the fan.

Nothing keeps me from thinking about Rhett and Liam. Crazy to think this time yesterday, I was in Rhett's bed, probably enjoying my second or third orgasm of the day. The way his body told me what his words didn't have to—that I was right-sized, beautiful as is, no edits or omissions necessary—God, my toes curl at the memory of it.

I taste the salt of tears on my lips. They trail into my hair, onto the pillow.

Somewhere in the house, I smell my grandmother's weed. Funny, but there's a definite lemon hint to it.

Good for her.

I wonder if I'll ever get to that level of self-possession. Rose always lived life on her own terms, and I'm pretty sure she's enjoying a bitchin' stretch of old age because of it.

I'm trying to do the same. Only I keep getting crushed.

The universe keeps making a fool of me, and it makes me wonder if living this way—keeping the faith, staying soft, staying hopeful—is right, or if it just makes me a chump.

I miss Liam. His screams of delight and the smell of his hair. Our morning routine. The way he'd light up when I walked into a room.

Does he still have a fever? Should I text Junie to find out?

I feel a stab of pain at the reminder I've lost the Beauregards. Again.

I can't go through this again. I need to pull a Quarterflash and harden my heart already.

Only the idea makes me cry harder. It feels wrong, like I've introduced an extra organ into my chest that definitely doesn't belong there. But whatever. Rhett doesn't belong there either, and if this is what it takes to scoop him out of my body, then screw it.

I'm in. After all, quitting is what I'm best at.

Case in point? My heart, being the stupid jerk it was before, would've leaped every five seconds at the prospect of Rhett barging through Rose's front door, begging to see me. Begging to make things right.

Now I know better. My heart is dead, and so is any hope of reconciliation. Rhett isn't coming. Sounds dramatic, but I'm delirious and hot and desperate, and it's got to be better this way. Even if it doesn't feel like it at first.

Even if I know my mom's shaking her head, wherever she is.

Chapter Thirty-Four

RHETT

"Want to talk about it?"

I look up from my son, who's snuggled into my shoulder with uncharacteristic . . . chillness, I guess, to see Mom standing at my elbow, brow furrowed and arms crossed.

My chest clenches. Mom saw Amelia leave. She's taking in my puffy eyes and tearstained shirt. She knows something's up.

But I know if I talk about it, I'll lose my shit, and we have a sick baby to take care of.

"When was the last time you gave him Tylenol?" I ask, dropping my cheek onto the top of his head. The smell of his hair, the feel of his little body tucked into mine—it's a comfort, one I need.

"Just did while you were in the bathroom. His fever hasn't broken yet, but the pediatrician said—"

"That we should take him in at the forty-eight-hour mark if that's the case. I know. He take his fluids okay?"

"Yes. He drained his sippy cup before bed, and I may or may not have made him a milkshake because I'm the grandma, and grandmas get to spoil their grandkids. Isn't that right, Liam?" She taps his chin, and he smiles. "Poor baby." She looks up at me. "Both of you are pitiful this morning."

I roll my eyes. *I'll be fine.* But the words get caught in my throat, making my eyes sting. I squeeze them shut.

"Think you could help out with Li this week?" I manage.

Mom puts a hand on my back. "Of course. But you need to tell me what's going on, son. I'm worried about you. Did you and Amelia get in a fight?"

"Yup." Breathe. I just need to keep breathing. I open my eyes. "I'm sorry if you heard any of that."

"It didn't sound good, whatever y'all were discussing. I came downstairs to make sure everything was all right."

I begin to rock Liam, keeping my cheek pressed to his head. "She's gone, Mom."

"Gone?" Mom blinks. "For the day?"

"For good. We"—I clear my throat—"we, um . . . couldn't work things out."

"Oh." The disappointment in her voice kills me. "Oh, Rhett—"

"Look, I know y'all love Amelia more than you love me—"

"That's not true."

I manage a smile. "Thanks for saying that."

"There's more to this than the two of you just not 'working it out.' Did something happen in Charleston? I could tell Amelia didn't want to go."

"We-wa," Liam mimes. The word sends a stab of pain through my center.

"I don't want to talk about this now," I growl. Anger: always so much easier than pain. "Besides, there's not much to say. I appreciate you helping us out until I can find another nanny."

Mom gasps. "You fired her?"

"She quit."

Like he knows what's going down, Liam starts to cry.

"Aw, buddy, I'm sorry." Patting his back, I swallow hard. "I'm so sorry you're not feeling well. Here, let's go watch Mickey."

"Lili watch Mi-hey," he says, voice pitiful and small.

Mom holds out her arms. "I'll take him. You go shower and get a little sleep. Maybe then you'll talk some sense."

"Mama, please." I give Liam one last kiss and hand him over. "I'm doin' my best here."

She gives me a once over, frowning. "I know you are, son. Go get some rest."

I'm hurting. I'm hungover. I'm ashamed of both.

Spearing a hand through my hair, I look away. "Holler if you need me. Thanks again, Mama."

"Rhett, wait. This is the last thing I'll say: if I could've traded all the money your father ever made for just one more good year with him, I would do it in a heartbeat. Think about that, son—*one year.*"

I take a breath and flatten my palm on the countertop, the cool marble a welcome antidote to the bloat of heat that fills me. "Daddy didn't make the kind of money I do. The amounts we're talking about are different. Night and day, Mom."

"But the risk is the same. And listen, it's not just the CTE. It's time spent away from your son. It killed your father, literally, knowing he couldn't get those years back. You can't get those years back with Liam either. It was also different for you. You had your older siblings. You had me. I say this with love, Rhett—but if you're in Vegas with Liam for the next however many years, we won't be in his life as the anchor I was for you kids."

Right. Because he doesn't have a mom anymore.

Closing my eyes, I take another breath. I hadn't thought about it like that. All of this—everything I want, how I feel about myself, the path it's led me down—it all comes back to the fact that my dad wasn't around much, and when he was, he wasn't well.

Would my son really want me over money?

I remember what Beau said. *Liam doesn't need a trust fund. He needs you.*

My head swims. Gut churns. Fuck. *Fuck.*

But it's too late to change course now. I've already jerked everyone around enough. I planted my flag in the sand, and it stays there.

It has to stay there.

And I gotta get in the shower. I give Mama a quick kiss and head for my bedroom. My feet are lead weights. The knocking in my head has become so acute I feel sick.

Whatever. Nothing some sleep, Gatorade, and ibuprofen can't fix.

But then I climb into bed, and I'm hit by the scent of Amelia's shampoo rising off her pillow, and I wonder if I've ever felt more wretched in my life.

Wretched. Who do I think I am, a character in that *Bridgerton* show Samuel won't shut the fuck up about?

It's just the only word that feels horribly unique enough to capture this feeling. I'm being crushed to death by a mound of defensive tackles while simultaneously getting drilled in the head by, well, a literal drill bit.

My heart feels like it's been chewed up and spit out.

My saliva thickens. I make it to the toilet just in time. I lose the contents of my meal, plus what must be a half-gallon of whiskey, into the bowl, heaving until there's nothing left. And then I dry heave some more, arms shaking as I attempt to hold myself up on the seat.

There's a rap on the door.

"Rhett?" Mama says. "Rhett, sweetheart, are you all right?"

Falling onto the floor beside the toilet, I rest my back against the wall. "I'm fine, Mama."

"I left more Gatorade on your nightstand."

Because I don't feel like enough of a shitbag. "Thanks. Thank you so much, Mom. I'm sorry."

"I know," she says softly. "I'm here if you need anything."

Hanging my head between my knees, I can only think of one thing: *low point.*

I only have up to go from here, right?

We're waiting for you, she calls, waving her racket. Come play!

Sunset catches on her hair and shoulders. She's smiling wide, all white teeth and full lips, and my dick throbs at the memory of those lips around it, my head disappearing into her mouth as she sucked. Teased. Gave.

My gut twists with guilt. I want to be the giver Amelia always was, but no matter how hard I try, I just end up taking.

Liam is standing beside her in the backyard. He waves too, his little face red from running around all afternoon.

He's getting good at badminton, Amelia says. He's an athlete, just like . . . me.

I laugh, and the twist hurts a little less, but I still can't get my feet to move down the steps into the yard. I'm stuck inside the house, shivering because the AC is cranked way up. I wave to them and ask them to help me, but they just wave back, still smiling like they can't understand what I'm saying.

It's because the doors are closed. They can't hear me through the glass. I try shouting; I bang on the door, but they just shrug and turn away from me. Amelia tosses a birdie into the air and hits it toward Liam, who dashes after it, his little bare feet kicking up the grass.

They laugh and play, happy on their own.

Happy without me.

I see all the badminton stuff spread out in the yard, and I realize there isn't an extra racquet for me to play with even if I could get out of this damn house.

Maybe Amelia and Liam don't want me to play after all.

Amelia, who's bent over with Liam's little hand in hers, teaching him how to hit the birdie, pauses. Looks at me.

Don't be an idiot, she says. And then she turns back to Liam and helps him send the birdie flying over the top of the mountain.

I wake up freezing.

Looking around, I see the covers are rumpled at the foot of the bed. For a split second, I wonder why I'm wearing boxers, and then it hits me: Coach Scott. Charleston. *You haven't changed.*

Mom is here watching Liam. God, what would I do without her?

Then again, I wondered what I'd do without Amelia, but she left. I let her walk out because I'm a coward and a drunk.

I cover my face with my hand. My mouth tastes like the inside of a dumpster.

Grabbing my phone, the pain in my gut intensifies when I see two calls from Miguel but not so much as a text from Amelia.

We have to make this a clean break. I love Liam, but . . .

Fuck. I need to get up. Get moving. Start working out.

That's what I need.

When I finally make it to the kitchen, Mom is tucking some leftovers into the fridge.

"Hi," I croak. "How's the little guy?"

"Definitely fussy this morning, but he ate a great lunch and just went down for his nap." She frowns at me. I hate when she does that. "How are you?"

"Feel like shit. But it's what I deserve, so I'm not gonna complain."

Silence settles between us, heavy with questions neither of us are willing to ask. *Are you going to apologize to Amelia? How do I stop drinking? Why are you doing this?*

"I'm worried," Mama says at last. My stomach flips.

"I am too." I grab a glass and turn on the tap to fill it. "I think—do you mind if I get in a workout? I don't want to keep leaving you with Liam, but I need to sweat it out. Work always clears my head. It'll be an hour, tops."

Mom watches me gulp the water. "You do what you need to do."

"I'll grab us some dinner on the way back. How do you feel about burgers? I can run to that new place downtown—Beau said they have a great kids menu."

"Sounds good to me."

I kiss her cheek. "I know I keep saying this, but I really am sorry."

"Are you sorry for the right things, though?"

"What does that mean?"

"Think about it," she says, meeting my eyes. "Just—think about it, okay? Enjoy your workout."

It's ninety degrees with seventy-five percent humidity. Tom wants to take the workout inside, but I refuse. I take off my shirt and tuck it into the waistband of my shorts, and I get to work in our usual field behind my house.

Tom must sense I'm in the mood for punishment because he has me start with an AMRAP—as many reps as possible—of twenty push-ups, twenty burpees, twenty sit-ups, and twenty squat jumps for twenty minutes.

Doesn't sound like a lot of time. But when you're hungover and your heart rate skyrockets to 180 and hangs out there from the first rep onward, it feels like an eternity.

Sweat pours down my face and drips into my eyes. The humidity presses in on me from all sides, making it difficult to breathe. My lungs burn, and so does the skin on my shoulders and back.

This is right, I tell myself as I drop into plank position. This is where I should be, working.

This sucks.

My biceps and abs are on fire as I curse through another set of twenty push-ups. My arms are shaking again.

"You all right?" Tom asks, looking up from his watch.

"Yeah," I grunt. "How much time left?"

"Fifteen minutes."

I rest my knees on the grass, baked to a dried crisp by the heat, and squint up at him. "Fuck off."

"If you're not feeling it—"

"I can push through."

"If you say so. But you tell me if you start to get dizzy."

We go through some footwork next. It's not nearly as taxing as the AMRAP, but I still find myself cursing through it.

"Come on!" I shout, as much to myself as to Tom. "You got this. Let's fucking go."

"There he is," Tom replies. "You're doing great, Rhett."

I wait for the endorphins to kick in. And they do—my arms stop shaking—but even when I don't feel like dying, I still find myself wishing I was home.

I shouldn't be sweating bullets in a field with some dude who says shit like *LFG*.

I should be home, taking care of my son.

I shouldn't fucking be here right now.

But work is the answer. Always was.

I made my choice. Even if it feels all kinds of wrong right now.

Chapter Thirty-Five

AMELIA

Liam rubbed off on me, literally: I wake up with a fever and a sore throat.

Rose, bless her, drives me to the doctor, who informs me I have strep throat.

"I think I was twelve the last time I got strep," I say to my grandmother on the ride to the pharmacy.

She pats my leg. "Bad things come in threes. You've knocked out two of them, so you just have to get through one more, and you'll start to see the light."

"Thanks," I say with a wry chuckle. "I wonder what will befall me next."

I pick up some antibiotics and Pedialyte, and then we head home. I have some of Grandma's chicken noodle soup for a late lunch—the salt and the heat make it taste good when pretty much nothing else does—along with some biscuits smothered in butter.

Popping a pill from my Z-pack, I'm already feeling better when I climb into bed.

"You need to call Rhett," Rose says, tucking the blankets around my legs. "Chances are Liam has what you do, which means he needs meds too."

My stomach seizes at the thought, but she's right. Poor little dude. I *hope* he doesn't have what I do.

I glance at my phone on the nightstand. Rose takes my hand. "Want me to stay?"

I shake my head. Swallow. "I'll be all right."

"One bit of unsolicited advice: be kind. Even if he isn't."

My eyes film over. "The world doesn't deserve you."

"I know." She squeezes my hand. "Good luck, lovie."

She closes the door softly behind her, and I grab my phone. My heart pounds as I wait for Rhett to answer, making the pain in my throat throb. I wonder if I've ever felt more miserable.

I'm sent to voicemail. I can't tell if I'm relieved or bummed. Either way, I begin to leave a pitiful, rambling message, trying to keep my voice even.

Just when I'm getting to my diagnosis, my phone beeps.

Rhett is calling me back.

Hand shaking, I end the voicemail and pick up.

"Hey," I say.

"Sorry I missed you," he replies gruffly. "I was in the shower."

I swallow again. Look down at the quilt and pick at an errant thread as I shake my head. "It's all right."

"You don't sound all right." A pause. "In fact, you sound like shit. What's going on?"

The concern in his voice makes the tears in my eyes spillover. I hate talking like this—carefully, like we're strangers feeling each other out.

"I have strep throat," I say on an exhale. "I'm worried Liam might have it, too. How's he doing?"

"Oh, Amelia. Amelia, I'm so fucking sorry you're sick. How are you feeling?"

"Not great. How's Liam?"

"Also not great. Shit." I imagine him running a hand up the back of his head. "Y'all got each other sick, didn't you? Okay, I'll call the pediatrician as soon as I hang up. I was going to do that anyway in a bit if his fever hadn't broken yet. Points to—"

"An infection," we say together, and despite everything, we both laugh.

"Since when do you finish my sentences?" he asks.

"Since right now, apparently. We're such dorks."

"We're damn good at our job."

"Are we?"

"Keeping Liam alive? He's sick, but we're handling it." Another pause as the two of us let that word sink in: *we*. "Trying to handle it, anyway. What do you need?"

"What do you mean?"

"You need food, saltines or soup or whatever? I can bring some groceries over."

Closing my eyes, I shake my head for what feels like the hundredth time today. "Why are you doing this? Being nice to me after being *such* a dick?"

His voice is gruff again. "I still care about you, A. Just because we broke up doesn't mean I can't help out. Tell me what you need."

I need to see him. Shake him. *Let me love you.*

"Rose has it handled."

"You sure?"

"I'm sure." I take a breath. I don't want to end the call—my God, I miss his voice, the feeling of just *being* with him—but I'm done being a softie. "Let me know how it goes at the pediatrician's office, okay? I haven't stopped thinking about Liam."

"Okay."

He sounds so *not* okay that my heart twists. I do my best to ignore it.

"Bye, Rhett."

"Bye. No, wait—Amelia, I'm sorry. About being a dick. I was a dick. I am a dick. Yikes, that's a lot of dicks."

I'm laughing again, even as I'm hit by a fresh wave of emotion. "I appreciate the apology. Doesn't change anything."

"I know," he replies quietly. "I'm sorry."

I'm sorry. Seems to be the phrase of choice from the men in my life. Always sorry.

I'm sick of hearing those words, so I say, "I should go. See ya."

He says goodbye, and I hang up. My screen is smeared with tears, and I wipe my phone on the quilt. Tell myself over and over again that not only does his apology not change anything but it also doesn't mean anything. If he was truly sorry, he'd—

I guess he'd be here. Telling me he'll make good on his promise to put us first. Me, Liam, and him. He'd show me, somehow, he really is the man I fell in love with. The one who isn't afraid of the unknown. Of a future he can't see yet.

Then again, that's unfair because I still am afraid.

I think about Rose, and I think about my mom. They were probably afraid too, but they always kept going.

Grabbing my laptop and notebook off the nightstand, I decide to keep going too. I probably should get some sleep, but who am I kidding? Even sick as a dog, I'm not going to be able to pass out knowing Liam's at the doctor's, and Rhett is . . . well, not here.

So I call for my grandmother. She pulls up a chair beside the bed, and I grab a pen—pink, naturally—and open my notebook to a blank page.

"A *fresh* page," Rose says. "You can make it look however you want."

I manage a smile. "I like that idea."

"Before we job hunt, let's brainstorm." She sits up in her chair, then leans forward, elbows on her knees, her thumbs pressed thoughtfully into her chin. "Tell me what happiness looks like to you. I'm talking big picture stuff. What does your ideal day look like? How does it start? Who do you see, and what do you do? Most importantly: what about it makes you happy? I think the answers to those questions will lead us in the right direction."

Her words bring me a glimmer of hope.

It may feel like the end of the world right now. But that can change.

I can change that.

So I think, despite the growing throb inside my head, I think, and I talk, and I research. Rose provides gentle guidance as I work my way through some ideas: getting a grad degree. Expanding Head Start programs in the greater Asheville area. Raising money for free programs for preschool-aged kids around town, like the one Emma and I worked on at Blue Mountain Farm.

I love kids. I also love interacting with adults on a regular basis. I love making a difference. I love being outside.

After a while, my stomach begins to hurt, but I blame that on the exhaustion and the stress.

Really, it's the effort it takes not to include Rhett or Liam in my plan. It physically *hurts* not to incorporate them into this new version of my life, whatever it ends up looking like.

But I do it anyway. Just because I can't envision a future without them doesn't mean I'm doomed.

"Only means you need time," Rose says. "And patience. You're learning to trust yourself all over again, Amelia. You're learning to trust, period. That takes time."

I drop my pen. "What do you think Mom would do?"

Rose thinks about this for a minute. "Your mother would do what's right for *her*. One step at a time."

So I do what's right for me, one excruciating step at a time.

And you know what? That glimmer of hope grows the longer Grandma and I talk. Not by much, granted. My stomach and my throat are killing me. But I keep going, and that feels good.

It's not the first time life's take an unexpected turn. Which means it's not the first time I've had to figure out what to do when things don't go to plan.

I can do this. As Rose said, I just need to trust myself.

I know that's what Mom would want me to do too.

Chapter Thirty-Six

RHETT

"Lili want Dada. Dada!"

I startle at the wail. Cracking an eye open, I see my son on the screen. He's standing up in his crib, face screwed up as he cries.

"*Dada!*" he repeats.

It's dark outside the windows. The kind of dead-of-night dark that means it must be two, three in the morning. I must've drifted off sometime after midnight. I got in bed as soon as I put Liam down at seven—after a hellacious workout, a visit to the doctor, and very little sleep over the past day, I was wiped—but I ended up staring at the ceiling for hours, unable to pass out.

I get out of bed, groaning at the full-body soreness that assaults me as I move. Shuffling upstairs, I open the door and wince. Liam is crying. Hard.

That kills me too.

I'm worried about Liam, for one thing. Turns out he does have strep throat. Meds should be kicking in soon, though, so hopefully, he'll start to feel better.

And then I'm worried about Amelia. She did not sound good on the phone. Caring for my son is what got her sick, so there's some guilt there. I also can't shake the sense that I should be with her. While I appreciate the fact that Rose stepped in to help out, I want to be the one Amelia calls.

I want to be the one who cares for *her*. But I forfeited that right the second I called her a quitter—really, the second I let my doubts get the better of me—so I can't go to her, and that kills me.

Fuck what Beau said. I am a piece of shit. And my little boy is paying for that.

I lift Liam out of his crib and hold him for a few minutes, gently rubbing his back. Then I give him a dose of Tylenol, followed by a good slurp of water from his sippy cup. Then I sit in his rocker and hold him some more. He cuddles into my chest, turning his head to rest on my shoulder, and I swear the iron bands of agony wrapped around my insides loosen with him tucked against me this way.

We rock. I try the skier, swooping my finger over the slopes of his little face, and he finally calms down. The bands loosen some more.

We keep rocking, the soft whirr of Liam's sound machine the only noise in the room. It could be an hour, could be fifteen minutes. Whatever the case, I don't dare move. Having a sick kid is no fun, but I'll take these snuggles all day, please and thank you.

Just when I think Liam is asleep, he lifts his head. Looks me in the eye. I can just make out his smile in the darkness.

"Dada rock Lili," he says.

My face cracks open with a smile—a smile that feels totally different from the ones I shared with Miguel and Scott in Charleston. This one hits my ears. My chest swells, and so does my throat because the fact finally penetrates my sleep-deprived haze: Liam called for me.

This time last week, he cried for his mom. He wanted *her* to comfort him.

Now he wants me. And I can't help but think it's because I stuck around and stuck it out.

Something the selfish idiot I was before didn't have the balls to do.

Holy shit, I have let go.

I have changed.

I've moved on to things that aren't necessarily bigger, but much, much better. Things I deserve because I'm a person, and every person deserves a shot at happiness.

If I'm capable of putting my son first, I can put the rest of my family first too.

Amelia is my family. No question.

"Yes, sweet boy," I say, holding him a little tighter. "Daddy will always stay with Liam. I love you so much."

A part of me thinks I have no business making promises after all the ones I've broken.

Another part knows with bone-deep certainty that this is a promise I'm going to keep. As I sit here with my son in my arms and my heart in my throat, the truth crystallizes: I'm so in love with this boy I'm helpless.

I can't put him down.

I can't leave him.

I can't raise him around strangers in a place where I have no plans to set down roots. Choosing money over family is not a lesson I want to impart. He deserves better than that.

Yes, he can be a pain in my ass sometimes. Yes, raising him is turning out to be so much harder than I thought. But despite all that, being his father is a privilege. One Jennifer may have never given me.

I would have never felt the contentment of Liam snuggled up against me this way. I would've never heard his voice or jumped through sprinklers with him or been pummeled by joy when he houses his dinner.

I have to see this—him—as a gift. A heavy, life-affirming gift. It's the most precious, perfect thing I've ever been given, and I want to share it with the most precious, perfect human I know.

Amelia. Because I'm so deep in love with her too, and I can't stay away.

Now I'm the one who's crying. Christ, I've cried more in the past week than I have in the past ten years combined.

I never saw Daddy cry. He only moped or raged.

I suddenly see what I didn't before—that my life is my own. That it's more important to raise a son who knows it's okay to cry than it is to raise a son who's obsessed with money and winning.

That my present is more important than my past.

I want to do better for my son. I want to teach him things I was never taught, and that begins with setting aside this bullshit idea that money equals power equals respect. He'll never be happy believing that, and neither will I.

I want to do better by Amelia too. I just don't know how.

I have no idea how I'm going to clean up the mess I've made. How do I convince Amelia I'm for real? That the new contract is dead and so am I without her?

I rock and I think. And I thank God Liam came into my life when he did. Clearly, I needed a swift kick in the ass, and boy did this kid deliver.

I just hope it's not too late to fix things with Amelia. Because this right here—my little family? It's not complete without her.

I have a call with Miguel in the morning. We're supposed to hash out the details of my new contract, but obviously, the agenda for this meeting has changed since we last spoke. I'm nervous, but more than that, I'm relieved. I wake up tired as hell—I'm beginning to learn this is just how it is when you have little kids—but the weight I didn't know was on my chest has lifted.

I can finally breathe, which clears my head and allows me to see the future. It's a year in Vegas, learning how to make family life work, learning how to say goodbye to football. It's helping Amelia make whatever new dreams she cooks up for her career come true. It's settling down right here on Blue Mountain after that. It's badminton and night swimming and waking up way too damn early with Liam, mainlining caffeine in the kitchen beside Amelia (coffee for me, tea for her). It's trying to give up booze because it's long past time I stopped drinking. It's taking up an instrument because I want my son to be well-rounded, and I might as well learn to play the guitar alongside him (will Hank give us lessons, I wonder?). If only so we can have musical accompaniment to the dirty nursery rhymes Amelia and I write.

It's the three of us,—her, me, and Liam—building a whole new life together.

I can't fucking wait.

I think I'll always wonder *what if*. I'm only human. Making this choice doesn't magically erase all my fears and doubts. But maybe that's just, well, life. There is no such thing as complete certainty, and if I wait for that, I'll be waiting forever.

There is, however, such a thing as being completely in love.

Love wins.

Maybe I do too. It'll be a quiet victory, quieter than winning a Super Bowl. But it already tastes so much sweeter.

Only problem? That victory is far from guaranteed. Everything hinges on Amelia accepting my apology and giving me another chance. Not likely, considering the way I've behaved.

Still gotta try.

"Yo." Samuel breezes into my kitchen and goes right for the refrigerator. "You got food, right?"

"Not likely," Milly says, hot on his heels. She sets her bag and laptop on the kitchen counter and straightens her pencil skirt.

"What the hell are y'all doing here?"

Milly looks at me like I just shot her. "We're here to babysit, dumbass."

"Beau is babysitting because Mom is at the dentist," I say slowly. "I told him, and only him, that I needed help for an hour tops today. Just gotta get through a call. Liam's still asleep, anyway."

Samuel frowns at the contents of my fridge. He points at a Tupperware container. "That ravioli comes from a can, doesn't it?" He shakes his head. "Tragic."

"Not as tragic as your outfit," I shoot back. He's wearing pink and purple plaid shorts, a white Louis Vuitton belt, and a pink polo shirt that is inexplicably embroidered with tiny naked mermaids. He's topped it all off with Givenchy pool slides and round sunglasses with studded frames that he's hiked onto his head. "You look like a gigolo."

Milly laughs. "A very expensive, very large gigolo."

"Hey," Samuel snaps. "This is a five-star resort. I have to set my prices high in keeping with Blue Mountain's clientele. I also have a sizable bag of tricks, so. Yeah. You get what you pay for."

I glance longingly toward the front hallway. "Beau is still coming, right?"

"I'm here!" he says from behind me, and I whip around to see him come in through the back door. "Everything all right?"

"Why did you invite everyone over to babysit?" I ask. "You're the only one with the experience I need—I've got a sick little boy, Beau."

He turns on the sink and washes his hands. "More the merrier. Also, we're here to stage a mini-intervention."

"We heard you're taking the extension," Samuel says, finally closing the fridge.

"We also heard you broke up with Amelia," Milly adds. "Two wrongs don't make a right, Rhett."

I just stare at them. I'm touched. I'm also annoyed.

"What's that face about?" Samuel asks. "Did we get it wrong?"

I shake my head. "Yes. And no. I was going to accept the extension, but I changed my mind."

"Good," Beau says swiftly. "We were prepared to tie you to a chair and pull out your fingernails one by one until you agreed to turn it down."

Samuel retrieves a pair of pliers from his pocket. "For real, though."

My eyes bulge. "Stop."

"Yeah, I may have grabbed these pliers to work out an electrical issue in the cellar earlier. But they would've worked real nice as a torture device too."

"Y'all are sick," Milly says. "And well prepared."

"Thank you." Samuel turns to me. "What about Amelia?"

I swallow. Look away. "I gotta get her back, guys."

"You fucked up pretty good, didn't you?" Beau asks.

"Yeah."

"Lord save us," he mutters. "You got a plan?"

"Not yet. Although I do know I gotta stop drinking."

Beau's eyebrows jump. "That's a big commitment."

"It's one I'm going to make. I'm sick of feeling like shit all the time."

"Hangovers *are* horrible," Samuel says.

"It's not just the hangovers, although they are awful these days. It's also making epically bad choices when I'm drunk. I'm always apologizing, you know?"

Beau nods, a small smile on his lips. "I think you're making the right call. Cold turkey?"

"I'm gonna try, yeah."

"You'll need help," Milly says.

My turn to nod. "I know. I'll do my research. Talk to my old therapist, see if he has any resources to recommend."

"I'm proud of you, brother," Samuel says.

"Thank you," I reply, eyes welling.

I glance at my siblings. They've gathered on the other side of the kitchen island, the concern on their faces making my throat tighten. They all have important jobs, but they've taken time out of their days to stage a freaking intervention. Makes me think of Mama's words because she was right: I may not have had a daddy for very long, but I did have a loving mother and these idiots for much, much longer.

This right here—*this* is what I want for my son. For my girl too.

This is the kind of love and support they deserve. It can be smothering, don't get me wrong. But it's also what'll get us through the hard times. Times like this.

Milly rounds the island and curls an arm around my shoulders, dropping her head into the crook of my neck. "As far as getting Amelia back is concerned—romance is my bread and butter. We'll figure out something appropriately extravagant. Then again, Amelia's not into the fancy stuff, is she? Let's go subtle, then. Subtle but meaningful." She grins. "Am I good, or am I good?"

Samuel whistles. "That's a slice of humble pie right there."

"Was your wedding not the best party ever?" she replies, and that shuts him up.

I take my sister's hand and give it a squeeze. "I appreciate that. Gimme some time to think, all right? In the meantime, I'm gonna hop on this call. Monitor's right there on the counter—charger is in the drawer."

"Good luck," Beau says. "You got this, brother."

"I'm trying."

"What'd I miss?" Hank appears just as I'm exiting the kitchen, a green plastic tractor tucked underneath his arm. "Sorry I'm late, y'all. Stevie's still in town."

"Say no more." Beau holds up a hand. "I've heard your quickies before. I don't need to hear *about* them."

"Same," Milly says.

"You don't need to worry about being late because you weren't even invited," I say, pausing at the threshold to the hallway. "But sure, stay a while. Bring more toys while you're at it. At this rate, I'm gonna need a bigger house just for all the stuff y'all give Liam."

"You're welcome," Hank says, smiling broadly before turning to Beau. "So, are we pulling out his fingernails or what? Rhett's, not Liam's, obviously."

"No need," Beau replies proudly. "Our little brother here made the right choice all on his own."

Hank turns back to me. "Well, would you look at that? We raised you right."

"Mom and Dad raised me right. Y'all just gave me hell for being the favorite." I hold up my phone. "I can't turn down the contract if I can't make the damn call. Can I go now?"

"Go!" everyone says at once.

"I'll get some groceries delivered and make some breakfast," Samuel calls after me.

"And I'll come up with a plan to get your girl back," Milly adds.

"Can I help?" Hank asks her. "I just did that myself, and I gotta say, I'm pretty freaking great at it."

"Are you?"

"It worked, didn't it?"

Smiling, I close my office door behind me.

This time, I don't hesitate. I'm not conflicted anymore, which makes sitting down at my desk and hitting Miguel's number easy. My pulse drums. Nerves are shot.

I keep breathing. One breath after another. I feel my heart rate begin to slow.

"There he is," Miguel answers with a chuckle. "How're ya feeling, buddy?"

Buddy. That grates. This man is so far from my buddy it's not even funny. Buddies care about what's best for their friends, not what's going to make them the most money.

276

"Don't you sound fucking chipper," I say.

"You actually don't sound so bad yourself."

"Listen, Miguel—"

"Rhett, before you—"

"*Listen*. I don't want to waste your time, so I'm gonna get right to it. I'm not taking the contract. I'm also not your client anymore."

A pause. And then another chuckle. "You're fucking with me."

"I'm not."

"How about you think about this a little more? Take—"

"I have thought about it. And I know in my bones I'm done after this season. I'm done with you too. Final answer."

"But we still have time, Rhett. Plenty of it. I think it's a mistake to make a call so soon. Think about how rare it is to hit it off with a coach the way you hit it off with Scott. C'mon—"

I look up at the *thud* just outside my office.

The front door being slammed shut.

It's followed by footsteps. Fast ones. Someone's running.

My stomach flips. Something's wrong.

Miguel is talking, but I don't hear it. I get up and yank open my door. There's a commotion in the kitchen, so I stalk in that direction.

My stomach flips again when I see Emma standing there, tears in her eyes.

"What's wrong?" I say, mouth going dry.

"It's Amelia," she replies. "She's in the hospital."

This time it's my phone making the clatter as it falls to the floor. Blinking, I bend down to pick it up. Then I sprint to the kitchen. Hank grabs my keys off the counter and tosses them to me.

"Mission?" I say.

"Yes," Emma replies. "Drive safe!"

"Who are you kidding?" Samuel asks.

He's right. I drive like a bat out of hell, tossing the only bill I have —a hundred—at the hospital valet guy before I dash through the sliding doors.

I've never run faster than I do sprinting through the maze that is Mission Hospital.

Chapter Thirty-Seven

AMELIA

I stare down the dented cup of red Jell-O on the plastic tray that covers my lap. I'm not hungry, but the doctors say I need to eat.

I stick my spoon into the Jell-O and bring it to my mouth. The artificial cherry flavor doesn't agree with me, so I drop the spoon and reach for my water instead. My stomach hurts much less than it did when I was admitted last night, but it still doesn't feel great. Morphine helps. It also makes me feel a little loopy.

The blows just keep coming. Am I ever going to feel like myself again? Not just physically but mentally and emotionally too.

My grandmother left a little while ago to find some lunch for herself. I feel terrible for putting her through all this drama. Because really, that's all my life has been lately—one shitstorm after another. It's embarrassing.

I just want this part of my story to be over already.

Turning my head, I look out the window. The view is less than inspiring—a roof dotted with squat air conditioning units, a sliver of forlorn parking lot—and the sky is gray. Rose said it's supposed to rain today, and I'm kinda glad. Shitty weather makes being stuck in a hospital bed slightly less depressing.

I miss him.

I miss both my boys.

Then again, they're not really mine anymore.

Rose drove me to the hospital after my fever spiked to 104°, and my stomach hurt so badly I was curled into the fetal position on the back seat, unable to move. I am so, so grateful she was there, but the whole time I found myself wishing Rhett was too. He always made me laugh just when I needed it.

Turning my head the other way, I carefully lift my Kindle off the bedside table. The motion draws the IV line taut, making the back of my hand sting where the needle is inserted. I draw a sharp breath. I'm admittedly a sissy when it comes to pain, but when everything hurts, and you haven't slept in nearly forty-eight hours, even the tiniest jabs make you see stars.

I downloaded a few historical romances by Olivia Gates. Historicals have always been comfort reads; give me a brooding highlander, a governess he can't handle, and a foreboding castle where they're trapped together for *reasons*, and I am one happy camper.

Only today, I'm not. I try to focus on the words, but my thoughts keep straying. My head keeps throbbing too.

That's why I don't startle at the commotion outside my door. At first, I think it's the sound of my pulse inside my ears. Then I think it's thunder. Only when I hear a familiar voice growl, "Where is she?" do I sit up.

Pulse thumping, I lean forward. Did I imagine that?

It has to be the morphine messing with my head. No way is Rhett—

"Nurses. God, y'all, I love you. Sincerely. You do God's work, even though you sure as hell aren't paid like it. I'mma try to remedy that. But first, you gotta tell me which room Amelia Fox is in. *Where* the *fuck* is she?"

A murmured voice, female. Followed by the man saying, quieter this time, *thank you, and I apologize for cussing, but the girl I love is hurt, and I don't know what happened, and I know she's scared, and I gotta get to her. Please tell me where she is.*

A beat later, the doorknob turns, and my heart explodes, and Rhett bursts into the room, sweaty and red-faced.

I can't speak. I just look at him, throat welling.

He takes in the machines gathered around my head like a beeping, mechanized halo. His eyes rove over the IV drip, the sad little cup of Jell-O.

His eyes lock on my face, and that's when they soften.

Relief.

Guilt.

Love.

My heart, its million pieces scattered across my torso, beats.

It beats again. And again and again and again, infusing my blood with oxygen, my bones with light.

His shoulders collapse, and his chest caves on an enormous exhale.

He is so handsome—set jaw, disheveled hair, searing eyes. *He came.*

I start to cry.

"Aw, honey." He crosses the room in one and a half-giant strides, and then he's beside me, taking my hand—the one without the IV—gently in the paw of his own. "How are you feeling? What happened? I'm just—" His voice cracks. He sniffles. "How the hell are you?"

I nod. Bite my lip. It tastes salty.

"Apparently, I had a bad reaction to the antibiotics they gave me," I manage. "I got this really intense stomach pain—hit me out of nowhere. At first, I thought it was part of the infection, or maybe, I don't know, a side effect of having my heart crushed or whatever."

Rhett's brows curve upward. He swipes his thumb across the back of my hand. He clears his throat. "What kind of douche canoe would do that? Crush your good, perfect, enormous heart?"

My voice wobbles. "An enormous douche, naturally."

"What's the prognosis?"

"Good. It may take a few days to feel better. Or, hell, years . . ." Rhett winces. I continue, "but the morphine drip will tide me over until then."

"Giving you the good stuff, huh?"

I manage a tight smile. "Guess so."

"I came as soon as I heard. What can I do?"

"I'm all right. Rose is here somewhere. She's taking good care of me."

His Adam's apple bobs. "What if I wanna take care of you too? Would you let me?"

Ugh, more tears. I wipe them away with my free hand. "Depends."

He shifts his weight on his feet, eyes never leaving mine. And then —slowly, silently—he gets down on one knee.

"What are you doing?" I ask, beginning to panic.

"Showing you I mean business." He brings my hand to his mouth and kisses my knuckles. "Let me put you first from today until forever."

I stare at him. "But that makes no sense."

"I turned down the extension this morning."

I keep staring. My mouth opens and closes several times.

"Y-you did?" I stammer.

"I also fired Miguel." His thumb is on my wrist now, pressing down gently. "He thought he could change my mind. Believed I was the same man I was two, three years ago. Nine years ago. That guy would've ponied up for the extension real fast."

"Wow," I say.

"I called you a quitter, and I'm really, really sorry about that. I was confused and scared as hell, and I took it out on you, which was wrong and really shitty of me."

I nod, tears falling left and right. "Yup."

"But then I started to think about it, and I realized that being a quitter isn't necessarily a bad thing. When you quit shit that hurts, it can be awesome."

"Yeah," I manage, nodding. "I like that idea."

"I quit the wrong thing, Amelia. I quit you when I should've quit football. I want to be the right kind of quitter this time around. One *you're* proud of." He searches my eyes. "Liam called for me last night. I don't know how to really explain it, but as I was rocking him back to sleep, I realized that he trusts me. You only trust someone if they show up when you need them. I've shown up for my son in a way I didn't believe I could a week ago. It showed me—well, it showed me two things. First, that I can trust myself to do the right thing because I'm not a reckless idiot anymore."

"Hmm."

He laughs. Sniffles. "And second, that actions really do speak louder than words. I said some really stupid shit, and I'm—Jesus, A, I'm so sorry about that. But I hope you can see that at the end of the day, I make my family a priority. Y'all will always come first, and I'm here to prove it to you. I'm done acting a fool. It's obvious my drinking is a problem, and I'm going to try to stop."

My heart skips a beat. "For real?"

"I made an appointment with my therapist this afternoon to talk about my anger and my drinking. I don't know where to begin, but I figure that's a good place to start. I can't promise perfection, but I am gonna try my hardest, honey. Won't be easy—"

"And that's okay."

"And *that's* why I love you. Are you still willing to come to Vegas with us? For the season? Because I want you to marry me, Jabba."

It's my turn to laugh. Tears spill out of my eyes left and right, soaking my hospital gown. Rhett reaches up and wipes them away with his thumb, his touch gentle. Familiar.

His blue eyes are so earnest it almost hurts to look at them.

"This is quite the turn of events, Vader."

"Hey, you were the one who told me to chase the wild, right? So let me do something wild. I don't have a ring, but I have this." He pulls a small children's book—blue cover, cardboard—out of his back pocket. He clears his throat again. Starts to sing to the tune of "Mary Had a Little Lamb." "*Amelia has a little band, little band, little band, Amelia has a little band, it's made up of Rhett and Li-am. Please would you consider marrying us, marrying us, marrying us? Please would you consider boning Rhett, let'smakedirtymusictogetherfor-e-ver.*"

I'm laughing, and I'm crying, and I can't believe this is his proposal. "That was *terrible!*"

His shoulders shake as he laughs too. "I know. Sorry. Best I could come up with on short notice. But A for effort, right?"

"Right," I say, wiping away a tear. Joy? Sorrow? Both?

"I also have this." His phone magically appears, and he pulls up a blurry image that appears to be a bunch of trees on the side of a mountain. "Can you see it?"

"What is it?"

"It's a piece of land on the far side of Blue Mountain. Closer to Rose's—not by much, but enough to count. Thought you and I could draw up our dream house while we're in Vegas, one that's a little more family-friendly than mine. Get to building it so we can hopefully move in when we're back in Asheville next year." His gaze moves over my face. "Let's set down roots here, honey. Starting right now. Let's make our own family—you, me, and Liam. Well, for starters, at least. I want him to call you Mama. I want him to be your son too."

Looking at Rhett, I feel full to bursting. He's doing it.

He's offering me the family I've dreamed about for years. *Our* family. Our happiness.

Without thinking, I fling my arms around his neck. My IV stings, and my stomach protests, but I don't care. I hold him to me fiercely, tears falling left and right, smiling harder than I've ever smiled in my life.

"Yes," I breathe. "Yes, I'll set down roots with you, Rhett Beauregard. I'll come to Vegas, and I'll marry you."

"Amelia Fox, you got yourself a deal."

"And a douche canoe with a really cute kid, apparently."

He laughs loud enough for the whole floor to hear, and I revel in the joy of that sound. "I'm not perfect. But I'll try my best to make sure that douche canoe never shows up again."

"Good."

A nurse pokes her head into the room. "Everything all right here?"

"Yeah," I say on a sob.

Rhett raises his head to look at her. "We just got engaged."

The nurse smiles. "Congratulations, y'all! But save the celebrating for when she's recovered, all right?"

"Done," Rhett says. "Also, I'm really sorry about the cussing."

She waves him away. "We've heard worse. Here, I'll close the door, but no funny business."

"Now *that* is a promise I'm not gonna make," Rhett says.

"Thank God for that," I murmur into his neck. "I've missed you. So much."

He runs a hand over my back. "I'm gonna make sure you never miss me again, honey. Now, how about we chase a little wild?"

And we do, if you count a session of gentle making out in a hospital bed "wild."

Wild has never felt so damn wonderful.

THE END

EPILOGUE

Rhett

I wake up fresh as a fucking daisy. One of the many benefits of sobriety.

Has quitting booze been easy? Hell no. But with the help of a therapist, a sponsor, and my family, I'm doing it, one long fucking day at a time.

It's early. The desert sun that streams through the windows above the bed is thin. Pink.

Different from dawn in Carolina, but not half bad.

The house is quiet. I glance at the monitor on my bedside table and see that Liam is snoozing peacefully in his crib, a wilted Pup Pup on the mattress beside his head.

There's a rustle. A hot mouth on my neck.

Grinning, I turn my head to see Amelia looking up at me, brown eyes lazy with sleep as she nicks my skin with her teeth.

My dick gets hard, and I say, "Don't start somethin' you ain't gonna finish, honey."

"I would never." She wraps a hand around my dick and gives it a tug. Every muscle in my body tightens. Blood warms. "Good morning."

"Morning." I reach over and return the favor, slipping my first two fingers through the folds of her pussy. "Damn. You dream about me or something?"

"Yes. Most vivid dreams ever. It was bizarre. And delightf—" She gasps when I circle her clit. Her legs fall open, and I glide my fingers farther into her slit, finding her entrance. I slip one inside her, and she tightens around me, immediately responsive.

"Whoa, you weren't kidding. You gonna come already?"

She shuts her eyes and smiles. "Maybe."

I can't help it. I lean in and kiss her mouth. When I first did this a few months back, Amelia would always protest. *Morning breath*, she'd say. And I'd say, *I love it because it's yours.*

Now she doesn't say anything at all. She just smiles and kisses me back, the way she's doing right now.

"I wanna come when you're inside me," she breathes, hips rolling into the strokes of my fingers. "Please, baby."

God, I love it when she calls me that.

Because I can't ever say no to this woman, I roll on top of her. Kiss her jaw, her neck. Her tits.

"Oooh," she hisses when I take a nipple in my mouth.

I go still. "That doesn't sound good."

"Yeah. My boobs are sore."

"Do you need to stop?" I ask, furrowing my brow.

Amelia grabs a fistful of my hair and gives it a tug. "Don't you dare. Just be gentle with the nips, all right?"

"You think this could be a sign?"

She looks at me and I look back. "Maybe, yeah."

We've talked about having a baby. A lot. We haven't been trying, per se, but we haven't done anything to prevent it either. We're not married yet, sure, but Amelia doesn't want a big wedding, and she keeps mentioning how fun it would be to "elope" here in Vegas. Just me, her, Liam, and Elvis. Oh, and Rose too.

I kinda dig the idea. To be honest, I'll marry Amelia any way she likes. I just wanna make her mine for good.

I smile. "I don't wanna get my hopes up, but that would be a really, really awesome way to start our Tuesday."

"I know." She smiles back. "I'll take a test when we're done, all right?"

"Okay."

We don't say another word as we move. We don't need to. I guide her knee to my hip, giving her thigh a soft squeeze. She reaches down and guides me to her center. I rock my hips and sink inside her, quietly and slowly, and her head falls back as I fill her to the hilt.

She feels like heaven. Hot, swollen, sweet.

She trails her fingertips through the hair at the nape of my neck, and my eyes roll to the back of my head. I begin to move, baby thrusts at first, and when I open my eyes, I see that she's studying my face, a smile on her lips.

I nudge her nose with mine. She nudges back and wraps her arms around my neck, pulling me closer. My chest brushes against her erect nipples.

"That hurt?"

"No," she pants. "That's—so good, Rhett."

I swivel my hips, doing my best to hit her where she wants it. She bites her lip. Plays with her clit for half a second, and then she comes without warning.

She never makes much noise during morning sex—my place in Vegas is smaller than the one I have on the farm, so we have to be quiet—but today, she cries out, her pussy clamping down on my dick like a vise.

Clawing at my chest, Amelia kisses me hard and keeps coming.

"My God," I manage.

"No kidding," she says when she can finally speak. "Wow, wow, *wow*."

I come with a grunt. "You're welcome."

I stay inside her for a minute. We stopped using condoms after we both got tested, so I feel myself seeping out of her. Raw sex is messy. I love it, and judging by the way Amelia clings to me, she does too.

"How about I make you some tea?" I murmur. "I'll get breakfast going too. What are you in the mood for?"

She smiles up at me, and my heart swells. Damn, she's gorgeous.

I still can't believe this woman is mine.

"Nothing too fancy. Toast is fine."

I frown. "But you're working today. Work requires energy. Which requires real food."

Amelia is working with my family to set up free educational programming for preschool-aged kids on Blue Mountain Farm. It's the coolest idea ever. Amelia's overseeing it all and is involved in every aspect. Beau and Hank volunteered to help her with fundraising to provide scholarships for underprivileged kids, while Samuel, Emma, and Milly are helping her develop a farm-based curriculum. There will be everything from swimming lessons at the pool to a mini-farmer camp in the gardens, where kids will learn about their veggies and how to grow them. Even Mama's helping out with a baking class that's all about cookies.

Amelia's got big plans. I couldn't be more excited for her.

"I'm not all that hungry, to be honest." It's her turn to frown. "Maybe once I get moving, I'll change my mind."

"Great. I'll make Samuel's eggs for us, then."

She grins. "Liam's favorite."

"Yours too." I kiss her mouth one last time before rolling off her. "You want some company while you take the test?"

"You mean do I need you there to watch me pee on a stick? I'll be okay."

I know I said I didn't want to get my hopes up, but I'm still a bundle of nervous energy as I pull on some shorts and pad to the kitchen. Before we left Blue Mountain, I had Samuel give me a crash course in cooking for a crowd. Well, a small crowd, but the idea was the same: I needed all the tips and tricks he had for keeping my family fed.

He taught me how to make a mean BLT (secret is the mayonnaise, which he jazzes up with fresh herbs) and the best mashed sweet potatoes you've had in your life. I learned the ins and outs of white chicken chili and the right way to roast a tray of veggies (3 tablespoons olive oil, 1 teaspoon kosher salt, 400 degree oven). He even taught me how to make chocolate chip cookies, which Liam, Amelia, and I devour by the dozen.

My hands shake as I fill a kettle with water and turn on the burner. Shake some more when I turn on the coffee pot and grab eggs, butter, cream cheese, and chives out of the fridge.

"Amelia," I call, too excited—too nervous—to worry about waking Liam. It's past seven anyway. He's usually up by now. "How's it going?"

"One more minute!" she calls back.

Right on cue, I hear Liam say, "Dada. Hi, Dada!"

I dash upstairs and change his diaper on the bed beside his crib. The poor little guy has diaper rash again, so I lather him up with diaper cream and try not to jump down the stairs two at a time with him on my hip.

Like I do most mornings, I glance at the two picture frames on the shelf opposite Liam's crib. One is of his mom and him the day he was born. She has happy tears in her eyes; it's obvious she loved him with all her heart from the first time she saw him.

The other photo was taken just before Amelia, Liam and I left Blue Mountain. It's of the three of us in the backyard, a candid shot that Milly took. I love it. Liam's screaming with laughter as I hold him above my head; Amelia is tucked into my side, a big old smile on her face.

It's pure joy.

"Dada, Mama?" Liam says.

I blink. Smile. He started calling Amelia "Mama" a couple weeks ago.

"Yes, little man, let's go find Mama."

We head down the stairs. It's all I can do not to take them two at a time.

"Dada fass," Liam says, and drops Pup Pup on one of the steps. "Dada, Pup Pup!"

Groaning, I turn around and grab the stuffed doggie. "You're giving me a run for my money this morning, aren't you, Yoda?"

"Yeah," he says, and smiles.

Amelia is waiting for us in the kitchen. She smiles, and my heart leaps into my throat.

"So?" I pant.

She wags her eyebrows and strides over, taking Liam out of my arms. "So what?"

"You're killing me here. What did the test say?"

Amelia nods at the counter over my shoulder. "See for yourself."

I whip around. Pick up the plastic stick and stare down at two pink lines.

This isn't the first test Amelia's taken. I know what two lines mean.

My heart thumps, and I look up. Meet her eyes. They're filled with tears. So are mine all of a sudden.

"Seriously?"

She grins. "Seriously." She gives Liam's belly a little tickle. "You ready to be a big brother, Li? I think you're going to be very good at it."

My son. He's going to have a sibling.

Amelia and I are giving him one of the best gifts ever.

Amelia and I are having a baby.

"Aw, honey, get over here," I say thickly, and I curl my growing family into a group hug. Liam naturally pushes me away, starting to fuss. Amelia laughs. I cry.

"Why the tears?" She teases. "Be glad it was *this* test that came back positive, not the one I took in high school."

"Thank God for that," I reply. Cupping the back of her neck in my hand, I lean my forehead against hers. "I'm gonna do it right this time. Thank you. For giving me another chance. Amelia, I'm so fuck—freak —*freaking* excited."

"Freak?" Liam parrots, momentarily pausing his wails.

"You okay with this?" I murmur.

She nods. "It's all I've ever wanted."

"I love you." I kiss Amelia hard. Then I kiss the top of Liam's head. "Y'all are my everything. I love *you*. Now how about we eat some breakfast, and then I'll kick your behinds at badminton?"

Amelia smiles. "Sounds perfect."

Thank you so much for reading SOUTHERN PLAYBOY! Want more Rhett + Amelia? Need to know if they have a boy or a girl? Download your free bonus epilogue by signing up for my newsletter at www.jessicapeterson.com!

Thank you so much for reading Rhett + Amelia's story. I hope you loved it as much as I do.

If you haven't read the rest of the North Carolina Highlands books, start with SOUTHERN SEDUCER, Beau + Annabel's story. If you have, be sure to check out my bestselling Charleston Heat series next! I kick off the series with SOUTHERN CHARMER, a slow burn, hot new neighbor romance.

I'd love to hear from you. Here are ways to keep in touch:

- **Check out Jessica Peterson's City Girls, my reader group on Facebook for giveaways, serious discussions of seriously hot guys, and more**
- Check out my website, www.jessicapeterson.com, for a list of my books, my recommended reading order, plus lots of other goodies
- Follow my not-so-glamorous life as a romance author on Instagram @JessicaPAuthor
- Follow me on Goodreads
- Follow me on Bookbub
- Like my Facebook Author Page
- Drop me a line at jessicapauthor@jessicapeterson.com

ACKNOWLEDGMENTS

There are books that are a joy to write. And then there are books that suck you dry.

This was one of those books. By the time I finished, I honestly couldn't tell if I had a hot mess on my hands or a story that, by some miracle, actually made sense.

When I got my first feedback from a beta reader telling me this was her favorite book of mine yet, I cried. Relief. Giddiness. Pride in my ability to stick with the story to the end, despite wanting to quit every damn day I sat down at my computer to write.

I had the ability to keep writing because I have an incredible team behind me. Y'all cheer me on, and you constantly push me to be a better writer, manager, and business owner. I needed that push this time around. Thank you.

Thanks to my PA and right hand woman, Jodi. Working with you through revisions made me fall in love with this story, and made me fall even more in love with you.

Thanks to Nina and the gals over at Valentine PR. My career has grown by leaps and bounds since I began working with you.

Thanks to my beta readers, Julia and Quinn, and to my editor, Marion, my copyeditor Jenny, and my proofreader, Karen. As usual, you guys saved my ass over and over again with this story.

Thanks to my reader group admins, Emily, Tara, Ingrid, and Kenysha, for holding down the fort so I could spend my days scribbling away in my writing cave.

This is my first nanny/boss, secret baby romance, and I had no idea where to start when it came to things like child custody laws, the educational requirements of preschool teachers, and destruction of property. I reached out to my reader group for help, and I was bowled over by all the offers and information. Thanks to Joseph Roth, Michelle Rodriguez, and Lona Speeney McCombey for your expertise on all things child welfare related. Thanks to my sister, Maggie Peterson, and to Tina Snider for helping me figure out what Amelia's path would look like in early education.

Thanks to my ARC team for always supporting my work. Your enthusiasm for my books is what keeps me going on the hard days.

Thanks to Nick for help with the business side of things.

Thanks to Joe, Julie, and the rest of the BlueNose Audio team for helping me produce top-notch audiobooks for this series. Y'all are a joy to work with.

And finally, the biggest thanks of all to my readers, my family, and my friends. Happiness can't be found in work alone. You are my joy, my *why*. I love you all dearly.

ALSO BY JESSICA PETERSON

Lessons in Losing It (Study Abroad #4)

ABOUT THE AUTHOR

Jessica Peterson writes smokin' hot romance set in her favorite cities around the world. She grew up on a steady diet of Mr. Darcy, Edward Cullen, and Jamie Frasier, and it wasn't long before she started writing swoon-worthy heroes of her own. She loves strong coffee, stronger heroines, and heroes with hot accents.

She lives in Charlotte, NC with her husband Ben, her sweet baby Grace, and her smelly Goldendoodle Martha Bean. You can check out her books at www.jessicapeterson.com.

Printed in Great Britain
by Amazon

68052081R00174